The Other Woman

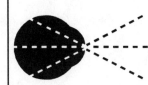

This Large Print Book carries the
Seal of Approval of N.A.V.H.

THE OTHER WOMAN

DIANA DIAMOND

THORNDIKE PRESS

An imprint of Thomson Gale, a part of The Thomson Corporation

Detroit • New York • San Francisco • New Haven, Conn. • Waterville, Maine • London • Munich

Thomson Gale is part of The Thomson Corporation.

Thomson and Star Logo and Thorndike are trademarks and Gale is a registered trademark used herein under license.

Thorndike Press® Large Print Core.

The text of this Large Print edition is unabridged.

Other aspects of the book may vary from the original edition.

Set in 16 pt. Plantin.

LIBRARY OF CONGRESS CATALOGING-IN-PUBLICATION DATA

Diamond, Diana.
   The other woman / by Diana Diamond. — Large print ed.
     p. cm. — (Thorndike Press large print core)
   ISBN 0-7862-8862-0 (hardcover : alk. paper) 1. Politicians — Fiction. 2. Politicians' spouses — Fiction. 3. Adultery — Fiction. 4. Washington (D.C.) — Fiction. 5. Women authors — Fiction. 6. Publishers and publishing — Fiction. 7. New York (N.Y.) — Fiction. 8. Large type books. I. Title.
PS3554.I233O84 2006b
813'.6—dc22   2006018797

Published in 2006 by arrangement with St. Martin's Press, LLC.

Printed in the United States of America on permanent paper
10 9 8 7 6 5 4 3 2 1

THE OTHER WOMAN

ONE

Pam Leighton should have seen it coming. She knew when John Duke was named a candidate for a position in the administration, he would have to tidy up all the messy corners of his life. She was one of those messy corners.

It wasn't that she was naive. Pam was a reasonably bright college graduate with an advanced degree in economics who held down a responsible research post for a Washington trade association. She knew that married men who wandered from home were usually on short leashes. Deep down she understood that John Duke would never leave his wife, Catherine, no matter how sincerely he claimed that they were no longer in love. Love meant different things to men at different stages of their lives. Maybe his romantic feelings for her were stronger than his feelings for Catherine, but that didn't mean he wanted to leave his wife. Pam had always understood that if push came to shove, she would be the one pushed aside. It was just that it was hard to believe. Hard, because her two-year affair with her boss wasn't the typical affair.

Pam wasn't a kept woman. She earned her money and paid her own rent. The only thing she depended on John Duke for was affection. Their relationship wasn't centered on the bedroom, even though it might have been. Pam was a very sexy woman, on the cusp of thirty, when youthful attractiveness softens into mature interests. Her coloring — dark hair with blue eyes — looked like it was the result of the mating of an English stallion and an Italian mare somewhere back in her bloodlines. Her skin tone, high cheekbones, and full lips came from her Mediterranean heritage. Her straight nose and sharply cut jawline were inherited from Nordic raiders. Her figure was a bit too curvaceous for a runway model, but without the bounce that draws applause from construction workers. There was just enough flow in her movements to turn heads on the street, and to raise eyes over the tops of restaurant menus.

But she wasn't a sex toy. She had no drawer of transparent nightwear, nor were there leather outfits hanging in her closet.

She slept in pajamas, or in nothing at all, depending on the occasion. Her bathrobe was terry cloth, her underwear white cotton, and her bras unpadded. When John came to her apartment, she was as apt to smell of a lemon fish marinade as of an exotic Parisian fragrance.

In their typical evening together, they worked side by side in the kitchen, generally sipping the wine intended for the saucepan. They shared a lively conversation over dinner and often fell asleep in front of the television. On weekends, when he was in town, they sat around in pajamas passing sections of *The Washington Post* back and forth before they settled down to the crossword puzzle.

Some evenings, they worked together. The Electric Energy Institute's real business was lobbying government officials to make sure that no legislation hostile to the electric utilities, or regulation distasteful to their executives, would ever be passed. Pam often needed guidance on exactly what politically attractive conclusions her research should yield. John would sometimes ask her advice on a recalcitrant senator. How big a donation was he looking for? How many votes could he deliver?

What they shared wasn't that much different from any marriage between urban professionals. Much more than just casual sex, their affair was a commitment of time, interest, and affection, from which intimacy flowed naturally and guiltlessly. It truly seemed that it would last forever.

They had to be discreet, of course. In the Electric Energy Institute offices, they exchanged greetings in passing that held no hint of affection. "Good morning, Pam!" "Good morning, John," when they met in the lobby. "I'll have those figures you asked for this afternoon" and "Thank you, Pam," when they interacted in the office. If they found themselves at the same table in the cafeteria, they invited others to join them. They never booked luncheon reservations at the same restaurant.

When they had an evening out together, it was never at a fashionable downtown restaurant or at one of the Georgetown clubs. As director of the institute, John was immediately recognizable by most senators, congressmen, and their staffers, as well as power industry executives. As the institute's top researcher, Pam would be recognized by most second-level Washington officials and many of the executives of the institute's sponsoring companies. Both of them were well known to the lobbying industry, with its offices stretching for block after block along K Street. Within hours after their appearing together in the District, it would have been universally acknowledged that they were an item.

Instead, they would often travel north to Baltimore, where they could get lost in the crowds at the harbor. They could drive west to Leesburg, where the county was exploding so rapidly that no one knew anyone. Or they might head south to Charlottesville and join the chaos of student revelers. When business called for them to travel together, they would find separate rooms in the hotel, even though one of those rooms would go unused. Or if Pam was joining John in a major resort city, they would book separate flights on different airlines. The subterfuge bothered neither of them. It was accepted as a necessary arrangement in their relationship, just as a husband might put up with a two-hour daily commute.

Over the two years of their relationship, there had been several close calls. One time, at a resort in the Bahamas, John had excused himself from the dinner table only to run into the president of a sponsoring company in the lobby. While the two men shared a drink at the bar, Pam had slipped away, leaving two untouched dinners behind. They had checked out in the middle of the night. On another occasion, Pam had seen a man from their office at an airport gate where John's flight was arriving. Suggestively, she had led him off for a cocktail. For weeks after, her colleague had hinted around the watercooler that she was hitting on him. Only once had Pam and John been caught red-handed, when they glanced across the aisle of a theater and saw a congressman they both knew staring back at them. Fortunately, the woman with the congressman was from an escort service, and both couples silently agreed not to acknowledge one another.

Pam had been delighted when John told her that his name was in play for a position in the new president's cabinet. He had modestly dismissed the implications. "Lots of names get kicked around. It's no big deal." But it was a big deal. The incoming administration was pro-business, particularly favorable to energy producers. The new Secretary of Energy would be responsible for turning the industry's wish list into public law. More important, she knew that John wanted it. Instead of courting important men, he would be the one being courted. The position would be his entry into public life, with all its social and financial perks. The repute that came from rubbing elbows with the president would lead to book advances, speaking fees, maybe even a university chair. All heady stuff for a man who was a paid flak for a stolid industry.

Pam knew that John would go through a detailed vetting. The new president's team would scrutinize every detail of his life, looking for breaches of the law or of public morality that could embarrass the administration. Ideal candidates had been unceremoniously dumped because the family maid was an illegal immigrant, or because they didn't pay a nanny's Social Security. A vice presidential candidate had lost out when it was discovered he had seen a psychiatrist. A Supreme Court candidate had been rocked by charges of sexism. More than likely, they would ask John about the state of his marriage.

He would have to tell them about her, because there was every chance that they would find out anyway. From the day his name came up, detectives had probably been following him. A panel truck full of radio equipment was probably homing in on his cell phone calls. More than likely, someone at the post office was watching his mail. But even when he told them, Pam didn't think their affair would be critical. Hadn't presidents carried on affairs in the White House? Weren't congressmen balling their interns? By comparison, her relationship with John was proper and discreet.

He had a lovely wife who presided over a household in Connecticut to which he frequently returned. She was the daughter of a politically connected family that had made its fortune in shipping, running molasses and hardware to the Caribbean, and bringing back rum and slaves. Two of her forebears had served as state representatives to the United States Congress, and two recent presidents had dined with members of the family while campaigning in the state. One of her cousins, Benjamin Porter, was the majority whip in the House. She was known to politicians of every stripe, and Pam had no doubt that her influence had been critical of John's selection for a cabinet post. Catherine was at his side in all his official photographs and joined him at important functions, always smiling at him adoringly even though they had separate bedrooms. She was the woman who would be at his side when he was sworn in, and she would be photographed with the president's wife. She was the perfect companion for his public life.

He also had a mistress, who was invisible to the outside world. She had no desire for notoriety, was content to live backstage, and would never do anything to embarrass his wife or jeopardize his public image. She was a perfect companion in his private life. It all worked very well, so why should the administration's inquisitors be concerned? Surely they had more incendiary issues to deal with.

He came to her apartment on a Monday night after spending a weekend in Connecticut, gave Pam a distracted kiss, and opened a bottle of a modest wine they both liked. He put the bottle on the table that Pam had already set, went to the stereo, and slipped in a jazz CD. Then he eased onto the sofa almost as if he was afraid of crumpling a cushion.

"How was your weekend?" she called from the kitchen.

"Okay," he answered unenthusiastically.

Pam knew something was wrong. John always clung to her when he returned from home, demonstrating how much he had missed her. By now he should have poured the wine, toasted to her beauty, and then plunged into the food preparation, taking every opportunity to brush against her.

"A problem?"

"Sure. There's always a problem."

She dried her hands and stepped out of the kitchen. The table was close to the front door, across from the kitchen counter. He was sitting at the far end of the room, tapping his fingers on the armrest in time to the music. She lit the candles, her signal that dinner was ready. "Anything you want to talk about?" she asked as she poured the wine.

He got up heavily, showing none of the zest he usually brought to their table. "No . . . well . . . there is. But not now. It will keep until after dinner."

They began silently, John plainly lost in his thoughts and Pam wondering what dreaded topic was hanging over them. She couldn't take the tension.

"What do you think?" she said, gesturing toward the fish she had served.

"Wonderful! What did you marinate it in?"

His eyes were glazing over before she finished listing the ingredients, but she went on with the details of preparation, trying to keep the conversation alive. "Delicious," he interjected when he realized she had stopped talking.

She tried another tack. "How was the flight?"

"Uneventful," he said without glancing

16

up. "The best kind."

"Did Catherine pick you up?"

"No, she was busy. I took a limo."

"What was she busy with?"

"The usual nonsense. Nothing important."

Pam wasn't going to give up. There had to be something they could talk about. "Let me tell you about my weekend," she started, but she was cut off by the clatter of his fork falling onto his plate.

"She knows," John said, breathing out the words rather than saying them. "Catherine knows about us." He reached for his wine-glass and drained it.

"So?" Pam asked. It wasn't a frivolous question. They had often speculated that his wife might already know of their affair and, if not, that she would probably find out. Both of them assumed she would live comfortably with the arrangement, or perhaps demand a divorce. Whichever, it would be a quiet and dignified resolution. Catherine wasn't into scenes.

"So," he answered softly, "she wants this ended."

Pam set her fork down and pushed her plate aside. She felt a cold chill of fear and a knot tightening in her throat. She couldn't even pretend to eat. "How does she want it

17

ended?" she managed.

"Just ended! She doesn't want me to see you anymore." He refilled his glass and then tried to pour a bit into Pam's glass. His hands were shaking. He looked up at her, but he couldn't hold eye contact.

"What do *you* want?" she asked, even though she could already guess his answer.

"What I want doesn't matter. It's what I have to do." He seemed distraught, on the verge of tears.

"What do you have to do?" she asked. He half-turned away from her. "Do you have to give me up?"

He nodded. "That's Catherine's price."

She didn't understand. Price for what? What was John's wife holding over his head?

"Her price for my nomination to go through. Catherine has connections all over the government. If she makes it known that she would rather not have me burdened with the demands of public life, the administration will find a more available candidate. Christ, the only reason my name came up in the first place is that the new people are trying to suck up to her family. They'd love to get her cousin in their pocket."

He jumped up from the table, went to the stereo, and snapped off the jazz combo. Then he sat down on the sofa, this time

18

heavily, as if he were falling into a great, black hole. Pam followed and took a chair across from him. "If I understand you, I'm not sure that I'm being dropped because of Catherine. It sounds more as if I'm losing out to a job in the new president's cabinet."

He shook his head slowly. "Catherine isn't giving me any leeway."

"No," Pam corrected. "It's your ambition that isn't giving you any leeway. You want the job more than you want me."

"That's not true," he wailed. "You know I love you. But Catherine has me by the short hairs." He was up on his feet and pacing in front of her. "I think she knew about us from the beginning. She's been biding her time, playing right along with us, just waiting for the moment when she could crush me like a bug. Now she has it. She pushed my nomination just so she could dangle it over me."

Pam caught his arm and turned him toward her. "If there's no nomination, then she has nothing to dangle over you. Call her right now and tell her you've decided not to join the administration. You'll still have the institute, and we'll still have each other."

"It's not that simple," he answered curtly. "Catherine could make one hell of a scene."

"And drag her illustrious family through

the tabloids?" Pam reminded him. "Catherine will never let that happen. She'll accept the present arrangement or arrange a very quiet and dignified divorce. Either way, we'll still be together."

She looked toward the telephone, and his eyes followed. But when he saw the handset on the end table, he turned his head away. "Damn it! It's not just a phone call. It's a lot more complicated."

That was true, Pam thought. She had never been able to explain why she was in love with John, or why their relationship was the anchor of her life. She couldn't expect him to explain why a short-lived position in the executive branch would be such an aphrodisiac for him. Sometimes people, or places, or titles, or opportunities simply became irresistible. Few people could explain all the choices that had shaped their lives, so it wasn't fair to demand an explanation.

"What are you going to do?" she asked sympathetically. She was trying to help him focus rather than demanding an answer.

"I don't know. It's all so sudden. A few days ago I had everything. Now I'm afraid that I'm going to lose it all."

"Is there anything I can do to help?"

"Just bear with me for a while." He

reached across the table and touched her hand.

TWO

Pam understood why he wouldn't stay the night. She was even grateful. How could they lie together while each of them was thinking how they were going to live apart? Lovemaking would be artificial. Conversation would be distracting. Sleeping together guiltlessly was a mark of their commitment. Now the commitment itself was being debated.

She was completely unnerved, unable to find a comfortable position in bed and too distracted to read or watch television. For the first hours of the night she wondered what arguments John was having with himself.

She couldn't picture him in his bedroom because she had never been above the ground floor of his town house. She had been in his living room, dining room, and kitchen when he had given small parties for the staff of the institute. On those occasions, caterers had passed cocktails and canapés for exactly an hour, then served dinner at his long colonial table. Pam had blended in with the other staffers, respectful of her boss and clearly one step down from him in the business pecking order. But often she had found herself glancing toward the stairs, wondering how the second floor was furnished, and what kind of bed he slept in when his wife was in town.

She had guessed a four-poster, probably one with a canopy over the top. The facades of all the homes on his Georgetown street were Federal, pretending to have been built in time for the Adams administration. The interior furnishings were generally colonial, usually with a copper kettle hanging over a seldom-used gas log. John had added to the illusion by hanging prints of the Founding Fathers in elaborate frames. So it was reasonable to assume that there was a washstand with basin and pitcher in his bedroom, perhaps even a long-handled bed warmer resting near the upper fireplace. The four-poster seemed a given.

Was he tossing and turning the way she was, weighing the alternatives and evaluating the consequences? For John, the choices were simple: fame and fortune or love and contentment. The argument was one-dimensional. How much would he give for the power and notoriety of a cabinet position? Were his ambitions worth a brutal separation from the woman he loved? For her, the choices were complex. What would she do if he said he wanted to stay with her? Could she believe that he was giving up the opportunity of a lifetime without resenting the limits on his future that their affair demanded? Wouldn't that resentment grow to frustration and anger and eventually destroy the very love he was trying to save?

What would she do if he told her that it was over and that they had to make a clean break? Could she go on with her life as if nothing had changed, continuing at the institute and seeing him when their business paths crossed? Or should she launch herself into an entirely new life, among different people in a different place?

All Pam had were questions. There could be no answers until John told her what her choices were. She was disposable at his whim, and that fact began to fuel her anger. In a sense, he had already decided she was a burden. What he was weighing now was whether the burden was too heavy for him to carry.

By the time the morning light began to leak through the blinds, she was angry at herself. How could she have loved without reservation when her total commitment wasn't returned? How could she have missed seeing that she was only a part of John's life, and that his sole enduring love was for himself? She knew she should have seen it coming, and that made her mad at herself. She knew that he was concerned only with his future, and that made her furious at him. And yet Pam hoped with all her heart that in the end he would decide she was the most important thing in his life. She could forgive his wavering. She loved him that much.

He phoned seconds after her alarm clock rang. His voice was exhausted. "I've had a terrible night," he moaned. "Maybe the worst night of my life."

"It wasn't a beauty rest for me either."

"We need to talk."

She winced. "All you have to say is that you don't want to join the cabinet. That's not a lot of conversation. It's just a simple declarative sentence."

He let the opportunity pass. "I think I have a solution," he said without any great enthusiasm.

"Am I part of it?"

"Of course you are. That's why we have to find a place to talk."

"Won't you be coming here tonight?"

John hesitated and then said, "That might be a bit risky."

It was all the information she needed. Being seen with her would risk his appointment. So the cabinet post was the new love of his life. "Okay," she answered. "Wherever you say."

"In my office at the end of the day. I'll find something that we have to discuss and set up a meeting."

The day dragged at a painful pace. Pam pretended to be involved in a study of the industry's finances and let most of her calls go unreturned. All she could think about were the plates that were crashing under her feet, and the giant fissure that threatened to swallow her up. Why was he prolonging her pain? It was obvious that if he had decided he couldn't live without her they would discuss it over dinner in her apartment. The trumped-up office meeting meant he wouldn't be coming to her apartment. And that meant he had decided to abandon her.

But despite the flawless logic, she still held hope that he might choose her. She should have been preparing herself to receive the devastating news with dignity. Instead, she continued to nurture the possibility that he would decide he couldn't live without her.

She saw him in the office dining room, sitting with the public relations director of one of the new energy marketers. His expressions and gestures were all business. If he was torn by the same agony that she had felt since his announcement, John was certainly hiding his pain. She knew he had seen her come into the room, yet he never spared her a glance.

During the afternoon, Pam jumped at her phone whenever it rang, hoping it would be the call to his office. At three o'clock she was tempted to call his personal secretary, Marion Murray, to make sure she was on his afternoon schedule. Marion was her closest friend inside the institute. Their social life was limited by Pam's need for secrecy and Marion's devotion to a woman she lived with, but they had shared an occasional evening at the movies. By four, Pam sat on the edge of her chair with her arms wrapped around herself, staring at her desk phone. When it rang, she jumped as if it was the last thing she expected. She forced herself to let it ring a second time before she lifted the handset.

"Pam, this is Marion. Mr. Duke wonders if you could stay a bit late. He needs to see you, but he won't be free until six." In her role as the director's secretary, when Marion asked "if you could," she wasn't really asking.

"Sure," Pam said. "Any idea what it's about?"

"Not a clue! Whatever you're working on, bring it along."

Did she know? Pam wondered. A personal secretary usually knew even the most intimate details about her executive's life. The phone number of his favorite restaurant and the maître d's first name. His wife's birthday and the kind of flowers she liked. His haberdasher and his shirt and sock sizes. Pam had always wondered whether Marion knew about her. Was it Marion who bought the wines they shared, and booked the hotels for their out-of-city liaisons? If she did, she would certainly know that Pam was about to be jettisoned.

Marion called back at six. "He'd like to see you now," she said. "I'm leaving, so just walk right in." Pam was relieved that she wouldn't have to face the secretary, but then the woman added, "Good luck!"

She knows, Pam guessed, and she's on my side. "Thanks," she answered.

John stood up when she entered his office. He took a furtive glance over her shoulder to be sure no one was watching before he closed the door. Then he gave her a quick, meaningless kiss and led her to the furniture grouping at the far end of the room. He gestured her to the sofa and waited until she was seated before he took the chair across from her. His manner was all business. Pam felt as if she were on a job interview.

"You can't imagine the agony I've been going through," he began. "I think this has been the most miserable day of my life."

Just say it, she thought. He wouldn't have needed to agonize about how to tell her he was staying with her.

"But I think I've found a way."

She leaned forward to show that she was listening intently, even though she didn't expect the news to be good.

"You know how important a cabinet post is to me." She nodded slightly. "I've come to a fork in the road. In one direction there are unlimited possibilities. Risks, to be sure, but the opportunity to push my career into a much higher orbit. The other direction really leads nowhere. I can go on being an industry flak, but I'll always be a second-team player. I'll always be doing someone else's bidding."

He paused to gauge her reaction. Pam

nodded again to show that she had followed him so far. Those were certainly the choices.

"You know me well enough to know I'd never take myself out of the race. I don't have to tell you that I want the opportunity. But the truth is, it won't mean anything unless you're there with me."

Her eyes widened. She couldn't hide her spontaneous smile. John reached across the coffee table and took her hands in his. "The point is," he continued, "that once I'm established in the position, Catherine's connections won't matter. Right now, while I'm a candidate, I'm vulnerable. But a year from now, I'll be established. It won't matter whether I have her support, and no one will care if I show up with a different woman on my arm. This isn't the Vatican! People don't get thrown out of Washington for getting a divorce."

He was talking enthusiastically. He believed he had solved their problem and delivered the good news. But Pam wasn't enthused. "A year?" she asked.

"Maybe a bit more. Maybe even less. We'll just have to see how things are going. But it won't seem long. We'll still be seeing each other."

"How are we going to manage that? Won't Catherine know that you've lied to her?

Won't she walk out on you?"

"We'll have to be very careful," he hastened to agree. "We can't be living in the same city or meeting at business affairs. Obviously, I can't be coming over every night. But we can still be together."

"How?" she repeated. But she wasn't completely puzzled. The conversation was beginning to sound familiar.

"I'll get you a place in Baltimore, down near the harbor," he answered. "And I'll line up a job for you on the staff of one of the power companies. The place will be yours, in your name, so you can take it over once you get settled." He paused, giving her a chance to react.

"And?" she asked. Obviously, there was more to his idea.

"We'll get together every time we can. I can easily arrange to have business in Baltimore a couple of days a month. And there will be a lot of travel to places where we can arrange to meet."

She took back her hands and looked away.

"I know it's not perfect," he pressed on. "I won't like being away from you. But it's just for a while. Just until the time is right for me to confront Catherine."

Pam knew when she had heard it before. It had been two years earlier, when he first told her he loved her and couldn't live without her. He had admitted that a clandestine affair was far from perfect but assured her that it was just for now. It wouldn't be long before he would be able to divorce his wife. She hadn't believed it any more then than she did now. But then she had wanted to believe it.

John Duke had been visiting the Electric Energy Institute when he was introduced to Pam. He was a top executive with a New York public relations firm working to get a rate hike for one of his clients. Pam had joined him in the conference room and briefed him on the rate increases that other utilities had been granted. He had thanked her by taking her out to dinner. In the course of the next two months they had conferenced a dozen times. The dinners had started earlier, with cocktails, and ended later, with his coming up for a nightcap. On the day their business was concluded, John had stayed the night, and most of the next morning.

For the following months, he had seized every excuse to be in Washington, and their relationship had opened up like a flower. He had never lied to her. He had admitted to being fifteen years older than she was, even though he could have claimed a much younger age. He had made it plain that he was still married and had described a relationship that had gone cold, his fault as much as his wife's, and a house that was lifeless since his two daughters had left. "But I'm not a cheat," he had insisted. "I haven't been catting around. You're the first woman I've been with for too many years."

As he had told it, he wasn't looking for anything more than a dinner companion the first time he had asked her out. It wasn't until their third evening together that he realized he loved her. "I found a new life with you," he had told her, and Pam had found no reason to doubt him. The first time they'd slept together he had held her close throughout the night, "afraid that if I let go you wouldn't be there when I woke up."

Then, miraculously, he had been offered the top position in the institute, and he had accepted it with neck-snapping speed. He loved her, and now they could be together all the time. Marriage would have to wait, of course. He couldn't simply destroy his wife, even if he no longer loved her. Besides, she was a powerful woman with important Washington connections. It would take time. He would have to find the right moment to broach a divorce.

"You told me all this two years ago," Pam said.

He bristled. "It was true then, and it's true now. I love you, Pam."

"And will it still be true two years from now, when you're offered an even bigger job?"

"What are you talking about? What job?"

"Suppose you're such a wonderful Secretary of Energy that they want you to run for vice president. Catherine will still be a well-connected woman. Will you ask me to wait around for just another few years? And where will you send me to live? Someplace in the Orient?"

"You're not being fair," he protested. "There was no way I could have foreseen this opportunity."

"John, that's what marriage is. It's two people pledging themselves to each other even though neither of them can foresee the future. That's what we should have done two years ago. It's what we should be doing now."

He labored to his feet and paced away toward his desk. "I can't. Not now. I just need a little more time."

"How much more time? Because I'm going to hold you to it. I'm going to sign up a caterer and send out the invitations."

He took a paper from his desk and held it up triumphantly. "Do you know what this is?" She shrugged. "It's the invitation for me to appear before the Senate Energy Committee. The president has named me. That's how close I am."

She rose and started toward him. "Good. You can tell them about me."

He sagged, letting the paper drop to his side. "You know I can't do that." He reached for her hand, but she didn't respond. "I'm sorry. I didn't mean to upset you. Let's just give it a couple of days, and then we'll talk again."

"No!" she snapped. She was surprised at her vehemence. "No," she repeated softly. "Not another couple of days. The decision is right here between us. If you love me, take my hand and we'll walk out together, ready to face all the things that neither of us can foresee. I can't put my life on hold until you have all your bases covered. I can't go on loving you in the hope that someday I'll be a safe bet."

She extended her hand. "Come on. Let's take our chances."

He rolled the paper carefully and held it with both hands. "I can't. If you can just give me some time."

Pam leaned forward and kissed him on

35

the cheek. "Good night, John. I'll see you in the morning."

She was halfway to the door when he called her name. She stopped and turned slowly. "Please," he begged. "Let me get you set up in Baltimore. Or anyplace you want . . ."

She knew what he meant. "You want me out of the institute, don't you?"

He writhed in his embarrassment. "I think it would be best. Even when I leave, I'll still be meeting with the institute. We don't need to be running into each other."

She smiled, the truth of the situation beginning to get through to her. "You even want me out of town."

"No, that's not what I want. It's just . . ." John didn't know how to explain.

"Who then? Catherine? Was this one of her conditions? You don't just have to stop sleeping with me. You have to make sure that you never even run into me."

"She wants a clean break," he mumbled.

Her anger flashed. "But you wanted to hedge it. I was supposed to stay in touch just in case you needed a good fuck!"

"That's not true!" he snapped back.

"Well, you can call and tell her that you did it her way, and that Pam Leighton is gone for good. I'll be back in the morning to clean out my desk."

"Pam, wait!"

But she never broke stride.

THREE

Her office desk was easy. There was one cactus plant that had taken to the artificial light and nearly outgrown its pot. There was a framed portrait in which she was in a cap and gown, surrounded by a buoyant family. Hanging on her coat tree was a simple white sweater that she put over her shoulders whenever the air-conditioning got too aggressive. From her lower desk drawer she took a pair of sneakers she kept there in case she found time for a brisk walk.

The rest of her baggage was computer disks. The official backups for her statistical studies and her field reports were company property, so Pam carefully weeded those out and left them behind. What she took were a few dozen CDs that were her working files, her notes, and her personal records.

As she packed, the word exploded like a flash fire throughout the office. "Pam is leaving? Why? Does she have a better offer?

Who's going to take her place?" She answered all the questions with a smile. "Career differences," she said. "I've been here long enough."

No one believed her. It didn't seem likely that she would just get up one morning and decide to change jobs. Something must have been simmering that had suddenly flamed up. But, at least in her presence, her colleagues pretended to accept her abrupt explanation. Around the coffeemaker, they speculated on everything from a breach of ethics to a fatal disease.

Marion stopped by to help her carry her things, relieving her of the embarrassment of being escorted to the parking lot by a security officer. "I'm sorry we're losing you," she said. Then she added, "Personally, I think Mr. Duke is making a terrible mistake. There are more cabinet secretaries in this town than trash collectors." Her face was impassive. But her comment seemed to say that she was aware of the choice John had had to make and that she thought he should have chosen Pam.

Cleaning out her apartment was a much more difficult chore. She was breaking a lease, so there were negotiations with her landlord. She needed a moving company to put her furniture into storage. Utilities required notice to terminate their services. She had to decide about her car, a red Miata ragtop that rarely left the garage. She should sell it, although she loved the occasional drive she was able to take on the back roads of Virginia. Her biggest problem was her computer. Pam had three years' worth of floppies and CDs, plus a twenty-gig hard drive. It would take days to go through the files and decide which records she should load onto her laptop and which ones could go into storage with her furniture. That decision, in turn, depended on how soon she would be able to find a job and decide where she was going to live.

She gave herself a month. Go through her files, decide what part of her experience to bet her future on, put together a résumé, then let her new employer dictate the city. It was going to be a melancholy exercise. The time she had already invested in the institute and in her life with John Duke was going into the wastebasket. She was starting anew, as if she had just stepped off the stage with her degree in hand.

The floppy disks were ancient, going back to the day she had arrived in Washington and joined the institute. There were letters to long-forgotten classmates, exchanges with her parents, thank-you notes for gifts, words of sympathy to relatives she couldn't remember, explanations of why she had to decline invitations, and even an irate letter disputing a credit card bill. The only thing of value she came across was the résumé that had gotten her the interview at the institute. The rest of her recorded history she erased with the touch of a key.

The CDs started with her involvement in her job. There were her daily things-to-do lists, which served as a calendar of her interactions with her electric company sponsors and the government officials they were courting. There were the notes she had taken in hundreds of meetings, and the conference reports she had prepared. There were dozens of for-your-eyes-only memos to John and the directors, and memos of telephone conversations with industry leaders and congressional aides.

She found two CDs of John's correspondence. Many times, when they were talking shop over dinner, he had gone to her computer and crystallized ideas while they were still fresh. There were also notes and memos that were too sensitive to put through the institute's computers, where they would leave a traceable record. Most of them Pam had never seen.

On her hard drive, together with dozens

of never-used programs and hordes of personal trivia, she found e-mail files that covered two years of energy industry correspondence. John had copied her in the blind on hundreds of memos so that he could work on them at her apartment.

The memos and the e-mails recalled the events that had inspired them. There was, for example, John's memo to an institute director that said, "TL thinks we should be able to do more than ten. The Clean Air Bill could cost us billions." Pam remembered the incident when the electric companies had donated ten thousand dollars to the campaign fund of Senator Thomas Lawrence. The senator had sent the check back, and an aide had delivered his message. "If you want this thing killed, you better add another zero." John had been furious with his directors. The senator was chairing a committee that could either kill an antipollution bill or send it on for a vote. Compliance with the new law would have cost power generators over $3 billion. "What do these idiots think?" John had ranted as they were preparing dinner. "Do they think they can buy a committee chairman for pocket change?" Pam remembered clearly that the directors had gone along grudgingly and raised the institute's contribution to $100,000. John hadn't been surprised in the least when the bill died in committee.

Another memo concerned the "honorarium" that was to be paid to an assistant Secretary of Energy for speaking at the industry's convention. "We can probably get him for the standard five thousand dollars," John had told the convention organizers. "But if you want him to say what you want to hear, you'd better go higher." They had. The honorarium was raised to twelve thousand.

As she sorted and read, Pam began to realize just how valuable her time at the institute had been. She knew firsthand how things worked. She knew how the lobbyists on K Street shaped the laws of the nation, how elected officials were enticed to do their bidding, and how the entire arrangement was hidden under a camouflage of public service. She had become an insider in a scheme that allowed only a limited number of insiders. She had a clear view of an industry that preferred to work in the dark.

Her records were talking to her. She wasn't starting from scratch. She had a wealth of valuable knowledge, and two years of hands-on experience. Any interest group eager to bend the federal or state governments to its will would see her as a prize catch. The list would include nearly all the trade associations in the country, most of the public relations agencies, and every political action committee. Her job search probably wasn't going to be nearly as difficult as she had feared.

But her optimism was dampened by the news reports of John Duke's procession through the Senate and his coronation on the White House lawn. First, he was photographed behind a felt-covered table, leaning into a microphone as he answered the softballs thrown up by the Senate committee members. He was squarely for reliable energy, at low cost, and with clean air as a by-product. Would he insist that energy generators cap their stack emissions? As soon as economically possible. Would he drill in the Alaskan reserve? Yes, as long as provision was made for the migrating caribou. John managed to come down on all four sides of any issue, all positions that Pam had helped to develop at the institute.

Next he was in the Rose Garden while the president praised his credentials. He was standing a step to the right and one step behind the president, an adoring Catherine at his side. She was gazing into her man's eyes with reverential awe, as if he were

Moses coming down from the mountain.

Finally, there were pictures of him carrying a box of personal items to his desk as Secretary of Energy. The first thing he set on the desk was a framed portrait of Catherine, retouched to remove the extra skin and the crow's-feet.

He was, indeed, moving to a higher realm, his climb lightened by the baggage he had shed. It was hard for Pam to be optimistic about a new career while watching her old one move beyond her reach. John seemed completely content with his new office and with the old wife clutched to his side. Pam felt completely miserable, rejected from the role that she had created. Judging from his smile, he had little regret for having dumped her.

The more she thought about it, the more obvious it became. He had never truly needed her. All she had been was a convenience during one stage of his relentless march to the top. It had always been about him. When she suited his purpose and tended his needs, he had wanted her nearby. When his needs changed, he wanted her out of the way. What *she* needed had never been part of their relationship. The realization boiled her self-pity into anger. Anger at John for being such a bastard. Anger at herself for letting him use her so shabbily. Pam tried to soothe her rage by putting all her efforts into packing. The sooner she got out of Washington and away from him, the better off she would be.

She decided on New York. It was the headquarters of the public relations industry and home base for the news and publishing industries that best fit her experience. There would be hundreds of opportunities for her skills in shaping public opinion and focusing it on the government and business leaders who could be pressured. She sorted through her PalmPilot and quickly found the names of ten New York executives she had worked with on one project or another. Then she made phone calls and arranged appointments. The responses were encouraging. Everyone was shocked that she had left the institute and delighted to help her find the right position in the Big Apple. John Duke and Washington lobbying would soon be left behind.

She was taking her final ride in her car before delivering it to a dealer who had offered her the top price. The farther she drove into the countryside, the more she regretted the sale. She loved accelerating into the turns, raising the speed until she heard the tires chirp and felt them bite. Somewhere along a stretch of road bordered by white paddock fences, she thought about writing a book. Could I ever blow the lid off the lobbying business, she thought. She smiled at the idea of the Secretary of Energy reading the details of his "another zero" payment to stop the Clean Air Bill. She could do a whole chapter on all the concerned-citizens' groups he had invented to launder the bribes his members were paying to elected officials. Living with another woman wouldn't even make the list of reasons why he would be banished from the capital.

As she thought through all the computer memos and documents she had just inventoried, the possibilities for revenge became delicious. But could she really do it? Wasn't it too petty to strike back at the career John had chosen over her? Wasn't her sudden need for revenge beneath her? Shouldn't she be ladylike and keep her hurt to herself?

Hell, no! she answered as she pressed down on the accelerator. What was she supposed to do, swoon whenever his name was mentioned? What was so ladylike about letting him wipe his feet on her as he left her? She had been naive and dumb, but he had been cunning and deceptive. Was it good breeding to go on being naive and dumb? Should he get away with being cunning and deceptive?

Of course, she still had feelings for him. She had given herself to him without reserve and poured her affection over him. Those weren't torrents that could be shut off like a faucet. But the fact that Pam loved him made his betrayal all the more heartless. If he had felt a similar torrent of emotion for her, he had managed to turn it off in the space of a weekend.

Back in her apartment, surrounded by the mover's cardboard cartons, she found another problem. Could she write a book? She had written reports, press releases, and articles for trade magazines, some running to twenty-five thousand words. But a book? That was probably too ambitious.

She went back to the names in her PalmPilot and found Glen Hubbard, an editor at a major New York publishing house. They had met when she was helping with a power industry story he was publishing. Why not sound him out for some professional advice?

FOUR

Pam met Glen for lunch between her meetings with real-estate agents. She might not have recognized him if the bar had been crowded. But he was the only one waiting there, and he seemed to recognize her. He delivered an overly familiar kiss to her cheek, told her how happy he was to see her, and gestured to a waiter that they were ready to be seated. He had picked a small table at the back that offered privacy.

They went through the usual rituals of people who don't really know each other. She looked great. It was wonderful of him to take the time to see her. Of course he would be delighted to help. They didn't hit on a real topic until Pam expressed her frustration in finding an apartment. "You wouldn't believe what they're asking for a studio without a view," she said.

"Yes, I would. It's probably what I'm paying."

"Where should I be looking?" she asked him

"Jersey City, or maybe Philadelphia," he answered with a smile.

Glen was Pam's age, handsome despite thinning hair and eyeglasses that were a bit too thick to be fashionable. He was an executive editor, specializing in business management books, with Thomas Howell, a major publisher. One of his books, the story of a merger of two fashion designers that had destroyed both firms, was in its twelfth week on the nonfiction bestseller list. Pam had been an important source on a book about a power company that had bellied up in spectacular style, putting the industry's best face on the lurid details. They both thought they owed the other a favor.

Glen was able to deliver immediately. He had an associate who was going to be out of the country for six months and would be leaving an empty apartment. "She can't sublet it, and when she comes back she'll pay twice as much for something like it. I think she'd love to have someone take it over while she's away, just to have the rent paid."

"That would be perfect," Pam bubbled. "It will get me off the street and give me time to get settled."

"It isn't cheap," he warned. "Three thousand dollars a month."

She choked on the water she was sipping. Then she asked, "Is it closer to midtown than Philadelphia?" He laughed, and she decided. "I'll take it. Now, unless you want to see your friend stiffed, you better help me find a job."

They ate slowly. First a salad with a ginger dressing tart enough to make her wince. Then an omelet with Greek cheese. Finally a pear cooked in wine. Pam did most of the talking, describing her experience at the institute, and what she thought were her insights into the ways things really worked. When the coffee was served, she got into her sales pitch. "I think I could write a book on the corruption of government by well-financed lobbies. Elected officials are always passing the hat, and the lobbies are always ready to donate, naturally expecting something in return. If they don't get it, they stop throwing cash into the hat. It's the way the public's business gets done, and it's not a pretty story."

Glen told her it was a great idea but one that had already been done. "People know this stuff goes on. I'm afraid no one really cares."

"They don't know what I know. Like the

names of the industry executives who wrote our new energy bill. Or the list of congressmen who can be bought and each one's asking price."

Now he was genuinely interested. "You'd be willing to write that kind of stuff? Name names, and places, and amounts? A real exposé?"

"Yes, and not just about the power industry. On some of these deals, different trade organizations collaborate in their common interest. They combine the contributions so they can have a big impact."

"That would be quite a book," Glen said after whistling softly through his teeth. "But wouldn't you be indicting yourself? You know all these things because you were part of them. I don't think you'd ever find a job in any business that needs to be friendly with the government."

She agreed. "You're saying whistle-blowers don't have much of a future."

"I'm saying whistle-blowers don't even have a present," he corrected. "Once the light of exposure burns out, they generally get crushed. I did a book about a guy who thought one of the cars his company made was too dangerous to drive. While they were in the spotlight, they called him a hero, gave him a raise, even handed him a plaque at the annual meeting. A year later, they fired him for sexual harassment. That was four years ago, and he's still out of work."

"But, if I was willing to do it . . ."

"Then I'd be willing to publish it. Assuming, of course, that it's all you say it is, and that you write it in a popular language, like English."

Pam smiled. "I may be crazy, but I'd like to give it a try. How do I get started?"

"Just start! Give me an outline, indicating the people and the events you'll be talking about. Write the first chapter and maybe one other chapter. That will show me the material and how it's going to be presented." Then he corrected himself. "I said 'give *me* an outline,' but it's not just me. Even if I decide not to do it, that's the kind of information any other editor would need." He asked her where she was staying. "I'll send some proposals over for you to use as guidance. They must be pretty good because I bought all of them."

"But you'll take the first look," Pam said, trying to assure herself that this wasn't just a polite brush-off.

"You'd better give me the first look," Glen chided. He glanced at the bill the waitress had left on the table. "I've already got seventy-one fifty invested in you."

As they were leaving, she reminded him about the colleague with the apartment. He promised to put the two women in touch.

True to Glen's word, the woman called her and set up a meeting at the apartment the next morning. Then a messenger came to the desk of her hotel and dropped off the sample proposals Glen had mentioned. Pam spent the evening in her room, reading the proposals and checking her laptop to find the kinds of information she could use. She was still working at midnight and was amazed to realize she hadn't even paused for dinner. A story was already outlining itself in her mind.

The title would be *Fouling the Air,* and the story line would cover the power industry's efforts to avoid limits on the stack gases belching out of its generating plants. The plot would center on the donations to Senator Thomas Lawrence and the deals wrangled to gain his support. But there would be numerous subplots, involving the destruction of data, the harassment of an environmentalist, doctored figures concerning health effects on children, coal industry involvement, and even the use of the FBI to intimidate opponents. She wouldn't have to offer conclusions. The facts would speak for themselves. And even though she would be writing about one incident in one industry, readers would see that the methods applied to any industry seeking government support for its financial interests. She was excited at the prospect. Now her task was to get that same excitement into her proposal.

She was out early in the morning. Jean Abbott, the woman who needed a temporary tenant, had suggested meeting at eight A.M. Pam had agreed with enthusiasm. She needed to move in as soon as possible to get out from under the daily rate at her hotel.

The building, a fifty-year-old apartment house on the Upper West Side, had little curb appeal. It was a brick block, squeezed between two identical brick blocks. Three casement windows, edged in metal, defined each of the five floors. The double-door entrance was flanked by two columns in a poor imitation of classical façades. Cars were double-parked along the street.

Pam pushed the button next to Jean Abbott's name and was buzzed in after a greeting from a pleasant voice. The elevator, a dark box with fake wood paneling on the walls, creaked up to the third floor. It didn't seem to have the energy to go any higher.

The door opened on an even grimmer

hallway, poorly lighted, with thick-troweled, tan, plastered walls. Down the hallway, a young woman's head poked out a door. "Pam," she beckoned. Pam put on her best smile. But she was already thinking of excuses for not taking the apartment. She knew she would have to compromise on her dream of penthouse living, but this was a total defeat rather than a compromise.

Jean looked to be about Pam's age, but her face was more motherly and her figure fuller. Her smile was genuine, and there was a pleasant lilt to her voice. She seemed a happy person, and the apartment reflected her personality. To her surprise, Pam liked it instantly, a beam of sunshine in an otherwise dreary building.

It was just one room, with a small alcove that served as a bedroom. The kitchen was simply a countertop and appliances along the wall that could be closed off with sliding doors. The bath, Pam guessed, must be a room off the alcove. But the space seemed much larger than it was. For one thing, the back windows had been replaced with tall French doors that let in a flood of daylight. The walls were nearly pure white and received the light easily. The furnishings, all Danish with simple lines, took up a minimum of room, which seemed to increase the floor space. The color came from a series of edge-framed Picasso prints that hung on the long wall.

"This is gorgeous," Pam said as a genuine compliment.

Jean smiled in appreciation, then threw open the French doors to reveal a small balcony that overlooked a rear garden. The entire atmosphere was pleasant. Pam also noticed the door-sized desktop that fit into the corner, just inside the doors. It would be a perfect place to set up a computer and get into her new career as a writer.

They sat over coffee while they agreed on the arrangements. Jean would be moving her personal things out and shipping them to her new address in London, where she was on loan to the English office. She would leave behind the pots and pans, bed linens and towels, television, vacuum, and all the other hardware of housekeeping. Most important, she wanted to leave behind her computer, from which she would erase all her files. That meant Pam could leave her own tower computer in storage and simply load her files onto Jean's machine. All Pam would have to do was pay the rent and utilities, and handle any maintenance. She promised to move out within thirty days of

Jean's announcement that she was returning.

Pam phoned Glen Hubbard to thank him once again for the lead and tell him that the apartment would be perfect. Then she went back to her hotel, packed her things, and moved into her New York career. She couldn't wait to get started on her book.

She had been in the apartment for nearly a week, putting in twelve-hour days, when Glen rang up from the lobby. "Have you had dinner?" he asked.

"No," she answered into the intercom, sure that she was about to be taken out on a publisher's expense account.

"Good. Because I brought it with me, and it's starting to leak through the bag."

When Pam opened the apartment door, Glen thrust a brown bag into her face. "It's the latest in Chinese cuisine, but it loses some of its flavor when it spills out onto the floor. I think you should rush to get this into some kind of dish." He opened a bottle of wine he had brought while she spooned an aromatic dinner out of soggy paper cartons. Then they settled on the floor, using the coffee table as a dining room. Pam ate quickly and realized that she hadn't taken a break for lunch.

"How's the proposal going?" Glen wondered.

"It's finished, but it's just a first draft."

"Can I see it?"

"Now?"

"Yes, now. I can't write off this expensive dinner unless I do some useful work."

She laughed, got to her feet, and circled to the desk, where she gathered up her most recent printout. "Can you wait until after we've finished dinner? I won't be able to eat if I'm waiting for your reaction." He set the pages next to his plate and lifted the top sheet with one hand while he manipulated the chopsticks with the other. "You've done this before," she commented.

"If it wasn't for take-out Chinese, nothing would ever get published," he told her. He paged through quickly, letting pork and vegetables hang in the air while he focused on the text. Occasionally, his head would nod in agreement with something. Or he would purse his lips, as if something he had read was painful. When he turned the last page, he switched his attention back to the half-eaten dinner.

"So?" she asked.

"Good," he answered.

"You like it?" Pam was cautiously pleased.

"I was talking about the food," Glen told her.

Her eyes widened. "You bastard! Are you going to keep me hanging until you finish the last mouthful of rice?"

He laughed and pushed the plate aside. "It's damn good," he said.

"The Chinese," she teased.

"No, your proposal. It might get by just as it is. But I think we can make some improvements so that it's a sure thing. Get a pencil and come around here. We've got work to do."

They sat cross-legged, leaning over the table, while Glen went through the draft line by line. He beefed up her descriptions of events and toned down her personal comments. "You want to be an objective reporter," he said. "You're like a kid with your nose pressed against the glass of a candy store window. You see everything, describe everything, but you never let yourself go inside."

Then, at another point, "Break this narrative right here. Right in the middle of the conversation. You shouldn't always complete what you've started. You want the reader dying to see how the conversation finished."

"Isn't that a bit contrived?" she challenged.

"It's theater, Pam. That's what we're trying to do. Keep the audience on the edge of their seats."

He worked with her for two hours, pausing only when she got up to fill his wineglass and then to put on a pot of coffee. His pencil marks were all over her pages. When he climbed to his feet, he had to kick to restore feeling in his legs and then stretch his back to crack the tightness. "This is damn good, Pam," he told her, which surprised her after all the things he had found wrong with the proposal. When he started into the bedroom alcove, she had an instant of fear that he might be planning on staying the night. But he turned in to the bathroom for the first time since he had arrived. When he came out, he was pushing up his tie, and he crossed quickly to the chair where his jacket was draped.

"How long do you need to make the changes we discussed?" he asked.

"Just a few days. A week at the outside."

"Okay, I'll be here for another working session a week from tonight. The dinner will be on you."

"Does it have to be Chinese?" she asked.

"Hell, no! I'm hoping you're going to do a steak."

He pecked a kiss onto her cheek and let

himself out. Pam stood looking at the closed door. A *steak?* She laughed to herself as if the idea was ridiculous. But then she thought of all that had happened during her first two weeks in New York. She had found a job, moved into an apartment, and taken the first steps into a new career. Glen Hubbard had been her guardian angel, responsible for each of her successes. So what was wrong with a great steak? She owed him much more than that.

FIVE

John Duke stood at the head of the reception line, beautifully tailored in white tie and tails. Catherine, who stood beside him, her face in a frozen smile, was equally glorious, in a floor-length Empire gown of gray satin. Stretched out to his left was a line of some hundred well-wishers who had come to pay homage, each with a feathered and bejeweled woman on his arm. Included were the board of the institute, the CEOs of all the major power companies, all the senators and congressmen whose committees had even the slightest oversight of the nation's electric power infrastructure, coal and oil industry barons, and even three sheikhs representing Arab oil powers.

To John's right were undersecretaries of his department, staff attorneys, and assorted bureaucrats, again with their ladies in tow. As the guests filed past, each had a handshake and a word with the department officials, and a quick kiss for their wives. Old friends greeted one another with great displays of camaraderie. Newcomers repeated their names slowly to be sure they would be remembered.

The affair, a cocktail party to honor the new Secretary of Energy, was one of the many functions planned by the institute and bankrolled by industry executives. Ostensibly, it was simple tribute to an honored figure. Actually, it was intended to assemble the new lineups of the regulators and the regulated so that each of the players would understand his obligations and his privileges.

As the cocktails and hors d'oeuvres were circulated by white-coated waiters, the various factions fell into groups. The top executives clustered around the committee heads who could advance or derail the laws under which they labored. Senator Thomas Lawrence, the valued "friend of the industry," rubbed elbows with presidents of generating companies and trading companies that marketed and delivered blocks of power as if they were crates of tomatoes. Oil executives gravitated toward Congressman Charlie Flowers, who was leading their crusade to drill in the Alaskan preserve. Jane Bonce, the stylish young head counsel at the department, was listening attentively to a half dozen attorneys advancing opinions on the laws blocking the burying of nuclear waste.

Beneath the learned discussions, tunnels were being dug that would carry the flow of money. Without ever mentioning his financial requirements, Senator Lawrence alluded to the tough campaign he would be facing in two years. The executives surrounding him understood that they would be asked to give generously to his fundraisers. Congressman Talbott was stating his case against expensive stack scrubbers to the head of the Clean Skies political action committee. The Clean Skies PAC was a coal industry front that backed candidates who were against strict pollution limits. Talbott was making sure he was on its friends list.

The flow of cash was complex, but it moved in only one direction, from the industry's coffers to the public officials. Money might be parked at the institute before being spent in paeans of praise for the politicians who did the industry's bidding. Or it might be accumulated at one of a dozen industry public action committees before being deposited in a government official's pocket. Some of it wouldn't be paid over directly but would be used to finance travel and entertainment for Energy Department staffers. It all had one purpose — buy the loyalty of key public officials and, once they were owned, keep them in office.

"My feet are killing me," Catherine whispered into John's ear. He flashed a big smile as if she had just said something witty. "As soon as the reception line is over, I'll find you a chair," he whispered.

Catherine loved the attention. The men treated her as if she were Miss America, polite and reserved but excitingly beautiful. She already had four invitations to dance once the band began playing. And the women fawned over her as if they were handmaids to a queen. All were hoping to be included in the afternoon coffees they assumed she would be hosting. What better way to help their husbands than to capture the ear of a political icon.

But it was the power that truly excited her. Not so much the political power that had always attached to the family name, but the domestic power that had come with her husband's return to their marriage. Catherine was a bright woman and had guessed that John was cheating on her within a few months of his move to Washington. She wasn't shocked, because she knew there had been other women. But those had been momentary flings that flared hot for a few weeks and then burned themselves out. She had known of an affair with a client executive in Chicago that had been the cause of a dozen overnight business trips. It had ended when the young woman was fired. There was also a model who had appeared as a spokesperson for one of John's clients. Catherine had caught her on television twice and had to admire her husband's good taste. The stunning young lady had dropped John for an ad agency chief who wanted to use her in a national campaign.

They had fought when Catherine confronted her husband with each of his philanderings. She had threatened a divorce that would leave him living at the YMCA. He had denied his affairs despite damning evidence, in one case a credit card receipt for jewelry that he hadn't given to her. But the passage of time had healed her wounds, and he had eased his way back into her bed if not completely into her heart.

She, too, had trifled. She enjoyed a brief fling with the tennis professional at their club, which ended abruptly when she found that several other members were also enjoying his attention. And there was a long, simmering affair with the tenor in her church choir, which, while never actually consummated, reached the notoriety of gossip. But even if she had wandered a bit, her marriage to John was always her home base.

His affair in Washington had been a much different story. He had taken his love elsewhere and built a new life around it. She wasn't being cheated on but rather was being ignored. That had been more humiliating than any of his flings. Being discarded was much worse than simply being cheated on, but she had been helpless to do anything about it. To go public in a divorce would have exposed her as a discarded rag doll in a city where she was thought to be influential and powerful.

Her anger hadn't flashed like a gasoline fire that burns out quickly. Instead, it had simmered, like a fire deep down in a coal furnace. By the time it showed flames, every single coal of her being was white with heat. There was no confession, no apology, no abject pleading that could put the fire out.

When John came begging for her endorsement so that he could reach a higher station, there had been no question of forgiving him. The most there could be was a treaty for which each side would bargain in its own interests. He would demand that she take him back so he could use her family's image. She would demand the exclusive right to his attention, which she hadn't enjoyed for several years. Specifically, he had to end his affair with Pam and exile her to some place where he wasn't apt to see her again, even by accident. Given his ambitions, he had seen no choice but to agree.

They danced the first dance together to a sprinkle of polite applause, almost as if they were at their wedding. Catherine blushed at the attention and smiled in all directions. John kept his gaze fixed on her.

"When was the last time we danced together?" she asked.

"At the club, I think. Weren't we at the Spring Ball?"

"Not this spring," she said. "But it was at a Spring Ball. So that would be over a year ago."

"It doesn't seem that long," he answered.

"It does to me."

He led her to the bar and ordered her a cocktail. Then he found her a chair in one of the furniture groupings, where they instantly became the center of conversation. She told everyone how excited she was by her move to Washington. No, she hadn't come down from Connecticut just because he had become the secretary, she lied. They had been planning it since John had settled in with the institute. And, yes, it was very nice that he wasn't away all the time.

She played her part perfectly in public, and was every bit as convincing at home. Once John had agreed to her terms, she never broached the issue of his past sins, nor did she even subtly remind him that he was on a very short tether. Catherine had no interest in avenging her husband's neglect or any desire to embarrass him. What she enjoyed was that she was once again the center of his attention, and a full partner in his public acclaim. Whatever his admirers thought, she knew she was the one in power. She had no doubt that he knew it too. All she demanded was what she, as his wife, was entitled to.

She knew she didn't have his love. But, in truth, that was something she had learned to live without. Early in their marriage, long before John had first wandered, their passion had turned into accommodation. They had roles to play as parents, heads of a household, and up-and-coming forces in their community. John set off to conquer the business world and supply the wealth. Catherine threw her energy into the Junior League, church projects, and school board matters. The fires that had attracted them to each other burned out slowly. Love gave way to commitment.

Even their sex life had been crushed into routine. Whereas they had once tossed their clothes around wildly as they pursued each other to the bed, now their clothes were neatly folded and hung. Underwear went into the hamper. John even paused to put shoe trees into his tasseled loafers.

Lovemaking had found a precise place in their daily schedules, along with the 7:26 A.M. express to Manhattan, the seven P.M. choir rehearsal in the church hall, and the ten A.M. brunch at the country club. Two or three times a week, after the eleven P.M. news on television, they rolled into each other's arms. They made love quietly, so as not to disturb the children. Later, when their daughters were older, they kept their nightclothes on in case one of the children should come barging in. Still later, two or three times a week became Friday night, unless there was a late-night function at the club. What had once been the center of their relationship had been pushed off to the periphery.

Catherine still enjoyed intimacy with John, but, heaven knows, she didn't at all need it. If he was struck impotent, it would be disappointing, but it wouldn't change anything. The fact was that she hadn't been able to command her husband's love for many years. And, for a long time, she hadn't been able even to insist on his commitment. But now she could demand commitment, and attention, and exclusivity. John's ambition had given her that power. She intended to use it as a matter of their daily relationship. She intended to enjoy it for the rest of their lives.

When the evening ended, a chauffeured limousine took them to John's town house in Georgetown, and Catherine climbed the stairs to the upper chambers, which Pam had never visited. She changed into a nightgown and sat at the vanity in the master bath while she removed her makeup and brushed out her hair. She was already applying the cold cream when he appeared at her door.

"Tired?" he asked.

"It's been a long day," she said with a smile.

"But a good one, don't you think?"

"Marvelous," she agreed. "Your head must be swelling with all the accolades."

"Not accolades," he told her. "Just acknowledgments. I'm not the one sought after. I'm just the trading post where the favor seekers come to meet those who have real clout."

"Then you'll be moving up," she said.

He nodded. "I hope so. There's always something higher to reach for."

She stood, came to him, and kissed his cheek, leaving a small stain of cold cream. "Good night," she said.

He took a towel to wipe off the cold cream. "I'll be up working for a while. I'll crash in the guest room so as not to disturb you."

"Thank you," she answered. "I really am dead tired."

Six

"This is terrific. Absolutely terrific," Glen said as he dropped the typed pages onto the coffee table.

"You like it?"

" 'Like it' was when you told me about it. Now I'm crazy about it."

He climbed up from the perch on the floor where he had been reading Pam's revised proposal and joined her at the one-wall kitchen, where she was sautéing mushrooms. The steak, fresh from the broiler, was sizzling on top of the stove. Glen took the Cabernet he had brought for the feast and went to work with the corkscrew. He opened the glass cabinet, took down two oversized balloons, and poured a toast. "To *Fouling the Air!*" he announced. They touched glasses and sipped.

"How did you know where the wineglasses were?" Pam asked. "I found them only this afternoon."

"I've been here before," he answered, without the least embarrassment. "In fact, I gave Jean these glasses as a moving-in present."

She carried the steak to the table. "Do you work late hours all the time?"

"I have to. The day is taken up with agents on the telephone, meetings, financial matters, and long lunches with young authors who have just come into town. I do all my thinking after hours."

"I do my best work during the day," she answered, letting him know that whatever privileges he had enjoyed with Jean Abbott hadn't remained in the apartment.

Over dinner he told her that he intended to walk her proposal through his company personally. "I'll bring it up at the Monday publishers' meeting and tell them that we have to act on it quickly, before you show it to someone else."

"Where else could I take it?" She wasn't being coy. They both knew that she had no knowledge of the business.

"Nowhere," he said. "But if my bosses think there's no urgency, they'll take six months to read your proposal. Then they'll take another six months to dicker over the contract. I'm going to present you as a knowledgeable industry insider with an explosive story to tell, as a communications professional with dozens of publishing contacts. If we hesitate, you'll end up with another house."

"Wow!" She was a bit overwhelmed.

"With a little luck, I should have you under contract within a few weeks. So, you can start writing right away."

"Before dessert?" she teased.

"Right! You don't work at night. Well, get started in the morning. This is going to be a big book for both of us."

During dinner he probed. How had she managed to gather so much industry data? Pam answered that nearly all the member-company statistics were sent to the institute as fodder for her position papers. "We used what helped us and discarded what hurt us. But we did get to look over everything. We knew that our official figures weren't completely accurate." How had she gained access to private correspondence? "I had a password that let me into all of the institute's e-mail," she said, omitting that she had used John's password from her home computer. How did she find out about private conversations that took place when she wasn't present? "In many cases, the director briefed me on conversations and asked my opinion."

She could have put all Glen's worries to rest simply by telling him that she had been John Duke's mistress for nearly two years. That would explain how she had gotten into the industry's head and heard all of its whispered secrets. But it would mean exposing herself as one of those foolish women who believe that their lovers are actually going to leave their wives.

He helped her clear the table and start the dishes, then poured the rich, black coffee. When they were seated over dessert, he got into the schedule. "What are you hoping to deliver? How many chapters a week?"

"How many? I was hoping I might make one a week."

"You've outlined twenty-eight chapters. At that rate it will take us a year to get the book out. Some of your lead players might be dead by then. Or there could be changes in the industry that will make the story irrelevant."

"What were you hoping for?" she asked cautiously.

"Maybe three . . ."

"Three? Good God, that would be fifty pages a week. I can't do that."

"How about if I lend you a writer? Someone who interviews you, takes your notes, and gets the story down on paper. Then you could edit and rewrite."

"No," she answered with a vehemence that surprised both of them. "Let me see what I can do. If I fall way behind, then I'll ask you for help."

Glen agreed and told her that, in the interest of speed, she didn't have to worry about style or spelling. "Just get it down. We have copy editors who can work it into shape."

He left as soon as they had cleaned up the kitchen so that Pam could close the doors over it with a clear conscience. She went immediately to her computer, assembled her notes, and began working. She had thought getting started would be the most difficult part of the book, but the words came faster than she could type. She knew the material well, and she had decided to begin with the most dramatic part of her tale.

She opened with the moment Senator Lawrence had sent the institute's campaign contribution back and suggested that the industry add a zero. There had been no subtlety in the exchange. The bill had been reworked twice and was coming up for committee vote. Lawrence could let it go to the floor, where the industry could take its chances. In an open vote, there were probably a dozen key players, each of whom would be looking for a campaign contribution. But he could also bottle it up in committee, deciding that, even after its many revisions, it still was defective. He might even determine that the whole matter needed to be rethought.

She was going to stop her narrative right there, with the reader hooked and eager to find out whether the industry came up with the money. At that point, she was going to go back to the beginning, when the idea of smokestack regulations had first gained the government's interest. That part of her tale would also serve to introduce the key players. Then gradually, and with evidence offered to support each step, she was going to work her way forward in time to the point where her first chapter had begun.

When she came to a logical break in the opening chapter, Pam glanced at her watch. "Oh, my God," she yelled at herself. It was almost two A.M. How had she managed to stay awake? She scrolled back through her file. She had done seven pages in just four hours. At that rate, she could easily deliver Glen's three chapters a week. But she doubted she could keep going at this evening's pace.

She was up early and continued to work with the previous night's excitement. She had four more pages done by noon, when Glen phoned.

"How is it going?"

"Better than I could have expected," she said. "I think the book is already written in my head."

"Good! And I think I can save you some time by editing on the fly. I'll drop by a couple of nights a week and go over the pages you've completed. There's no point in waiting until you finish a whole week's work."

Pam thanked him and tried to sound enthusiastic over all the time and attention he was lavishing on her. Actually, she was wary. It wasn't that he had made any move, or even made a suggestive remark. But the ease with which he had insinuated himself into her life was unnerving. It was obvious that he had felt completely at home with the prior tenant of the apartment, coming and going whenever it suited his purposes. She knew their relationship had been professional, but she was beginning to suspect it might have gotten personal. Business associates didn't usually reach into your cupboards and help themselves to your wineglasses. Glen had apparently enjoyed many evenings with Jean Abbott, lingering after dinner. Pam didn't want to extend his franchise.

It wasn't that she disliked Glen. He was well mannered, soft-spoken, and very attentive. His conversation was bright and stimulating. He had certainly gone out of his way to help her get started in New York. But she still felt used and betrayed. She was just beginning to find her legs as a single, free, professional woman. She wasn't eager to have a man move into her space. Maybe in a year or two. Perhaps in some other part of the world. Certainly not here and now.

But it was just the next night when Glen buzzed up from the lobby. "I spared no expense on dinner," he said, then came to the door with a pizza and a straw basket of Chianti. "The best pizza north of Canal Street," he announced, "and the best Chianti that four dollars can buy."

He took a cutting board from one of her lower cabinets, laid the pie on top of it, and used it as a serving tray. Pam got out knives and forks, but Glen waved them away. He picked up a slice, folded it in half, and began eating out of his hand. She shrugged, sat at the table, and followed his lead.

They still had half a bottle of wine left when the pizza was finished, and they brought it with them to the floor beside the coffee table that seemed to have become their workplace. She watched while he made pencil corrections, replacing words and rearranging paragraphs. As he worked, he mumbled, "Good . . . terrific . . . ," and threw in an occasional "Ugh . . . no." When he was finished, he had a completed opening chapter stacked in front of them.

"Wonderful," he said. "I'll take these with me. I'll have a copy editor working on them tomorrow." He patted the top of her hand as if paying a compliment to a child. "Congratulations! It's a terrific beginning."

They talked about the next chapter while sipping the wine. Pam outlined the text, and Glen nodded or interrupted with suggestions. She got caught up in their work and relaxed completely for the first time since John had announced their breakup. The effects of the wine were suddenly strong, and the words tumbled out of her mouth. She threw her head back and laughed as she told him about John carrying on business negotiations in a ladies' room. A senator's aide had used a trip to the bathroom as an escape from John's nearly religious sermon about an industry need. He had walked right at her heels, pressing his case, and followed her into the women's lounge without ever realizing which door he had entered.

"You were pretty close to John Duke," Glen observed innocently.

Pam caught herself before babbling out an answer. "Well, I suppose so. We had a great deal of confidence in each other."

"Were you sleeping with him?" he asked, as if the question were no more intrusive than asking about her astrological sign.

"Isn't that a bit impertinent?"

He wasn't at all apologetic. "I was just wondering how you got so much inside information."

"Do you think I was some sort of Mata Hari, offering sex for information?"

"No, of course not. But having a fountain of industry information gushing over in your bedroom would explain a lot of what you know. It might even explain why you want to write this book. I was wondering if such lively prose was the work of a woman scorned."

She stood and picked up the empty glasses. "Would it matter?" she asked as she went toward the kitchen.

He lumbered to his feet and followed her with the empty bottle. "I suppose it would if people could dismiss the book as the peeving of a neglected mistress. Critics might ask."

"If they do, I'll tell them the same thing

I'm telling you. It's none of your damn business."

Glen nodded. "Okay, we'll leave it at that. When should I plan on picking up the next chapter?" He made his way to the door and let himself out.

Pam went to her desk to get started on her next chapter. But she was too troubled to concentrate. Was that what all this was — the peeve of a neglected mistress? She was angry at John and knew that her rage would continue burning for quite some time. There was something delicious about treating him as shabbily as he had treated her. But was that her only reason? She couldn't pretend to be simply a concerned citizen who was exposing the corrupting power of money in government. She had been part of that corruption, and probably still would be if John hadn't decided to become a member of the cabinet. Nor could she use the book's title, *Fouling the Air,* to pass herself off as an environmentalist. Hadn't she arranged data to suggest that smokestacks had nothing to do with air pollution? Why was she taking such relish in writing about influence peddling in the halls of government? Was her work nothing more than a tantrum?

Maybe it had been, when she first thought about the book. She had to admit that she had enjoyed the idea of embarrassing John and making him squirm. But now the book was taking on a life of its own. It wasn't about John, even though he was one of the characters. It wasn't even about the industry he had promoted. It was really about the inner workings of Washington, a cautionary tale to show readers that their government was slipping out of their hands. People would see that their elected representatives were hired out to the largest donors while the important business of the country went unattended. Yes, she had been part of the conspiracy, but now she was making a clean break.

Pam decided that she would say exactly that in her introduction. I did it. Others are still doing it. Her private relationship with John Duke wasn't the story. The story was the public things they had done together.

Seven

John Duke came through the doors of the Hotel Washington, glanced into the lobby, and spotted his mark. Senator Lawrence was sitting on a sofa in the corner, one hand wrapped around a glass of his favored sour mash, the other dipping into a dish of salted peanuts. He didn't notice John until the Secretary of Energy reached the sofa and settled into a stuffed chair on the other side of the coffee table.

"Senator," he said in greeting, and Lawrence returned, "Secretary." John signaled a waiter, who nodded and headed straight to the bar. Over the past two years, all the waiters in the small hotel had learned his preference for a pricey single malt. It was his constant after-hours drink.

"How are things at Energy?" the senator asked in his trademark Tennessee drawl. "Are the tree huggers giving you fits?" John nodded and elaborated that the environmentalists and the coal lobby had one thing in common. They both thought he was the enemy. They exchanged small talk until John's drink arrived and then toasted the health of the nation. With the niceties out of the way, John reminded Lawrence that he had asked John to "stop by if you have a minute." In the senator's idiom, that wasn't a casual invitation. It was a summons.

"What do you hear from that young woman who used to work over at the institute?" Lawrence asked as his opener. "You know, that good-looking woman who used to grind out all those industry numbers?"

"Pam Leighton?" John pretended to wonder, even though he knew the senator would have been briefed about every detail of Pam's life.

"That's it! Pam Leighton. Her looks were distracting whenever she appeared before us. I used to be wondering more about the kind of underwear she was wearing than about her testimony." He sipped his sour mash. "Have you heard from her lately?"

"No," John answered with a shrug and shake of his head. "I have no idea where she went."

"New York, I think," Lawrence said, as if he were recalling some vague rumor. "Did you know that she was writing a book?"

"A book? Pam?" John's surprise was genuine.

"So I'm told. Some sort of a tell-all about the institute and its lobbying activities."

John was amazed. "I had no idea Pam was working on a book."

"You might want to look into it. My understanding is that both of us are mentioned. My sources tell me it's not very flattering."

"Pam?" John was still trying to come to grips with the notion.

"I assume you people had some sort of nondisclosure agreement. Certainly she's bound to respect confidential information."

John wasn't sure what kinds of agreements they'd had. But he told the senator that Pam had signed something, and that he would look into it.

"I think that would be a good idea, Mr. Secretary. And then take a look at what she's writing. There may be some things that neither of us would want aired in public. People jump to some damn foolish conclusions about the way we work on the country's business. I'd hate to have Miss Leighton adding fuel to the fire."

John was nodding before Lawrence finished. "I'll certainly do that, Senator. And I appreciate your letting me know. Knowing

Pam, I don't think we have anything to worry about. But I'll certainly check things out and get back to you."

He knew he could find her. The institute had to have been in touch with her over a variety of matters, like her health coverage and pension assignments. And the new director would go to any lengths to please the Secretary of Energy. But John wasn't sure exactly how best to approach her.

Go to New York and take her to lunch, he thought. But if it ever got back to Catherine that he had been to see his former mistress, the consequences would be dire. He could get her on the telephone, but she might very well hang up at the sound of his voice. He couldn't write to her or send her an e-mail. These weren't things that you wanted to commit to writing. Maybe he should send an aide who would simply express the institute's concern and ask to preview her work. But the more he thought about it, the plainer it was that Pam wouldn't pay any attention to his messenger. It was an errand he was going to have to handle himself.

When he arrived at home, the cook was just setting the meal on the table. Catherine came down in a skirt and blouse, an outfit that flattered her figure without holding out any invitation to intimacy. They sat across from each other and waited in silence while they were served breasts of chicken and wild rice. The butler poured a nice Chardonnay. Catherine went into a pleasant review of her day, which had included bridge with another cabinet member's wife and then a quick cocktail with a lobbyist's wife and her friends. All very pleasant. Nothing consequential.

Then John described his meeting with Senator Lawrence and said that Pam Leighton was writing a book. Catherine stiffened and set down her fork. "Is she writing about you?"

"No, no. Nothing personal. Just about the industry and its lobbying efforts. I haven't seen it, so I don't really know how detailed it is." He was trying to appear unconcerned. "But the senator is pretty skittish about people revealing inside information. I promised him I would look into it."

Catherine wasn't fooled for an instant. "So you're going to meet with her."

"Well, that would be the best way to calm the senator. But I know it might also be upsetting to you. That's why I'm bringing it up."

"It is upsetting," Catherine said. "Can't you send someone else?"

John had anticipated her response. "I

could, but that would mean one more person would know about . . ." He let the thought die without mentioning his adultery. "I guess I need to know how you feel."

They went into silence, the only sounds the rattle of ice cubes and the ringing of silverware against their plates. Then Catherine reached her decision. "If you fly up and back on the same day, no one could charge you with an indiscretion."

"That's what I thought," he agreed. "We'll meet for lunch in a public place."

He phoned the institute the next morning and had Pam's new address and telephone number within an hour. He stared at the phone for a full minute before he picked it up and dialed. She answered on the first ring with an abrupt "Hello," as if he had interrupted something important.

"It's John," he said.

There was a terrible moment of silence. Then, "Hello, John."

"How are you doing?" he asked.

"Just fine, thank you. And how are you enjoying the president's cabinet?"

"Would you believe I haven't seen him since I was sworn in? It seems that energy is on the back burner."

There was another awkward pause. Then she asked, "Why are you calling, John?"

"As a matter of fact, I'm going to be in New York tomorrow. I thought you might like to have lunch with me. God knows, we have enough things to talk about."

Another silence before she answered, "I don't think that's a good idea. I think we should leave the past in the past."

"I'd really like to know what you're up to."

"I'm writing a book," she answered with no hesitation.

"Oh, I'd like to hear about it. I'll be coming in early in the morning. Couldn't we meet somewhere for an early lunch?"

"What if your wife finds out?"

"For God's sake, Pam, it's just lunch. I know that you and I are . . . over."

"That's the problem, John. Deep down inside, I don't think I've admitted that yet. I don't think sitting across the table from you is the best way to put the past behind me."

"Please," he said. "I really think we should talk."

She agreed to meet him at a sidewalk café across the street from Lincoln Center. She hoped she wouldn't regret her decision.

John already had a table when she arrived. He jumped to his feet and took her into a hearty embrace, careful to make it friendly and not intimate. "Pam, you're looking fabulous."

"You look tired, John. I hope you're getting your sleep."

"The government is a bit of a madhouse," he said. He signaled the waiter and ordered a bottle of water while they glanced at the menu. "So, you're writing a book! Tell me about it."

"I'll bet you already know about it. Isn't that why you're here?"

He was taken aback by her directness. "I've heard only that it's about the institute. Nothing of the details."

She answered, "There aren't many details. I just started working on it. And it won't be just about the institute. It takes a much wider look at the lobbying business."

"When can I see it? I assume that I'm one of the characters."

"You are, and I'll send you a copy when it gets published. I'll even autograph it."

He laughed and seemed satisfied until they had ordered their lunch. But then he got back to the book. "Senator Lawrence has heard about it. Apparently his sources think it puts him in a bad light."

"How would Senator Lawrence know what it says? The only ones who have seen it are my editor and myself."

John smiled. "You know better than that, Pam. The senator has friends everywhere. He's a very important man."

She remembered that Glen Hubbard had promised to rush the pages into production as fast as she delivered them. That meant any number of people might have handled the manuscript. Obviously, someone in the publishing house thought the senator ought to know.

"I've opened the book with our campaign contribution over the Clean Air Bill. The one that Senator Lawrence said needed another zero."

"Jesus!" John's face fell into his hands.

The waiter appeared with their salads. John ordered a glass of wine. Pam decided to stick with the bottled water. "Pam, you can't get into that," he resumed. "It makes him look like he's selling his vote."

"He'd already sold it," she said. "What he was quibbling over was the price."

"I'm sure you realize how embarrassing that incident would be for me. It makes me look like the senator's bagman."

"C'mon, John. You'll look like a winner. That had to be one of lobbying's finest moments."

He leaned closer to her. "You're accusing me of bribing a senator," he said in a muffled voice.

"I didn't use the word 'bribe.' At the time, you called it a campaign contribution, and that's exactly what I call it in my book. It's not a tirade, John. It's just a factual account of how things get done in government."

"Pam, don't kid yourself. This is a payback, isn't it? I hurt you, and now you're going to hurt me." She shook her head and started to respond, but he cut her off. "You said you loved me. You must still have some feeling for me. I did what I had to do. I was sorry then and I'm sorry now. But I never had a choice. Catherine would have destroyed me."

Her eyes locked on to his. "You had a choice, and you chose your own advancement over me. What I'm doing now isn't to hurt you. I'm launching my new career, and that means I'm going to take every possible step to be completely fair and accurate."

He moved the salad around on his plate and sipped his wine thoughtfully. "They'll never let you do it," he said. "When word gets out, they'll kill the book before it even goes to press."

"Who are *they?*" she asked defiantly.

"The industry executives. The board of the institute. The key lobbyists. Even the elected officials. People with deep pockets and enormous political clout. They like the way the system works right now, and they're not going to stand by and let you throw sand into the gears."

"Whatever happened to free speech?" she taunted.

"Don't be naive," he shot back. "You're putting your whole future in jeopardy just to get back at me."

She folded her napkin carefully and set it next to her plate. "This isn't about you, John. It's about me. I'm stepping out on my own." She stood and smiled. "Thanks for lunch. I'll send you a copy of the book."

She started to turn away, but he caught her elbow. "For your own sake, think about what you're doing. You're digging yourself a very deep hole."

She paused with a long, sympathetic glance. "If this was anyone but you, John, I'd think that might be a threat." He slumped back into his chair and watched her walk away.

EIGHT

Pam knew something was wrong as soon as she opened her apartment door. Something had changed, but it took her an instant to realize exactly what. The computer tower was on her desk instead of on the floor. The plastic case that held her CDs was missing. She called into the room, but there was no response. She closed the door behind her and started to the desk.

He came at her from the sleeping alcove and moved so quickly that she hardly saw him. She caught movement out of the corner of her eye but could turn only far enough for a glimpse at a figure in a dark T-shirt. Before she could scream, a gloved hand covered her mouth. Pam kicked and twisted, trying to break free, but the grips across her face and around her waist were tight and unyielding. Then there was the voice, whispering in her ear. "Take it easy, lady, I'm not going to hurt you."

He lifted her off her feet and turned her toward the alcove. She saw the bed, and the flash of anger that had powered her struggle suddenly became a dreadful terror — he's going to rape me. Should she fight to the death or give in meekly? Would begging do her any good?

But he pushed her past the bed to the door of the bathroom, then fired her through the opening. Pam staggered forward and caught the edge of the sink to keep from falling onto the hard tile floor.

"Stay in there!" his voice ordered. The door slammed behind him.

She had caught a quick image in the mirror over the sink. A nearly bald head, narrow eyes, a round face unshaven for several days. His neck was wide and his shoulders and arms powerful. He hadn't had to tell her not to come out. Pam threw her weight against the door to keep him from coming in.

It became deathly quiet. She was struggling to stifle her sobs when she realized that the apartment sounded empty. She hadn't heard the front door close, but she was aware that he must have left. She reached for the door handle, then decided to wait a bit longer before venturing out. She let the minutes drift past, pressing her ear to the door every few seconds. Finally, she felt sure he must have gone.

She eased the door open and listened carefully. There wasn't a sound other than a distant rumbling from the air-conditioning. She heard a bird chirp, which meant that the French doors must be open. When she stepped out of the bathroom, she saw they were.

She glanced about the sleeping alcove. The drawers from the night table were lying on the floor. The books across the top of the headboard were toppled. She stepped cautiously into the living room, listened, then went to the desk. There was a small pile of machine screws next to the computer tower. The tower cover was ajar. When she lifted it, she saw open spaces, loose connectors, and a few cut wires. Her hard drive and the motherboard had been ripped out. She pulled open the drawer and found that all her CDs and floppies were missing. The intruder had stolen every bit of digital memory that might have held any part of her book. As she searched more closely, she found that every space in the apartment had been opened and its contents tossed. Every page and file that related in any way to her book had been taken.

Pam went back to the door and checked

the lock. There was no sign of forced entry, not even a scratch on the metal surface. She tried her key, and the lock worked perfectly. She called down to the building superintendent and asked him to call the police. He told her there had been no tradesmen working, or any unusual deliveries. He doubted that anyone had even used the elevator. Then she remembered the French doors leading out to her balcony. They were open, but she couldn't remember whether she had left them that way. She was three floors above the garden, and two stories down from the roof. How could anyone have gotten to her balcony? Then she called Glen Hubbard and told him that the book had been stolen. He promised to be right over.

The police got there first, two uniformed officers in blue windbreakers. They glanced around, touching nothing, then settled at her dining table. One of them asked questions while the other noted her answers. The interview was brief.

She had been out for less than two hours, probably an hour and a half. She had no idea how the burglar had gotten in. The front door was locked, and even though the French doors were open, her balcony would have been impossible to reach from either the ground or the roof. At this point, the officer who was asking the questions ventured out on the balcony, looked down and then up.

Glen rang the bell, and Pam buzzed him through the front door. He arrived just as she was describing her assailant and listened while she explained how the man had held her from behind and forced her into the bathroom. "You could have been killed," he blurted out and took her hand.

She introduced Glen to the police and explained that he was the publisher of the book that was stolen.

"A book?" one of the officers asked. "I thought it was just computer stuff."

"It was! Computer memory and processors," Pam said. "But they contained notes and pages for a book that I'm writing."

The officer shrugged and jotted down a few words.

"It's the book that's valuable," Glen interrupted. "The computer hardware can easily be replaced. But the book has a great deal of value."

"How much?" the other policeman asked.

"I don't know," Glen answered. "We won't know until it's published."

The officers looked blankly at each other. Then the one who had been asking the questions tried to summarize. "Look, what we do in these cases is post a description of the stolen goods. If someone tries to sell them locally, we might be able to pick him up."

Glen felt his impatience coming to a boil. "No one will try to sell the hardware. They'll wipe the memory clean and throw the disk drives in the trash."

"And we'll file a report with the detectives," the officer went on, ignoring Glen's comment. "One of them will probably want to talk with you." They started to the door.

"Aren't you going to investigate? Don't you want to dust for fingerprints?" Glen asked.

The officers exchanged glances, one of them holding back a laugh. The other explained, "What we have here is a burglary. Simple case of breaking and entering. We save the stuff you see on television — looking for fingerprints and DNA samples — for the more important crimes."

Glen started to lecture. "This *is* an important crime. Someone tried to kill Miss Leighton to stop publication of her book. It's not just —"

The officer cut him off with a raised hand. "No one tried to kill Miss Leighton. She had the bad luck to walk in on a burglar, and sometimes these guys panic and do get violent. But this was a pro. He just put her out of the way so he could take what he wanted and get away clean. It's only a burglary. But like I said, we'll notify the detectives. One of them may want to investigate further."

"Should I leave things just as they are?" Pam asked.

"No, you can tidy up. But what you should do is keep a lock on those French doors. If I lived in this neighborhood, I'd have a roll-down steel shutter or something." He touched the tip of his cap, and the two officers filed out the door.

"Is everything gone?" Glen asked her as soon as they shut the door.

"Everything that was here."

"You mean you have it all backed up?"

"You have the outline and the first two chapters," she reminded him. "I have the originals of all my notes stored away with my furniture. We'll lose only a day or two. But that's not the point. What we should be worrying about is that someone is trying to stop publication. And whoever it is, they have a spy planted inside your company."

His eyes widened. "A spy? What in hell are you talking about?"

She explained that John Duke had come to New York because he had heard about the book. From his comments, she thought Senator Lawrence also knew about it, and maybe people at the institute. "How would they have found out about it so quickly," she reasoned, "unless someone in your place told them? No one else knows that I'm writing a book about the industry."

Glen was about to argue, but he could see her point. "Well, there's my secretary, and the copy editor. They're the only ones that have read the first chapter besides me. The legal department knows about the book, but they have no idea what it's about. All they've done so far is draw up the contract. And, of course, top management. But they haven't seen any of the manuscript." He threw up his hands. "My people either don't know or don't care about what you're writing. They couldn't be tipping anyone off!"

"John Duke found out," Pam repeated. "That's why he rushed up to New York. He wanted me to stop for his sake. He said the book would ruin him."

"How could he have found out?" Glen asked himself. "No one in my place would have told him."

"He also hinted that the book could ruin me. He said there were lots of important people and millions of dollars involved. He told me that the people would never let the book see the light of day."

Then Glen realized. "You were at lunch with John Duke while they were breaking in here and stealing your computer. Maybe that was his real reason for meeting with you: Get you out of the house and keep you out while the burglar did his work."

"I walked out on him before we had finished lunch," Pam said. "I got home before I was supposed to." She thought for a moment, weighing the implications of the scenario she had just sketched out. "John Duke was working with a burglar?"

Glen put an arm around her shoulder and led her to the sofa. He went back to the kitchen, retrieved a bottle of Scotch from the top shelf of one of the cupboards, and brought it to her along with two glasses of ice. "Let's just relax for a few minutes and see if we can figure this out. If it's your old friends from the power industry, we don't want to let them scare us off the story."

Pam pointed at the bottle. "How did you know about that? I never bought it. Jean must have left it behind."

"I brought it in," he said as he poured a small measure in each glass. He handed one to her. "I told you, I worked over here lots of times."

"Were you sleeping with Jean?" Pam demanded.

"Isn't that a bit impertinent?" he said with a smile, tossing her own words back at her.

"Glen, do you have a key to this apartment?"

He hesitated, then said, "Yes, I do."

"Do you have it with you?"

"No. Jean and I haven't worked together for several months. I think the key is back at the office in a desk drawer."

"Is that why she was assigned overseas? Because she and you broke up?"

"No, not at all. Jean and I worked together on and off for about two years. We had a very brief affair, maybe six months ago, that we both agreed wasn't going to work. She took an assignment in the London office because she wanted to try something different. She's working with a nearly unintelligible scientist, trying to get his book ready for publication. Jean didn't leave because of me, and if she comes back, that won't be because of me."

Pam weighed not just what he said but also the expression on his face. She didn't know why, but his explanation rang true. "I think you should find the key. If it's not in your desk, then maybe the same person who leaked the book has it. In the meantime,

I'm going to get the locks changed. I may even get that steel shutter. Right now I don't feel very safe."

"Throw a few things together," he said. "We'll have dinner and then you can stay at my place."

She shook her head. "No, I'd better get back to work. I've already lost today."

"You can't work without your computer," Glen reminded her. "Tomorrow, you get the locks changed and get your records out of storage. I'll have a computer brought over from the office, and I'll check on that key. There's nothing we can do tonight. Why should you stay here listening to things that go bump in the night?"

"I'll be all right," she assured him bravely. Her tone wasn't convincing.

"Pam, you can have the bedroom. There's a lock on the door."

She wavered. "Let's see how I feel after dinner."

"Okay, but get some things in case you decide you'd feel safer with me."

They spent dinner wondering who had broken in and stolen the manuscript. Pam leaned toward the institute. "Anyone who saw the first chapter would know that it concerned the institute, and the people there would want to protect John at all costs. Besides, he was the one who got me out of the apartment." But Glen thought it must have come from the government. "I don't think anyone on my staff would understand the importance of the book. And none of them knows about the key. If it's someone at Thomas Howell, then it's probably someone in our parent company who has a friend with government clout." He reasoned that it had taken real professionals, whether they unlocked the front door or found a way in from the balcony. He was thinking in terms of military types, or the FBI. But all of their ideas had obvious flaws. When the coffee came, they were no closer to a solution than they had been when they unfolded their napkins.

"I don't feel good about you staying at your apartment," Glen concluded. "At least not until you get new locks and a dead bolt for the French doors."

Pam wasn't at all sure she ever wanted to go back there. Certainly not tonight. She decided to take Glen up on his offer of a night's lodging.

His apartment was in a new building with windows looking out on Lincoln Center. He showed her into the master bedroom, which he insisted was hers for the night. He had a daybed in his office. They shared a nightcap and in a burst of bravado decided that they wouldn't let themselves be frightened off. But they would take precautions. He would continue to be the liaison for the project, picking up her pages as fast as she finished them. But he was also going to take personal charge of the production process, cutting his own company out of the loop. "As far as they'll know, nothing more is coming in until the manuscript is finished." Her part of the ploy would be to tell anyone who asked that she had given up on the project. She might even go out on some job interviews so it looked as if she wanted to get back to work. "They warned you," Glen summarized, "and they demonstrated that they could get to you. So what we'll do is make it look as if you've been frightened off."

Letting herself actually be frightened off wasn't that bad an idea, Pam thought as she closed the bedroom door behind her. The book was a very personal catharsis for her and, as she was beginning to believe, maybe even an important national contribution. But it wasn't worth having "military types" or the FBI breaking in on her. It sure as hell wasn't worth getting mugged for.

She changed into her pajamas and made a

point of not turning the key in the bedroom door. She guessed Glen would be listening for a click, and if they were entering a conspiracy together, she thought she should show that she trusted him.

She woke up to the sound of a distant door slamming, jumped up, and stared into the morning sunlight that was streaming through the window. She put on a robe and walked out to the living room. "Glen?" There was no answer. She glanced into the kitchen. The coffeemaker was gurgling. There were two places set on the small kitchen table. She looked around quickly; no note, or any hint of where he had gone. He hadn't said that he would be leaving. If something had come up suddenly, he could have told her or at least left a note. So where was he? Had the people who had thrown such a scare into her decided to warn her publisher as well?

She went back to the bedroom and changed into the slacks and sweater she had worn the prior evening. She took her Black-Berry into the kitchen and sent him an e-mail:

Glen, you weren't here, so I left. Call me at my apartment, because I'm worried.

She had just retrieved her bag when she heard a sound outside the front door.

Was the door locked? Pam moved quickly to make sure. But the handle on the dead-bolt lock began to turn. It clicked, and then the door began to open. She rushed it, threw all her weight against it, and felt it hit hard against the intruder. There was a quick cry of pain, followed by a curse. "Damn it!"

"Oh my God!" Pam recognized the voice and pulled the door open. Glen Hubbard was standing in his own doorway, his glasses pushed to the side of his face, a paper bag pressed up against his chest. "Glen!" she shouted.

He raised the bag. "I got some bagels."

"Oh, God," Pam repeated and threw her arms around him. "Are you okay?" She buried her face against his shoulder.

He stood motionless until she unlocked her arms and backed away a step. Then he straightened his glasses. "If I knew you were this crazy about bagels, I would have skipped the Chinese and the pizza."

"I thought you'd been kidnapped," she said, still standing in his doorway.

"No," he told her calmly. "I just went down to the corner. I even got some cream cheese."

"You should have left me a note," she chastised.

"May I come in?" he said.

"Oh, yes, of course." She backed into the living room.

"I knew I'd be back in a few minutes. It would take you that long to find a note."

"Well, you could have told me."

"Sure, I could have walked right into the bedroom. Except you might have been sleeping in the nude. Would you have believed that I had come in to tell you about bagels?" He went to the kitchen and shook a half dozen bagels onto the counter. Pam was right at his heels.

"I don't sleep in the nude."

"I'm sorry to say I don't know that for a fact," he answered. Then he asked, "Do you like them sliced and toasted, or broken and heated in the oven?"

"Any way is fine." She turned and sank slowly into one of the kitchen chairs. "I panicked. I thought surely they had come after you. What in God's name has gotten into me?"

"You were attacked and robbed yesterday. You don't get over something like that in a day." He dropped the sliced bagels into the toaster and brought a container of cream cheese to the table. "I'm a little jittery myself. When the door slammed back into my face, I thought someone had broken in."

Pam stood and pressed against him, kissing him gently on the cheek. "I'm sorry for being such a jerk," she said.

He started to draw her into an embrace but was interrupted by the bagels popping out of the toaster.

NINE

Pam met the locksmith at her apartment and watched carefully as he replaced the lock in her door and added a second dead bolt that could be accessed from the inside only. On the French doors, he installed dead bolts into both the bottom and top frames. They were key-locked on the inside so that someone couldn't open the locks simply by breaking a windowpane. The man was finishing the work when Glen called to say that the old apartment key was still in his desk drawer. But, they agreed, someone might have copied it and returned it. The new locks were still a prudent investment in her safety.

But the computer he had told her was "on the way over" didn't arrive. Pam waited through lunch and at two P.M. phoned him. She had to leave to retrieve her stored files from a warehouse in Long Island City. Glen traced the shipment; the new computer tower, along with a laptop, was to be delivered at three. She waited, then lost another half hour while the technician hooked up the new system. It was closing in on four P.M. when she found a taxi and gave the driver the warehouse address.

The taxi crept across to the East Side in Manhattan's perpetual traffic jam and reached the bridge in time to catch the first flow of commuters. It was nearly closing time when she reached the warehouse, and the clerk was visibly annoyed. "You got ten minutes," he warned as they rode up in a freight elevator that was nothing more than an open platform. "I don't get paid for overtime."

They got off at the fourth floor. He flicked a switch that turned on lights all over and led her through a labyrinth of corridors to a fire door with her number stenciled on the gray metal. He opened the padlock, reached inside, and turned on the lights in her vault. As she stepped inside, he reminded her, "Ten minutes."

"It may take a bit longer," Pam answered. "Can I let myself out?"

"No way, lady. Just make it quick!"

She looked around the vault and found her Washington furniture against the back wall. Her computer system was sitting appropriately on top of her office desk, locked under the same Bubble Wrap blanket that protected the desk. She should have summoned the clerk to cut and then reseal the wrapper, but she knew if she went down he wouldn't let her back up. She would have to make do with what she had at hand.

Pam scanned the cardboard boxes that held her china and kitchenware, each with a packing slip indicating its contents. The third box she checked contained kitchenware, and she peeled back the shipping tape. Inside, halfway to the bottom, was her set of chef's knives mounted in a wooden block. She pulled out a twelve-inch paring knife and went to work on the desk wrapping. It took only a minute to cut a window in the packing material, but still she had used up most of the ten minutes she was allowed.

She had copied all her files onto the computer hard drive before she handed the machine over to the movers. All she had to do was copy them onto new CDs and she would recover everything that had been stolen. But there was no power outlet in the storage vault, so she would have to lug the twenty-pound computer tower back to her apartment. She lifted it in both arms and carried it out of her vault. She set it down for the instant it took to turn off the light, close and lock the door. Then she picked it up and retraced her way through the maze of intersecting corridors. For a moment she thought she was lost, but she went ahead, trusting her sense of direction. She smiled when she saw the steel rails that guided the open elevator platform.

As she was walking toward it, she heard the motor start. Her timing had been perfect. When the clerk reached her level she could step aboard and tell him that everything was locked up. That wouldn't leave him much to complain about.

She stepped as close to the open shaft as she dared and set down the computer to rest her arms. She could see that the elevator was creaking upward, halfway between the first and second floors. Leaning out just a bit, she looked for the clerk and was about to shout down happily that she had finished just under the limit. But it wasn't the clerk. Even from the angled glimpse, she knew it was the man who had ransacked her apartment and forced her into the bathroom.

Pam turned and started to run, but her heels hit the floor like rifle shots. She stopped and kicked off her shoes. His head was beginning to appear over the floor level, rising inch by inch. In a second he would see her. She saw the heavy, industrial light switch that the clerk had pressed when they reached the floor. She lunged at it and threw the whole floor into darkness. Then she eased away slowly, backing along the wall of the corridor.

There was a beam of light shining up the shaft from the ground floor, getting smaller and smaller as the elevator filled the opening on her level. It was hardly visible when the platform stopped, but it gave enough backlight for her to see the silhouette of her attacker. She recognized the shaved shape of his head and the broad shoulders. He stepped out of the light and into the darkness.

She kept retreating, past one corridor and then another. She could make out his footsteps, but she couldn't tell which way he was going. Was he following her? Or was he searching for the light switch? If he found the lights, he would be looking directly at her. She backed into the next corridor and turned, so that she could move more quickly.

The footsteps followed, slowly paced as he worked his way through the dark. He was moving blindly, aided only by the walls and corners that were barely visible in the ambient light from the shaft. But Pam knew that he would soon gain his night vision and be able to move more quickly. She couldn't outrun him. She had to find a hiding place and hope that he would pass by her.

She came to another passageway that intersected the corridor she was on. She could continue ahead, or she could go right or left. Beyond the barely visible corners, all routes led into blackness. She chose to go left because that seemed to be the direction leading back to the elevator. She took a few cautious steps and then stopped to listen. The footsteps had stopped.

Pam held her breath. He must have heard her and stopped to figure the direction of the sound. Both of them were deathly still, probably no more than twenty feet apart. Had he decided where he had heard her moving? Was he easing toward her, or was he waiting for her to make the next move?

Her eyes were becoming more accustomed to the dark. She could make out the outline of the door to the vault nearest to her and two or three padlocks farther down. It would be easier for her to move. But she knew that his eyes were finding outlines in the blackness as well. If he got into the same corridor with her, he would be able to spot her movements.

He took a step lightly, but she could hear the footfall. He seemed to be in the distance, maybe still in the hallway that led from the elevator. If he was, then they were in parallel aisles, he moving away from the elevator while she went toward it. Her best move would be to continue in her direction. She might be able to get to the elevator when he was at the other end of the building.

Another step. This one sounded closer. He had turned into the hallway where she had made her first turn. She couldn't wait where she was until he reached the intersection. But she was too frightened to move. She heard him again, closer still. She stepped off as quietly as she could. She breathed so gently that she was suddenly aware of her heart pounding. He could certainly hear it, Pam thought. It sounded like a sledgehammer.

His footstep sounded from behind her. She was closer to the elevator than he was. She came to another intersection. If she had figured correctly, this new aisle ought to lead back to her original escape route. That would put the elevator only a few feet to her right. She started up, guessing that her pursuer was once again moving in the opposite direction in a parallel passage. She could see the end of the hall, glimmering in the sparse light from the shaft. Pam knew she had to reach that corridor before he followed her route and arrived where she had just turned. If she could get to the elevator while he was still searching the dark passages, then he wouldn't be alerted until he heard the sound of the elevator motor. By the time he retraced his steps, she might be halfway down.

In her panic, it was hard to keep from gulping in the air she needed, even harder to keep from breaking into a dash. She needed soft, measured steps, although her every instinct was to scream and run. She was almost there. The footsteps she heard seemed a long way behind her. Still, she managed to keep her steady, silent pace.

Pam reached the corner and eased her head out into the crossing corridor. Just to her right, the elevator girders were visible against the narrow light shining up from below. She started toward the shaft, struggling to move quietly.

She reached the edge and bent slowly to retrieve the computer. She stepped aboard the elevator platform and set the computer down gently. Then she put her hand on the elevator control lever. The clerk had pushed it forward when he brought her up. Pam pulled the handle back.

In the distance, an electric motor began to hum. Next to her, there was a loud crack as the cable to the counterweight tensed. With a creak, the platform began to lower. The movement was nearly imperceptible; quarter inches, then half inches. It seemed it would take forever to descend a full foot.

Pam heard a furious clattering of footsteps. She saw movement in the shadows. Then, in the growing shaft of light that brightened as the platform dropped below the level of the floor, she saw the man's form hurtling toward her. She recognized the face that she had glimpsed in her bathroom mirror. She pulled the handle back as far as she could, but it made no difference. The elevator continued to groan down at a painfully slow speed.

He never hesitated. As soon as he reached the shaft, he jumped and landed in the center of the platform. Pam spun toward him to defend herself, but her attacker was instantly balanced. Once again, the hand flew over her mouth and pulled her head back against his shoulder. Instead of clutching her around the waist, he used his free hand to pick up the computer. She twisted and kicked for an instant, but the hand tightened across her face. She stopped struggling. He could easily smother her, or break her neck like a twig.

The third floor rose slowly around them

as the elevator descended. He moved her to the edge, then forced her off, still keeping the iron grip across her face. He stepped off behind her and set the computer down. Then, with an arm around her waist, he lifted her feet off the floor.

She knew he could take her into any one of the dark corridors. He could kill her if he wanted. But he could have killed her the day before. It was the computer he was after. She reached out with a dangling foot and pushed against the top of the computer case. The machine toppled into the shaft. Even though it fell only a few feet, the case smashed open.

Her attacker hesitated. He would have to leap onto the platform to get the computer. But to do that he would have to let her go. He released the grip around her waist and leaned over the edge, reaching for the case. Pam was able to break out of his grasp. He touched the top of the case but wasn't able to take hold of it. At the same time, he reached out for her. As he swayed in indecision, she drove a vicious kick into his groin.

Pain flashed across his face. He groaned through clenched teeth and sank slowly to his knees. But he held on to her foot, dragging her toward him as he slumped. She punched at his face, but he ignored the blows. Contorted with pain, he had all he could do to keep her from getting away.

Pam wasn't running. At that moment, she was fighting. There was no escape into the dark corridors where he would find her sooner or later. She had to get on the elevator, now halfway to the second floor. Furiously, she raked her nails across his face and dug her thumbs into his eyes. He let out a loud scream, released her foot, and clutched blindly at her hands, tearing them from his face. He stood slowly, managing to hold on to her even though he was unsteady. He looked over the edge and saw the elevator platform, now past the second floor and still going down. He forced Pam toward the opening.

She twisted one hand free and, before he could catch it again, made another jab at his eyes. In his fury, he slapped the back of his hand across her cheek. Her knees buckled, and for a moment she thought she was falling. But she got her balance just as he grasped her free hand. With him holding her up, she aimed another kick at his groin and found the mark again. This time, though, she wasn't nearly as effective. He was able to keep her wrists locked even while struggling to stay on his feet. He dragged her toward him.

She kicked again, and he had to let go of one of her hands to catch her knee. Then her sharp nails were back in his face. He let go with the other hand and aimed a punch at her head. But he missed wildly and lost his balance. Pam stepped into him and pushed with all her might. He staggered backward until his left foot found nothing but open air. He felt himself falling and let go of her in his panic to find a handhold. But his weight was already over the edge, and he began to topple backward. He fell headfirst into the shaft.

The elevator platform was sliding past the first floor on its way to the basement. He fell three stories and hit hard, his head snapping against his shoulder. His body crumpled and splayed. He lay on his back, his eyes staring back up at Pam. Even from her height, she knew that he was dead.

TEN

Pam finally got the attention of an NYPD detective. Sergeant Peter Vitale, who arrived at her apartment the next morning, was nothing like the handsome law enforcers from television. He was short, no more than five feet, six inches, and round, probably tipping the scales at two hundred pounds. His hair was dark and thin at the top, but gray and thick around his ears. He had the eyes of a basset hound and the chin of a bulldog. Yet it all worked together, making the sergeant appear pleasant and certainly unthreatening.

Vitale had responded to a call from the warehouse clerk, who had awakened from a blow on the back of his head to find his attacker dead on the elevator floor. Together the detective and the clerk had climbed the fire stairs, calmed Pam, and led her down to the office. By that time, the emergency medical people had arrived, confirmed that the sprawled-out figure on the elevator was dead, and sealed off the platform with yellow crime-scene tape. Vitale had listened with great patience to Pam's hysterical account of the assault, the battle on the third floor, and her attacker's fall into the elevator shaft. Her appearance confirmed her story. Her blouse was torn and smeared with dirt as if she had been rolled across the warehouse floor. There was a welt on her cheek, and her hair was a mess. Every time she tried to talk, she trembled with fright.

In the meanwhile, other police vehicles had arrived, including a white panel truck labeled FORENSICS. The body had been photographed and the area dusted with the care and attention of a religious observance. Glen had come in response to Pam's cell-phone call and sat beside her while offering vague assurances that everything would be all right. Vitale had tried once again to get the details of her story and realized she had already been through more than she could handle. He had told Glen to take Pam and her computer home, promising that he would contact her again in the morning.

Glen had taken her to her apartment, donned an apron to cook a chop from the freezer, and found a bottle of ordinary red wine in the back of another cupboard. While he cooked, Pam had showered, used drops to take the blazing red from her eyes, and applied makeup base to cover the bruise made by the back of her attacker's hand. She had dressed in jeans and a T-shirt, cried on and off, then accepted his offer of a night's protection. She finally fell asleep in her bed, relieved that he was only a few feet away on the sofa.

They had been awakened by a call from the building superintendent, who announced that a "Sergeant Vitale is on his way up." They had dressed frantically in the previous night's clothes and tossed the bedding into the bathroom before the detective knocked on the door. Now they were sitting in the living room while Vitale tried his best to make sense out of his scribbled notes.

"You have no idea who he was?" the sergeant asked.

"Just that he was the same man who attacked me two days ago, when the police couldn't have cared less."

"Yeah, well, we care now," Vitale answered. "But we don't know who the guy was either. He had no identification on him. There were no tags in his clothes. All we had to go on were his fingerprints."

"And?" Glen asked, as if the fingerprints

should have revealed everything.

"Negative! Nothing in our files and, so far, nothing back from the feds. That brings me back to you, Miss Leighton. It's pretty obvious that your burglar wasn't *just* a burglar. He was after whatever it is that you keep in your computers. So I have to ask what is it that you're up to, and who might want to stop you?"

"I'm writing a book about my experiences in Washington. I used to work there with a lobbying group."

"Lobbying for what?" Vitale asked.

"The electric power industry," she answered, "but the book is broader than that. It's about how all the special-interest groups get the government to do their bidding."

The detective smirked. "Sounds like you're trying to make lots of enemies."

"There's not much in it that people don't already know!" she snapped. She was the one who had been assaulted. It was supposed to have been her body splayed out at the bottom of the elevator shaft. Why was he questioning her as if she was the criminal?

Glen tried to take over. He explained that he was the publisher of the book, knew its contents, and didn't consider it incendiary. "It will embarrass a few people and bruise a few big egos."

"Whose egos?" Vitale interrupted.

Glen threw up his hands. "Anyone who has been sending money to public officials. The lobbyists who dangle the money. The senators and congressmen who sell their votes. But these aren't the kinds of people who hire a hit man."

"But he wasn't a hit man. From what you've told us, he wasn't after Miss Leighton. He was after the information in her computer. When he broke in here, he had you in his grasp," he said to Pam. "And in the warehouse, he had every opportunity to kill you. So I don't think we're looking for someone who wants you dead. It seems to me we're after someone who wants to kill your book."

"That could be anyone," Glen had to agree.

Then Vitale asked Pam, "Can you give me a list of the people named in your book?"

"Of course not!" she exploded.

The detective tried to calm her down. "Look, Miss Leighton, all I'm doing is looking for someone who has a motive. I'm trying to be helpful."

Pam looked properly chastised.

Vitale stood and closed his notebook. "Try to put together a list," he said to her. "In the meantime, I'd like to go through the material in your book. I want to take your computer records back with me."

"Absolutely not," Glen protested. "The computer, and whatever is on it, is Miss Leighton's private property. Nobody has the right . . ."

Vitale rolled his eyes, indicating that he had heard it all before. "I'm on your side," he reminded Glen. Then he emphasized to Pam that he was "looking for the person who attacked you."

"I won't allow it," Glen hollered. "She needs those records to continue her work."

The detective shrugged. "I can always get a court order," he said.

Glen began sputtering that his lawyers would get involved, but Pam raised a hand to quiet him. "Will I get it back?"

Vitale nodded. "In a couple of days. As soon as we copy and transcribe the files."

"Then you can take the computer. It's right here." She pulled the broken tower out from under her desk.

Glen watched openmouthed as the detective lifted the machine and went toward the front door. Pam skipped ahead, only too anxious to open it for him. She closed it as soon as he was out of the way.

"Are you crazy?" Glen demanded. "How

long do you think it will be before John Duke has a copy?"

She reached behind the sofa pillow and took out a dull metal frame that had a series of colored wires protruding from its side. "He didn't get anything that John would be interested in," she said with a smile. "All he got was an empty case."

Glen's angry expression softened slowly into a smile. "You took out the hard drive?"

"All my records from the institute," she answered.

"Then we're still in business?"

"If you shut up, and get all of these files copied. The detective will be back as soon as someone tells him that the hard drive is missing. We'd better have two copies by then, in two different places."

He saw her smile and found that he was smiling too. "You're fantastic," he told her.

Pam answered, "I'll *feel* fantastic when you get back with the copies."

Glen returned the next morning, bringing donuts and flavored coffee. Pam set the table as they spoke. He explained that he had gone to a friend who had put two complete copies on compact discs. "I've already hidden one in my office. The second one is yours. You'll just have to copy it onto the machine I sent over."

"Is it safe for me to work here?" she asked.

"No, I have another place in mind. I want you out of town, where they can't find you."

"Where?"

"I'll tell you after we eat." He pulled out a chair and seated her in front of a cup of coffee and a plate of doughnuts. "We'll eat and then take a walk in the park."

They walked three blocks east and entered Central Park at the museum. Glen kept finding reasons to stop and glance around until Pam suddenly realized what was going on.

"Do you think we're being followed?"

"It could be," he answered. "Someone followed you to the warehouse. How else could they have known where you were going?"

"And bugged?" she said. "That's why we're out here in the park. You think my apartment has been bugged."

"Why not?" he responded. "The guy who took your computer was in your place all the time you were having lunch. He could have installed anything: microphones . . . cameras."

Glen had made his point, and Pam was suddenly eager to get away. "Where are you hiding me?" she asked.

He told her as they were walking across

an open, grassy field. He owned a weekend house on the eastern end of Long Island. "It's not a Hamptons mansion," he assured her, "and it's nowhere near the beach. But it's secluded . . . private. I don't think anyone will find you there." He wanted her to take just the bare necessities, leaving most of her things in her apartment. "Let them think that you're still living here in the city, away visiting friends or whatever."

"How long?" she wondered.

"Into the fall. Until it gets cold. The cottage has a fireplace, but there's no central heat."

"And how will I get chapters to you?"

"I'll come out on weekends, just like I always do. I'm not going to tell anyone in my office where you are or what you're writing. They'll be completely out of the loop."

"Do you really think that's going to fool anyone?" she asked, her expression showing that she thought the idea was far-fetched.

"For a while, yes. It won't take long for whoever is looking for you to figure out that you're not coming back. But if you don't make phone calls or write letters home, it won't be easy for them to find you."

"Won't they just pick you up and hang you by your thumbs?"

"Why? All I'll tell them is that you're off

someplace writing a book. I expect to hear from you when it's finished. I'll promise to get back to them as soon as I hear from you."

"What about my rent?" she asked.

"Give me a check when I come out to work with you. I'll mail it in Manhattan."

They found a park bench and sat while Glen suggested new diversions to confuse her pursuers. "I could send someone over to Europe using your passport, then have them come back on their own."

"The problem," Pam interrupted, "is that there's someone in your company who has friends in Washington. If we make even one small slipup . . ."

"I'll put the same word out in the company. You're off someplace working. Probably back home in Indiana. No one will get antsy until your manuscript is due and you haven't returned the advance. By then, we'll have a book."

"It's risky," she concluded.

"The alternative," he said, "is to drop the project. Then John Duke and his government friends live happily ever after."

ELEVEN

Pam had fallen in love with the cottage at first sight. It was a small saltbox of weathered, hand-split shakes, set back from the road in a wild undergrowth of leafy plants and scrawny trees. There were two shuttered casement windows flanking the tall front door, and a screened-in porch that reached into the foliage on the right side. It was unobtrusive, private, and quiet, the ideal place to hide and work on her book.

She used the key that Glen had promised would be waiting behind one of the black shutters and stepped into a living room that ran all the way to the back of the house. There, sliding glass doors looked across a wooden deck at a wetland filled with tall reeds. There was a door to her left that led to two small bedrooms, one with a queen-sized bed and the other with twins. Between them was the only bath, a small room with the simple necessities. The kitchen was along the left outer wall, an antique table serving as a countertop. A small dining table was on the kitchen side of the living room. A pair of chairs was set by the stone fireplace on the right wall.

Pam went out to the back deck and sniffed air pungent with the smell of the salt marsh. She heard the chatter and honks of seabirds nested amid the reeds. To her left, on the outside wall of the kitchen, there was a louvered cabana with a skylight in its roof, the perfect stop on the way back from the beach.

She carried in the few things she had brought in the rented car, a plain midsize sedan in an inoffensive gray. She had missed her red ragtop while driving the winding paths from the expressway to the house. They were the kinds of roads that cried for a sports car.

She took the bedroom with the large bed and hung her things behind the sliding closet door. Even the small supply of under-wear and tops she had brought with her filled the three small dresser drawers.

Her workplace suggested itself. She put the new computer under the kitchen table, and the keyboard and monitor on top. She could work with the glass sliders open or closed. Either way, the wetlands were hers to enjoy simply by glancing up.

The printer was on the floor behind the tower, amid the rat's nest of wires that came from the back. It was an ugly arrangement but practical for the time she would be staying. She had wrestled a bookcase from one of the bedrooms and put it next to the table to hold her supplies and pages. Together, all these pieces formed a workstation in the center of the room.

She was settled in within a few hours and hard at work before nightfall. She was in an early chapter, dealing with the coal industry's stake in blocking the environmental bill. Power plants burned coal because it was cheap. If they had to spend a fortune to process the coal before burning it, and more money on stack scrubbers to keep it from fouling the air, other fuels, like natural gas, might prove more economical. In a rare show of unity, both the mine operators and the labor unions had descended on Congress to block the bill. Together they had created a river of money from which the legislators could drink.

Pam had the source: the names of the manufacturers of coal digging equipment, the railroads that carried coal, the several unions involved between the mine and the power plant, the companies that ran mines, and the firms that financed them. She also had the calculations that utility accountants used to determine at exactly what point clean air would become price-competitive. She knew the story by heart and wrote most of it without needing to consult her notes.

She also gave herself some time off. Each morning she struck out shortly after daybreak on the two-mile run that had long been part of her routine. Until now she had done all her running in urban environments, either through city streets or on paths that wound beside parkways. She had used earphones to fill her head with music and block out the groans of auto engines and the incessant blare of horns. But now she was running along sandy paths that reached into the wilds and skirted the edges of marshes. She heard the daily explosion of sound as birds flew out into the fresh morning light. For the first time she began to doubt her career choices. As a well-paid urban professional, she realized, she was leaving many of life's pleasures on the table. Why had she been so dedicated to her rising career at the institute? Why had she been so flattered by the attentions of a powerful man?

"I love it here," she told Glen when he arrived on Saturday.

"So far, it seems to be working," he told her. "The only one who knows you're gone is Sergeant Vitale. He called me when he couldn't reach you. I told him that you were a country girl and New York was just too frightening. You had packed up and left for the old farm, someplace out west." Then he added mischievously, "I don't think he's going to miss you. He sent back the broken computer and never asked about the records. I guess the New York police have more pressing problems."

She responded with a suspicious glance. "No one? You mean your bosses don't care where I went with their money?"

"To be honest, your name did come up at the editorial meeting. The president asked how the project was coming along. He heard that you had fallen in among thieves."

"How did he find out?" she asked, suddenly quite serious.

"Police checking up on my involvement, I suppose. I guess I didn't strike Vitale as particularly cooperative."

"And what did you tell your president?" She was leaning across the antique countertop in anticipation.

"I told him the same thing. Two attacks in two days was scary, even for New York. I said that you were working elsewhere and I had no idea where that might be."

Pam had bought the makings of a salad, which they took out to the picnic table on the deck. There Glen got a bit more serious and explained the precautions he had been taking. He had resurrected a book by a long-ignored author and decided that his staff could whip it into a bestseller. He was keeping everyone so busy that no one was interested in *Fouling the Air* any longer.

"Thanks a lot!" she said sarcastically. "I didn't want you to make me a nobody."

"That's inside the company," he said. "What I'm really enjoying is making sure no one is following me on the outside, hoping that I'm going to lead them to you." He went into great elaboration on his life as a secret agent. He had hired an electronics expert to scan his apartment for bugs. There were none. And his private line at the publishing house. Again, nothing. He had made a point of taking long walks and turning quickly into storefronts to confound whoever might be following him. As far as he knew, there was no one. Then, like Pam, he had used a rented car for his trip out to the Hamptons, exited the expressway several times, and gotten right back on. No one who had pulled off after him had followed him back onto the highway. He had even kept an eye on a helicopter that seemed to be keeping pace with him, but it had turned south into a commercial airport. "If anyone is trying to follow me, I'm keeping a step ahead," he boasted.

Glen read the week's work, with Pam peeking over his shoulder and trying to make out his marginal notes. His comments were nothing more than "hmmms" and "hahs," until he got to the part where a mine industry labor leader lifted a senator's aide off his feet and tossed him aside on his way into the senator's office. "Don't ever send a kid out to brush me off," he told the senator. "You might get him killed."

"This is great," Glen exulted. "A labor goon talking down to a U.S. senator. Did this really happen?"

"I got it straight from the aide. He told me he was so scared that he upchucked his lunch."

Glen gathered the pages, promising to make his changes after hours, when his office was empty. Pam sighed wearily and settled into the chair at her makeshift workstation. Her hands were on the keyboard when she felt Glen's hands on her shoulders.

"That's enough for a day," he whispered in her ear. "Let's take the night off."

She turned the machine off, stood, and stretched wearily. "Do you feel like going to the beach for a swim?" She was walking away from him as she spoke.

He followed close behind. "I thought we might settle down here. I brought a bottle of champagne that really needs to find an ice bucket."

If he was trying to be subtle, he had missed wildly. The champagne was an obvious prelude to what he was suggesting as the main event. But Pam didn't think it was a power play. Glen wasn't hinting at his just rewards for helping her book into print. He wasn't suggesting a thank-you for the career chances he was making on her behalf. He had been testing her feelings more suggestively at each meeting. Their conversations had become less business and more personal.

At the same time, Pam had felt a growing affection for Glen. It was by no means a sexual yearning. She had simply recognized that he was a good man, honest and caring, who had been completely respectful of her privacy. He wanted to take their relationship to the next level. He was doing nothing more devious than asking how she felt.

"Glen," she started in a tone that was much too understanding.

"I know," he interrupted. "I presume too much."

"Not at all. I know what you're saying, and the suggestion is very appealing."

He brightened visibly. "Should I get the champagne?"

"Not yet," she told him. "I've just fallen out of bed and landed very hard. I'm still angry, still depressed, and maybe even still in love. I have to get my own life straight before I can attach it to someone else."

"Well, at least you've given me some hope."

"That's exactly what I meant to give you. Along with asking for a little patience. I'm just not ready."

Glen nodded. "So, how about a swim?"

They drove to the beach and walked through the dunes to the water's edge. A perfect half-moon was rising, tracing a silver path across the water. The breakers were wild, tossing up clouds of spray. They stripped to their bathing suits, let their feet adapt to the water temperature, then plunged in. They held hands when they ducked under the waves, and twice he scooped her up to keep her from tumbling under a breaker. They were both anxious as they awaited the next roller, frightened as it crashed over them, and then laughing in exhilaration as they were tossed up onto the beach. An hour went by before they fell exhausted into the sand.

"I should have brought the champagne," he teased. "I have you right where I want you: half naked and too tired to fight me off."

"I wouldn't put up much of a fight," she told him. Then she rolled away and got to her feet. "We'd better get out of here before we get ourselves arrested."

In the morning, Pam was happy that she hadn't let herself get caught up in the moment. She wandered into the living room and saw Glen out on the deck. He wore just his jeans and cradled a mug of coffee against his chest. She poured a cup for herself and went out to join him. The marsh was alive with the antics of the morning birds.

"I love this place," she said again, putting a hand on his shoulder.

"You can have it," he answered. "But I come with the property."

She leaned close and kissed his cheek. "Are you mad at me?"

"Of course not. It was my own fault. I should have opened the champagne to celebrate my good fortune. Then, when you were dulled by the wine, I could have carried you off to bed."

"What good fortune?" she asked, her eyes narrowed with suspicion.

"Didn't I tell you? I'm being promoted."

"No, you didn't tell me."

Glen pulled her down into his lap. "It seems that old Tom Howell has decided to stop publishing books and devote himself to spending his fortune. The brass at Intermedia want me to be the new president of Thomas Howell Publishers."

She smiled broadly and kissed his forehead. "Congratulations."

He looked disappointed. "You call that congratulations? That was two cousins meeting at a funeral. This is congratulations!" He drew her into a long, sensual kiss, and she softened into his embrace. But she suddenly pulled back and untangled herself from his arms. "That wasn't just congratulations," she said. "That was 'I better get back to work.' "

"You're right," he agreed. "I want four more pages before I leave."

"With your new job, can you still find time to work with me?"

"Sure. Intermedia is a big international. They have television stations, newspapers, and magazines all over the world. Thomas Howell is just the flea on the elephant's

behind. I'll still be doing what I've been doing all along, just a little more of it."

"It sounds great," she concluded. "Maybe
we ought to pop that cork."

Twelve

Congressman Carl Croft slipped into the golf cart next to Senator Thomas Lawrence and set his soft drink in the cup holder. "The usual?" he asked.

"I think so," Lawrence answered. "My putting hasn't gotten any better since the last time we played. Probably not wise for me to raise the stakes."

Croft laughed. "For God's sake, Tom, it's only a buck a hole."

Lawrence nodded. "Yeah, but you play to win. My business friends always let me win all the skins, so with them I go for a bigger bet."

They climbed out at the first tee and hit two respectable drives that stayed in the fairway. Then they bounced back into their cart and headed off for an afternoon of rest and relaxation.

Like most of their colleagues, the senator and the congressman spent a lot of time on the golf course. Over the years, it had proven a perfect political environment. With no photographers close by, and no reporters following with their recorders poised to take down every word, the members could speak frankly. In the halls of Congress, and even in the privacy of their offices, they were always on guard against the death quote. They couldn't let anything slip that might conceivably be offensive to their business supporters, their states' major industries, religious zealots, women's organizations, or any other constituency. On the golf course, a public official could express his true feelings on the issues of the day and perhaps even bond with others of like views. A committee chairman could weigh his support before sticking his neck out.

The rolling fairways were also the perfect venue for the darker side of political life. They were where weapons salesmen, drug manufacturers, insurance czars pitched their products and agendas, and where the lobbyists made their deals. How could the public possibly object to an elected official sharing an innocent game of golf, where ten or twenty dollars changed hands with a constituent? How would they ever find out that the friendly conversation on the tees had won the industrialist a $10 billion sale and the congressman a $500,000 campaign contribution? Who would know that it was in just such a game with a computer association's lobbyist that Carl Croft had first mentioned how much he and his wife would enjoy playing at St. Andrews?

It was on the third tee that Lawrence asked casually whether Croft was aware of a book being written by a former aide to the energy secretary. Croft paused, searched the thousands of bits of information his staff sent across his desk each day, and admitted that he had never heard of it.

After they had hit their drives, Lawrence filled his playing partner in on the details. "In the wrong hands, this stuff could be explosive," he summarized. "A lot of our people think it could be very easily misconstrued."

"People on the energy committee," Croft said, suggesting that those dealing with the offensive aide might very well be tarnished.

"It's more than that," Lawrence corrected. "Apparently the woman is taking a very broad swipe at government practices. For instance, I understand there's a chapter on how congressional travel gets expensed and paid for. She talks about your golf trip to Scotland."

Croft's eyes widened. "Jesus, I thought

that one was dead and buried. *The Post* bitched about it, and the TV guys pretended to be shocked. Then it turned out the media had been sponsoring junkets to get supporters for some of their station buyouts. They were more embarrassed than I was."

"This woman admits up front that she was in on some of the deals. She knows who, for what, and how much. Some of the labor people would like to bury her next to Jimmy Hoffa."

"So, let them." Croft laughed. "I'm not going to take them to task. I'm on the record as a friend of labor."

"First they'd have to find her. My sources tell me she's gone into hiding."

"What about her publisher? There must be something the publisher wants from us."

Lawrence explained that people were already at work on that. "But we have to be very careful. Publishers are always screaming about freedom of speech. A screwup there could be worse for us than the revelations." He let that sink in while they played another hole. Then he got to the real purpose of their outing.

"Carl, I was thinking that your influence with the intelligence community might be useful. There are aspects of this book that should concern the people at Homeland

Security." The congressman squinted inquisitively, thought for an instant, but didn't see the connection. What would Homeland Security have to do with lobbying? "The book," Lawrence went on, "is pretty damn specific about the operations of the electric power industry. I understand that it's an exposé of the weaknesses of the national electric energy grid."

The idea clicked into place in Croft's mind. "That's not something I'd like to see in the hands of terrorists."

"Neither would Homeland Security. And they can do something about it. In matters of this kind, they don't even need a search warrant. It seems to me that someone over there would want to take a good look at this book before it goes any further."

Croft was nodding vigorously. "Can we get John Duke to work on this? He could issue a confidential finding that the information would be dangerous in the wrong hands."

"I think we can count on John," the senator assured him. "He's in the book too."

THIRTEEN

Pam's days had found a routine. She ran in the morning, showered outside in the cabana, then took yogurt and fruit, or a bowl of cold cereal, out to the deck. By nine A.M. she was at the computer and, with the exception of a coffee break, worked until noon. Then she drove into town to do her shopping, treated herself to a cappuccino, and returned to the house for a quick lunch and an afternoon of work. She quit at five P.M. and drove to the beach, took an hour of the afternoon sun, then plunged into the surf. Dinner was a packaged diet meal that she gave a touch of civility by pouring herself a glass of wine. She went out on the back deck to take in the sunset, with its fiery red clouds, then put in another hour at her computer before going to bed.

Glen's house was the perfect workplace, open, airy, and free from interruptions. At the end of most days, she was amazed by how much work she had done, and delighted by the rising stack of printed pages. In just two weeks she was ninety pages into the work and had covered a quarter of the chapters in her outline. The memories of her moments of terror at the hands of the intruder had faded. The work was exciting, and the long, late-summer days in the Hamptons were idyllic.

She was in town shopping at a small supermarket when she was suddenly reminded that she was still in danger. "Excuse me," a voice called as she squeezed through a produce aisle. She turned to a tall, lanky man with long hair and a short beard that needed trimming. He was holding a melon under his chin like a shot-putter about to begin his launch. "Do you know how to tell if these things are ripe?"

"I haven't a clue," Pam responded, shaking her head in a gesture of regret. She turned away, but he moved closer.

"I know you're supposed to knock on them and then listen, but I don't know what I should be hearing."

She smiled politely. "I think you could get into a lot of trouble if you go around knocking on melons." Again, she turned up the aisle and began walking away.

"Maybe it's coconuts that you're supposed

to knock on," he called after her.

He maneuvered to be right behind her at the checkout counter. "Are you vacationing, or do you live here?" he asked. He was pleasant, a bit obvious in his pickup line. He wanted her to know that he was interested in her and not simply in the ripening of melons. She should have been pleased, or at least amused. Instead, she felt a chill of fear. Her defenses were up immediately.

"Just visiting," she said and pointedly busied herself putting her groceries on the conveyor.

"I've never developed a taste for yogurt," he went on as she put a few containers on the belt. "I mean, do you like it, or do you just put up with it?"

"It's an acquired taste," she answered without looking at him.

The cashier began processing her purchases, and she was happy for the distraction. Pam reminded herself that she was in hiding, and that making any new friends might be dangerous. Whoever was trying to stop this book had come after her before, and they could well be after her again. True, the man looked nothing like the lean, intense professional who had attacked her, but he seemed determined to find out who she was and where she could be found.

"Where do you hang out?" he asked as she was awaiting her change. "So far all I've found are teenagers and stockbrokers. Do you know a good spot?"

She turned angry eyes toward him. "I told you, I'm just visiting for the day."

"Not very nice of your hosts to send you out to do the shopping," he said with a wry smile.

He had seen through that lie immediately. Pam picked up her bag and walked away without looking back. What was he? A vacationer trying to pick up a date? That didn't make sense, because the beaches were covered with bikini-clad nymphs auditioning as sex companions. Or maybe an agent or private detective sent to find her. That would make sense if someone had learned the town she was in. All they would need would be to spot her and get an address.

Pam glanced back at the store and saw him standing at the entrance, a plastic shopping bag in hand. He was looking in her direction and making no effort to hide his interest. He seemed more intense and professional than he had on first impression. She tried not to look in his direction as she loaded her purchases into the trunk. She took a final glance back as she slipped into the driver's seat. He was still there, still looking in her direction. But now he was talking on a cell phone.

Her concern lingered through the evening, distracting her from her work. She closed the sliders out to the deck, fighting a vague fear that he might walk in on her. Several times she went to the front windows and peeked through the blinds. It was ridiculous, she knew. Government agents and mob hit men didn't wonder what they should hear when they knocked on a melon. He was nothing more than vacationer looking for company.

She had worked herself back to the episode in the opening chapter, where Senator Lawrence was demanding that another zero be added to his check. She had reached the part of her story where John Duke was scrambling to raise the money for the institute's patrons. The details were perfectly familiar to her, so the words should have come fast and easy. But she wasn't focused. It was almost two A.M. when she finished the chapter and fell into bed.

Pam came out the front door in the morning, spent a minute stretching on the wooden steps, then broke into a run down the sandy path. She was in shorts and a tank top, with a sweatband to hold her hair out of her eyes.

So far, it was a good story, and she complimented herself on the way she had handled the details. Even though the terms of the environmental bill were boring, and the many interests involved were nearly narcotic, she had captured the suspense of arranging the payment the senator had suggested. It had been a poker game played under a deadline, the outcome worth billions of dollars to the players.

Now she was trying to replenish her enthusiasm. She knew exactly where her story was going, the names of the principal players, and the amounts involved. What she needed was a clear head and the determination to keep up the pace of her writing. Running filled those needs. As the path drifted under her feet, her head cleared and her energy level rose. She knew that when she finished her route, and scrubbed the sweat away in the outdoor shower, she would be ready for another full day at her workstation.

She was gliding along the edge of a pond on a curving, downhill stretch that encouraged her to pick up the pace. At one moment she was at perfect peace. But at the next, without any real evidence, she knew she was not alone. She sensed another person behind her on the path and slowly gaining on her. She altered her stride just enough to look back over her shoulder. Still at a distance, she spotted a tall man in shorts and running shoes with a long, graceful stride. She slowed her pace a bit. She had no chance of speeding away from the runner, so she decided to let him pass her. She didn't want him following her when she made her turn onto the narrow, secluded path that led back to the house.

A few seconds later she could hear his feet on the hard-packed sand, and then his heavy breathing. Next he was beside her, slowing down so that he was matching her, stride for stride. She recognized him immediately, the bearded man from the supermarket.

"Should we run together?" he suggested impishly.

"Good God, don't you ever give up?"

"No, but I'm about to. I'm damn near dead from trying to catch up with you. Could we just slow down to a nice, easy walk?"

Pam slowed but jogged in place. "No, I've still got a way to go. I'm turning back home."

"Where's that?"

Her alarms went off. "Back behind us."

"What road are you on?"

Even if this was an innocent attempt at a pickup, he was prying too much. "I don't know the street name. I'm a guest at a friend's house along with several others." Anyone looking for her would expect her to be living alone, Pam reasoned, so sounding like a house groupie might throw him off. And if he was simply a man on the make, then the implication that there was a man waiting for her might be a turnoff.

She began running in the opposite direction, hoping that he would continue with his cooldown walk, but he turned and tried to keep up with her. "I swear," he said through labored breathing, "I was just out for a run, and I thought I recognized you when I came up behind you." He panted in obvious pain. "You're tough to catch. Couldn't we just stop for a second?" She didn't know what to do, but she broke stride and came to a stop, her head down and her hands on her hips.

He flashed a white smile, and his dark eyes danced mischievously. The shock of black hair fell almost to his eyes. Pam guessed that he was her age, maybe a bit younger. His attentions would normally be quite pleasant. But at the moment she was feeling the fear that had dogged her the night before. "What do you want?" she asked, making no effort to hide her suspicion.

"I want to introduce myself." He extended a hand. "I'm Pete Salerno."

She ignored his gesture. The last thing she wanted to give him — or anyone else for that matter — was her name. "What made you think I might want to meet you?"

"Well, I guessed you were living alone. You bought frozen dinners, a couple of yogurts, and a small can of coffee. There wasn't enough for two. Certainly not enough for a house full of groupies. So I thought you might like some company."

She had told him that there were others waiting at her house, and he had seen through that lie too. And since she was still here, she clearly wasn't a day-tripper.

"You're very observant. Are you a detective of some sort?"

He laughed. "Would you believe a math teacher?"

"Not for an instant."

"It's true! I'm a mathematician. Or, at least, hoping to be. I'm working on my doctorate at Columbia."

They were walking together, gradually catching their breath. He seemed sincere, likable, and nonthreatening. But they were walking toward the house. At some point she would have to find a reason to send him on his way.

"What's your thesis topic?" she asked.

He drew a breath as if he was about to answer. Then he shook his head. "It's too complicated. Telling you would make me look like a geek."

Pam stopped and offered her hand. "If it's complicated, I wouldn't understand it. I'll just wish you well and let you get back to your work."

He was startled. He'd thought he was beginning to win her over. "Aren't you going to tell me your name?" he asked.

"No, I don't think so."

"Why?"

She smiled. "It's a little complicated. Telling you would make me look like a jerk."

She turned away abruptly and began jogging in the direction she had been heading originally. She went a good distance before glancing back. Pete was still standing in the middle of the road, looking astonished. She breathed easily at the thought that he wasn't following her.

But her fears came back. Maybe he really was a scholar who had gone into isolation to work on a thesis. It was possible that he had noticed a woman who was apparently living alone and decided they would both enjoy a bit of companionship. But she couldn't take that chance. It was also possible he was another agent, who had been sent to find her. If that was the case, he was too close for comfort. True, she hadn't led him to her front door. But obviously he had gotten so close it wouldn't take him more than a few hours to have the address.

Would he be the one who would break in, push her into a closet, and ransack the house for her source material and written pages? He didn't seem the type. Her attacker in the city had been honed to peak physical condition. His expression had been emotionless, almost robotic. As she recalled, he had grunted only a few words. Pete, by contrast, was angular rather than muscular, and expressive to the point of being a caricature. She could actually picture him as a struggling student, still more a schoolboy than an academic fossil.

But if he had been sent to find her, it didn't matter who would be assigned to silence her. Her enemy, whoever he was, would have her address pinned down very soon. She had to be gone by then.

First, her records. She began copying all the notes, correspondence, and e-mail documents that were important to the book.

While the computer was loading them onto her iPod, she went through her bedroom and packed the few things she had brought from the city. She left her overnight bag on the bed while she retrieved the iPod.

She heard a car grinding up the hard-packed road. Then she saw it through the window, a small black Miata two-seater with the top down. Pete Salerno, his hair even wilder than at their first meeting, was driving slowly, leaning forward and squinting through the windshield.

FOURTEEN

Pam knew she had to hide the iPod, and she had only seconds to do it. She surveyed her options, then sprinted onto the deck. She jumped off to the sandy ground and pushed the small white case under the deck. At the same time, she heard a car door slam in her driveway. For an instant she thought about sliding under the deck herself. But her car, out front, announced that she was at home. Maybe she should work her way around to the front of the house, then make a dash for it while he was inside. She'd started edging along the side of the house when she heard him knocking on the front door. She froze, her back pressed against the outside of the screen porch, and listened carefully. She would hear him try the door and push it open. That would be her signal to make a run for her car.

The keys! The damn keys were with her overnight bag. He knocked again, this time a bit louder. And her car! It was a narrow driveway. He would have pulled in behind her, leaving her no room to back out. She would have to run. As soon as he was inside, she would make her break.

"Oh, there you are!" She wheeled in fright and saw him through the screening. He had started around the house and caught her hiding in the shadows. His smile was broad, and there was laughter in his voice. "I've had lots of women avoid me, but you're the first one who ever ran out of her own house."

"I was just . . ." Pam started to fabricate an explanation but then realized that it was her house, and he was the one who ought to be explaining. "What are you doing here?"

"I came to see you."

She walked around the porch to the front corner of the house where he was waiting. "I thought we went through that this morning."

"You asked about my doctoral dissertation. So I brought it over for you to read."

She went past him to the front door. "I was just making small talk. Besides, you said it was dull." As she opened the door, she turned back to him. "How did you find my house?"

"Your car," he said as he ambled toward her. "I watched you pack your groceries. When you were running in this section, I figured you lived nearby. So I drove around the neighborhood until I spotted the car in the driveway." He raised his hands as if to say, What could be simpler?

"I was packing to leave," she answered. "I have to get back to town, so maybe some other time." If he was legitimate, he would get the message that he wasn't wanted and go away. If he was after her files, he would have no trouble pushing past her.

He looked dejected, but he nodded in defeat. "Okay, but the probabilities aren't very high that we'll meet 'some other time.' That's what my paper is about — probability theory. With a little more information, I could work out the exact odds." He gave her a feeble wave and turned back to his Miata ragtop. "Have a safe trip."

He wasn't after her files. And if he had driven by just to pinpoint her address, then he wouldn't have stopped and knocked on the door. "I had the same car," she called after him. "Only mine was red."

He stopped and looked back, his eyes narrowing with suspicion. She had just given him a no-nonsense brush-off. Now she was offering a conversation starter, as if she had sat down next to him at a singles bar. "Isn't that your car?" he asked, pointing at the rental sedan in the driveway.

Pam came down the front steps and went to his car. "No, it's just a rental. Mine was exactly like this. I think probably the same year." She noticed the file folder with pages poking out. "Is that your thesis?"

He nodded. "Pretty close to being finished."

"You still want to tell me about it?" she asked.

"Sure." He leaned into the car and retrieved the folder.

"I hope it won't take long," she told him as they walked back to the house. "I really do have to make it back to the city." Her announced intention of leaving was her protection in case he lingered too long. He promised her the abbreviated version.

Inside, he was stopped by the computer workstation. "I thought you were vacationing. It looks as if you're working harder than I am. What do you do?"

"Research," she answered. "I do studies on business and industrial issues."

"Then you know mathematics," he said with delight. "You must know statistics, and that means you know probability analysis."

"Just the basics," she answered.

"Where do you work?"

She wondered whether he was just making small talk or whether he was digging for information. "In Manhattan for the past month. Before that in Washington."

"Both places where good-looking women get rushed," he observed. "How did you manage to stay single?"

"Did I say I was single?"

He smiled. "A married woman rushing home to her husband would probably be sure to wear her wedding ring."

Now Pam feared that he was coming on much too fast. "Let's talk about your paper, Peter. We're running out of time."

"Pete, please, now that we know each other." He slipped the pages out of the folder. They were covered with graphs and equations, with only a few lines of copy between the displays. "How much do you know about games theory?"

He sat close to her at the dining table, spreading pages across the tabletop. His opening was clear and well presented, but by the end of the third page, Pam was lost. Still, he talked on, becoming more enthused as his arguments grew more unintelligible. He talked for two hours, interrupted only when she took a break to make iced tea. She didn't understand much of it, but she appreciated his mastery of a difficult field and enjoyed his enthusiasm. It was hard for her to imagine why she had ever thought he was dangerous.

"I do have to be going," she finally interrupted. "I have a long trip."

He gathered up his papers and put them back in the folder. "When are you coming back?"

"I don't think I will. This job is pretty well finished."

He glanced at the computer system and supplies that she was obviously leaving behind. Pam knew she had been caught in still another lie. "Oh those!" she said, gesturing at the equipment. "They belong to the people who let me use the house. I have my own files packed."

"Why don't you print a copy for me? I'd like to read what you're doing."

She was startled, and she knew that it showed.

He added, "Put your phone number on it. I'll call you after I've read it and tell you what I think of it."

She rushed into another thoughtless lie. "I'm not sure where I'll be staying, so I don't have a phone number."

He had no trouble dealing with that. "Don't you have a cell phone?"

She had to put him off. "I don't have the time to print my work for you, and I don't like to give out my phone number."

He nodded. "That probably explains why you're still single." He took a page from his thesis, turned it over, and began writing on the back. "This is my phone number, and my address. If you're coming back, let me know. Or call from wherever you settle. I can always come and visit you."

She took the paper and folded it into her pocket. "I have to lock up now," she said.

He went to the door, turned back, and told her, "I'm serious. If you'd like to get together, give me a call."

"I will," she said, knowing that she never would. He was through the door and out to his car in just a few seconds.

Pam heard the motor start and watched the car back away. She waited a few minutes to satisfy herself that he was really gone. Then she retrieved her iPod from under the deck, gathered her things, and locked the door behind her. She kept looking for his car as she drove down the lanes to the village and then picked up the main highway. She never saw him and was pretty sure that she wasn't being followed.

She wanted to talk with Glen, but she couldn't simply use her own phone. They had agreed that calls from any of their listed numbers could be traced. Glen always went out to the street and used a pay phone to call her. She hadn't been able to use even that ruse, because her call would betray where she was. She would have to drive a good distance before she called.

Glen was startled when he heard her voice. "What's wrong?"

"Probably nothing," she answered, "but there's a guy out at your place who is either hitting on me or stalking me." She went on to describe Peter Salerno, how quickly he had tracked her down, and how curious he was. "I was sure he was dangerous. Then I was sure he wasn't."

Glen chuckled. "You're not paranoid if they're really after you," he said.

"I feel like a fool. I actually ran out of the house to get away from him, and ten minutes later I was stringing him along. It's probably nothing, but still I'm a little edgy. What do you think?"

"Tell you what," Glen decided after a short pause. "I'll come out tonight. I'll take tomorrow off and we can talk about it."

Pam felt better just because she would have some company. But then she thought that she was being a bit of a wimp. "I don't want to screw up your schedule. It's probably nothing more than someone trying to pick me up."

"All the more reason why I should be out there," he answered. "I'm on my way."

FIFTEEN

They met at the yacht club three hours later. If Peter took another ride past the cottage, she wanted him to find that she had left, just as she told him. She had parked her car in the public lot, where it wouldn't stand out, and gone to the lounge for a slow, leisurely lunch. After lunch she had taken her coffee to the verandah and watched the parade of yachts.

All the while, she had been stealing glances at the dining room entrance, and then at the far corners of the property. She could accept that their running on the same road might be a coincidence, although she was sure Peter must have asked around to find out where she lived. But if he showed up at the yacht club, that would defy his own laws of probability. Then she would really have something to worry about.

When Glen arrived he found Pam in an oversized rocking chair, her face turned into the sun. "Already?" she asked, amazed that he had made the trip from the city so quickly.

"I drove like hell," he said with a laugh as he kissed her cheek. "I couldn't risk leaving you alone with some horny surfer."

"He's a graduate student," she reminded him as they walked to his car. "Also, a bit of a bore. I didn't understand half the things he talked about." She filled Glen in on the bit she had gathered from Peter's thesis.

They left her car at the club and parked his near the house. As far as anyone could know, she had left and Glen had moved in. Inside she put a bottle of wine into the refrigerator ice-maker. Then she started assembling a salad. As she worked, she filled Glen in on the details of her encounter with Peter Salerno. "He was a nice guy, but he asked too many questions. And he could see right through me. I must have gotten caught in a dozen lies."

Glen promised to call Columbia when he got back to the city. "How many candidates could they have for a doctorate in mathematics?" he asked rhetorically. He would claim he wanted to reach the man about a potential book deal. If he really was a graduate student, they could assume that his appearance had been a false alarm.

They talked about her progress. Glen thought the material she had already delivered was "fantastic." Pam told him about the new chapter she had ready. It was about a golf junket to Scotland aimed at getting congressional approval for a gambling casino on an Indian reservation.

"The foursome was two senators and two congressmen. They and their wives were flown over in a private jet, put up at St. Andrews, and given tee times on three consecutive days. It cost the Indian tribe over a hundred thousand dollars. When they got back, the legislators pushed an exemption for the tribe through Congress in two weeks. The casino took in twenty million in its first year."

"How can they get away with things like that?" Glen asked, shaking his head.

"Supposedly, they were visiting Scotland as a potential market for reservation products. Can you believe it? Scotland, the land of wonderful woolens, importing Indian blankets?"

Glen poured a glass of chilled wine for each of them. When he sat down, he didn't return to his chair but settled close to her on the sofa. He stopped laughing at the antics of public officials and was suddenly very serious. "I'm worried about you," he said.

"I am too," Pam admitted. "It was awful today, being terrified because a nice guy tries to talk to me."

"Is it worth it?"

She was startled. "What do you mean?"

"The book. It's going to sell well and get you on a lot of talk shows. But these people are very protective of their dirty little secrets. It could get you hurt."

"We knew that once someone broke into my apartment," she reminded him. "We knew there were dangers. That's why you sent me into hiding."

He nodded. "As your publisher, I found you a place to work where you wouldn't be threatened. I was protecting Thomas Howell's investment. But now you're a lot more to me than a bestseller. I'm in love with you."

"Oh," she said softly. "That does change things, doesn't it?"

He touched her hair with his fingertips. "It changes everything." He drew her close and kissed her gently. "I don't want you taking any risks. I want to keep you nice and safe."

She did feel safe in his embrace, just the opposite of the way she had felt planning her escape from the house. She felt loved and wanted, emotions that had vanished from her life when John Duke decided to abandon her.

They went to the beach, frolicked in the breakers, then stretched out at the water's edge. Glen eased back into his suggestion that her project wasn't worth the risks. "Even if this guy turns out to be perfectly legitimate, it points up just how vulnerable you are. Anyone can come up behind you and toss you down an elevator shaft. The guy behind you at the checkout could be a hired killer."

Pam thought he was exaggerating. "The man in the warehouse didn't want to throw me down the shaft. What he wanted was the computer. He could have killed me in the apartment, but all he did was move me aside so he could wrap up the things he had stolen." She was thinking there were dozens of books appearing every month that tarred and feathered public officials. Of course, the politicians and the lobbyists would try to stop them. "But the United States government doesn't go around murdering its own citizens. It doesn't make any sense."

"Then what were you so frightened about?" he asked.

"Logically, I know that they'd need a better reason than my book to start killing. But emotionally, it gives me the creeps when I think someone is trying to infiltrate my life. I feel violated and exposed."

They took in the sunset, then headed back to the cottage for a simple dinner. Once again, Glen expressed concern. As he prepared the pasta, he worried about how quickly her pursuers had found her. "You've been out here for only two weeks, and we haven't left a single lead. No phone calls that they could be tapping into. Nothing mailed to this address. Still, they came right up to your front door."

She reminded him that they didn't yet know Peter Salerno had been sent to find her. He agreed but didn't like the coincidence. "If he doesn't check out as a graduate student, I think we should drop the project and find a secure place for you until they know you've dropped it."

Over dinner Glen didn't care whether Peter proved to be legitimate. "With your safety an issue, I don't think we should wait for hard evidence. We know they tried to stop you before. We know you could have been seriously hurt. That's all the reason I need."

Pam started back to work, and he took her latest pages out onto the deck. When he came back inside, he set the pages next to her and stood behind her. He reached over her shoulders and took her hands away from the keyboard. "This stuff is starting to scare me," he said. "What I just read, and what you're writing; they're never going to let you get to press. Each deal you write about brings a few more people into a conspiracy of those who would rather see you dead."

He came around, guided her up from the chair, and took her in his arms. "I don't want the book anymore. I want you."

She let him draw her still closer and then opened her mouth to his kiss. When he eased her toward the bedroom, Pam went without hesitation. When his hand moved under her blouse, she made no effort to stop him. She watched him start to undress and joined in the dance without deciding if this was what she really wanted. She was captive to the safety of his arms. She was the one who pulled down the bedcovers. They both settled in from the same side of the bed.

Pam awoke in the middle of the night and lay still in the darkness, listening to the rhythm of Glen's breathing. She could hear her own heartbeat, slow and steady. She felt deliciously relaxed. She didn't ask herself whether she was really in love with him, or try to decide if he was truly in love with her. At that moment she could easily give up the book, along with its dangers. She simply rolled closer to her protector and fitted herself into the curves of his body. He felt strong and warm.

But the light of day brought its own emotions. Her commitment to her book was there waiting for her. How could she have considered abandoning it when she had so much of herself invested in it? The man sleeping beside her wasn't her *protector.* He was her ally. They were working toward the same goal, and together they could achieve something important.

He woke up to the sound of her shower, staggered into the kitchen, and put on a pot of coffee. Then he went into the bathroom and climbed into the shower with her. His assumed intimacy was uncomfortable for her. One night together didn't mean that she had surrendered all privacy, and she stepped out before he could embrace her. "Don't be too long," she told him. "We have work to do."

When he came out of the bathroom, a towel wrapped around his waist, she was already dressed and involved with two English muffins. "Sex really excites you," he teased. "You're running like a two-cycle engine." He stumbled into a chair across from her and pointed to the coffee. "Hurry," he begged.

"We can't give up," she said as an introduction to the debate she knew they would have. "It's a solid story, backed by valid records. Our government is being auctioned off, and the book shows who, how, and why."

He sipped at his coffee. Then he said, "I want to fondle your body, not identify it in a morgue."

"All they're trying to do is scare us off. They'll steal my computer, put a spy in your offices, and send someone out here to find me. But they're not going to kill us."

He began buttering a muffin. "Let me tell you who 'they' are. They're federal agents who have been dropping bodies down wells all over the third world. They're the same military types who murdered Salvadoran peasants at El Mozote. They're the labor leaders who made Jimmy Hoffa disappear. They're the financial executives who launder drug money —"

"Don't be melodramatic," she interrupted. "It's just a book."

He looked up at her. "Which is the one thing in the world that absolutely terrifies them. They have a great little game going that makes all the insiders rich. They protect themselves with pious words about free speech, rising tides that lift all boats, and creating jobs for the poor and marginalized. The only thing they have to be afraid of is an insider like you, who knows how it all works and is willing to talk about it. 'Just a book!' I'll bet I could get you a million dollars if you promised not to write it."

"That's why I should write it," she countered, "and why you should publish it."

His expression hardened, and there was anger in his voice. "That's why someone broke into your apartment, why you were nearly dropped down an elevator shaft, and why it took one of their people just two weeks to find you at my summer house. Good God, Pam, what does it take to get your attention?"

"We don't know that the math student is a hired killer. He could be just what he says he is."

"Then why were you so damn frightened? You met the guy. You talked with him, and then you wanted to run."

He had trumped her argument. She sat quietly, openmouthed, trying to think of an answer.

Glen pushed his point. "Last night, I thought we agreed that it just wasn't worth it. I think we found a better relationship than the daring publisher and the crusading writer. I want to hang on to last night."

She weighed his argument for several seconds. Then she said, "Call Columbia. Find out if this guy is a plant or if he's legitimate."

"Pam, please! What do I have to say to convince you? I love you. I want to keep you safe."

He stood and went into the bedroom. When he stepped out a few minutes later, he was the button-down editor she remembered from their first meeting. "I'll go back to the city, where it won't lead anyone to you, and I'll have someone check out Columbia. I'll mention ten thousand dollars. If he's really a poor student, I won't have to wait long for a callback."

He reached out for her, and Pam kissed him affectionately. "Thanks so much, Glen. I don't mean to be such a nuisance."

"I'll drive you to the yacht club so you can pick up your car," he offered.

She decided she would leave it there and keep up the pretense that the house was empty. "Even if he's just a schoolboy, I don't want him dropping in on me again," she said. The yacht club was less than three miles away, so she could run over and pick up the car whenever she needed it.

Pam took her muffin and coffee out to the deck. Before she sat down, she stretched like a cat, content in her memories of the night before. That got her thinking about her now romantic relationship with Glen Hubbard. It certainly wasn't something that she had planned. But, she admitted, it was something that she had allowed. He had been straightforward about his interest in her. She had fended him off but had never said no. In all of yesterday's anxiety, she had easily taken comfort in his arms. But did she mean to begin a long-term relationship?

It was difficult for her to pin down her feelings. Glen had been enthused about her writing a book, arranged the contract, then helped her get started. His advice had been invaluable, and his approval had carried her through the moments of self-doubt. She had every reason to be grateful to him.

Even more important, he had rushed to her in every crisis. When she was burglarized, assaulted, and threatened, Glen's courage had been contagious, and his determination had inspired her. There was much to admire and respect about him.

But now he was ready to abandon the

project, even though he had already invested so much of himself in it. He was more concerned for her safety than he was about a successful publishing venture. Pam couldn't help but contrast his attitude with John Duke's willingness to jettison their two-year relationship for his next career step. Glen's commitment to her was obvious. What she couldn't pin down was her commitment to him.

To be in love, there had to be a willingness to take chances. Even the best-considered relationship had all the elements of a leap from secure footing into open space. Sometimes the tumbling through life with another person held all the ecstasy of free fall through a cloudless sky. Sometimes it ended in a bloody crash onto the rocks.

Was she ready to leap? Pam didn't think so. Her last leap into space had nearly destroyed her. She wasn't yet able to bring herself to take another chance, even with someone as safe as Glen.

The other thought she couldn't manage was the danger of going ahead with her book. John had warned her that powerful people would never let the book see the light of day. She had already experienced crude attempts to destroy her source material and her work. But if she had successfully vanished, and the people at Thomas Howell thought her book had gone into limbo, then the government and industry power brokers would be convinced they had no reason to fear the publication. They could congratulate themselves that they had scared her off.

She wanted to complete the book, for both altruistic and selfish reasons. The people had a right to know. Even though most Americans were aware of the cozy relations between lobbyists and their elected officials, few realized the extent to which their government was being corrupted. It was one thing for an industry to support a representative who advanced its causes. It was another for the politicians to advertise what donations they demanded and what favors they sought as the price for their votes.

But, Pam had to admit to herself, there was still a personal agenda. The opportunity to repay John for betraying her was nearly irresistible. Most other women simply had to accept the humiliation of being discarded. She could fight back!

There were still unsettled issues, but she couldn't solve them now. What she should do was get back to work. She turned on the computer and waited for the program greeting. She was irritated that the screen remained blank. It took her just a few seconds to realize that the hard drive had been wiped clean.

Someone apparently knew that her book had not been shelved. Someone also knew where she could be found. Suddenly, Glen's summer house was a dangerous place to be alone.

Sixteen

George Medovic wasn't the typical lobbyist. He hadn't been bred to any manor, didn't spend a fortune on English tailoring and Italian shoes, and had never learned to order wine at a French restaurant. Whereas most in his trade took serpentine routes to the topics they hoped to discuss, he was given to simple, declarative sentences. The K Street crowd had come up with dozens of polite vehicles — honorary dinners, speakers' fees, travel vouchers, consulting fees, phantom jobs for phantom workers, scholarships, medical research funds — to get money to the public officials whose endorsements they sought. George Medovic was more direct. He simply wrote a check drawn against his union's political action committee.

His background didn't lend itself to long courtships. In the labor movement, there were few nuances. You demanded the outrageous, settled for the reasonable, and paid your dues on time and in full. Businesses that worked with you got a hard day's work in return. Those that tried to shortchange you got job actions and sick days. Well-cut suits, cordovan loafers, and tables at fine restaurants weren't part of the scene.

Among lobbyists, there were good stories about Medovic as well as bad ones. He was rumored to have handed ten thousand dollars in cash to an elevator starter whose baby girl needed an operation. And it was said that when a congressional aide had tried to block the door to the congressman, Medovic had lifted him by the lapels and dropped him in a trash barrel. With Medovic, all that was important was doing the right thing for union guys. Whether it was socially acceptable, or even legal, was another subject.

He was dressed correctly for his meeting with John Duke — dark suit, white shirt with a starched collar over a striped tie, black, laced brogues polished to an ebony finish. He sat in the waiting room with both feet on the floor and flipped through a copy of *National Review,* reading only the headlines and photo captions.

"Mr. Medovic, the secretary can see you now," John's assistant office manager told him. She waited to guide him through the outer and inner offices that were arranged to keep the Secretary of Energy undisturbed. He smiled as he followed the young woman, admiring the gyrations of her hips. John had certainly jumped up a notch.

"George, what a pleasure." John came around his aircraft-carrier-sized desk with his smile and glad hand. He was in his shirtsleeves, with his cuffs linked and his tie knotted tight against his Adam's apple, the down-to-business image that the new administration was trying to project. He pumped his guest's hand as if they were long-lost brothers, then steered him to a casual setting of chairs around a coffee table.

"Nice digs," Medovic said, taking in the office. He walked to a framed portrait on the wall and squinted to read the inscription. It was an autographed portrait of the president smiling adoringly at John while he shook his new secretary's hand. "Very impressive," Medovic said, then turned back to his host, who was making himself comfortable in one of the chairs. "Did he do that just for you?"

John waved away the compliment. "Everyone gets one of those. The White House gets a discount on multiple prints."

They spent a few minutes in small talk, reminiscing about some of the political battles they had fought together and speculating on the demands of the immediate future. Then John asked directly why the vice president of the Operating Engineers Union, which handled heavy equipment at the mine sites, wanted to see him in such a hurry.

"You know about the book?" Medovic asked.

"The book. What book?"

"The one your former analyst at the institute is writing. I hear she has a great memory for names."

John went to his poker face, hiding any show of apprehension. "Oh, that. There's nothing to worry about, George. I think she's decided not to pursue a literary career."

"That's not what I heard," Medovic contradicted. "My information says that the guy who was supposed to get hold of her records got himself killed. I hear she took everything she needed and went off by herself to put her experiences down on paper."

The last update John had received had assured him that the New York Police Department had all of Pam's records. Supposedly the department was turning everything over to the FBI in the interest of national security. "George, I think we have everything covered. We're not on the outside anymore. We're the federal government, and the government doesn't want her writing about the secrets of the power industry." He smiled with a conspiratorial glimmer in his eyes. "We don't want terrorists getting inside information on the national electric energy grid, do we?"

Medovic wasn't amused. "I hope you're right on this, Mr. Secretary, because there are a lot of guys in my business who don't want to see their names in print. There are also a few who don't want to read anyone's new take on the Arthur Ries business."

"There's nothing on Arthur Ries," John said with certainty. "That was before I came to the institute, and before she got out of college. It was never discussed."

"I'm glad to hear that," Medovic said. "There can't be any surprises."

John Duke had always been slightly afraid of George Medovic, even while working side by side with him. He had formed the distinct impression that this was a man who didn't know how to lose gracefully. In his line of work, someone had to pay. "There won't be any surprises, George. We're on top of this."

Medovic looked thoughtful for a few seconds and then nodded to indicate that he was satisfied. "It's always good to see you, John. Just keep me in the loop."

The secretary took a few minutes to compose himself after Medovic left. John hadn't been completely honest when he had given his assurance that everything was covered. He knew only that the attempt to seize Pam's records had gone awry. He wasn't at all sure that the book was a dead issue. He guessed, from their conversation, that the man who had fallen into the elevator shaft wasn't one of Medovic's people. More likely, he thought, Pam's pursuer had been a government undercover agent sent at the behest of a senator or congressman. But he wasn't sure of that either.

The reference to Arthur Ries was particularly disturbing. Ries was thought to have been the bagman in a large and particularly naked payment from a big union to a very important congressman. He had either gotten religion or gotten greedy, but he was thought to have been talking to a federal prosecutor. The prosecutor had raised the alarm and begun naming lobbyists and industry leaders thought to have contributed to the payment. He was killed when his plane crashed into a mountain outside of

Pittsburgh.

John was certain that Pam knew nothing about Arthur Ries. What was clear was that several powerful people thought she might, and so wanted the book stopped. They expected that he, as Pam's former boss and mentor, was the one who should stop it. He had tried reasoning with her, but she had walked away from him. Someone else had tried to scare her off. Now he was hearing hints that more direct action might have to be taken. John knew he couldn't ignore the growing paranoia of the lobbyists and their congressional marks. He had to be seen as taking action to protect his constituencies. He had to get back inside his former assistant's life and make sure that her inside information never got to print.

John was morosely quiet that night as he and Catherine dressed for a dinner honoring a congressman who had been a fervent advocate of national energy independence. The high-sounding goal translated directly into more offshore drilling, and the top people in the oil and gas industry had anted up a thousand dollars a plate to pay tribute to his wisdom. As secretary, John was seated on the dais and would be called to the microphone to praise the industry's man on the inside.

"Is something wrong?" Catherine asked when his brooding became unbearable.

"Nothing important," John answered unconvincingly. Then he added, "It's that damn book. People are getting worried about it."

"The one your lady friend from the institute is writing?"

"If she's really writing it," he mumbled. "I thought I had her convinced that it wasn't such a smart idea."

"She certainly wasn't one of *your* smart ideas." Catherine rarely passed over an opportunity to ridicule her husband's affair. Then she asked, "How badly can she hurt us?"

He struggled with his bow tie as he answered. "She could embarrass a lot of people who don't like to be embarrassed. I'll probably come across as an arch-corrupter of government."

"Which means that no one of importance will have anything to do with you," Catherine concluded. "You'll become the political leper of the year."

John wasn't at all shocked by her grim prediction. He had been thinking much the same thing himself. "I don't think she'll go through with it. And, with a little pressure from the right places, neither will her publisher."

Catherine gave John her shawl to carry, then led him downstairs to the front door. Their limo was waiting at the curb.

"John," she said as he took her arm. "This isn't something you can leave to chance. You have to be certain that your little lady's book dies an early death. She humiliated me for two years. I won't let her do it again."

SEVENTEEN

Pam sat staring at the blank computer screen, weighing the implications. The day before, the computer had held her programs and all the source files for her book. Now its memory was wiped clean. She ticked off all the conventional causes of a total system crash and discarded them one by one. It couldn't be a virus. The computer wasn't connected to the Internet, nor had she introduced any new files. Probably not a power surge. The machine had been shut down, and there was a surge protector on the power line. None of the normal computer disasters seemed remotely possible.

That meant someone had come into the cottage, turned on the computer, accessed its files and records, then methodically erased them. Someone who knew who she was, where she was living, and what she was up to had made a new effort to stop her.

They had found her apartment. That

hadn't been difficult because she hadn't tried to hide where she was living. At the time, there had been nothing to fear.

Then they had found the storage warehouse.

Now she had been located at Glen's cottage. Either while she was waiting at the yacht club or while she and Glen were at the beach, someone had erased all her work. She had to think of Peter Salerno and his formulas of probability. He had met her in the supermarket, found her running, then located her house. Only a few hours later, someone had neutered her computer. What was the probability that it was a coincidence? Didn't the odds indicate that the newest arrival in her life was connected to the latest attack on her book?

Another fact seemed evident: The enemy was close at hand. No Washington bureaucrat or K Street lobbyist could possibly have known her hour-by-hour movements. Once again, it seemed likely that there was an informer in the Thomas Howell organization. Glen, she thought, probably suspected the same thing. That would explain why he had suddenly wanted her to drop the project. He was being promoted to president and could no longer keep close watch on the people who were producing the book.

He didn't want to leave her to the wolves.

After weighing all the evidence, Pam made some decisions. She could continue with the book, but she had to guard her work even more carefully. She would make multiple copies of everything: production copies for Glen, working copies for herself, and file copies that she would keep hidden. What she needed were enough hidden copies so that no one could be sure they had destroyed them all. Most important, there was no reason for her to stay at the cottage. Whether it was by Peter Salerno or by someone else, her hiding place had been compromised. Now the lonely cottage at the edge of a salt marsh was the perfect place for the next attack.

She closed all the blinds to keep anyone from seeing in. She reloaded the operating system and used the files she had hidden in her iPod to replace the erased records on the hard drive. Then she made herself three CD copies of her files and erased the hard drive. When Peter came back, he would find the computer exactly as he had left it. She would be gone.

She dressed quickly in her running shorts and top, took her cell phone, filled a water bottle, and, at the last minute, remembered to pocket the house key and car keys. In a final flash of intuition, she pulled thread from a pajama top and tied it from the top of the front door to the doorjamb. She left carefully through the deck door.

She ran down her lane and turned away from the route where she had met Peter, choosing another road that led to the yacht basin. Her plan was to wait on the breakwater until Glen had had enough time to get home. Then she would call him on her cell phone and tell him that she had been compromised. It wouldn't matter now if someone traced her call back to the Hamptons.

She kept her head up as she ran, scanning ahead and glancing back over her shoulder. She examined each house she passed, looking for anything out of the ordinary. She even took note of boats that were close to the shore. But she found no reason for caution and began to feel silly at being so suspicious. Her pursuers thought they had destroyed her project, and they were probably no longer interested in her.

She reached the yacht club and turned away from the gate. In just a few steps she was on a sandy beach, jogging toward a rock jetty that reached into the water. She walked halfway out, settled onto her haunches, and waited till she could call.

Her book was getting into material that she couldn't handle on her own. She was up to the techniques used for laundering the money going to elected officials. For that the lobbyists needed public service foundations with nonprofit status that would escape tax auditors. They would create organizations with high-sounding names, like Citizens United to Save Our Trees. The organizations existed only on paper, generally with some totally unaware public do-gooders as chairmen.

In truth, Citizens United was only a checking account that could receive funds and dispense them. A lobbying firm in the process of buying a congressman's vote would make a contribution to the organization. Then Citizens United would make the payment to the congressman, to his campaign fund or to another phantom organization run by the congressman's friends. Sometimes the payment would take the form of gifts, like paying for a fact-finding trip to St. Andrews.

The arrangements were purposely convoluted to give everyone deniability. The lobbyist hadn't made any gift to an elected official. The congressman could not be expected to know that Citizens United to Save Our Trees was really a lobbying group for the logging industry. No one had done anything wrong.

Pam needed information from people who had actually run such scams. She had to interview staffers who had actually written the checks to the charities and knew where the money had gone. One woman had been the accountant for several charities at the same time, opening one or another whenever a payment had to be made, then closing it as soon as its work was finished.

Would any of them help her? Each person whose name Pam remembered had a good job to hang on to. Why should any of them risk the displeasure of a president or managing partner? They all admitted freely over lunches or after meetings that there was something tawdry about their work. There had been many conversations about "getting out of this sleazy racket," but none of them had followed through. Pam had to admit that she would most likely be in her same office if John hadn't pushed her out, and she probably wouldn't have revealed any of the institute's secrets to a crusading author.

She checked her watch and decided to try Glen. "Nice to hear from you," he said as soon as he picked up. "I was thinking about last night."

"I hope you didn't forget what you were going to do this morning," she answered, reminding him that they had shared a serious discussion after they had shared the night.

"I have someone checking right now," he told her.

"That may not be necessary," she told him. "He came back."

"What?" Glen's tone shifted from casual banter to serious concern.

"He, or someone he works with. Somebody was in the house while we were away. The computer was wiped clean."

Glen quickly became authoritative. "Pam, get out of there right now! Get in the car and come straight to my apartment."

"I should be safe," she said, as much to buoy her own spirits as his. "They think they've destroyed everything. They have no reason to bother me."

"Don't be crazy! You're being stalked. Throw your things in the car and get out of there."

She tried to slow him down, explaining where she was. "I'd have to go back to the house to get my things. I'm sure it's perfectly safe there."

"Don't!" he shouted. "Don't go back to

the house. Just get into your car and start driving."

"Okay, okay," she agreed, trying to calm him down. "I'm on my way." But she had no intention of leaving her things at the cottage. It would take her only half an hour to drive back and pack the car. Nor would she go straight to Glen's apartment. First, she wanted to stop at the New York City bank where she kept some bonds and her passport in a strongbox. She wanted to lock one of her copy disks in a vault.

She picked up her car at the club parking lot and headed back to the cottage. She drove slowly so that she could take in each glimpse of the sound. She realized that she was smiling.

Glen had been insistent that she head home instantly. He was more worried about her safety than about the money invested in the book, or even his own safety. He cared about her. He cared deeply and without reservation. No wonder she was smiling, Pam thought. He was afraid for her. She, in turn, was responding to his fears. Wasn't that the way people who cared about each other acted?

She turned into the driveway, shut off the engine, and dashed into the cottage. In the bedroom, she tossed her few outfits into an overnight bag. She took all the pages she had printed, along with her disk files, and packed them carefully into her briefcase. For a moment, she thought of planting a set of the CDs in her hiding place under the deck, on the chance that something might happen before she reached the bank. But that didn't seem likely. Her enemies already assumed they had won.

She darted through the rooms to make sure that the gas and water were turned off. Finally, she retrieved her overnight bag from the bedroom and tucked the briefcase under her arm, leaving her right hand free for the door key. It was only then that she heard the grinding of tires in the driveway.

Pam knew it was Peter Salerno before she even looked. She stepped to the door, watched him climb out of his ragtop, and forced her biggest smile. "God, but your timing is lousy. You're always arriving just when I'm leaving." She stepped outside and locked the door behind her.

"But you just got here," he said, coming forward to meet her. "I was down this lane twice this morning and your car wasn't here."

She tossed her bag onto the backseat. Peter kept coming toward her. He was close enough to touch her. "Yeah," she agreed, trying to sound casual. "There were just a few things I forgot." She was moving around the front of her car, the briefcase still clutched under her elbow.

"I hoped you'd call me if you were coming back," he said.

"Well, I'm not really back. I'm just stopping by. And I really have to go."

"Is that your research project?" he went on, indicating the briefcase.

"No," she lied, then amended her statement. "It is, but only a small section."

"I'd like to read it." He had followed her around the car and was standing near the unopened driver's door. "I could help you get it published."

"Published?" she blurted out in surprise. "I thought you were a graduate student."

"I am," Pete answered. "But in academia, it's publish or die. I know a small outfit that specializes in books no one is ever going to read."

"I'll keep that in mind."

"We could talk about it over lunch," he persisted.

"No, I'm really in a rush to get back to the city." She opened the car door and swung it out between them.

"I know a restaurant in town that you'll be driving right past. Three courses in fifteen minutes, if you're in that much of a hurry."

"Peter —" she started.

"Pete," he corrected. "My mother is the only one who calls me Peter."

"Pete, then. I still have to go." She slipped into the driver's seat. "Please move your car so that I can back out."

"Okay. But follow me. I'll lead you to the restaurant. You can see for yourself."

"Peter," she said, then corrected herself. "Pete, I know who you are and why you're interested in me. You've won. I'm dropping the book. So there's really nothing for us to talk about over lunch."

He was wide-eyed with surprise. "Of course you know who I am. I told you. And what have I won? It seems to me I've done nothing but strike out with you." He stepped away so she could close her door.

He revved his engine and backed out with a squeal of tires. He kicked up sand as he pulled away and was out of sight before Pam backed onto the road.

EIGHTEEN

Glen was waiting in the lobby of his building and threw his arms around Pam as if
she had been away for months. "I've been
worried to death," he whispered, took her
overnight bag, and whisked her into the
elevator. "You could have been killed out
there by yourself."

At his apartment door he showed her two
keys. "One's yours and one is mine. I've
changed the locks." Inside, his investment
in her security made her laugh. The new
lock was a gray steel dead bolt that bulged
out two inches from the door. Nothing short
of dynamite would dislodge it.

"It looks like a bank vault," she teased.

"The people who installed it said you
couldn't get in with a sledgehammer." He
took her bag into his bedroom. "I've got a
security guy coming in tomorrow for you to
interview," he called through the open
doorway. "He's from the company that does

the security at my office."

"A bodyguard? Is all this really necessary?"

"It's necessary if you're determined to keep on writing. You've been mugged, beaten, and robbed. There's nothing more they can do but have you killed."

The reference to her writing caught her attention. "Oh, I have some more for you to see." She pulled the pages out of her briefcase and handed them to him.

He shook his head wearily, settled into the sofa, and began reading. She went to his kitchen and took a bottle of water out of the refrigerator. "Oh, God," she heard him groan. Then he called to her. "You're going to need a whole army of security guards."

When she returned, he told her that she was going much too far. "This stuff is criminal. Up to now, you've been showing what a cynical and unethical bunch of bastards we have running our government. But now you're charging them with crimes. You're saying that senators and congressmen screwed with the tax laws in order to hide who was paying their bills."

"That's what they did," she insisted. "And the way they did it wasn't illegal. I remember at the institute we paid for two legal

opinions before we started funding charities."

"But I can't publish this," Glen said, wav-
ing the pages. "These are unsubstantiated
charges. We'd be sued for libel."

Pam admitted that she needed substantiation. "I have to talk to people who have
done this. I need names, and dates, maybe
even check numbers. I have friends who can
help me."

He laughed derisively. "Why would they
help you? So they can end up in the grave
next to yours?"

"So, you think I should drop the chapter?"

"I think you should drop the whole
project," he snapped. "Then we can take
down the barricades and start living like
two people who are in love."

"You encouraged me to write the book,"
she reminded him.

"That was before I found out that the
United States government would stop you.
The whole government! The FBI, and the
CIA, and maybe Army Special Forces or
Navy SEALs." Glen knew he was going over
the top. He paused for a moment to gather
his composure. "Look, Pam, if you were
some seedy yellow journalist, I'd probably
want you to go ahead and finish the damn
book. But I love you. I don't want the

government to keep putting its dogs on you."

She was sobered. It was another reminder that he wanted her much more than anything she might write. But what did *she* want? Certainly not to crumble because of threats from the people she was exposing. She wanted to finish what she had started. Still, she didn't want it if it meant living behind bank locks and sharing her days with gun-packing private policemen.

Nor was she thrilled with Glen's easy assumption that they were two people in love. She liked him, enjoyed his company, and appreciated his interest in her and his concern for her safety. She had found him gentle and caring when they made love together. There were no regrets about the experience. Still, he was coming on awfully fast, and taking for granted feelings that she hadn't yet sorted through.

He had gone to the kitchen and set the makings of an omelet on the counter. "Cheese and chopped peppers?" he asked, when he felt her standing behind him.

"Sure," she answered, trying to sound enthusiastic.

"You can make a salad," he said. "It's in the refrigerator."

They worked side by side, neither at all

talkative. She asked about dressing. He mentioned that the cheese was cheddar. Then she wandered off to set the table. When he brought the steaming plates, he tried a joke. "You'll probably demand a chef instead of a bodyguard." All it earned was a smile. They began eating quietly.

After a few bites, Pam went to the issue that was hanging over them. "Glen, I don't want them to scare me off. I want to try to finish the book."

He set his fork down carefully. "Even after they have their fake graduate student break into your house."

"He may be exactly what he said he is. I accused him of stalking me, and the more I think about it it doesn't seem he had any idea what I was talking about."

"Pam, I checked him out, and he's a fraud," Glen said, almost as if he regretted having to tell her the facts. "There's only one Salerno in Columbia's graduate math program. He lives in Albany. They have no information about a Salerno who lives in the Hamptons. If this guy is really at Columbia, they don't know about it."

She took a moment to absorb the information. All it did was confirm what she had suspected. Based on his own math, Peter Salerno was probably the one who had erased all her files. But it was just as obvious to her that the man who wanted to be called Pete had no intention of harming her. He'd had his chance, and he had passed on it. "Couldn't a man living in Albany be a student at Columbia and be vacationing in the Hamptons?" she asked defensively.

"Not unless they're paying graduate students like company presidents," he answered.

She shook her head. "There are so many ways it could be true. He could be sharing rent, visiting relatives —"

Glen interrupted her. "I figured you'd want to forge ahead. That's why I brought in all the armor." He tipped his head toward the ugly locks on his front door.

"But I don't want to be locked up," she went on. "I know I've had some scares, and it's nice to know you're worrying about me. But I just don't believe that the government goes around killing its own citizens. Not because they're writing critical books. If they want to kill me, it has to be over something more than lobbyists buying votes. If there is something more, then it certainly won't be in my book."

He shrugged in defeat. Nothing he said was going to change her mind.

"I want to move back into Jean Abbott's

apartment and pick up where I was before all this nonsense started. And I want to go to Washington and get solid proof about the charitable funds."

Glen's expression was hardening as she talked. When she finished, he thought carefully before he answered. "It's not just the government. There are a lot of private interests who don't want to be accused of corrupting the government. And it's not just you they're trying to scare off. I'm beginning to feel the heat."

Her jaw dropped in surprise. "What? Who?"

"My own board. They're getting some grumbling from the unions. If the typesetters are unhappy, they can shut us down. Not just your book but everything we have in the works."

"The typesetters?" She obviously didn't understand. "Why are the typesetters unhappy with my book? I don't know anything about typesetters."

"I guess all the unions come together at the top. You've named national labor leaders who have been buying favors. Didn't you write about an investigation of a labor contract that got dropped after a senator was paid off? That sort of thing gives all unions a bad name."

"It's true!" Pam insisted. "Exactly as I wrote it."

"Well, the typesetters aren't so sure they want to have any part in a book that disparages their leaders. Or at least that's what was intimated to someone on the board. So I got asked whether this book was important enough to jeopardize all the other titles we're getting ready for press."

"What did you say?" Pam asked.

"That a publisher who could be bullied out of a book just because it hurt someone's feelings should probably find another line of business." She reached out and took his hand. Then Glen continued, "They said I was a credit to the industry, but then one of them asked if I was aware how much profit Intermedia was expecting from Thomas Howell. They suggested that I run my numbers to see what our profit would be if we took a thirty-day strike."

"Does that mean we're finished?" she asked.

"Of course not. Typesetters aren't going to risk a juicy contract in a wildcat strike. But you can see it's not just the government that's after you. There are people with lots of clout who aren't afraid to use it. Maybe even a few union leg breakers."

■ ■ ■ ■

In bed, the conversation shifted to their personal relationship. Glen admitted that he had made too much of a leap in suggesting a marriage. Pam denied that she was offended and said it was something they should talk about. "Then why did you turn mute when I brought it up?" he asked, more as a tease than as an accusation.

"It was sudden, and in a terrible context. 'If we got married, we wouldn't need extra locks on the door.' "

"That's not what I said."

She smiled. "That's what it sounded like."

He pulled her close and promised that his next offer would be made on one knee with a diamond in his hand. But her mood was unresponsive. "Please, don't do anything until we've both had a chance to think about it and talk about it." She turned away from him with a heavy sigh. "Right now, we both have our plates full." She mumbled a good night. His arm wrapped around her, and he snuggled up close.

In the morning, Glen was bubbling with optimism. He brought her juice and coffee in bed, and announced French toast for breakfast. When Pam came to the table rubbing the sleep from her eyes, he joked that he didn't expect to see her quite so natural until after the wedding. He kissed her forehead and led her to the door so that she would be certain to lock it behind him, then left for his office. She turned the lock.

She dressed, packed her briefcase and her overnight bag, and let herself out. In the lobby, she used her BlackBerry to tell Glen she was going back to Jean Abbott's apartment. The doorman got her a taxi.

Pam hesitated outside the door. There was still the vivid memory of opening it into a burglary scene, and she knew she would never want to repeat the experience. She took a deep breath and turned her key.

The apartment seemed friendly and familiar. Jean's computer had not yet been repaired, so Pam went to work with her laptop. Within minutes she was on to another subject, a lobbyist who'd raised $1 million from a client but needed only half that amount to sway the appropriate house committee members. Because of the tangled machinations under which the money changed hands, there were no records of exactly how much was involved. So the lobbyist put the difference in his pocket.

She opened the locks that had been installed on the French doors and took the laptop out to the balcony. The trees around the small garden below were in full color, and the tall grasses surrounding the lawn were turning to gold. Pam was thrilled. In this tiny patch of nature, she had no reason to worry about who was threatening her book.

She went shopping and bought a week's supplies — fresh vegetables, fish that would have to be eaten that night, and chicken breasts she could put into the freezer. Then a bottle of milk and a box of cornflakes. Finally, she added a couple of bottles of cheap wine, a six-pack of beer, and two bottles of Pellegrino water. With all the bottles, her shopping bag was heavy, so she arranged for a delivery to the apartment.

She picked up her mail in the lobby, a large packet bulging out of the small mail-box. She should have asked the building manager to empty it for her each day she was away.

She went out on the balcony to sort through her mail. There wasn't much of interest. A stack of circulars and promotions were addressed to her as "occupant." There were offers of opportunities to go deeper into debt from credit card companies. Two Fifth Avenue stores sent invitations to sales. Then there was a large manila envelope, addressed in perfect script, with a row of first-class stamps that had been applied by hand. She turned it over and found no return address. She studied the cancellation on the stamps and found a postmark from the District of Columbia. It had been mailed a week earlier.

The flap was taped, so she went to the kitchen and used a paring knife as a letter opener. She slipped out a batch of newspaper clippings from *The Washington Post* and was surprised to see that they were from three years earlier. She carried the clippings back out to her balcony, wondering why anyone would send her old newspaper articles with headlines that meant nothing to her.

POLICE SEEK MISSING LABOR OFFICIAL was the headline of the first article. It wasn't a banner but a small two-column headline, probably from an inside page.

Pittsburgh, Pa.: Federal Attorney Donald Parker has issued a warrant for the arrest of Arthur Ries, a union official who failed to appear as a witness before a grand jury seated here. Ries, who claimed to have information on a union attempt to bribe a United States senator, is a key witness in an ongoing investigation of corruption by coal industry labor unions.

There was nothing sensational about the story. A witness had apparently changed his mind and bolted. Police intended to pick him up and bring him to the prosecutor, who would charge him with contempt in an effort to force his testimony. She went to the next clipping.

POLICE FEAR FOUL PLAY IN WITNESS'S DISAPPEARANCE. This piece had appeared three days after the first one, again on an inside page. There was no groundswell of media interest in where Ries might have gone. According to the same Donald Parker, there was speculation that Ries had been kidnapped and perhaps killed by union enforcers to keep him from testifying. "We may be looking for a body," Parker was quoted as saying.

PROSECUTOR DOUBTS WITNESS WILL BE FOUND. This one was two weeks later and had a single-column headline from the middle of the paper. Police, it reported, had called off their search for Arthur Ries. "We have been advised by people close to the case that Mr. Ries probably went 'up in smoke,' a source within the federal attorney's office said."

According to the story, someone familiar with the area had revealed that troublemakers sometimes disappeared into coke furnaces. Ries, he implied, had probably come down somewhere in eastern Canada.

Pam shuddered. She picked up the next clipping, this one from a Pittsburgh daily. It reported on the crash of a small commuter airliner shortly after takeoff on a flight from Pittsburgh to Washington. Cause of the crash was unknown but under investigation by the FAA. The list of victims was short — three crew members and eight passengers. In the listing, someone had circled one of the names. It was Donald J. Parker.

She recoiled. Undoubtedly the same man who had served as the federal attorney in the Arthur Ries case. She instantly wondered if he, too, had "gone up in smoke." Now she could speculate on why the clippings had come to her. Someone in Washington was offering her a new line of investigation.

The next clipping carried a bold, four-column headline, a front-page story with several columns of run over. CRUSADING PROSECUTOR KILLED IN LOCAL CRASH. The story confirmed that the Donald Parker from the plane crash was the same one from the grand jury investigation of bribes to a senator. The second paragraph said, "Parker had spent the last month trying to revive an investigation into union corruption that collapsed when his star witness, a union whistle-blower, vanished under mysterious circumstances."

The next paragraph said that Parker had found new sources and was on his way to Washington to question an unnamed informant.

Pam put the clippings aside and sat staring out over the garden. Obviously, buying favors from public officials wasn't anything new. Then, as now, the payments were disguised as legal expenditures, laundered in a process known only to a few insiders. Ries probably was one of those insiders, and for some reason had blown the whistle. What was she supposed to do about it more than three years after the fact?

Parker didn't give up even after he lost his star witness. From the newspaper clipping, it sounded as if his case had been back on track when the plane crashed. She could take it that his death was purely accidental and that the article had been included to tell her how the investigation had ended. But whoever had sent the material had put all the clippings together. Apparently he, or she, thought the two deaths were related.

But again, what was Pam supposed to do about it?

The answer hit her like a lightning bolt, suddenly and with terrible force. This was a warning. Whistle-blowers go up in smoke. Those who persist despite violent warnings have only themselves to blame for the flaming accidents that kill them. Someone was showing her what would happen if she went on with her exposé.

She stood, went inside, and began to pace the apartment, her arms folded across her chest. Glen's warning from the night before seemed prophetic. He had mentioned senators, congressmen, lobbyists, business leaders, labor leaders. What they had in common was power that they would certainly use to maintain their positions at the top of the pyramid. Anyone who challenged them would be crushed like a bug.

The clippings proved the point. Arthur Ries, the heroic whistle-blower, never made the front page. Donald Parker, the crusading prosecutor, was praised only in his obituary. Neither of them was so much as a ripple on the pond. They had challenged the arrangement and gone up in smoke. As far as she knew, no one had taken up the battle.

That was the warning the clippings were

meant to deliver. She might think her book was important. She could even believe that, by throwing light on the daily auctions that passed for representative government, she could change things for the better. But to them, she was only a minor nuisance, a fly buzzing around the table that would be dispatched with the swat of a rolled-up newspaper. See what happens, the clippings advised, and learn the lesson the stories teach. You can't win. No one will even notice when you lose.

Her doorbell startled her. Glen was the only one who knew that she had returned to the apartment, but he wouldn't have come without calling. Pam tiptoed to the door, holding her breath. She peeked through the peephole, and broke out in laughter. A dark young man, trying for a mustache, was staring back at her over the top of her box of groceries.

As soon as he left, her chill returned. Pam felt the hairs on the back of her neck and the sweat on her palms. She hoped Glen would call. She wanted to tell him that he was right. It was too dangerous to continue. It was time to trash her book and try to find a more normal life.

The call came at six o'clock, about the time Glen would be leaving his office. She snatched up the phone and answered "Glen?"

An officious voice asked if she was Pam Leighton.

"Who are you?" she asked without revealing her name.

"This is admitting at Roosevelt Hospital. Are you Miss Leighton?"

She hesitated. Then answered "Yes."

"Mr. Glen Hubbard has been admitted. He requested that you be notified."

"What happened to him?"

"He was burned in a fire at his office. EMS brought him here."

NINETEEN

Glen was at a meeting on another floor when the fire bells rang. "Eve," he called out to the receptionist at her desk just outside the conference room. "Will you find out if that damn thing is for real? And if it's another false alarm, see if you can turn off the bell."

He looked at the faces around the table. Procedure required that they all walk quickly to the stairwell and start working their way down. "Let's give it a minute. By the time we get all the way to the street and back up, we'll forget what we're talking about." No one appeared to be anxious. There were no sounds of panic in the hallway and not the slightest stench of smoke.

The bell stopped. "Okay," Glen tried, "where were we?" But he was interrupted by a recorded voice. There was a fire on the floor above. Everyone was ordered to leave the building.

"That's my floor," he suddenly realized, and he was up and out the door in an instant. The others followed at his heels to the fire stairs. At the landing Glen began climbing up to the next floor.

"Don't go up there!" a voice shouted.

"I have to get something!"

"Leave it!" a calmer voice advised him.

He kept charging up to the next level and pulled open the door. He was greeted by a stampede of editors and assistants, rushing through on the way down. "Don't go back," a production manager said, grasping his arm. Glen pulled free. "Just for a second," he explained. "There's something I need."

He could smell the smoke in the secretarial area. There was a sooty haze rolling along the ceiling. He reached the corridor that led to the executive offices. The smoke seemed to be getting heavier.

The fire, he could tell, was in his office. The smoke was puffing out, lit by the wavering light of flames. When he reached his door, the heat backed him away. He crouched and spread a handkerchief across his nose and mouth. When he looked in, he could see the credenza behind his desk. There was an inch-high manuscript at the far corner with several computer disks lying next to it. The credenza was burning, and pages were turning up at their corners. It was Pam's manuscript and records.

Glen dropped to his knees and tried to crawl under the heat. He was stopped by flames that seemed to be flowing along the surface of the carpet. Pages of the manuscript broke free from the stack and rose as burning embers into the air. Then he was burning, not in flames but in the intense, roasting heat. He started to back away, but he was crawling into another puddle of fire that had broken out behind him.

There was a sudden hammering sound. A flood of rain began falling around him, dousing the flames and cooling the room. The sprinklers had gone off, turning the entire area into a fountain. Glen fell on his side and rolled through the dying fire out into the hallway.

Firemen in their rubber coats and over-sized boots came running toward him. The first two hurtled over him and checked the other offices. Then one of them was kneeling beside him, pushing an oxygen mask against his face. Glen gulped, felt his awareness return, and staggered to his feet. With the mask on his face, he let himself be led through the rainstorm and out to the fire stairs.

Almost instantly they were pushing him onto a gurney that looked like a wire basket. "I'm burning! Put out the fire," he blurted.

"It is out! You're going to be okay," a firefighter said.

Then a medic stood over him with a syringe. He felt the prick and let himself drift off to sleep.

He woke up briefly as they were shifting him into a hospital bed. His hands were heavily bandaged, and he could see the edges of a bandage under his eyes. He mumbled that they had to notify Pam and stayed alert long enough to give them the particulars. Then he fell back into empty space.

They had tried his apartment number, and when they got no answer, they used the cell-phone number he had given them. Pam rushed into the room only a few minutes after she had taken the call.

He looked terrible. The face and hands that protruded over the blanket were covered with thick gauze. One of his legs was intentionally out from under the covers, with bandages from the top of his foot up to his calf. There was an oxygen tube, an intravenous line, and half a dozen monitor wires hanging over him. He was in an unconscious sleep that seemed frighteningly close to death.

"He'll be fine," an intern said as she came up behind Pam. "The burns are superficial, and his lungs are clear." Pam looked at the motionless form in the bed and grimaced her doubts. "Honestly, it's not as bad as it seems," the young woman continued. "He shouldn't even have scars. But he is in pain, so we'll keep him sedated."

"What happened?" Pam asked.

"His office went on fire, and he went back to get something. Not very smart, but he was lucky."

"His office?"

The intern shrugged. "That's what I heard. The fire department people tried to talk to him, but he was in la-la land. They said they would be coming back."

Pam stepped out into the hall, where food carts had claimed the right-of-way. She dodged over to the nurses' desk and asked when Glen would be awake. The nurse looked at his chart and smiled. "Not during my shift. You may be able to talk to him in the morning."

Pam decided there was no point in waiting and took a taxi back to her apartment. She thought she knew what Glen had tried to save from his office. She hoped she was wrong, because if he had gone back to save her book, she would be indebted to him forever.

Pam was up early in the morning and realized that she had left the French doors open all night. She closed and bolted them. Glen had thought they were still in danger. Pam saw the fire that had apparently destroyed her work as further proof he had been right. She had always suspected there was someone inside his office. Was it possible that the spy was much more than a snitch? Maybe an arsonist?

When she reached his hospital room, Glen was still sedated, and she joined a fire department investigator waiting outside his door. "Just routine," the investigator said. "We try to determine the cause of every fire." But in half an hour's conversation, Pam gleaned that the fire had been unusually intense. "In a fireproof building, you don't expect a fire to find much to feed on. This one found plenty of fuel."

Glen woke up late in the morning and waved away an additional shot of painkiller. He welcomed Pam into his bandaged hands and assured her that he was all right. Then the fire inspector took a few minutes to ask his questions.

Was Glen storing anything flammable in his credenza? A cleaning solvent, perhaps, or a can of touch-up paint? He wasn't.

Was he using any unusual electrical equipment? A sunlamp, for instance? Again, he wasn't.

Glen listened patiently to several questions, none of which applied. Then, showing a bit of irritation, he said, "I've been in that office for only a few weeks. I was promoted recently, and the office came with the job."

"Any rivals for the position?" the investigator wanted to know.

"No, no one."

"One last question," said the investigator. "Was there anything in your office that someone might want to destroy? Records that might prove embarrassing? Photographs of people in compromising situations?"

"No! Nothing at all," Glen snapped. Then he asked, "Why are you asking these questions? Wasn't it an ordinary fire? Do you suspect arson?"

"Not suspect. We're certain it was arson. There was so much propellant in your office that it was puddling on the floor."

Glen was shocked. "Are you sure?"

"There's no doubt. The question is who

and why. What was in your office that someone might want to destroy? Who knew you were going to be out of your office for a while? Would someone who knew your schedule have any interest in something you were handling?"

He took out a business card and offered it to Glen. Glen waved his bandaged hands to show that he couldn't hold a card. The investigator placed it on the table next to the bed. "Call me if you think of something. I'm sure we'll be talking again as the investigation moves along." He smiled at Pam. "Take good care of him."

After he left, Pam moved next to the bed. "It was my book, wasn't it?"

Glen nodded. "It was on the credenza. I could see it beginning to burn, but I couldn't get to it."

"That's why you went into the burning office. You were trying to save my manuscript."

"Yeah," he admitted. "I kept the whole project away from the staff just to make sure it wouldn't be compromised. There were no copies, no edited versions on anyone's computer. Just that copy and the disks. I had to save it."

"Why? You knew I had backup, so why were you risking your life?"

Glen lay back on his pillow. "Yeah, but your backups don't have the edits. You'll lose a lot of time."

Pam went to the window and glanced down at the busy street below. Hundreds of people were rushing from one place to another. Cars were swerving to gain a few feet in the jammed traffic. People were too busy to give a damn about the way their government worked. Her book wouldn't change anything.

"I'm sorry you got hurt," she said and came back to his bedside. "I was stupid, and stubborn, and you paid the price."

"Hey, remember. I thought it was a great idea," he offered in consolation.

"But I'm the one who kept after it even when we knew that it was getting danger-ous. I won't keep at it any longer, though. They destroyed the manuscript. So be it!"

He nodded. "I think that's the right thing to do. But don't make sudden decisions. Sleep on it!" He held up his hands. "I'm not going to be doing any work for the next couple of days anyway."

She kissed him gently, careful not to put any pressure on his burned face.

"See if you can rouse that nurse with the

painkiller," he said. "I'm beginning to hurt again."

When she got home, Pam sat out on the balcony, looking down on the garden that was nearly a miracle in the shadows of old apartment houses. Just yesterday she had been working joyously, excited about her book and its prospects. Now she felt stupid and childish. Her delicious exposé had almost gotten Glen killed. Who did she think she was that she could take on the whole lobbying establishment? What did she expect when she went up against powerful, well-funded people who had no intention of losing their grip on the throat of the country?

Her book hadn't really been destroyed. Pam still had all her notes and records hidden in a bank vault. Along with the records, she had copies of all the pages she had drafted. More than ever before, her story was a complete entity in her mind. She could go on without missing even a single beat. What had been lost was the benefit of Glen's editing, the cuts, rearrangements, and additions he had made to add drama and interest to the story.

The other victim was her false sense of safety. She had traveled from naïveté through crippling fear to overconfidence. The fire was the final warning that she had no reason to feel confident.

There was also her relationship with Glen. He had gone back into the fire to save her work even though he didn't want her to pursue it. No one, certainly not John Duke, had ever made that kind of commitment to her. She would have to take very seriously Glen's informal proposal and force herself to decide exactly how she felt about him.

Her cell phone rang, and she lost seconds trying to find it in her purse. When she got to it, the caller had hung up. The call forwarding gave her a number and a name. The number was in Washington, and the name was Marion Murray, John Duke's former secretary.

TWENTY

Marion picked up on the first ring and greeted Pam warmly. After the "How are you?" and "How are things going?" she got down to business. "Did you get the package I sent you?"

"It came from you?"

Marion claimed the newspaper clippings. "I thought you might find them useful for the book you're doing."

Pam laughed out loud. "God, I'm glad to hear that. I thought it was someone threatening me. Why didn't you put in a note?"

"I didn't know who would be reading your mail. Everyone at the institute is going crazy trying to figure out what information you might have taken with you. I thought they were probably watching your house."

"Somebody has been," Pam said. "They've taken three shots at destroying my records. I suppose your name in my mail could end your career at the institute."

It was Marion's turn to laugh. "I've already ended that relationship," she said. "I followed your lead. I quit and entered the ranks of the unemployed. Some of the things we were doing," she went on, "were a bit more than I could stomach."

She got specific and told about a recent institute success in blocking revisions to the Clean Air Bill, which they had privately ridiculed as the Mercury Enhancement Bill. Instead of limiting the amount of mercury that power plants could belch into the environment, the bill allowed generating companies to buy certificates of compliance from power plants that used cleaner fuels. The key lawmakers who had pushed the new rule through didn't get just generous campaign contributions. A group called the French Experience was hosting them on a three-week tour of atomic power plants in Provence and Bordeaux. "Imagine how educational that will be." Marion chuckled.

Next, she asked about the book Pam was writing. "I hear John Duke gets top billing among the snakes of the earth."

"Who told you that?"

"Our old boss talks to the new director about it, and I guess I listened in. And there was a two-week campaign around here to find every confidential memo our esteemed

Secretary of Energy ever wrote and feed it to the shredder before there was any interest from the Justice Department. We've got enough confetti for the next inaugural parade."

Pam told her about the book and the excitement involved in shining a bit of light into dark corners. But she admitted the problems. The lobbyists and their friends were blocking her at every turn. She needed a lot more information on the roundabout way payments were made, and corroboration for some of her allegations. "I don't know whether I can finish it, and I'm coming to believe that it's too dangerous to try," she said. She explained the most recent setback. "I'm backing off," she concluded. "Part of wisdom is knowing when you're beaten."

Marion was sorry to hear that the book was dead. "I've got a batch of stuff that you could have used. I made a lot of copies of things that no one was supposed to see."

"Why?" Pam wondered.

"I resented the same old fat cats walking off with all the goodies. I guess I'm burdened with an honest streak. You know that I used to be in the convent."

Pam had no idea and expressed her surprise.

"Until 1983," Marion added. "It was the same thing then. The bishops and the priests got retirement plans. The sisters got soup kitchens."

"Maybe we could get together," Pam suggested. "I'd like to see some of your copies. I'm not sure I'll do anything with them, but at least I'll know what's available. Could I take the shuttle down tomorrow?"

"Tomorrow's great," Marion said. "I'll tell you about the convent."

Pam regretted her decision as soon as she ended the call. She should spend the day at the hospital, where Glen would be in less pain and more talkative. She couldn't excuse herself by explaining that she had to be in Washington getting more ammunition for the book. She had told him the book was dead.

Still, she was eager to see printed proof of deals she knew had been made. She wanted to share her work with someone else who had been on the inside and get informed feedback. Pam was realizing that, no matter how she might try to persuade herself, the project was still very much alive in her gut.

She phoned Glen's room early in the morning and got his drowsy voice on the line. She had a dear friend in town, she lied, and her day was going to be hectic. She would try to get to see him in the evening, as soon as she was free. She wasn't sure he fully understood what she had said but was pleased that he agreed without any hint of disappointment. An hour later she was at LaGuardia Airport, boarding the shuttle to Washington.

Pam took out the notepad on which she had written Marion's address and was at once aware that she was headed into an unfamiliar part of the District. There were clusters of luxury condos along the Potomac, historic neighborhoods in Georgetown, and a few of the in-close circles where most of the government officials lived. There were also nice neighborhoods in nearby Maryland and Virginia. But Marion's address was in the eastern heart of the District, in a neighborhood generally considered dangerous. The residential rows, built in the twenties to accommodate a growing army of federal bureaucrats, had become a nearly impenetrable ghetto that posted one of the highest murder rates in the nation.

K Street people simply didn't live there, at least no one with the importance of a personal secretary to a director. Pam had never been there, even on her route to someplace else. She was amazed that this was where Marion had been living while serving in the halls of power.

She joined the cab queue at Reagan Airport and gave the address to the driver. He seemed surprised. They drove up the Washington Parkway as far as the Pentagon, then crossed the bridge. It was easy to tell when they had left the area where the government functioned. Suddenly, everyone on the street was Afro-American. Buildings were old and run-down, with clusters of people idling on their steps. Most of the parked cars were from another generation.

The driver found the address in a row of white-brick two-family houses. When Pam paid the fare with a generous tip, he gave her a business card. "If you call, I'll come and get you. You won't have much luck finding a taxi around here."

Marion opened her door with a joyous greeting and a familiar hug. Pam felt instantly welcome even though they had never been close friends at the institute. A few times, they had gone to a movie together. But they had never spoken of personal things or socialized in the same circle. Pam had been pleasantly surprised when Marion had comforted her at the end of her affair with John and helped her carry her things from the office.

The apartment was the top floor of the building, a railroad arrangement, with the living room in front, a kitchen in the center, and two bedrooms at the back separated by a single bath. It was neat and nicely furnished. Pam settled in the living room and carried on a conversation with Marion in the kitchen, where she prepared coffee.

"There are two of us here. Nuns, I mean. Sister Jane and myself. She works at a soup kitchen on the next block on a government project that pays next to nothing. I took the institute job so we could handle the rent." As she explained, there had been seventy nuns living in a Maryland convent. There were five left, three in an assisted-living home, Jane, and herself. The two working nuns were paying the nursing home expenses for their retired sisters.

She brought coffee and scones and set them between Pam and herself. "Not what I expected when I joined the convent," she concluded. "But when the bishops didn't need us, they just turned their backs. No point in throwing good money after bad, I suppose."

Pam tried to apologize. "I must have seemed awful to you, living well with a married man," she said. "Isn't that everything you hate?"

Marion shook her head vigorously as she tried to move crumbs from her chin into her mouth. "No, not at all. I thought you were a victim just like me. Being used while you were helpful but sure to be discarded when Mr. Duke no longer needed your service. I don't hate anyone. Sisters aren't allowed to. But I can dislike intensely, and that's how I feel about John Duke and his sponsors. They use everyone. They take everything for themselves. To them, God is money and power. They don't care what happens to the people they hurt."

Pam reflected as she sipped her coffee. Then she said, "I wish my motives were as altruistic as yours. Sometimes I think I started this book just to stick it to John. I mean, these are things people should know. But I don't have any calling to be the messenger for truth and justice. It may be that all I am is the scorned woman venting her fury."

Marion excused herself and a few seconds later staggered back into the room under the weight of a paper file box. "I started collecting a few years ago, when I opened my eyes and understood what was going on. John had me sign on as a trustee of something called Energy for America. I asked what it was, and he was happy to tell me. It was a way to bypass House ethics rules, which he called 'something of an oxymoron.' You put money in one end, and it disappears. A congressman takes it out, and no one knows where it came from. Pretty funny, don't you think?"

The two women started through the file, and within minutes Pam knew she had found a gold mine. In the case Marion had just mentioned, she had copies of the group's establishment filings, the names of its officers and its members. She had a notice approving its tax-exempt status. There were copies of the checks that had been paid into its account.

There were also copies of disbursement vouchers, information a tax-exempt foundation didn't have to report. Several had gone to campaign funds through private groups and political action committees.

There were similar transactions with other groups and evidence of the institute's participation with other industries. The stain of influence peddling grew wider and wider. There were instances in which the lobbyists had bilked their clients and where public officials, facing sudden pressure from another quarter, had double-crossed the donors. There was even an instance of a senator delaying a bill so that he would have an opportunity to solicit more donations.

"It's not so much what they do," Marion said, "as the style with which they do it. Tuxedos, limousines, baby lamb chops, caviar." She announced each excess as she found an invoice in her records. "They're the best people, meeting in the best places, and talking about the virtues of 'this great land.' It doesn't bother them that they're stealing everything that isn't nailed down. The only thing that matters is that each one gets his share."

Pam stoked her own anger throughout the afternoon. The theft of government was even more outrageous than she had realized. Marion's evangelism was getting through to her. But she had to warn her newfound friend. Glen's office had been torched to destroy Pam's minor testimony. If elected officials and their lobbyist conspirators knew what was in Marion's file, they would burn down the whole block.

"If I use any of this, I'll give you full credit," Pam said. "But I don't think either of us should talk about anything in these files until after the book comes out, *if* a book comes out. As I told you, people involved with me seem to get hurt."

Marion wasn't impressed. "They'd never come after me. None of them would set foot in this neighborhood if their lives depended on it." Then she noted, "You said 'after the book comes out.' So you've changed your mind. You're going to finish it."

"I also said 'if it comes out,' " Pam replied. "I may have caught some of your religion, but I still have to convert my publisher."

TWENTY-ONE

Pam went to the hospital directly from the airport and was surprised to find that Glen had been discharged. She called his apartment and was greeted by a petulant voice. "Where were you? It would have been nice to have someone bring me home." He was too tired to see her right then. Maybe if she wasn't too busy she could come over the next morning.

She did and found him in a much better mood. He welcomed her with an embrace and a kiss. "I'm sorry I was such a prig last night," he confessed. "My hands hurt, and my face looked ugly. I was up to my chin in self-pity when you called."

For her part, Pam admitted that she had gone to Washington, pleading that he would have been upset if she had told him where she was going.

"Damn right I would have been upset. In fact, I'm upset now. Those guys are playing

249

rough," he said, holding up the hand that was still bandaged. "They wouldn't appreciate your nosing around."

"But wait until you see what I've found," she interrupted and took out the short stack of files she had brought home on the shuttle. He reached out reluctantly and took a few folders. "This is just the beginning," she said. "The rest is being shipped to me. There was too much to carry."

He began reading reluctantly, but within minutes his eyes were wide open. "Where did you get this stuff? This is incendiary!"

He seemed enthused, so she explained about the woman who had been copying industry correspondence and documents for two years. She held her arms out to describe the size of the file box that was full of documents. "It's almost too heavy to lift."

Glen put the folders aside. "You're back on the case, aren't you? You're going to finish the book?" Pam shrugged and gave him a sheepish look. He shook his head. "I wish you wouldn't. You're going to get yourself in big trouble. Besides, I can't help you. Thomas Howell will never publish it. With the threats, and the fire, they wouldn't let me bring your manuscript through the front door."

"I understand," she admitted reluctantly.

"You've already gone beyond the call of duty. I couldn't ask you to stick your neck out any further."

"But you're going ahead? In spite of everything: the threats, the attacks, the strains on our relationship. I can't even find you another publisher. What am I going to say? 'Hey, here's a great book for you. We can't do it because some of the people named in it tried to burn down our office.' "

"I have to," she said.

"Why?"

"Because it's right."

"Right? That's the worst reason I've ever heard." He stormed off into the kitchen.

Pam was right at his heels. She waited while he took a bottle of water from the refrigerator. When he reached for a glass with the bandaged hand, she grabbed the bottle and poured him a glassful. Then she watched while he drank. "Let me tell you about the woman who gave me these records. She was John Duke's secretary, and she quit the institute because all the lying and stealing got to be too much for her."

"Why? She wasn't getting her cut?"

"She didn't want a cut. She's a nun who sends most of her salary to an old-age home to support the last few sisters in her order."

"Oh, wonderful. A nun who steals confidential records from her place of employment," he said sarcastically.

"Because she was morally outraged. That's not an emotion that I'm very familiar with. But I'm beginning to understand it."

"Pam, please, you won't like standing on a pedestal. It's a very lonely place." He wandered back into the living room and flopped into a soft chair.

She pursued him. "Do you know why it was possible for me to give up on this book? Because I didn't have a good reason to write it. I started it because you thought it might make us some money and I thought it was a great way for me to get back at the bastard who dumped me. And once I got into it, I found it exciting. Imagine me, blowing the whistle on the entire government. Look at me, taking on all the sleazebags who are robbing us blind. All reasons for writing it, but not one of them a good reason to stick my neck out —"

"And that's exactly where we are," he interrupted. "It was a good idea, but not worth the risk of falling down an elevator shaft, or getting burned to death."

"Marion has a good enough reason: Because it isn't right! A bunch of high-living thieves have taken over the government and run it to keep their pockets full. They don't give a damn about what happens to the country. She has a roommate who works in a soup kitchen. And she has a few million dollars in receipts from the posh watering holes where these people dine while they're making their deals. She thinks it all stinks, and she's morally outraged. We should be too."

Glen offered a condescending smile. "Pam, the first American politician who was treated to dinner by someone seeking a favor was probably George Washington."

"Then shame on George Washington."

"It's the way the government works."

"You mean the reason it doesn't work."

"And you think you're going to change it?"

"No, but it's a damn good reason for finishing the book."

They fell into an angry silence. Glen folded his arms and looked over his shoulder and out the window. Pam settled quietly into the far corner of the sofa. In the awkward silence, both heard the refrigerator motor turn on.

Pam gave in first. "We don't have to fight over this. It can just be what I do. You don't have to stay involved."

He nodded in agreement. Then he said, "I guess I'm just afraid for you."

"I appreciate that." She stood and gathered the files he had discarded.

Glen said, "I'll still help you with the editing. It can't be in my office, and probably not here. But I can stop by at Jean's apartment the way I did in the beginning."

She thanked him and promised she would welcome any help he could give her. She kissed him affectionately and went to the door, where she was brought to a halt by the sight of the oversized lock. "Can you get your money back on this?" she asked.

"Probably not," he said. "So why don't you take it and install it at your place? You're going to need all the security you can get."

TWENTY-TWO

John Duke always talked to the press. As an advocate, he had learned early on that you couldn't get very far by stonewalling reporters, and that you could make lifelong enemies by lying to them. Plead ignorance of subjects you don't want to discuss. Give them all the background material that supports your cause. Never be quoted as disagreeing with anyone powerful. And, by all means, pick up their bar tabs. David Tillis had always been kind to John, even when they didn't agree on an issue. So John stepped out of a meeting when he heard that Tillis was on the line.

"David, it's been a while. What have you been up to?"

"Same old beat," the reporter said. "But I must say it's getting tougher. Your replacement at the institute isn't nearly as helpful as you've always been."

"Mort?" John laughed, referring to Mort

Zucker, who had come from one of the power company PR departments to run the institute. "He's a very bright guy. I'm surprised you're having problems with him." Then he volunteered, "Is there anything you'd like me to talk to him about?"

"No, but there's something going on that I think you ought to know about. I got one of those don't-tell-anyone tips from a Senate aide. I'm told that your good friend Tom Lawrence is looking into the citizen's groups you set up to handle campaign contributions."

John felt a stab of fright. "I set up?" he mumbled.

"Supposedly the senator is checking to be sure they were legitimate. He's scrupulous about adhering to the letter of the law. Personally, I think he's planning to wash his hands of even the appearance of impropriety."

John thought quickly. This was a time to plead ignorance. "I haven't heard a word about it, Dave. Sounds like he's just making sure that everything is neat and tidy. But he'll have no problem with me. At the institute, I got two legal opinions before I put change in the poor box." He was chuckling when he said good-bye.

But his expression was serious as he stared

at the phone he had just hung up. He was distracted when he returned to his meeting. Why would the senator be leaking suspicions about his own fund-raising? That was one area where elected officials didn't invite scrutiny. In public, they claimed that their donors were interested in nothing more than good government. There was no link between a $100,000 donation from the lumber industry and a vote to open public parks to logging. The donations from PACs came from small groups of concerned citizens who had decided to pass around a hat. Why had Dave Tillis thought the leak was focused on the institute?

John's suspicions swung to Pam's book. There must have been new developments that linked the senator to payments from the power companies, and as Dave had hinted, Lawrence was washing his hands. Who knew? He might even be planning to challenge the propriety of some of the donations himself, to take the sting out of a tell-all book. If that were the case, John knew he was in the perfect position to take the fall.

He bounded out of his meeting to his own office, where he could use his private line. Quickly, he dialed Senator Lawrence's office and listened while the connection went through. A secretary announced the senator's name, acknowledged the Secretary of Energy, and asked for "just a moment." John found himself listening to patriotic marches by the Marine Corps Band. Easy enough, he thought. He'd simply ask Lawrence if there was "anything new on that book we were discussing." His latest report was that the publisher was no longer interested in taking the book to press, which should mean that the senator had nothing more to worry about.

"Mr. Duke," the senator's secretary cut in, ending the music. "Senator Lawrence regrets that he can't speak with you at the moment. He's tied up now, and he expects to be unavailable right through the weekend. He asks that you call on Monday."

John felt weak. That was about as rude a brush-off as Washington's rules of decorum allowed. Lawrence could have promised to call back as soon as he had a moment. Or he could have had an aide answer and at least pretend to be helpful. The distancing, it seemed, had already begun. He could almost see the feigned shock on Thomas Lawrence's face as he announced that some donations made to him might not have been as they appeared. He would demand an investigation to assure that the Secretary of

Energy, while he was director of an industry organization, had done nothing improper. By the time Pam's book came out, if it ever went to press, John Duke would long ago have been hung out to dry.

But the more urgent necessity was to find out what the senator knew that he didn't. There must have been some development. Pam had been determined to write the book. Then, he understood, she'd been wavering. The latest he had learned was that the publisher had pulled out. None of that would account for the senator's sudden coolness.

The only person who could tell him for sure was Pam herself. He called Catherine to explain the situation. Then he buzzed his secretary and asked her to arrange a plane ticket to New York for that evening. He added a hotel reservation at the Trump Tower, just off Columbus Circle. He hoped she was still living on the Upper West Side.

Pam was completely immersed in her story when she received John's call. He was coming in on business, he told her light-heartedly, and would like nothing more than to have dinner with her. Her guard went up instantly. Not that he would be trying to stir up old romantic embers. He was too practical to take that big a risk. But he most certainly wanted something from her. Maybe it was just another effort to talk her out of the book. Or maybe he had a specific interest in the carton of institute records she had just received from Marion. Whatever, there was no reason for her to see him.

She pleaded exhaustion, said that she had been working very hard and was in no mood to dress for dinner. But he begged. His situation had changed, and there were things he had to tell her. She caught a hint of desperation in his voice that she had never heard before. He suggested a quiet place on Eleventh Avenue better known for its food than for its decor. It guaranteed privacy, and she could "come as you are."

Pam agreed. She had no intention of telling John where the book stood. But maybe she could find out what kind of reception was being planned for it in Washington. She might even learn who had torched Glen Hubbard's office, or whether Peter Salerno was a government agent. She put on a man-tailored shirt, decorated it with a scarf, and went off to her meeting with the man who had once sworn he loved her.

The restaurant was even less than he had described, a dark little room with candles on the tables, lighted for the most part by the neon beer signs that decorated its windows. The waiter, probably the owner's son, had the physique of a bouncer and spoke in grunts.

"John," she joked, "do you plan to kill me and leave me here where no one will ever find my body?"

He apologized that this wasn't the place he remembered, but they agreed it provided the privacy they needed. They tried a few minutes of idle talk while they were served a bottle of Chianti. Did he enjoy his work in the cabinet? she asked. What was it like to be rubbing elbows with the president? He asked how she was enjoying New York. He eased into the implications of her writing career.

"I need to ask you about your book. How's it coming along?"

"Good," she answered, knowing that it was no answer at all.

"I hoped you would have forgotten about it by now. As I said, it could be very embarrassing to a lot of old friends."

"Oh, there have been all sorts of suggestions that I give it up. For instance, did you know that when I got home after our last meeting I was mugged by an intruder?"

The shock in his expression seemed genuine.

"No one knew I was there," he assured her. "Except Catherine, and what could she possibly have to do with it?"

Pam filled him in on the destruction of her computer records and the attempt to steal her backup files in the warehouse. She told him about the mismatched struggle on the edge of the elevator shaft and how her attacker had stumbled to his death.

"Jesus," he said, his face sinking into his hand. "I had no idea. . . ."

She continued with the man stalking her on Long Island, the break-in at her publisher's cottage, and finally the apparent arson of his office. John's expression grew grimmer with each detail. Finally, she admitted that Thomas Howell had pulled out of their agreement. As of the moment, she had no publisher.

"I tried to warn you," he mumbled. "I know I have no credentials as your friend, but I swear I've been worried about you. You're taking on a whole branch of the government and maybe a third of the country's power brokers. You were bound to get hurt."

During their dinner, John added more cautions. He wasn't at all surprised that a first-rate house like Thomas Howell had pulled out of the contract, and he would be amazed if any other publisher picked it up. "Your charges will clearly be challenged as libelous, tying a publisher up in court before he can begin to recoup the investment." He mentioned the pressures anyone attempting to publish the book would feel from banks, labor unions, maybe even chain stores.

Pam nodded sadly. "Thomas Howell was hearing threats from labor unions," she told him. "They were trying to pull out of the project even before their offices were torched."

Having brandished the stick, John showed her the carrot. "You know, I still have contacts all over the energy industry. I could find you a spot with a great future. And I mean that sincerely . . . no strings attached. I wouldn't be any part of the deal."

"A job doing what? Putting the same happy spin on industry crimes? Finding ways to funnel still more money to the politicians? Trying to sell the benefits of mercury in the daily diet?"

He waved away her speech with the back of his hand. "C'mon, we're not that bad. Half the time we're just defending ourselves against the other side's lies. It's the way things get done. Whoever gets on the eleven o'clock news wins."

She nodded wearily. "I know. You're right.

Nothing is going to change."

"Then let me find something for you. Maybe a pure research job where you're not involved in lobbying. Something where you don't have to sell the wonders of mercury."

She smiled, and then he laughed. They settled quietly over their coffee until he introduced another subject. "Do you still hate me?"

She denied that she had ever hated him. "It was humiliating to see how far down I fell on your scale of values. I was disappointed in you, and angry at myself. I had made assumptions about our life together, and they didn't turn out to be realistic."

He took her hand and held it even when she tried to pull it away. "I'm sorry," he said. "I did a terrible thing. If I had to make the decision all over again, I would have stuck with you."

"And given up a cabinet post?" she challenged skeptically.

"Maybe! Maybe not! I think I could have told my supporters that I was in love with another woman and that I was about to ask Catherine for a divorce. I could have warned them that she would try to derail me. They could have had me as the secretary or not. But you would have been nonnegotiable."

Pam agreed that it would have been flattering, but that it probably would have cost him the appointment.

"I've learned that I don't love the job," he said. "I love you."

She was instantly on guard. Was he coming on to her? Did he really think he was going to talk his way back into her bed? Was he proposing that she stay in reserve until he found it convenient to leave his wife?

Suddenly he was busy paying the bill. "I have to get back to the hotel," he explained while signing the check. "Early meeting and then a flight back to Washington."

When they stepped outside, a light rain was falling. John insisted that she wait inside until he commandeered a taxi, and he was soaked by the time he found one. Pam feared an awkward moment when they reached her building, but John was without guile. He held the taxi while he took her to the safety of her lobby. "I'm happy that you're dropping the book. It would have brought you nothing but grief. And I meant it when I said I could find you a top position. All you have to do is call."

She watched the cab pull away and took the elevator to her floor. The apartment was exactly as she had left it. Her computer was on, showing her screen saver. A half-empty bottle of beer stood next to the keyboard.

Marion's shipping carton, bulging with files, was under her desk. John had assumed she was abandoning the book because she didn't have a publisher. Maybe he was right that it would never see the light of day. But that didn't mean she wouldn't put it all down on paper. When it was finished she'd worry about getting it printed.

TWENTY-THREE

In the morning, Pam rooted through her papers, looking for a page that she had pushed into her briefcase. It could have gotten mixed in with any of her notes, or even the manuscript pages that were burned in Glen's office. But she spotted it behind the briefcase flap, a sheet of math equations with captions between them. She pulled it out and turned it over. His name was there, and a telephone number, scribbled across the back of one of his thesis pages. Pete Salerno, the graduate student she thought had been stalking her in the Hamptons. The area code was for eastern Long Island.

She dialed it, listened to three rings, and then heard a woman's voice. "Peter Salerno? No, he doesn't live here. He was just a tenant." She thought she might have his address, and after a long wait in which Pam listened to background conversation, the woman came back on the line. She had an address on 121st Street, and a phone number with a Manhattan area code.

The address was only a few blocks from Columbia University. So the man who was claiming to be a graduate student at Columbia was probably telling the truth. He had seemed to be interested in her. But that was while vacationing at the seashore. Would he still have any interest in helping her?

Pam called and left her name and number on an answering machine. She added a comment about being the one who was always leaving as he was arriving. She tried to sound cheery. Then she took her laptop and Marion's box of files out to the balcony and got back to work. She had papers piled on her lap and a pencil clenched in her teeth when her phone rang. Her "hello" sounded more like a growl.

"Pam, is that you?"

She dropped the pencil, and the files spilled out of her lap. "Yes, it is. Peter?"

"I recognized your voice in your message, but now you sound as if you have a mouth full of marbles. Should I call back?"

"No, no! My hands were tied up, and I had a pencil in my teeth."

He laughed and said, "Okay, I'll try again. Hello, this is Pete Salerno. I'm returning a call from Pam Leighton."

She returned the chuckle, apologized, and launched into the usual small talk. She had gotten his phone number from his Hamptons landlady. She hoped he didn't mind. When had he come back to the city? What was he up to? He was glad that she had found him. Right then, he was between two classes he was teaching. His thesis had been submitted, and he was waiting for the tenured faculty to pass judgment on his work.

Finally, she turned to the reason for her call. She was in the market for a publisher, and he had mentioned a small publishing house that did a thriving business in academic titles. No, it wasn't just for a research project. Actually, she explained, she was in the process of writing a book.

"Without a publisher?" he asked. "You certainly are brave."

Pam said it was a little more complicated than that. In fact, it was too complicated to explain on the phone. Perhaps they could get together sometime so that she could fill him in.

Peter didn't seem overjoyed at the prospect. Not today, because he had a class to teach and another to prepare. And not tomorrow, because he had to be on hand for a faculty meeting. "Unless," he suggested, as if the idea had just flashed before him, "you wouldn't mind coming up here tomorrow."

"Sure! It's been years since I visited academia," she answered, trying not to sound too excited.

He gave her his office address and then apologized. "It's not much of an office. More like a closet with a beaded glass door. But there is one decent chair."

The next day she taxied uptown and walked through Columbia's gates with throngs of what appeared to be street people carrying backpacks. Bathing and shaving didn't seem to be highly regarded among the students. The lobby of Peter's building was papered with handbills and announcements. There were calls to boycott and calls to arms. A young man with heavy, brooding brows checked her briefcase for contraband before directing her to an elevator. Peter's office was at the end of a dim hallway that seemed to wind into the top-floor dormers. His office door was every bit as depressing as he had promised.

But his welcome was cheery. He directed her among piles of clutter to a sunlit corner where a comfortable leather chair waited. "We could have had much more fun out in the Hamptons," he said, and laughed.

She countered with "What did you do to get the department head so mad at you?"

"My office? You think this is a punishment? For a teaching assistant, this is pretty plush. It means I've been kissing the right asses."

In his environment it was very easy to believe that he was exactly what he claimed to be. The endless file cabinets and the chalky blackboards would never suit a government agent. He was in khakis and an open-collared sports shirt. His beard was a bit scraggly, indicating that, like the students, he had relaxed standards of appearance. But when he settled into the folding chair he had moved into position, he seemed fully attentive and even anxious to hear her story.

She started with her background and her two years at the Electric Energy Institute. "I was in charge of research," she said but readily admitted, "It was mostly self-serving research put out to show that the industry was good for the environment. We allied with the coal industry to explain the topographical benefits of strip mining, and with cell-phone companies to demonstrate that electromagnetic radiation actually retarded the growth of cancer cells."

Pam omitted her two-year affair with the director of the institute, and how the end of that affair had contributed to her leaving. She said that she had simply decided to try another line of work. That brought her to Glen Hubbard and Thomas Howell Publishers, and the decision to try a tell-all book on her experiences with the lobbying industry. "When I met you, I was working on the book. But I have to tell you why I was working in my editor's summer cottage. And that will explain why I was so damn unfriendly."

Peter's pleasant expression turned grave when she got into the break-in at her apartment and her near fatal encounter at the warehouse. She explained that she had been in hiding when he had talked to her at the supermarket and caught up to her on the road. "I thought you were a government agent who had found me. I had to get away from you as fast as I could."

His smile returned. "Wow! A secret agent. That would certainly be more exciting than an obscure point in mathematics. Do you know exactly who was stalking you? Because I'd like to apply for a job. I'd stalk you for a fraction of what the other guys are getting paid."

Next Pam told him about the threats to her publisher and the fire that had destroyed some of her work. "Thomas Howell decided that they were up against the whole government, and that it would be prudent to bow out. So here I am, looking for a publisher."

Peter got up and brought back two paper cups of water. "Here's to your muckraking book," he toasted. She responded, "And here's to that obscure point in mathematics." He circled twice before sitting down across from her.

"I was trying to impress you, so I may have overstated my connections in the publishing field." He saw the disappointment in her face. "I know a publisher, and he does put out good books. He has my thesis manuscript right now. But he's kind of a one-man business. More like a publishing agent, really. His daughter is his secretary. He prints just enough copies of scholarly works to fill the needs of academic libraries, so we're not talking about doing bestsellers. His books are controversial, but only to people who can get excited over a new subatomic particle with left-hand spin. No one would hire an arsonist to get rid of anything he published."

Pam conceded that he didn't sound very promising. "It was a long shot," she admitted.

"But let me introduce you to him," Peter

hastened to offer. "Even if it's not his thing, he may be able to recommend someone."

Pam said she didn't want to intrude on Peter's time. He answered that he had made the original offer in the hope of spending some time with her. "I'm still offering, probably for the same reason. Also, I hate to see a few industry-government conspirators keep a book from being published. It violates my sense of fair play."

They set a date when they would meet at the office of Carl Weiss Books, just a few blocks from the Columbia campus. Then Peter rode down with her in the elevator so that he could head off to his staff meeting. Pam found a taxi to take her home.

Glen came over that evening, free from the bandages, with only a few red blotches left of his burns. He brought a bottle of expensive French vodka and, in the process of creating a fashionable martini, talked about the fire investigation. The blaze, he reported, had been started with raw alcohol spilled in his credenza. The fire had burned invisibly until the finish and the wood caught. Then the flames had literally exploded out of the cabinet.

"It was definitely someone with everyday access to my office," he said as he poured an electric blue mixture into classic martini glasses. "So you were right all along. Someone working for me has been reporting back to Washington."

He handed her one of the drinks. "To us." They both wet their lips at the edges of their glasses. Glen sucked in air as if he was tasting a fine wine.

"Very nice," Pam declared.

"Maybe too minty?" he wondered. He took another sip.

"What happens now? Are they going to try to find out who it was?"

"Sure," he answered. "It would be pretty easy if they knew what was burned. They could probably find someone who was making a lot of calls to Washington. But we're mum! Our official position is that we have no idea what anyone would have wanted to destroy. Intermedia, our owner, wouldn't want Thomas Howell to do anything that might anger members of Congress. They're in the process of filing for an FCC exemption so they can buy more stations."

"Why did they let you take on the book in the first place?" Pam wondered.

"They didn't give a damn about Thomas Howell as long as we made our numbers. It wasn't until the trouble started that they realized what they had. Now they don't want anyone in Washington to know they were ever involved with *Fouling the Air.*"

Halfway through his drink he pronounced the martini definitely too minty, took both glasses, and decided to do something more conventional. The exotic French vodka, he told her, tasted better unaltered.

They were sitting on her miniature balcony when Glen got to his message. Naturally, he would help her with her book in any way he could if she decided to continue with the project. But there wasn't much he could do for her. He couldn't publish it or recommend anyone else. He couldn't get too involved in the editing. "But in a way, this may be all for the best," he said. "It was that damn book that brought us together, but I think in the end it was coming between us. If we put it aside, I think it will be easier to take our relationship to the next level. That's what I want. You're much more important to me than anything you might write."

He paused. It was her turn to say how important he was to her, but she remained thoughtfully silent. She wasn't going to tell him she was already looking for a new publisher. That would only place new burdens on their friendship. Glen had already shown that he was on her side. He had nearly gotten himself killed. If she told him her plans, he would either have to join her for her sake or put distance between them for the sake of his career.

"Jean Abbott is coming home in a few months," he told her. "She wrapped up her assignment faster than anyone expected. You should be hearing from her that she'll need to get back into the apartment."

Pam remembered that the apartment had come hand in hand with her book deal. The deal was over. "Wow! I hadn't even thought about that. I better get looking."

"I already have a place for you," Glen said. "That's what I meant about the next level. I'd like you to move in with me."

She was stunned. Only two nights ago, John Duke had tried to rekindle their old flame. All she had to do was drop the book and he would find something wonderful for her. Now Glen wanted her to move in. There was no commitment to marriage, but a definite commitment to the next level, which was only a vow or two short of marriage. Of course, that assumed she was through with her dangerous ideas about publishing an exposé.

Pam wasn't ready to move in with Glen, and she wasn't quite ready to give up the book. For an instant she thought of John, who had put his career and his work ahead of the woman he loved. Was that what she was doing? Except she had never been sure she was in love with Glen, nor had she ever made a commitment to him. Moving in would imply a commitment, at least by her standards. Then she would be obligated to put her book into the background.

"Glen, you know how much I care about you. But I have too many loose ends. I'm not ready to join up with you, not yet." She watched his head sink to his chest. She knew she had disappointed him. But it was the truth. She did have too many loose ends.

"It's an open offer," he said. "In the meantime, if you find yourself out on the street, you can bunk at my place. Separate bedrooms unless you get terribly horny." He kissed her cheek. "I'll call you in a couple of days to see if I can help."

Pam locked the door behind him. Glen would always be welcome in her life, but for the time being she was erecting a symbolic wall between them. She wouldn't let her work on the Washington exposé spill over into his life, where it could cost him his career. Nor would she let his feelings for her radiate into her space, where they would rob her of her independence. She was going ahead on her own, and the dangers would be hers to face.

She took her phone out to the balcony and dialed Marion Murray's number. There were several beeps before she was greeted with a recorded voice that told her, "The number you have dialed is no longer in service." She called the information service for Marion's area code and gave the name, address, and telephone number. This time it was a human being who came on the line to tell her that the phone had been disconnected.

"That's impossible," Pam said. "I talked to her only a few days ago."

"One minute," she was told, but the answer came back more quickly than that. "I'm sorry, but the line was disconnected yesterday. There's no forwarding number."

There were any number of reasons why Marion might have terminated her phone service. Maybe the nun she lived with required separation from her clients and a degree of professional privacy. Probably Marion would call her soon with a new number where she could be reached. Still, Pam was uneasy.

Twenty-Four

Carl Weiss Books was a second-floor office in an ancient, five-story office building on Upper Broadway. The directory listed three lawyers, a doctor, two chiropractors, and an answering service along with the publisher. The entrance was a double wooden door with the name affixed in raised brass letters. Small though the company was, Carl Weiss gave a touch of class to an otherwise uninteresting building.

Pam met Peter and noticed immediately that he had tidied himself up. His beard was neatly trimmed, his cheeks shaven, and his hair combed. He wore the same khaki slacks, but he had changed to a fresh, pressed sports shirt. Most impressive was the corduroy jacket with leather patches on the elbows. Today he looked more like a professor and less like a student.

They stepped into a reception area that had a large desk and padded benches for visitors. The walls were decorated with dozens of dust jackets from books she didn't recognize. There was a bell on the desk with a hand-printed note advising that they ring for service.

The woman who responded was pleasant faced, probably in her early twenties, wearing jeans and a colorfully patterned blouse. Her eyes sparkled behind wire-rim glasses that, along with her nearly shaved head, gave her an iconoclastic appearance. It seemed quite possible she had read many of the complicated titles that adorned the walls.

Peter introduced himself, saying that he had called.

"Oh, sure! I'm Ronda. You wanted to discuss a nonacademic book."

"That's right," he answered. "It's a book that has been under contract to Thomas Howell. They've decided not to publish it, so it's free to all takers."

Ronda laughed. "We don't get much fallout from Thomas Howell." She beckoned them to follow her. "My dad's been expecting you."

They walked past four empty cubicles that presumably had been occupied in better times. Carl Weiss's office was at the end of the hall. He was a small, dark man with bulging eyes behind thick glasses and wore a yarmulke on a nearly bald head. He shook hands with each of them, wrapping the hands they offered in both of his, as if they were being welcomed into a secret society. "You have a book that needs a home," he said to Pam. She smiled, liking him immediately.

Pam described the project in a nutshell. Then she went into all the problems — the burglary of her apartment, the attempt to steal her computer, the break-in at the editor's summer home, and finally the fire at Thomas Howell's offices. "Apparently, there are people in government, or at least in Washington, who don't want this book published," she concluded.

Weiss listened to the whole account, shaking his head in sympathy. Pam half-expected him to wrap his arms around her and bring her home to dinner. "You poor child," he commented more than once. But when she ended her story, he was ready with answers.

"First, no one could find your book in my office. My manuscripts are typeset in China. It's cheaper there! My printing is done in England, and a Mennonite house in Pennsylvania handles the binding. The book is nowhere and everywhere at the same time.

"Second, I don't like censorship. Chances

are, if a government doesn't want a book published, that's all the more reason why it should be published.

"Finally, I'm pretty hard to threaten. I don't have government contracts, and I pay my taxes. So what are they going to do? Sue me? My wife's brother is a lawyer."

Pam was laughing before he finished. Carl Weiss was a simple man with simple principles. He was anxious to publish her book because he thought it spoke the truth. Maybe he didn't understand all the nuances involved. In fact, he didn't understand half the books he published. But the fact that the government didn't want the book to appear was reason enough to make sure it got into print.

"I can give you the first half in a few days. The rest will probably take me another month," she told him.

Weiss took out a form contract that obligated him to print a small number of copies and send the bills to Pam. But if sales reached higher numbers, he would underwrite the cost and she would begin receiving royalties. "If it's a book that nobody wants to read, you pay for it," he said. "If it's a bestseller, I pay for it. From what you say, I think it should find a decent audience."

Ronda took them through the formalities of the contract and promised that she would personally handle the publication. "My father can hardly read anymore," she said. "But he still decides what books we're going to publish. I think the fact that someone is trying to stop you is why he wants to do the title. So I'll make sure it gets done."

Pam asked again if they appreciated the dangers. Even though there should be no way for anyone to find out where the book was being published, she couldn't guarantee that the same people who had attacked Thomas Howell might not come after them. "They've proven to be very resourceful. So far, they've followed every move I've made."

Ronda shrugged. "Like my father says, a book doesn't hang around here very long." Then she added, "In fact, I can give you the Web site of the typesetter in China. You can send your text directly over the Internet. That way the Chinese will be the only ones who know you're dealing with us."

"What do you think?" Peter asked as soon as they had cleared the lobby.

"I think he's wonderful, but I'm still afraid that I might be putting them in danger."

Peter smiled. "I think he probably loves the idea. After publishing things like my thesis, I bet he loves getting involved in something exciting."

Pam insisted she could see herself home, but Peter was adamant that he would accompany her to her door. That led her to ask if he would like to see her apartment even though she was about to lose it, and him to say that he would like that very much. When they arrived, she offered him a drink, which he promptly turned down. Instead, he dove into the stack of reproduced manuscript pages and then into the files she had gotten from Marion Murray. Pam went to work while he sat and read.

He took a deep, audible breath when he had read enough, and she turned away from her computer. "What do you think?"

"I think it's great. I sort of suspected that the average guy was getting screwed over. But I didn't know that stealing from the public till had become a growth industry. I can see why you want to write this story, and I can see why a lot of powerful people don't want it published." He went on thoughtfully. "You know, my book isn't going to change anyone's life. It doesn't matter whether I'm right or wrong. I mean, to my fellow mathematicians, it might be a big issue. But to the world at large, it's meaningless. But what you're doing is going to affect a lot of people. It might keep us all from being bought and sold. I'm glad you have the guts to stick with it."

Now, why in hell didn't Glen say that? Pam thought. Why were they discussing who might be offended and who might try to keep it from getting published? Why were her safety and his career the most important considerations? Wasn't the important thing that the wheeling and dealing in which money was more important than the public welfare be exposed and stopped?

Peter ambled out of the chair, stretched his back, bent over, and kissed her on the forehead. "Good luck," he said. "I'd like to help you in any way I can. Just give me a call." Then he was moving toward the front door with Pam scrambling at his heels so she could get the door open.

"When do you have to be out of here?" he asked.

"The next few weeks. Maybe a month," she guessed.

"If you get stuck, and you can survive in student housing, give me a call. I can probably find something for you."

With that he was gone, pulling the door closed behind him. So what was that? Pam wondered. More of a polite brush-off than an expression of interest. He had run all over East Hampton trying to get a date with her. Now he had gotten to spend a day with her and he seemed to be bowing out gracefully. Was it her, or the book she was determined to write? Was she too idealistic, or just too silly? The last two men she had been with had given her proper, sisterly kisses before rushing out her door. She felt very much alone.

She worked until nearly midnight, pausing once to dine on peanut butter crackers and later to try Marion's number in the hope that her line might be back in service. Once again she heard the recording regretting that the line had been disconnected. She left her French doors open, when she finally slipped into bed. There was a hint of fall in the night air, and the distant street sounds seemed to connect her with the city.

TWENTY-FIVE

Pam woke to what she thought was her alarm and wasted several seconds slapping at the night table until she found the clock. At that moment she realized it was her cell phone and bounded out of bed wondering where she had left the phone. By the time she found it, under papers on her desk, it had stopped ringing. She focused slowly on the caller ID display, which showed a Washington area code with a number she didn't recognize.

She set the phone down and made her way carefully to the open kitchen, where her coffeemaker should have been gurgling. "Damn!" The timer wouldn't turn on for another half hour, and she needed coffee now. Pam turned the coffeemaker on, then bent down to see the first drips fall into the pot. Satisfied that she would survive until the coffee was ready, she stepped past her messy bed and into the bath. She fell into a semiconscious state under the shower of hot water and didn't emerge until her skin was pink and puckered. Then she wrapped herself in a towel and padded back to the kitchen, where the aroma of fresh coffee was intoxicating.

She was sitting out on her balcony, still wrapped in the towel, when the caffeine reached her brain. Immediately she remembered the phone call and thought of the Washington, D.C., area code. Of course! Marion had either reconnected or gotten herself a new phone. She was calling to tell Pam about her abrupt loss of service and resume the conversation they had started in her apartment. Pam took a minute to dress in shorts and a sweater, and another to make her bed. Some command left over from childhood compelled her to make up her bed before she started with the work of the day.

She dialed the call and sat back into her sofa, prepared for a long conversation. After a few rings the phone was answered with a simple "Hello."

"Marion?" Pam said. "Where have you been? I've been trying to reach you."

There was a moment of silence. "Who is this?" someone asked. The voice was not at all familiar.

"Pam Leighton. You called me this morning."

"Oh, yes, Miss Leighton. This is Jane Sample, Sister Marion's roommate."

"Of course," Pam answered. "Marion told me all about you. Is she ill? Is anything wrong?"

Jane was having a great deal of trouble speaking. "I have terrible news to share with you." There was a sob deep in her throat. "Marion died yesterday. She never recovered consciousness."

Pam felt a scream of grief building up in her chest. "Died? How?"

"You knew about the break-in?" Jane asked.

"No! What happened?"

Jane tried to gather herself. "I've talked to so many people I don't remember who I've told. Our apartment was broken into the day before yesterday. Marion was at home. I was at work."

Pam felt a chill spreading up her spine. "Jesus," she mumbled.

"The police feel it was probably locals looking for drug money. That sort of thing happens a great deal here. They ransacked the place, which was unnecessary because Marion would have simply given them any money she had. I'm sure she didn't resist them. But they hit her with something heavy. The police think it was most likely the crowbar they used to break in, because they couldn't find anything in the apartment that intruders could have used."

Pam began to shake.

"I found her when I came home," Sister Jane continued, and then she choked. "I called the emergency medics, and they said she was still alive. They took her to the hospital and put her in intensive care." Another suppressed sob. "I was right there, all the time." Jane's voice trailed off. "She never woke up."

"Oh, dear God!" Pam sighed. "Oh, God . . ."

"Your name and telephone number were on our refrigerator. Isn't it crazy? They took all her papers. Even her address book. But they never touched the numbers that were posted on the door of the refrigerator."

"I'm so sorry," Pam managed. "I'm . . . devastated."

Jane told her that funeral arrangements had been made, and Pam wrote down the information.

"It's the cemetery at our motherhouse," Jane continued. "There used to be seventy nuns living there. Now there's just the groundskeeper."

"I'll be there," Pam said. "Can I send flowers, or anything?"

"Just donations to our order. There are a few older sisters that Marion and I were trying to take care of. Anything would help."

When she hung up, Pam held her hands over her face for a full minute, her mind whirling with grief and guilt. She suddenly screamed in an outpouring of pain, turned facedown on the sofa, and began crying hysterically. It was nearly noon when she was able to get control of herself.

TWENTY-SIX

Pam didn't believe that it had been a random break-in. Marion and Jane had been living in the neighborhood for two years, had served its needs and given away what they had whenever they were asked. None of the locals had any reason to harm them. Of course, it was possible that some cracked-out loser, desperate for the cost of a fix, had killed Marion in a rage. It was likely that such an intruder would tear her rooms apart looking for something of value. But there was no reason why he would tear up her address book and rummage through stacks of papers. The pieces just didn't fit. Pam couldn't shake the conviction that Marion's death, just a few days after she had shown her files to Pam, was too connected to be a coincidence.

It fit the pattern of violence that had followed every move she had made to work on her book. Somehow, somebody knew her every step. When she began writing, her computer files were trashed. When she went to retrieve her own computer, she was attacked in the warehouse. When she moved out to Glen's summer place, the house was quickly discovered. When her manuscript made it to Glen's office, the office was set afire. Then she had visited Marion to find hard proof of her allegations, and just a few days later, Marion was killed. Pam had guessed that she was being betrayed by someone who worked at Thomas Howell, and that had proven to be the fact. But Glen had moved to a new position and isolated Pam and the book from his former staff. So it couldn't be an internal spy who had linked her to Sister Marion.

The only answer was that she was being watched. When she had traveled to Washington, someone had followed her, or called ahead to have the plane met. She was sick at the thought that she had led an assassin right to Marion's house. Now there was another terrifying thought. Had she also pointed her Washington enemies at Peter Salerno? Had she led them to Carl Weiss? Was she spreading the danger to every person she involved? She had come close to getting Glen killed. With Marion, it seemed she had succeeded.

Pam thought of the files Marion had shipped up to her. She had pushed the carton under her bed more to get it out of her way than with any thought that she was hiding it. If Marion's killers knew about them, they would already have come after them. But how long would it take them to figure out what Marion had shipped to her? She had to move them to a safe place. Where would that be? Not with Glen, who had already been targeted. How would she move them? Whoever was watching could hardly miss seeing her with the carton clutched to her chest.

Peter Salerno seemed to be her best hope. His department's building had round-the-clock security in the lobby. Even though government agents would have little trouble getting by the student guard, they might not want to risk being identified. Besides, in the warrens of the top-floor offices, there had to be a hundred places to hide a box of files.

Just as important, Peter could come and get them. Tomorrow, when she left for Marion's memorial service, anyone following her would stay with her. She could leave Peter a key, and he could simply let himself in and take the files back to his office.

Pam left her apartment and walked a

meaningless pattern of streets. She couldn't be sure she wasn't being followed. She had never noticed anyone suspicious lurking around her building or following her. But somehow they knew her every move. She found a pay phone in the back of a coffee shop and called Peter's number. His machine answered, and she left a message giving him the number at the coffee shop. Then she settled into the booth next to the phone and ordered lunch.

She watched the door as she ate. People came and went, mostly to pick up orders in brown paper bags. A few sat at the counter and ate quickly. She realized that she had no idea how a person following her would look. Any one of these customers could be her tail, or perhaps she was being watched from a car parked across the street. Most likely she was making every mistake that amateurs fell into.

The phone rang, attracting the attention of the waitress. Pam picked it up and sighed in relief when she heard Peter's voice. She explained her plight, reminding him of the files he had looked through. Then she told him about Marion's death and why her records were extremely dangerous.

"She was killed?" he asked in disbelief.

"By someone who broke into her apartment in the middle of the day. The police are passing it off as the work of a strung-out junkie. I think it's the same people who set the fire at Thomas Howell."

He was silent. "So, if I pick these up and store them at my place, I can expect to be burned or murdered. Why doesn't this sound like such a great idea?"

"It isn't," Pam said. "Helping me seems to be a very hazardous occupation. But the fact is that you're the only one I can turn to. You said you wanted to help. You were even going to try to find me a place to stay."

"Sure," he said, laughing. "But that was before I knew your friends couldn't get life insurance. If I do this, I'm going to want a payback. A very big payback."

She knew he was joking in the face of a very dire situation. "How big?" she teased.

"Dinner," he suggested. "Someplace cheap that I can afford."

"You drive a hard bargain, but I guess I have no choice." Pam told him that she would be gone the entire following day. She felt certain no one would be watching her building. She told him she would leave the key on top of the doorjamb of the apartment next to hers.

"You sound as if you know all the CIA tricks," he said.

"No, but I'm starting to learn some of them."

At home she used her phone to make her plane reservations. Anyone listening in would learn exactly what she wanted them to know. She locked the French doors and checked the lock on the front door, not that she thought for a second that door locks would keep out the people who had killed Marion. It was just that she no longer felt safe working in the fresh air by her balcony.

In the morning she got up early, had toast and coffee, and put on a modest, dark dress. She walked to the corner to hail a taxi, glancing around without seeing anyone who had any interest in her. As the cab drove past her front door, she found no one who might be watching the building. Looking back over her shoulder, she spotted no car that could be following. But if they already knew where she was going, there was no reason to follow her.

Pam landed in Washington, picked up a compact rental car, and followed Jane's directions into Maryland, where the funeral was being held. The motherhouse turned out to be an estate behind a high stone wall. The building, probably a century-old mansion, was in obvious disrepair. The grounds were badly overgrown. She could imagine the activity when seventy women had lived there, studying, praying, and preparing for their ministries. Now the place was awaiting a wrecking ball. Most likely it would be replaced by a tower of condominiums.

Paper signs posted inside the gate directed mourners to the nuns' graveyard. People had already arrived and were standing somberly at the corner of a small field of tombstones. The stones, only a few inches high, were nearly buried in the neglected grass.

Pam didn't recognize any of the mourners. There were a few older ladies, and half a dozen street people, mostly Afro-Americans, tattered and unkempt. But then cars began to arrive, bearing a more distinguished-looking group. Pam saw people from the institute approaching and walked to greet them. They had all worked with Marion and were genuinely saddened to be there. Minutes later a limo came close, and John Duke stepped out with his wife. Several chauffeured cars followed immediately, bringing people Pam recognized as lobbyists who had worked with the institute, and congressmen and aides who had benefited from the lobbyists' generosity. Marion had been right. They all flaunted great style.

They drew close to the street people but never offered the courtesy of a smile. Those who knew where money was to be had weren't comfortable with those who had no idea of where to get it.

Then came the hearse, an old car with its finish showing years of wear. A white-haired clergyman stepped out and turned to assist a small, plainly attired woman who, Pam guessed, was Sister Jane. The guests assembled around an open grave and watched silently while a plain pine coffin was carried from the hearse and positioned over the grave site. The clergyman opened a black leather book, cleared his throat, and began reading the prayers for burial. It seemed that Marion's order didn't make a big thing out of death.

Pam was standing directly across the coffin from John, whose head was bowed in a somber pose. Catherine, clinging to his arm, seemed to be looking in every direction except straight ahead, which would have brought her face-to-face with Pam. Did Catherine recognize her? In all likelihood John had never shown her a picture. But it was probable that she had seen Pam in the dozens of telephoto black-and-whites that her detectives must have taken. John may even have warned her that her former rival might be at the funeral. From the way she avoiding looking directly across the top of the bier, Pam guessed that Catherine had made the connection. But she had no fear of an awkward scene. John's wife was too self-assured to acknowledge that he had ever lived with another woman, that someone like Pam could even exist.

The clergyman interrupted his prayers to sprinkle the casket with holy water from a plastic bottle. Then he droned on, informing the mourners that life was eternal despite the evidence before them. Pam tried to listen, but her mind kept wandering to John. Did he know that Marion had taken copies of his most confidential records? Did he know that people were going to break into her apartment in order to get them back? Had he arranged the break-in? "We're used and then thrown away," Marion had said. Did John know who had thrown her away?

What about the other lobbyists who were standing by the coffin, trying desperately not to get mud on their shoes? Did any of them know Marion was dangerous? Had one of them decided it was best to defuse the ticking time bomb?

That led logically to her next question: Did any of them know what had happened to Marion's copied files? Without doubt many of them knew Pam had tried to write a book that could be extremely embarrassing. But did anyone know that she was going ahead with the project, and that she now had the files which would make the book devastating? If someone did, might he decide that she too had to be defused?

John was right and Glen was right. Common sense dictated that she should drop the project. The plain pine coffin at her feet showed just how dangerous it could be. But the woman lying inside the box was the reason she had to go on. Marion had given her the files trusting she would use them to expose the scale of corruption. In taking the files, Pam had implied a promise to do just that. So, whatever happened, there could be no turning back now.

The clergyman dropped a handful of dirt on top of Marion's casket, symbolizing that she was being returned to the earth from which she had come. The prayers were over. He turned to Sister Jane, embraced her, and kissed her cheek. Then Jane turned to the mourners, who were assembling in a line to pay their respects. She knew the people from her soup kitchen and greeted them warmly. When the guests from the capital reached her, she could only nod and smile and mumble that Marion would have appreciated their being there.

Pam introduced herself, and Jane lit up in recognition. She said that Marion had told her of Pam's visit and that they had worked together wrapping the carton. She knew Marion was happy to have the material in Pam's hands.

"I need to talk to you about those records," Pam whispered, as if she was offering words of condolence. "I'll call you during the week. In the meantime, please don't mention them to anyone. It could get me into a lot of trouble."

Jane pulled back. "Did we do something wrong?"

"Not at all," Pam said. "Marion and I agreed that it was the right thing to do. But there are a lot of people here who don't agree with us. They want to get them back."

Jane's eyes registered confusion. It was obvious that Marion hadn't shared with her why she'd kept the files, and why she had chosen to send them to Pam. Nevertheless, she agreed that there was no reason for her to tell anyone about them. She said she would look forward to Pam's call.

Pam lingered in the parking area, chatting with friends from the institute, all of them stunned to have learned that Marion was a nun and shocked that she had died violently. John Duke joined the group for a moment and then took Pam aside. "I hope you're still weighing my offer," he said pleasantly. "I know of two spots that would be great for you, one in Florida and the other in Washington."

"I think I will be looking for something very soon," she lied. "I'll give you a call."

His smile at the news of her decision was so genuine that Pam couldn't believe he knew anything about the circumstances of Marion's death.

TWENTY-SEVEN

As soon as Pam landed back in New York, she telephoned Peter and heard him bubbling like a true conspirator. He described his taxi trip to her apartment and claimed he had circled her street several times just to make sure he wasn't being followed. He had found the key atop the door of the next apartment and let himself in quickly so that he wouldn't be seen. He had listened at the door before he left to make sure the hallway was empty and then had used the fire stairs so he wouldn't run into anyone on the elevator.

He had walked to the corner for a taxi, then directed a few random street changes to be sure he wasn't being followed. "It was just like the movies," he said. "I felt like James Bond, except that Bond never would have carried a heavy box by himself. He would have gotten a leggy blonde to handle it for him."

He told her that he had hidden the files in the Science Department offices. "There must be a thousand boxes of files in the closets and hallways. I'm not sure I'm going to be able to find it myself."

"You said you could get me into student housing," Pam reminded him.

"God, I have to be careful what I say to you. First you take me up on a publisher. Now on finding you a place to live. I'm glad I never said that I'd walk through fire just to get to your front door," he teased.

"Call me when you have something," she said. "Don't mention 'apartment' or tell me an address. Just say that we should get together. I'll be packed and ready to move."

He sounded suddenly serious when he said, "I have to tell you, you're beginning to scare me."

"That's because I'm a little scared myself. There are several things I have to tell you about."

Riding in a taxi to her apartment, she realized she was putting all her trust in a complete stranger. She had known Peter Salerno for only a few weeks and still didn't know anything important about him except that he really was a mathematician working on a doctorate at Columbia, and that he seemed to be taken by her. But she had to trust him because there wasn't anyone else. She knew she could always turn to Glen Hubbard if things became desperate. No matter what he thought of her persistence with her book, he would never let her drown in her own stubbornness. But he had already risked everything for her, even his life. She couldn't ask him to risk more. That left Peter as the only person who wanted to help her and could.

She knew she was taking advantage of his feelings for her. She had to surmise that he was not so much working for her cause as trying to work his way into her life. Most likely the moment would come when she would have to put that fantasy to rest, but in the meantime she would let him hope. What she couldn't do was draw him into the dangers that now surrounded her. She would have to make certain he understood exactly what the danger was, a point that had been driven home by her standing so close to Marion's dead body.

Pam didn't think she had yet placed Peter in jeopardy. As far as she could tell, no one from the other side knew who he was or had any idea that he was helping her. She would have to make certain no one ever did. She wouldn't tell anyone about her move into campus housing but would simply disappear from her present apartment. She wouldn't involve him in any of her contacts with the publisher. In fact, once she was settled in, there would be no need for her to have any contact with Peter. He would understand why separation from her was in his best interest.

She unlocked the door to her apartment and swung it open ahead of her. She gasped when she saw a light on and heard something move. Someone was inside waiting for her. Instantly she pulled the door closed and started for the fire stairs. She heard her door rattle open behind her.

"Pam," a voice called. It was Glen rushing out to catch her.

She turned angrily. "Jesus, you scared me. What are you doing here?"

"What do you think? I came to see you."

She took a deep breath to vent her fear. "You should have called me," she said as she walked back to her door and into his embrace.

"I did. You didn't answer. I figured you were out and I'd catch you when you got home."

"How did you get in?"

"With a key," he answered. "Remember? You gave me a key when you changed your lock."

"Of course," she said, and then she began an apology.

"Where were you?" he asked.

Pam realized that she had never told him about Marion's death. She hesitated for a moment, wondering whether she should involve him any further. But she didn't want to lie to him. "Washington," she admitted.

"Dear God!" His head shook slowly in frustration.

"I had to go. You remember I told you about Marion, and the records she had copied?"

"Marion," Glen snapped. "She's the last person you should be visiting."

"She's dead. She was killed in her apartment. I was at her funeral."

His first reaction was wide-eyed shock, but that quickly gave way to concern. "Killed? How?"

Pam went into the facts she knew. A break-in. The apartment ransacked. All her papers thrown about. "She was hit over the head with a blunt object. Police speculate it might have been a crowbar. The door had been jimmied right off its hinges."

As she spoke, Glen sank into grief. "Jesus," he mumbled each time she added a new detail.

"The police think it was a junkie looking

for drug money," Pam continued. "But I don't buy that. Marion would have given anyone who came to her door whatever he needed. The neighborhood people would have known they didn't have to break down the door. Besides, why would a junkie take the time to go through her papers and tear up her address book?"

His head snapped up. "Was your name in her book?"

"Maybe. My name and number were stuck on the front of her refrigerator."

"You think she was killed because of those records she showed you?"

"I don't know," she answered. "But it's a hell of a coincidence, isn't it? You try to help me and your office is torched. Marion tries to help me and she's murdered. For God's sake, who's doing these things? And how do they know my every move?"

"It could be anyone," he answered instantly. "A public company that bought millions of dollars' worth of favors. A lobbyist who thinks you have information that could send him to jail. Maybe a labor leader who has a few senators doing his bidding. But if I had to guess, I would say it's someone involved in the Arthur Ries disappearance. Your book could embarrass a lot of people. But information about Ries could get someone indicted for murder. That's someone who would kill to keep it from being published. And you're the leading candidate to become the next victim."

"I've thought of that," she said softly. "I'm scared stiff."

"Then drop it!" he shouted.

"I have," she said. "When you were burned I told you I was giving up. Then Marion had this information and I wavered. I didn't just have a story. I had hard proof. And I had leads to Arthur Ries. But this morning, standing at the grave, I was frightened. If Marion was killed for her records, it was because the killers didn't know she had sent the records to me. If they knew, Marion would have been looking at my coffin."

"Where are her files?" he demanded.

"I got rid of them."

"How? Where?"

Pam knew Glen would do anything to protect her. She was determined not to involve him any more than she already had. "Down the incinerator chute," she lied.

"Did they burn?"

"I went to the basement to be sure. All I found were barrels of ashes."

"But Marion's killers don't know that," he reasoned. "They'll be coming here. You've got to get out!"

She nodded. "Now you know why I was scared to death when I found someone in my apartment."

He bounded to her and clutched her in his arms. "We'll go to my place. I still have the dead bolt on the doors."

She pulled away. "I'm not going anywhere I could bring you more trouble. They set fire to your office. They could just as easily set fire to your apartment."

"But you can't stay here," he warned.

"I know. I'm getting out and I'm going into hiding. I'm not telling anyone where, and I won't come back until all this is over. God, I may even change my name."

"But I have to know where you are. You know how I feel about you."

"If you know, you'll be in danger. This won't take long. Once they know that there's no book and no records, I can come back. Then we won't need all those locks on the door."

"I can't let you do this," Glen pleaded.

"I've thought it through. This is the best way. No one can get hurt for what they don't know."

"When are you going?"

"Right now," she said. "I'm going to pack one bag and get a cab to the airport."

"I'll take you there. Let me drive you."

"No, damn it! If you take me, then you'll know where I'm going. Please, Glen. It has to be this way."

He shrank into a dejected pose. "Pam, I'll wait. You know I'll wait for you."

"I know." She leaned to him and kissed him affectionately. "And I'll be back. I promise."

As soon as he left, she began packing a small suitcase. Underwear, a pair of jeans, and a couple of tops, along with her toiletries and cosmetics. But she had no idea where she was going. It was only twelve hours since she had asked Peter to find her a room. There was little chance he had already succeeded. She would wait until she was outside before phoning him. She reasoned that her apartment was most likely bugged. She hoped she had been overheard when she swore off the book and announced that she was going into hiding. That was the last thing she wanted everyone to know about her. Everyone except Peter, the stranger to whom she was entrusting her life.

TWENTY-EIGHT

Peter hadn't found her a place to live. The truth was, as he freely admitted, he hadn't even begun looking. But, of course, she could stay at his place, if she didn't mind the clothesline stretched across the bathtub. She did mind, but there wasn't anyplace else available. She taxied up to an address on West 116th Street, climbed the stone steps, and rang a bell outside the front door.

"Yeah?"

"It's me, Pam."

"Third floor," Peter directed, and then he buzzed the lock on the front door.

She stepped into a dimly lighted hallway with an apartment door to her left and a flight of stairs to her right. Before she could get her bearings, a door opened at the back of the ground-floor hall, and two young women came bouncing out. They were dressed in the student fashion she had seen on campus: worn jeans, oversized ponchos, and knit hats. The women were so involved in their conversation that they ran around Pam without even looking up. She glanced down at the outfit she was wearing. She might as well have had a reflective sign across her back that said, "I don't belong here."

She made the second floor without effort, but she was panting when she reached the third. Peter was standing by an open door at the front end of the hallway. "Welcome to the Ritz," he said and reached out to take her bag.

The apartment, which was the front half of a railroad flat left over from the turn of the twentieth century, was actually quite spacious. The living room, with two windows looking out over the street, had a setting of modern furniture centered on a woven carpet atop a highly polished wooden floor. There was a stereo system stack under the windows and speakers in each corner. Behind that was a dining area furnished with a small butcher-block table and four cane-back chairs. The bedroom, along with the tiny bath, was to the left of the living room, over the building's front door. As best Pam could see, there was no kitchen, only an electric coffeepot, a hot plate, and a toaster oven on a shelf in the dining area.

"I'm so sorry," she began. "I know this is inconvenient for you."

"You don't know the half of it," he said. "I had to cancel the dancing girls who were coming to spend the night."

He carried her suitcase into the bedroom, which had a single-size mattress with no headboard or footboard. "This is yours," he said with no elaboration, "except that I may have to come through to get to the bathroom."

"No, I can curl up on your couch," Pam insisted.

"If you do, you'll be lying on top of me. So leave your things and we can go down to a coffee shop. I've got to hear what's been going on that couldn't wait until tomorrow."

Instead of a coffee shop, they went to a noisy student bar where undergraduates stood around raised tables drinking beer from bottles. The decor was drab and dreary, but the sexual tension in the room was electric. Men were leaving their friends like electrons breaking free from a nucleus and flying unerringly to atoms of young women. Overnight pairings seemed to be forming by an insistent law of physics.

Peter elbowed up to the bar, ordered two beers, and came back with chilled bottles but no glasses. He clicked his bottle against hers. "Okay, so tell me. What in hell is going on?"

Pam had no clear answer. She tried to explain the fear she'd felt when Marion's body was being lowered into the ground and, at the same moment, her resolution to finish her book no matter what. But the two thoughts didn't fit smoothly together. It was hard for her to explain how she could be both determined and terrified. "Anyhow, I had to get out of the apartment where they could find me. If I was going to finish the book, I had to vanish."

Peter was peeling the label off his beer bottle with his thumbnail. "You know, when I saw you in that store in East Hampton, I thought, Now there's a good-looking woman who seems to be living by herself. I'm embarrassed to say that the only thing I had in mind was getting into your pants. Now I find out that you're on the FBI's most wanted list and that federal agents are apt to nab me as a coconspirator."

"I'm sorry," Pam started. "You have every right to toss me out —"

"No," he said, cutting her off. "This has to be the most interesting pickup I've been involved with. Usually all I get is a few minutes of small talk and a faked orgasm. But you're like *Candid Camera.* I can almost hear the emcee wondering how long this idiot is going to believe such a ridiculous line before he realizes that you're part of the game."

"It's not a game!"

"I know that. I know you're on the run and the danger is real. It's much more than small talk, and I don't expect there's going to be an orgasm, faked or otherwise. So I'll hide you until I can find a place for you. After that, I'll help you in any way I can, so long as it doesn't involved getting killed."

"Fair enough," she said with a smile.

He nodded. "Okay." Then he went back to the bar for two more bottles of beer.

Pam awoke to the flush of a toilet. Next she heard the shower running, and then Peter's voice humming a show tune. She got out of bed, went to the sideboard in the dining room, and tried to figure out the electric coffeepot.

When Peter came out of the bedroom, he was wearing trousers and an undershirt. His bare feet left wet footprints on the floor. "Don't worry about coffee," he said. "I've got an early class. I'll eat at the student union."

"I'll get out of your way as fast as I can," she offered.

He seemed insulted by the idea. "You're not in the way. Make yourself at home. With any luck, you'll have a place of your own tonight." He went back into the bedroom, returned wearing a shirt and shoes, and picked a windbreaker off the clothes tree by the door.

"Thank you," she called after him.

"No sweat," he called back.

She heard his footsteps bounding down the two flights of stairs.

Pam found herself smiling. Peter's light-heartedness in the face of danger was contagious and, more important, it looked as if she had made a successful escape. No one knew where she was. Most likely her Washington enemies believed that she had given up her book and destroyed all the dangerous evidence. There wasn't much reason to continue hunting her down. She took her laptop out of her suitcase and set herself up at the butcher-block table. It wasn't much of an office, but it was completely safe.

TWENTY-NINE

The Kennedy Center was awash in light, the perfect setting for an international love fest that would bring American and Italian leaders together over an Italian opera about the American frontier. The lobby was filled with power brokers, all in white tie, and their ladies, dressed in couture fashions. Ambassadors congregated at the foot of the main stairs together with a sprinkling of jurists. The elected representatives were in clusters brought together by their state affiliations, committee memberships, or fields of interest. Lobbyists buzzed like bees from flower to flower, showing ivory smiles and offering perfectly manicured hands.

John Duke stood with members of the Senate's energy committee, laughing at a joke about an Italian environmentalist who wore white socks when he crushed grapes. Catherine was chatting with a senator's wife about the opera they were about to see, raving about the performance she had heard at La Scala. She felt a hand touch her arm and turned to the smiling face of her cousin Benjamin Porter, the House majority whip. "Ben," she gushed as she embraced him and accepted a kiss on her cheek.

"Catherine," he responded, and reached to shake John's hand. His rank changed the geography of the group as he immediately became the center of attention. There wasn't much that could make it through the gears of government without Congressman Porter's approval, so his every word was mined for hints of his preferences.

"How's that clean water bill doing, Ben?" one of the senators wondered.

"Oh, I'm sure it will pass," he answered. Then, with a roguish twinkle in his eye, he added, "Of course, there will have to be a few amendments."

Laughter exploded among the group. They all got Benjamin's meaning, that the high-sounding bill would be emasculated before it came to the floor. He stood still for a few more seconds of small talk but then managed to draw John aside. "I missed you at the coal panel meeting," he said as an opener. "Are you waning in your support of the nation's most abundant fuel?" Congressman Porter was a faithful ally of the coal mining industry, and his panel brought industry lobbyists together with legislators and their staffers.

"Not at all," John answered. "But there was a funeral I couldn't miss. My personal secretary at the institute, Marion Murray."

"Ah, yes. I heard about that. What was she doing living in that neighborhood? She must have known it wasn't very safe."

"I told her exactly that time after time. But she was a religious woman and spent her free time working with the neighborhood people."

"Commendable," the majority whip allowed. Then he got to his subject. "Any new information on that book we were discussing? The one your girl at the institute was thinking about writing?" Benjamin always said "your girl" when referring to Pam. John was never sure whether it was a reference to an employee or a mistress. Had Catherine told her powerful cousin about her husband's philandering?

"I have it on the best authority that the project is dead," John answered. "The publisher has pulled out, and the author has abandoned the idea. I think she's planning to look for a research job back in the power industry."

Benjamin smiled. "Well, that is good news.

It will make a lot of people very happy. And may I ask about the reliability of your source?"

"The most reliable." John beamed. "The young lady herself."

A chime toned, announcing that it was time for the audience to take seats. When John turned back to Catherine, there was a broad smile on his face. He was sure he had left the impression that he had stopped the book personally. That should show the House leader he was the kind of man who could be counted on.

"What was that all about?" his wife asked as he led her down the aisle.

"The book we were worried about. I was able to get it killed. Your cousin was very grateful."

"John, sometimes I'm amazed at how naive you can be," she whispered. "Do you really think you were the one who had the book killed?"

THIRTY

"What do you think?" Peter asked once Pam had had a chance to look around the room. "It's great," she answered, trying to sound more enthusiastic than she was. It was a typical dormitory room: a desk and bookcase, a single bed, a soft chair with a reading lamp, and a small closet with sliding doors and a built-in dresser. "Is there a bathroom?"

"Sure! It's the next door to your right. You share it with three suite mates — graduate students, so you probably don't have to worry about all-night keg parties or glue on the toilet seat."

"Do you think I'm going to fit in? I'm four years out of grad school."

"You'll be writing and they'll be writing. That's what graduate students do. As far as the bathroom goes, it would help if you got a tattoo. That seems to be the rage among college girls. Maybe a rose on your breast, or a peace symbol on the small of your back. Those are both very popular."

Pam dropped her suitcase on the bed, turned to him, and kissed him gently on the cheek. "I really appreciate this. Somehow, I'll find a way to thank you."

"You already did. And tonight's the night!"

She backed away a step. "What's tonight?"

"The dinner you promised. I'll pick you up at eight. And wear something scruffy so I don't have to get dressed up."

When he left, she took a closer look at the room and then ventured out to see the bathroom. She found two sinks sunk into a long countertop, two toilet stalls, and two showers, each with a curtain for privacy. The clothes hooks were on the outside wall, which meant undressing and dressing in the open area. She smiled at Peter's suggestion that she should add a tattoo if she really wanted to blend in.

She unpacked her few things, set up her desk with the laptop computer and a box of blank CDs. She put her printed notes and pages on one of the bookcase shelves. The important CDs, with her background notes and drafted pages, she dropped inside the removable lining of her raincoat, then she hung the coat in the closet. Anyone who found her would take the computer and the disks lying next to it. They might even go through her drawers and dig into the pockets of the clothes in her closet. But they wouldn't take her raincoat. Once she felt secure, she got down to work.

Peter showed up right on time, wearing a cotton sweater over corduroy trousers. He surveyed Pam in her slacks, loafers, and tailored shirt. "Don't you own anything drab and worn out?"

"That was never a goal for my wardrobe," she answered. "This is as casual as I generally get."

He nodded. "Okay, we'll try for a dark table in the back, where no one is apt to see us. Tomorrow I'll take you clothes shopping. After all, I have a reputation to protect."

The restaurant wasn't nearly the sty she had been expecting. It was dark, with plaster chipped off the interior walls, and the plumbing and air-conditioning ducts exposed between the ceiling beams. But the dozen or so tables had white tablecloths and colorful place settings. Most of the tables were taken, some by well-dressed couples who obviously weren't involved with the university.

"You said a place you could afford," she

reminded him as they were being seated. "This seems a bit upscale."

"I do dishes here on weekends," he teased. "They give me a break on the prices. Besides, if it gets too steep, we can always put it on your credit card."

She frowned. "That, I'm afraid, is one thing I can't do. All the government would have to do is check my account number to find out where I was spending my money. Credit cards leave a very detailed trail."

"My God, you really are with the CIA."

"I'm worried about you as well as about myself. I warned you, I'm a very dangerous dinner companion."

Over their meal they discussed a working arrangement. Pam would go on campus once a day when Peter planned to be in his office. She could go through the box of Marion's files and take what she needed for the part of the book she was working on. Her coming and going would seem perfectly normal. The dorm room was only a block from his department building.

For his part, Peter intended to keep a close watch on the files and give Pam use of his office for reviewing and copying them.

"Won't I raise suspicions by spending so much time in your office?" she wondered.

"I don't think so. It will just look like a

teacher hitting on a student. Nothing out of the ordinary."

Their conversation turned personal when the coffee was served. "What made you decide to write a book?" he asked casually.

She stuck to the essentials. She had been an important lobbyist and had gathered a great deal of information on how the business worked. An editor friend had suggested that she talk about it.

"But weren't you kind of sticking it to your friends in the business?"

That was harder to answer. Her metamorphosis from angry vengeance to vague idealism was too long a story. "Not to the good guys. Just to the bad ones, and there are enough of those to fill a book."

"Well, if lobbying is so seedy, why did you go to Washington in the first place?"

That was easy. "Because I was a naive student who suddenly needed a job. I answered an ad for a research assistant at a Washington business council. Coming from Indiana, it seemed like the most exciting opportunity on earth."

"Did you like Washington?"

She shrugged. The truth was that she hadn't really involved herself in the capital. Instead, she had become her boss's other woman, and spent more time hiding than exploring. Pam didn't want Peter digging into the darker corners of her past, so she flipped the subject to his past. "Enough about me. What brought you here?"

"A teaching fellowship when I graduated from SUNY in Albany. I liked abstract math, and it was a chance to study with some of the best in the business. I had to put my life on hold, but I have no regrets. Now, with a little luck, I may even get a salary."

Pam realized that she liked this man. He spoke simply and honestly, with a self-deprecating sense of humor, just the opposite from the influence peddlers who had populated her life.

They put their plan to work the next day. She wrote in the morning, quickly learning to ignore the slamming doors and loud voices. She had one interruption, when a student named Brooke knocked and barged in before Pam could answer. She introduced herself as "the girl next door" and condensed her life story into a single paragraph. She was working on her master's in sociology and planning to get married at the end of the school year. Pam said that she was a doctoral candidate in political science, the first cover that came to her mind.

"The other girls are okay," Brooke told

her. "You'll probably meet them in the shower. Marsha is a chemist, so she's kind of focused, if you know what I mean. Ellie majors in medieval poetry. She has a rich father, so she can study anything she wants." Brooke popped out just as abruptly as she had popped in, leaving Pam to ponder the embarrassment of meeting Marsha and Ellie in the shower.

She found a small delicatessen on the corner and carried a sandwich and coffee up to Peter's office. He dragged the carton of files to an empty desk, where she went through the material and began to catalog the documents. When she had the ones she needed, she took over his desk and copied the important facts and dates onto a disk. Then she packed up and headed for home.

The routine worked well, and she produced an amazing amount of work in just the first week.

She also found leads in the Ries disappearance, although nothing conclusive. There were e-mails from a former director of the institute to another lobbying organization saying that important contacts "we have spent three years developing" were very upset over the activities of AR. There was also a memo of a meeting with coal industry officials suggesting that they encourage the union to rein in their man before "he does great damage to important contacts we have been cultivating." It seemed the electric power industry feared a loss of influence in Congress if AR testified as planned.

Pam met her other two suite mates in the bathroom and exchanged condensed résumés. Her distinct impression was that they were children and that it must be obvious she was too old to be a student. She took an inventory of tattoos and found an exciting array of designs to share with Peter.

Her biggest shock came early one morning as she tried to sneak a shower before her rivals came barging in. She entered the bathroom just as a naked figure stepped out of the shower stall. The surprising thing was that it was a man, who didn't seem at all disturbed to have a woman walk in on him. "Tim Condon," he said, offering one hand while the other held a towel around his waist. "I'm Brooke's friend." Then he announced, "I have to run. I have an early class," and he sloshed past her, leaving a drippy trail behind him.

"Tim Condon," Peter said in surprise when Pam told him about the embarrassing encounter. "He's a tenured professor in the Sociology Department. What's he doing in your bathroom?"

Pam explained that he was apparently the intended of one of her suite mates. "That will certainly come as a surprise to Mrs. Condon," Peter said. Apparently Tim had discovered qualities in one of his graduate students that needed further development. "Hitting on students is like shooting fish in a barrel," Peter said.

Pam had enough material to begin sending pages to the Chinese typesetter. She chose a computer in the university library so that her personal address wouldn't show up on the transmission. In a two-hour session, she sent nearly two hundred pages over the Internet. She used a pay phone to call Carl Weiss Books, and his daughter congratulated her on her progress. The typeset pages would come back as a computer file for copyediting. Pam should be able to pick them up in about a week.

She stayed true to her work schedule, gathering a few more of Marion's files each day to use as the basis for the next day's writing. Her work in the dorm room was mostly uninterrupted. Brooke's visits were her only diversion, and Pam listened patiently to the younger woman's blissful accounts of being in love. She also confided her plans for marrying Associate Professor Condon, "sometime after graduation, as soon as his divorce is final." Pam asked only enough questions to show polite interest, but even with sparse information, she was pretty sure that Brooke was headed for a devastating letdown.

There were moments when Pam wanted to tell the truth about her own past and give Brooke the benefit of her experience. She was certain that Condon wouldn't be trading in a faculty-approved wife for a young master's degree candidate. She guessed, from a few comments Peter let slip, that Tim might drop Brooke as soon as another nubile student came to his attention. But Pam decided she had to stay focused and incognito, and Brooke was old enough to fend for herself.

THIRTY-ONE

It was a Wednesday afternoon when Pam finished the book's concluding chapter and went to the library's computer center to e-mail the text to China. She stopped by Peter's office to share the good news, and he suggested a modest celebration. "Dinner at my place. Eight o'clock!"

She laughed. "Let's make it a restaurant. You don't even have a stove. And I can begin paying bills again. I'll be gone by the time they can trace me to this part of town."

"Why don't you lie low until the book is in print?" he advised. "Then you won't be worth killing. They'll charge you with libel and haul your ass into court, but there won't be any reason for you to have an accident."

"You think I'm still in danger?" she asked, implying that she had already won.

"Maybe not. But it's a good reason why we should eat at my place instead of a restaurant. I can produce miracles without a stove."

Pam stopped at a flower shop on the way to her dinner date. It seemed appropriate that the guest should bring a gift. It should be something sensational, she reasoned, because she was grateful for more than just the dinner. Peter had put himself at risk on her behalf, and had rearranged his life to support her work. But she had no idea what would be the perfect gift for him. Flowers was about as personal as she wanted to get.

She waited to be buzzed into his building, then climbed the two flights of stairs to his floor. He was waiting in his open doorway. The smell of garlic and spices filled the air. "You can't get those aromas out of a hot plate," she said suspiciously as he showed her in. The butcher-block table was set with a checked cloth and a short candle in a Chianti basket. There was a vase of fall leaves in the center. The aroma was coming from an electric skillet simmering a brown sauce. Pam gave him the flowers. "I brought this for the table, but I like yours better."

Peter took the bouquet, stood it in a pilsner glass, and set it on the low living room table. "So, what do you think?" he asked as he squeezed past her to pull out her chair.

"I think you're a fraud! No mathematician knows how to set a romantic table, or cook with real spices. I'll bet your doctorate is in art history."

"Why do people always think mathematicians are one-dimensional?" he asked, acting as if his feelings had been hurt.

"Because no one understands what they're talking about. How can you have a conversation about imaginary numbers?"

He carried her plate to the sideboard and served her from the skillet. "Chicken Marsala, with portobello mushrooms and fresh capers," he announced. "With a side of whole-grain linguini." He set the dinner before her. "And, of course, wine. Tonight I've chosen . . ." He paused while he raised a bottle of straw-colored wine. "Tonight I thought a Pinot Grigio from the North." He set out a wineglass and carefully poured in a small measure. Then he set the cork beside her plate and stood at attention with the bottle raised to eye level.

She took her time with the cork ritual, examining it and rolling it in her fingers before testing the aroma. She lifted her glass to the candlelight, tipped it, and studied its faint traces of color. She raised the glass to her nose, then let a small taste fall on her lips. "This will do nicely," she said.

"Madam is pleased?"

"Madam is very pleased."

"Good," he announced. "Because that's the only bottle in the house."

He filled his own plate, sat down, and made a great show of shaking out his napkin and letting it settle across his lap. He raised his fork and waited for her to begin.

"This is marvelous," she said after her first bite. Then her eyes narrowed. "Did you really do this by yourself?"

"No," he said. "I have an Italian lady who does my cooking. I like her because she doesn't wear any underwear."

"You really did cook this . . ." It was more a question than an admission.

He smiled. "I did have a bit of help. There's an Italian restaurant on the next block that does takeout. But I had to keep it hot without burning it. The chef also recommended the wine, but it was up to me to get the cork out."

"And the flowers?" she asked.

"The florist picked them out." He grinned. "So what do you want to do? Should we talk about imaginary numbers?"

They laughed, but then she grew serious. "What I want to talk about is how grateful I am to you. You rescued me and supported me. You kept me calm when I was terrified and kept me laughing when I probably should have been crying. I don't know how I'm ever going to thank you."

He was ready for the opportunity. "Why don't you stick around a little longer? It will be at least a month before they find out that you're not a student and kick you out of the dorm. It will be a good place to work on your edits and changes. Besides, I've gotten to like seeing you every day."

"No," she answered. "I've imposed enough."

"Does that mean you've seen enough of me?"

"God, no," she said. "I enjoy being with you. Probably I enjoy it too much. But there are issues in my life I have to work out. There are things you don't know about me."

"Well, tell me. Then I'll know and I can make up my own mind. I mean, if you're a serial killer, there's probably not much sense in my waiting around. But if you were just mean to your sister . . ."

"I had a two-year love affair with a man I trusted completely. As it turned out, I shouldn't have trusted him at all."

He leaned across his plate. "That wasn't part of the life story you told me."

"No, it wasn't. I was lying to you the same way I was lying to myself."

"Forget lying," he said. "At the time, it wasn't any of my business. But now I'd like to make it my business. So why don't you start from the beginning? And don't spare any of the salacious details."

Pam told him about her life as John Duke's other woman, the thrill of being involved with an important man, and her expectation that somehow it would all work out. "I was as dumb as my suite mate Brooke, who thinks your friend Condon is going to give up everything to marry her," she said. "I should have known better."

She was much more guarded in explaining her relationship with Glen Hubbard. He had helped and encouraged her, and nearly gotten himself killed for his efforts. He was protective of her. "Maybe a bit too protective," she allowed. "His solution to my problems was to put more locks on the doors. It seemed as if that would have given him too much control over my life."

Peter thought he understood. "But when you leave here, he's the one you're going back to."

"I'm not going back to anyone," Pam said sharply. Instantly, she regretted her vehemence, so she explained, "When you've been lied to, you begin to suspect that everyone is lying to you. It's irrational, I know. But I find myself looking through people and wondering, What do they want?"

"I already told you what I want," he interrupted. "My intentions are totally dishonorable."

She laughed. "That I can deal with. It's the con games that go along with it. Like, why does Condon keep Brooke believing that he's going to leave his wife for her? He must know she's going to get hurt."

"It will be over soon," Peter said, trying to ease her concern. "There's a new graduate assistant in his department. He mentioned that she has great legs."

Pam started to pick up the dishes at the end of the meal, but Peter stopped her. "Leave them," he said. "I have no place to put them until I wash them in the bathtub."

He offered her the chance to stay the night and didn't seem at all surprised that she refused. Instead, he put on a pullover sweater so he could walk her back to her dorm. Pam praised the dinner and thanked him for celebrating with her. She repeated her gratitude for all he had done for her and finished with "I hope you're not angry that I wouldn't stay."

He shrugged. "No, I didn't think you would. But I've learned that you never get anywhere if you don't ask. There's no telling when someone will surprise you."

He delivered her to the security desk on the ground floor of her dorm, where a young woman checked Pam's ID. She held out her hand for Peter's identification. "I'm not going up," he told her. Then she asked Pam to look in on Brooke. "She was a real mess when she came in a few minutes ago. She'd been crying so hard she couldn't even talk. I asked her if I should call the police or medical emergency. She just shook her head."

"Maybe you'd better come up," Pam suggested. Peter flashed his identification and followed her to the elevators.

While they were riding up, she wondered aloud whether Condon had told Brooke about the new assistant with the great legs.

Peter shook his head. "Condon would have gotten someone else to tell her."

There was no answer when she knocked on Brooke's door. Pam tried the knob, found it unlocked, and pushed the door open. The room was empty, but Brooke's hat and poncho were lying on the bed. Maybe the bathroom, Pam suggested, and Peter followed her across the hall and waited at the door while she went in. A second later he heard Pam's scream.

She had pulled back the shower curtain

and stepped into the stall to turn off the water. There at her feet was the body of a young woman, her clothes soaked through. She was lying over the drain, causing the water to flood out beyond the shower sill. The spilling water was stained with red.

Pam went to her knees and lifted the woman's head. "She's cut her wrists. Get the towels out of her room."

Peter ran back to the room and took the towel hanging in the closet. When he returned to the bathroom, Pam was kneeling in the water, with Brooke leaning against her. Her hands were wrapped tightly around the bleeding wrists. He cut the edge of the towel with his pocketknife, then tore it into strips. Together he and Pam tied them over the gaping slashes.

"Is this Brooke?" he asked while he worked.

"Yes, it's Brooke. I should have warned her what she was getting into."

Peter was back on his feet. "I'm going to call down to security and get an ambulance!" He rushed out.

Brooke's eyes opened slowly and panned up to Pam's face. She looked bewildered. "You're going to be okay," Pam said, trying to sound certain when she had no idea whether the girl could draw her next breath.

Brooke seemed like a child when she let her eyes close again.

The next few minutes passed in a blur. Other students came in, gasped at the sight, then helped Pam carry Brooke's colorless body out of the shower and into her bedroom. Peter blasted in to announce that the ambulance was on its way. Brooke kept passing in and out of consciousness. Sirens howled outside, and then medics rushed into the room. Seconds later there were policemen everywhere. Brooke was on a gurney rolling to the elevator. Then she was loaded into an ambulance. Pam, who had held her hand from the moment the medics arrived, was pushed in next to her. They were roaring through the nighttime streets, Brooke regaining color as the plasma flowed into her veins.

When they reached the hospital, doctors and nurses were waiting. Pam followed them into a pale green corridor, where photographers pressed close and flashes went off in her face. Brooke and her medical entourage disappeared behind a curtain, and Pam stood by herself, listening to a babble of medical code words that she didn't understand. She turned and walked wearily into the waiting area. For the first time she realized that there were bloodstains all over her shirt and slacks.

Reporters rushed to her, thrusting small recorders into her face. Who was the victim? What had happened to her? Was she attacked? What was Pam's relationship to the victim? A police officer intervened, freeing her from the reporters. But then a detective had questions for her, a repeat of what the press had been asking. The police went into more detail, and they seemed to ask everything twice.

Peter arrived. He had taken a bus to the hospital to offer Pam whatever help he could. When someone spotted the blood on his shirt, he was lionized by the reporters and the policemen.

In the midst of the commotion, a doctor came out to tell Pam that her friend was going to make it. "She's lucky you got there when you did," he said. "The cuts were deep. It wouldn't have taken long for her to bleed to death."

Then Pam and Peter were in a taxi. She was cradled in his arms, but her eyes were wide open, staring out at the dark faces of the buildings. She got out without asking where they were and let herself be led back into his apartment. Their dinner dishes were still on the table.

He settled her on the sofa, where she

found herself staring into the bouquet she had bought only a few hours earlier. Jesus, she thought, so much had happened since then. Peter came to her with a small glass of liquor, which she took without protest and sipped immediately. She was jolted by the burst of flames in her throat. She doubled over in a coughing fit.

"What was that?" she asked when he had finished slapping her on the back.

"Tequila," he said. "It's all I have. We drank all the wine."

"You thought that would make me feel better?"

"No. I hoped it might jolt you out of the doldrums. I was afraid you were going to die of melancholy."

"Are you trying to get me drunk?"

"That too!" he said proudly.

She glanced around. "You don't mind if I stay here, just for the night?"

"Stay as long as you want. I'll get something less primitive than tequila."

She stood. "Can I take a shower?"

"Sure!"

"And maybe you could go to my dorm in the morning and get me something to wear?"

"No problem. I'll enjoy going through your underwear."

Pam smiled, leaned to him, and kissed his forehead. "Will I be safe staying here tonight?"

"Probably. Unless you tackle me while I'm squeezing past you to get to the bathroom."

"Thanks for everything," she said, taking her leave and closing the bedroom door behind her. Seconds later Peter heard his shower turn on. He slipped out of his shirt and trousers, stretched out on the sofa, and settled into sleep. As he heard the water running, he tried to picture Pam in his shower. But he had to block out that image if he had any hope of getting to sleep.

It was only an hour later when he awoke to the touch of her hand on his cheek. She was wrapped in the blanket from his bed, her hair still wet from the shower.

"I can't sleep," she said, hovering over him with her silky breath touching his face.

Peter held out his arms, welcoming her into his embrace. She threw the blanket over both of them and snuggled onto the sofa, pressing in close to him.

"If you fall asleep," he warned her, "I'm going to kill myself."

Her face was already under his chin. Her breathing was relaxed. She sighed as he stroked her back. But within seconds she was deep in sleep.

THIRTY-TWO

Pam awoke on the sofa, wrapped snugly in the blanket from Peter's bed. She stretched, letting the blanket slip to the floor and was shocked to find that she was naked. At the same moment she heard a key rattling in the door, then the door opening. She sat up abruptly, tucking the blanket under her chin.

Peter turned into the room, his arms laden with packages. "I got you a cranberry muffin that you're going to love," he announced. "And I have your clothes, which you may like or hate, depending on what kind of mood you're in. Finally, I have the morning tabloid, which I think will make you mad."

He was in the room but was ignoring her compromised figure as he went to the dining room and dropped his parcels on the table. He tossed her the package of clothes he had pirated out of her dresser drawers. "I hope you like these, because I'm not going back. There are policemen all over the dorm."

"How did I get here?" she demanded, nodding toward the sofa.

"Your excuse was that you couldn't sleep. Actually, I think you were trying to seduce me. But I was a gentleman to the end."

Pam stood, wrapping the blanket securely around her. Then she took her clothes and headed for the bedroom. Peter watched her leave, turned back to his packages, and laid out the muffins and paper cups of coffee.

She came back seconds later. "I like what you picked," she said, modeling the jeans and sweater. "You have excellent taste."

"Wait until you taste the muffin." He held her chair while she sat at the table.

Her eye caught the morning tabloid that he had set beside her plate. She glanced casually, and then her eyes widened in a second look. "Oh, my God!"

"I know," he teased. "It's not your best side."

The front-page photo showed the gurney being rushed into the hospital emergency room. Two medics bent over the victim, and Pam was leaning over the medics. Hers was the most visible face in the picture. She went to the caption and found she was identified by name, along with the comment

348

that she was the roommate of the woman who had slashed her wrists.

"Everyone who knows me will recognize this," she said softly.

He nodded. "When you're living undercover, it's never a good idea to get your picture in the paper. Particularly on the front page."

"I'll have to get out of here," she concluded.

He agreed. "At least out of the dorm. And you'll have to stay off the streets." Then he added, as if the idea had just come to him, "I suppose you'd better move in with me."

"I couldn't do that," she answered quickly.

"I suppose not. The mattress *is* a little lumpy. On the other hand, you can get from here to Carl Weiss's office without going near the campus or past the dormitory. If people who see your picture stake out the university, they won't find you."

"Peter," she started.

"Pete," he corrected once more.

"Pete, I don't want you to be the next person to get burned. Or killed."

"That's my point. They can't find me unless they find you. It's in my best interest that you stay here."

She knew he was right. Where else could she go? Not back to her apartment, which would probably be staked out again, and not in with Glen Hubbard, who was already a highly visible partner in her attempt to publish her book. Nor could she rent a place without providing background and references that would give away a new address even before she moved in. She didn't like the way Peter had brushed off the danger, pretending it was in his interest that she stay there. The best thing she could do for his safety was clear out before anyone could put them together. But clear out to where?

When they'd finished breakfast, Peter left to teach his morning class. Pam carried the dishes to the bathtub and tried to envision how her new relationship might play out. It would be too dangerous to go back to the dorm to get her things. If anyone had made the connection, the dorm would be the first place they would watch. Peter couldn't go there either. When he claimed her things, he would identify himself as her ally, and that would lead them to his apartment. The clothes didn't matter. She could take a bus downtown and buy whatever she needed. But her laptop was there with the text of the entire book on its disk memory. There were also the disks hidden in the lining of her raincoat. She had to get those back!

Or do I? Pam asked herself when she was

putting the clean plates back on the dining room shelf. All the computer held was the book that would soon appear. What difference would it make if the government people got an advance look? They still wouldn't know if it was going to be published or by whom. All her transmissions had been made by e-mail to a company in China. She had used a library computer as her mailbox. In the same way, she had no real need for the copies of her notes. Her enemies would gather that she was working from hard information, but nothing in the notes would lead them to Carl Weiss. Besides, if she ever needed the notes for the record, she had another copy locked in her safe-deposit box.

The more she thought about it, the more sense it made that she should move in with Peter. But she would have to make it clear that she wasn't *moving in with him* in the usual sense. It would still be his home; they weren't sharing it. And it would be his bed. They wouldn't be sharing that either. She would be a guest for only as long as was absolutely necessary.

When Peter returned from his class, Pam went into her speech. He was right. This was the best place for her to stay. But she looked at it as a business arrangement. She would repay all the costs involved as soon as she could safely write a check. She warned that they had to be careful not to let her need for safety lead their relationship. Whatever they were going to be to each other would have to wait until they weren't forced to be under the same roof. She made her distinction between *moving in together* and her acceptance of his hospitality very clear. She didn't stop until she found that she was repeating herself.

Peter followed her entire speech with interest, nodding in agreement and interjecting an occasional "absolutely" or "of course" for emphasis. He allowed a long moment of silence when she finally ran down, just in case she thought of something more to say. Then he announced solemnly, "Never in the history of personal relationships, probably going back to when man first stood upright, has any woman taken so many words to tell a man that he wasn't going to get laid."

She stared at him. Then her face split with laughter. She laughed at herself until she cried.

"I think I know why the guy you were living with dumped you," Peter added. "He was probably bored to death. Couldn't you just say 'I have a headache'?"

She continued laughing. When she stopped, she looked at his deadpan face and started in again. Finally she was able to say, "I just wanted everything to be clear."

"Oh, it's perfectly clear! The only thing you and I are going to discuss is imaginary numbers." He shuffled to his feet. "I'll go back to the dorm and get the rest of your things." He was startled by the vehemence of her "No!" Pam took him through her reasoning, and he agreed. She explained that she would buy new clothes. "But you're going to need clothes that fit the neighborhood," he said. "So I better be going with you."

They took a bus down to Columbus Circle, then past Central Park to Fifth Avenue. A few streets farther south she found a women's outfitter famous for knockoff prices. Peter followed her around the racks in complete amazement and admitted he hadn't been in a women's store since he bought his mother a birthday present.

He waited outside the dressing room, and Pam came out to model each outfit. He laughed at some and shook his head at others.

In the lingerie department he was enthusiastically helpful, tending toward the thongs and the see-through bras. His favorite color, Pam decided, was bright red. She took her selections as well as his into the dressing room and carried her choices out to the counter in a shopping bag. "So what did you get?" he asked, reaching for his wallet.

"You'll find out soon enough."

He grinned broadly. "I will?"

"Sure. It's all going to end up on the clothesline over your bathtub."

When they returned to the apartment, Peter had to leave for a department meeting and an afternoon class. He gave her the address of the Italian restaurant where he had gotten the takeout, and two ten-dollar bills. "I expect change," were his parting words. Pam walked to the old building where Carl Weiss had his offices. Weiss's daughter gave her the computer files that held her first round of typeset pages. "I see you made the front page of the *News*," Ronda said. "It was a good photo. Looked just like you."

Pam winced. "I was hoping it wasn't recognizable." Then she explained that, as a result of the unwanted publicity, her computer was "unavailable." Ronda lent her one of the company's. "It's a little slow," she apologized.

But it was more than adequate, and Pam was thrilled when she saw the typeset pages of her book. Her words had become reality, and her thoughts took on a new importance. She began scrolling through the text, answering the copy editor's queries and making corrections as needed. She was in the homestretch.

She took a break from her work to get their dinner at the restaurant, accepting the owner's recommendation of the lobster ravioli. For this meal he recommended an Ovieto that seemed even paler than his previous recommendation.

Pam had been in Peter's apartment for only a day, but they were already settling into a routine. Each morning she could return the pages she had reviewed to Carl Weiss and pick up the new ones that had come in. Peter would go out in the morning for their breakfast, and she would be responsible for picking up the dinner. Probably she would bring in fast food every now and then, just as a change from the rich Italian dishes. Her best guess was that she would be finished with her edits in no more than ten days.

She was working with the laptop on the table when she became aware of footsteps on the stairs. They were slow in coming up, each footfall placed carefully so as not to make a sound, but the squeak of the old steps was unmistakable. Peter usually bounded up the stairs, his footsteps exploding. This was someone else. Someone who was unexpected.

THIRTY-THREE

Pam stood and eased quietly to the door, leaning close so she could hear better. The footsteps had reached the top of the stairs and hesitated. Then she heard them again, moving in the hall toward her. When they stopped, she could hear the heavy breathing on the other side of the door.

There was a knock. She had no intention of answering. At best, it was a student or faculty associate who had business with Peter. She wouldn't want to introduce herself as his roommate. At worst, it was someone looking for her. She didn't want to be found.

Another knock, this time heavier and more demanding. She stood perfectly still, holding her breath. She knew that any movement could be heard through the door.

"Pam. It's me, Glen. Let me in. I have to see you."

Glen? She recognized his voice, and it

took her only a second to understand how he had found her. The picture in the paper, and the link to Columbia University. Glen would easily link Columbia with Peter. She unhooked the chain and opened the door. Glen was still breathing hard from climbing the stairs.

"Are you all right?" he asked as soon as she had shut the door.

"Yes, of course, except I'm frightened out of my wits. You keep showing up where I don't expect you."

He leaned toward her and kissed her on the lips. "I was frightened for you. I'm glad I got here in time."

"In time for what?" she asked.

"Pam, it took me one day to find you after I saw your picture in the paper. I was afraid they would be faster than I was. You have to get out of here."

She weighed his words and then decided. "Glen, I think I'm safer here than I would be anyplace else. You found me because you know about Peter Salerno. They don't know Peter. They'll go through Columbia's files trying to find out where I live, and all they'll come up with is that I'm not connected to the school."

She sat on the sofa that Peter used as a bed, and Glen sat close to her. Once again he reminded her that she was dealing with professionals. Her best course was to give up on the book.

"It's too late for that," she said. She went to the table and brought back the first of her typeset pages. "It's not just an idea anymore. It's real, only a few weeks short of going to press."

He looked at the pages. "Where were these set?" he demanded.

"Someplace in China."

"China?"

"I don't know where. All I have is a Web address. The book is too far along for anyone to stop it."

"Anyone but you," he countered.

"I won't stop it," she answered simply. "I have too much of myself and of you invested in it."

He stood wearily, showing the despair of his defeat, and glanced around the small apartment. Then he walked to the bedroom door and glanced in. Her nightgown was folded at the bottom of the bed.

"I sleep there," she said, "and Peter sleeps out here on the sofa. There's nothing between us, if that's what you're thinking."

"No, I was thinking of what a dismal place you're living in. I want so much more for you."

"This is just for a short time," she told him.

"Then you're determined to stay here?" he asked.

She nodded.

Glen went to his trouser pocket and pulled out a wad of bills. "You're going to need some cash. I brought you a thousand dollars so you won't have to use credit cards or write checks." He held out the money, and she took it.

"I don't know what to say, Glen. You're always there for me."

He bent and kissed her, this time on the cheek. "I can only hope this place is as safe as you think it is."

Pam didn't tell Peter about Glen's visit. She didn't want him to know how easily she had been found. She lied about the money, claiming she had risked cashing a check in a branch of her own bank. "I went downtown, so even if they trace it, they'll be looking in the wrong neighborhood."

"You didn't have to do that," he said. "I could have carried you a little longer." He took the money she owed him. "From now on I'll be able to bring home the better bottle."

Each day she went back and forth to Carl

Weiss, getting the most recent typeset and copyedited pages. Peter kept Marion's files and brought the records Pam needed when he came home each night. It was four days after Glen's visit when he came home early and unannounced. "We've got to talk."

"They've found me," Pam guessed.

"Maybe not you, but they've found your book. Carl Weiss's daughter has been kidnapped."

THIRTY-FOUR

Pam sat mute for a few seconds, trying to come to grips with the news. She had been basking in the heady freedom of seeing her work finally completed. Now she was shocked to find that the freedom was only an illusion. All the power brokers were still out there, with their tentacles reaching into every corner of her world. They could find her anywhere and do whatever was necessary to bend her to their will.

She and Peter rushed from the apartment to Carl Weiss's office. The old man was alone, sitting calmly at his desk, staring at his telephone and waiting. It had been Ronda who called. "She said she was being held in an apartment by two men and a woman. She didn't know where. They were interested in your book and wanted to talk to you about it. They'll get back to me, she said."

"Whatever they ask," Pam promised. "I'll

do anything to get her home safe." She reached across the desk and took his hand. "I'm so sorry I involved you in this."

He patted her hand. "You told me it was dangerous. You came right out and said so. I wanted to publish your book, probably because you said that the government didn't want it published. I figured, What can they do to me? My business is just making arrangements. I don't own anything worth stealing." He shook his head slowly. "Who could believe that the people who run our country could do something like this?" He asked, "Who are they? Who are the people who really run the country?"

"Not the ones we think," she said. But then she reassured him. "But whoever they are, I'll give them anything they ask. We'll get Ronda back."

She and Peter sat with the old man, exchanging an occasional word or glance. Peter offered to bring in lunch, but no one was hungry. He got coffee for Pam and himself, and tea for Carl.

The waiting became unbearable. Twice the old man picked up his phone just to assure himself that it was still connected. Peter paced until his constant movement became irritating to Pam. Then he sat quietly, perusing the books on obscure academic subjects that were Weiss's specialty. They all jumped at the sound of a knock at the front door.

Peter was there first and opened the door to a short man in shirtsleeves who held a large mailing envelope. The man looked at Peter, then leaned to look over his shoulder into the office. "Where's Ronda?" he asked.

"She stepped out."

He was still trying to see who else was in the office. "Who are you?"

"A friend of Mr. Weiss."

"Is Carl here?"

Carl's voice boomed in the background. "It's all right, Harry." Peter stepped aside.

"This came to my office by mistake," the man said, handing over the envelope.

"Do you know who delivered it?" Peter asked anxiously.

Harry spared Peter a glance, but he directed his answer to Carl. "I don't know. A messenger, I guess. It was shoved under the door. But it's for you. Look, your name and office number."

They stayed calm until Harry had left. Then they tore into the envelope. There was a single printed page together with a fine silver chain. Pam recognized the chain as the one Ronda had worn at their meetings.

The note was straightforward. Weiss was to assemble everything related to the book

Fouling the Air — the original manuscripts, the typeset pages, all related business records. The author was to gather all notes, files, and records, electronic and printed documents. Everything should be packed into a suitcase with wheels and an extended handle. The author would deliver the suitcase at a time and place to be specified. Simultaneously, Mr. Weiss's property would be returned to him.

"It's all the things they tried to take in the beginning," Pam said.

Carl studied the page. "And everything that's happened since." He looked at her. "Are these people idiots? Do they think they can stop a book just by stealing a lot of papers? There's already how many; three, four, a dozen people who have read your book? What are they going to do? Erase our minds?"

"They don't care about a dozen people," she said. "They can ignore a dozen people. But a book can start a firestorm. Once a book creates an issue, then they have to deal with it."

"Carl has a point," Peter interjected. "They can take every record you have, but you could find another safe house and start over again. How can they be sure that you didn't keep just one copy? One hard copy, one CD, or a couple of floppies, and all they'd accomplish would be to delay publication by a few weeks."

"What's your point?" Pam asked.

"My point is that they don't want your papers. They want you."

"They had me lots of times. They didn't harm me. It was the files and notes they tried to destroy."

Peter wasn't buying her argument. "Then they were trying to scare you off," he said. "Now they know they can't."

"We have to do whatever they ask to get Ronda back," Pam reminded him.

"Give them what they ask," Peter argued, "but don't you deliver it. It's too dangerous."

"But, Peter, they must be watching this place. They must know I'm here. If it was me they wanted, that package wouldn't have held a letter. It would have been a bomb."

Carl broke in. "They want everything. What good is it for them to get all the pages if they don't get you? And what good are you to them if they don't get the pages?"

Pam had no answer. She had come to believe that she had already won her battle with the business leaders, the elected officials, the unions, and all the other special interests. They had dropped out of sight.

But that might have been because she had convinced them her book was a dead issue. Now something had alerted them that it was nearing publication. Maybe the picture in the paper identifying her as a student had persuaded them that she was still hard at work. Maybe they had picked up a careless comment by Ronda, or Carl, or even Peter. Or perhaps they had kept her under surveillance all the time. But right now, none of that mattered. The only issue was winning Ronda's freedom.

Carl began to search his offices for any copies of the typeset pages, and for contracts and correspondence that mentioned the book. Peter walked Pam home to his apartment, looking back repeatedly for anyone who might be following. They were amazed that there was no one. "They had to be watching Weiss's office," she insisted. Peter surmised that her enemies had no need to follow her. They already knew where she was going.

Pam went upstairs to scan her CDs and locate all her records. Peter found a store that sold the kind of suitcase they needed, then went to his office and packed Marion's copied institute files. It was nearly nine o'clock when they arrived back in Carl's office and packed Carl's material in the suitcase along with their own.

"Is that everything?" Carl asked.

Pam remembered the copies she had left in the bank vault. "Everything!" she said in a loud, clear voice. Weiss's offices might now be bugged and she wasn't going to say anything compromising. Particularly, she wasn't going to mention the copy she had made of the complete typeset book.

"There's one provision," Peter announced. "No matter what they ask for, Pam isn't going to meet with them."

"They said I was to bring everything," she reminded him.

"A messenger will make the delivery."

"What messenger?"

"Me," Peter said, "and while I'm trading the suitcase for Ronda, you're going back into hiding."

"No!" Pam answered without a moment's thought. "If it's not me, they might walk away and take Ronda with them. We have to do whatever they tell us."

Carl shook his head. "No, we can't let you go. It's too dangerous."

Pam reminded him that it was his daughter who was in danger. She told Peter that she couldn't let him do it. She had already involved him too much.

Carl said Ronda wasn't in danger. "They

gain nothing by hurting her. You're the one they have to silence." Then he came to his conclusion. "It's my daughter. I'm the one who should go to her."

They were in the midst of their argument when the telephone rang. Carl looked at the receiver for a second before he lifted the handset.

"Daddy?" It was Ronda's voice.

"Ronda, are you all right?"

"I'm fine! I have a message for you. You better write it down."

"Of course, of course." He took a wooden editing pencil from a jar on his desk. "Go ahead."

"Pam should bring the suitcase to the Staten Island Ferry Terminal at the Battery. She should catch the eleven-twenty boat to Staten Island. There will be a red panel truck parked on the car deck with the name 'Leighton' printed on the side. She should open the tailgate door and put the suitcase inside. Then she should go to the upper deck. If everything is in the case, she'll find me inside the terminal when the boat docks."

"Fine, fine," Carl agreed. "Except it won't be Miss Leighton. I'll be bringing the suit-case."

Pam snatched the phone out of his hand.

"Ronda, I'll be there, just the way they specified. Whatever you told your father, that's exactly what I'll do."

"There's one more thing, Pam," the girl said. "You have to come alone. If there's anyone with you, the back door of the truck will be locked."

As soon as she hung up, Peter told her, "I'm not going to let you do this."

She came back at him in a cold, determined tone. "I don't need your permission. It's my decision, and I'm doing exactly what they told me."

The men looked to each other. Carl shrugged.

THIRTY-FIVE

Peter went back to his office, searched his desk for his safety razor, and used the soap from the dispenser in the men's room. Painfully, he shaved his beard, drastically altering the face that Pam knew. He used desktop scissors to cut the loose ends of his long hair until there was nothing hanging down over his collar. He stuck his head in and out of colleagues' offices until he spotted a foulweather outfit — a long, dark raincoat, a broad-brimmed, waterproof hat, and an umbrella — hanging from a coat tree. He searched the colleague's desk and added a pair of drugstore reading glasses to his disguise.

He looked ridiculous in the bathroom mirror. The hat was too big, and he had to move the glasses down to the end of his nose so that he could see over them. He recognized the long, narrow chin that had been the reason he had grown a beard. He felt stupid, but that wasn't at all important. What he liked was that he could hardly recognize himself. Pam would probably know him if they got close and she took a good look. But anyone who had been stalking them would never know who he was. As a final touch, he took the leather briefcase that he had received as a present when he graduated from high school. Now he could be any one of the thousand back-room drudges who walked from Wall Street to the ferry terminal each night.

Peter took the subway to the Battery at the tip of Manhattan. It was ten-thirty when he approached the ferry terminal, much too early for the eleven-twenty boat. He took a detour, circling back into the Financial District. He didn't want to be the only one waiting in the terminal in case Pam got there early. He needed a crowd to blend into while he tried to spot her.

He refreshed his memory on the instructions. When Pam got to the ferry, she would go to the lower deck and watch the cars that came aboard. A red panel truck with her name on it would be easy to spot. She would wait for the truck to stop and then watch to see if anyone got out. Then she would walk along the deck like a driver going back to his car. As she passed the panel truck, she would open the back door and lift in the suitcase.

That was the moment when it would be easiest to take her. As she reached in with the suitcase, a pair of hands could grab her arms and pull her in with it. They could have their people in the car parked behind the truck. Someone might get out to block the view of bystanders and motorists in the surrounding cars.

But there would be many opportunities. Pam would be walking out in the open, dragging a rolling case that would clearly identify her. Someone could brush against her and finish her with the thrust of a knife. A passerby could bring her down with a silenced pistol fired out of coat pocket. What better place to dispose of a body than in the middle of New York Harbor?

Peter's job was to keep her in sight. He couldn't let himself be distracted for even an instant. In addition to what anyone else might do, Pam was just stubborn enough to have concocted a plan of her own. If she made any move to renege on the transfer, he had to be ready to act.

He circled back to the terminal, where cars were lined up and a steady tide of passengers was flooding into the waiting room. Peter blended in well. Fall coats and briefcases seemed to be the commuter costume. There were dozens of men just like him.

He went to the window and bought a round-trip ticket. As he turned away, he spotted Pam. She had come through the terminal door and was walking toward the ticket window he had just left. She was easy to spot in the student garb they had bought to make her less conspicuous around campus. Most of the women coming in from the Financial District were dressed in business suits.

Peter slipped over to the newsstand and bought the evening paper. Then he found a bench seat and peered around the newspaper at Pam.

Pam had left Peter's apartment less than an hour earlier and taken a taxi down to the ferry slips. During the trip her confidence had steadily drained. Bravado had come easily when she was surrounded by friends who were anxious to protect her. Now she was by herself, headed for a meeting with the people who had set fire to her publisher's office and bludgeoned Marion Murray to death.

She had been confident that all they wanted was the book and that the suitcase was all they would take. Probably what they wanted from Marion had been just the copied files, but Marion must have put up a struggle. Pam had no intention of offering any resistance. But Carl and Peter had raised strong arguments. Why would they take just the copies, only to have her start all over again? The only certain way to kill the book was to destroy the manuscript and the writer.

When she entered the terminal, Pam looked around carefully. Not that she had any idea who she was looking for. She caught a young, athletic-looking man eyeing her as she passed. She had learned long ago to ignore, then to enjoy, men who found her worth a lingering glance, but now every look was menacing. Another man darted away from the ticket counter hiding behind a newspaper. Was that a suspicious person, or just an exhausted commuter looking for peace in the little privacy that a paper offered? Then, when the clerk closed the ticket window in front of her, directing her to another window, she was certain that they were all part of the scheme. She was being routed right into their arms.

With her ticket in hand, she joined the crowd pressed against the door and watched the ferry make an uneventful landing. There were few passengers and even fewer cars coming off the boat. At this hour all the traffic was headed out of Manhattan.

The door opened, and she jostled in the line. As soon as she was aboard, she found the stairs and moved to the lower deck, where trucks and cars were being guided aboard. She stood at the foot of the steps and watched carefully.

The red panel truck was easy to spot. At first she couldn't make out the name on the side, but as the truck moved forward in the center lane, she could make out her own name in scripted letters. Her heart was beginning to pound.

More cars and trucks came aboard and pulled up close to the vehicles ahead. For an instant Pam was concerned a car might pull so close to the panel truck that she wouldn't be able to open the rear door. But the car that came behind the truck left nearly three feet of space. A lucky break, she thought.

The crew pulled the gate across the car deck. Overhead, the passenger gangways lifted away. The diesel engines groaned, and a rush of water sounded behind the boat. The ferry moved quickly out of the slip.

Pam watched the truck. No one got out of it. She glanced around the deck. Several of the drivers had gotten out of their cars and were gathered at the edge of the deck for a better look at the New York skyline. There were enough people moving about that she wouldn't be conspicuous.

She stepped out on the deck and wove her way among the autos to the truck. She turned the rear door handle, and the door opened easily. Inside, there was nothing but the truck bed. Looking forward, she could see only a dark wall. The driver's section was curtained off. She lifted the bag, eased it over the bumper, and slid it inside. Then she closed the door and walked away.

Pam stole a few glances backward to see if anyone approached the truck, or if there was sudden action inside. But no one seemed interested. No lights appeared in the truck windows. She started up the steel stairway that would bring her to the passenger deck, where she couldn't see the truck. She knew she was being watched, but no one seemed to be following her. There was a man coming down the steps, and she moved aside to let him pass. The instant he was by her, she took her next step up. Then she felt a hand close across her mouth.

Before she knew it, she was being lifted onto the outside handrail. Then her mouth was free, but hands gripped her ankles. She got a glimpse of the furious water rushing past the side of the boat. It took an instant for her to realize that she was in free fall.

Pam tried to scream, but she hit the water too quickly. She landed in a belly flop that felt like landing on pavement. Then the wash from the ferry caught her, carried her like a wave, and crashed down on top of her. She was in black darkness, the pounding of the propellers exploding in her ears. The fall had driven the air out of her lungs like a punch in the gut. She knew she was sinking fast.

Her first struggle was to get her arms moving, clawing at the water as she tried to right herself. Then her legs had to kick, propelling her upward. But high over her head, the ferry's wake was pouring downward. All her fight wasn't enough.

Then the boat was past her, and the downward pressure gave way to a wild churning. She was caught in a powerful riptide driving her away from the boat, tumbling over and over again helplessly. She knew that the rapids would move away with the ferry and that in the calm it would be easy for her to reach the surface. But she was desperate for air, and her limbs were quickly exhausted. Wet clothes weighed her down.

Peter, who had been moving cautiously to

get behind Pam without being seen, had watched her deliver the suitcase and start for the stairs. He had given her plenty of room. She was already on the stairs before he started toward them. He would let her reach the top before he took the first step. He hadn't seen the man coming down until he was abreast of Pam. Then the man had moved so quickly that Peter had no idea what was happening. Had she lost her footing? Was he catching her to keep her from falling? Was he mugging her? Or was this the assassin that Peter and Carl had dreaded?

Then she went over the rail and hit the water close to where Peter was lurking. He was dumbstruck. He looked up the stairs, but the man was gone. Then his head snapped around to the water that was roaring past. There was no sign of Pam.

The next instant, Peter was in full motion. He screamed, "Man overboard," the cry for help that he had read in books and seen in movies. He took a few quick steps to the stern gate, where two crew members were enjoying their rest between landings. "A woman just fell overboard," he screamed into their faces. They lost a moment looking at him as if he was crazy, then looking at each other. "Where?" one of them managed to ask.

"Into the water!" Peter screamed. "Stop the boat."

One of the crewmen raced to the life ring that hung at the stern. He worked it out of its mounting and hurled it into the boat's wake. As soon as it hit the water, a white lamp turned on. The point of light began rushing away behind them.

Peter tore off his hat and raincoat. "Get them to stop the boat," he repeated. He stepped to the edge.

A crewman caught his collar. "Don't be crazy," he screamed into Peter's ear.

Peter tore out of his grasp and jumped into the churning wake.

"Stop the boat!" someone screamed. "Stop the boat!"

Pam felt herself being lifted up. The violent churning had stopped. Now all the water the boat had pushed down came rising up behind it. She blasted out of the water and into the reflected light from the downtown skyscrapers. She got a quick breath before she sank again, but in an instant she bobbed back to the top. Then she was afloat, treading water, her face barely clear of the lapping waves.

The poncho that was part of her student disguise was getting heavier by the second. Pam slid it over her head and left it floating beside her. She felt as if she had cut free from an anchor. Now she could keep her face and shoulders above the surface with much less effort. She tried to calm herself and slow down her rapid breathing. Then she began to think.

It was easy to get her bearings. She could see the Statue of Liberty in the distance, which indicated the New Jersey shore. The lighted towers of Manhattan were right in front of her, and the lower lights of Brooklyn were to her right. She turned in the water and found the ferry moving away at top speed. There were no signs of an emergency response onboard, nor any indication that the ferry was turning back. Probably no one had seen her go over.

Manhattan was the closest shoreline. The ferry hadn't traveled very far. She was even able to identify the light of the terminal. But it was still a long way. She would exhaust herself before she was halfway there.

How long could she tread water? What were the chances of someone finding her? Close to zero at night. Unless someone on the ferry had seen her fall. Then they might organize a search. They would know where to look: on a straight line from the boat to the slip they had just left. But how far might she drift off course before anyone could get to her? Pam didn't think she could last until morning. The water was warm enough at the end of summer, but she probably couldn't survive in it for the six hours until sunlight. She was tiring already.

She turned back to the ferry. Even if her scream had been cut off, someone might have heard it. But the boat was still moving away, rushing to make an on-time landing in Staten Island.

She had no choice. Somehow she had to keep herself afloat.

Aboard the ferry, one of the crewmen darted through the hatch into the engine room, where there was a phone to the bridge. He got the captain in the wheelhouse and breathlessly told him about the man who had just jumped overboard.

"Who reported it?" the captain demanded.

"I saw him. He ran to the stern and told us a woman had fallen in. Then he jumped over after her."

The captain didn't hesitate. He ordered the engine to dead-stop.

The boat became eerily quiet, the sound of the rushing water the only noise.

"Fuck!" the captain cursed. He grabbed the whistle cord and began blasting out the repetitive bursts of the emergency signal. Then he ordered the forward engine started. The ferry was still charging ahead, but once he got power to the propellers on the front of the boat, he could stop it in a hurry.

THIRTY-SIX

Pam heard the ferry's whistle, and the repeated blasts told her that the boat's crew knew it had an emergency. But she couldn't make out the reaction. The ferry was just a cluster of lights still moving away from her. She knew the boat would come back, and she guessed the captain was already on his radio calling for a search and rescue effort. She would be all right if she could just manage to stay afloat.

She also saw that she was getting closer to the shore. The current was bringing her back toward the ferry terminal. That gave her even more hope. Even if the searchers couldn't find her, she might get close enough to swim for it.

"Pam!"

She gasped at the sound of her name coming from the darkness. It couldn't be. She raised up in the water and looked in the direction of the voice. Her name sounded again, stretched out into a long, frantic call. Then she saw a light, a white flash blinking as it bobbed up on a wave and fell down into a trough. Again she heard her name.

"Over here!" she called toward the light. "Over here." She caught a glimpse of something floating in the lighted halo. She started swimming toward it.

"Pam?" This time her name sounded more like a question. "Is it really you?" And she recognized Peter's voice. But that was impossible. It had to be her imagination.

"Pam. Jesus, it's you!"

She flailed at the water, trying to swim faster toward the light and the voice. But she was getting nowhere and losing the bit of strength she had left. Then his arm was around her, pulling her close. "Hang on," Peter told her and pulled her arms across the life ring.

She stared at him. In the suddenly bright light she could see that it wasn't him.

"Hang on!" he repeated. "We're being pushed to the shore. In a few minutes you'll be able to walk away."

She wasn't looking at the city lights that were drawing closer. Her eyes were locked on the face only inches from her own, brightly illuminated in the glow of the rescue light. It *was* him. Without the beard and the mustache, without the long hair. But how?

He sensed her questions and saw the bewilderment in her eyes. "I was following you," he said. "I saw what happened. I didn't think I'd ever find you."

Still, she couldn't speak. The pieces didn't yet fit together. He had come looking for her, which meant that he must have jumped in after her. He had grabbed the life ring and leaped into the water.

They were startled by the blare of the ferry whistle. The boat was closer, moving slowly back toward the slip. There were floodlights shining down from the upper decks. But it wouldn't get close enough. It was headed on a straight line to the pier it had left just minutes ago. In that short time, Pam and Peter had drifted well to the west.

"They'll see the light," Peter said hopefully.

"No!" Pam said, her first word since she had reached the life ring.

"Maybe if we hold it over our heads for a few seconds," he went on. "We could wave it back and forth —"

"No! Kill the light. Turn it off!" Pam dragged herself on top of the ring so that her body blocked the light.

"But . . ." Peter had no idea what was the

matter with her. Why was she dimming a chance at being rescued?

"They're on the boat," she said. "The people who threw me over."

Now he understood what she was saying.

"They think I'm dead. I should stay dead."

Peter searched the life ring and found the battery pack that provided its power. He felt the wires that ran to the base of the lamp. He hooked his fingers around the wires and tugged until one of them pulled out of its connection. The light went out.

Pam looked up at the shoreline. "How much longer, do you think?"

"I don't know. We're moving pretty fast. It must be the tide flooding into the harbor."

"I'm freezing," she said.

"We could swim this thing toward shore. It would get us there faster."

Pam slipped her body from atop the ring into the water. It was warmer than out in the night air, and the effort of kicking and paddling with one arm seemed to bring her a new bit of energy. They were already past the ferry terminal, and no more than fifty yards from a row of rotted pilings. They could hear auto traffic.

Then there was a new sound. A helicopter flew near, low over the water, with a searchlight illuminating a large area below. It was moving slowly, its rotors pounding, kicking up a fine spray.

"They won't find us," Pam said.

"Not if you don't want them to."

"I want to be dead," she said.

They pushed between the pilings and in toward the splintered, sloping base of an old pier. It would be only a few seconds before they were able to drag themselves onto dry land.

"Where do you want to be buried?" he asked.

She didn't understand. "What?"

"You're dead. Where am I taking you so that no one will find you?"

Her only thought had been surviving the water. Now she needed a plan. Where could she go?

She clutched an oily cross brace between pilings and pulled herself up to the rotted pier. Then she sprawled across the surface and got to her knees. He came up behind her. They were a hundred feet or so from a street where cars were whizzing past. Farther away, they could see the entrances to the ferry terminal.

"If we walk close to the road, we can get one of those taxis," he said. He was pointing toward the cabs that were dropping their fares at the terminal.

Pam nodded. She labored to her feet and began to walk behind him across a field of packed earth and broken concrete. Lighted buildings surrounded them, and they were momentarily caught in the glare of head-lights, yet the sunken pier and razed ground could have been the ruins of a long-destroyed city. The parked taxis now seemed to be impossibly far away.

Where could she go? Peter's apartment was too dangerous for both of them. It would probably continue to be watched until her attackers on the ferry confirmed that she was gone. Jean Abbott's apartment might be bugged. That left her just one safe haven, but it was a place she didn't want even to consider. She had taken torturous turns to avoid involving Glen Hubbard more deeply in her problems. But now she had no choice.

Peter flagged a taxi that slowed but then passed him by when the driver got a look at his potential passenger. Soaked through, and stained with tar and oil, he looked like one of the homeless who lived in vacated buildings and under bridge approaches. Peter reached a parked taxi and pulled the door open before the driver could react.

"I'm off duty," the driver said as soon as he got a look at his fare.

"I've got money," Peter assured him, sliding across the seat and pulling Pam in after him. He reached out a handful of soaked, wadded bills.

The cabbie mumbled a curse as he turned on his meter. "Where to?" he asked, but he never touched the money. Pam gave him Glen's address. He pulled into the flow of traffic and headed uptown.

"What happened to you two?"

Peter answered. "We were mugged and thrown into the river."

The driver was skeptical. "Yeah, you were mugged, but they didn't bother to take your money."

"We fought them," Peter responded, elaborating on his story.

"Do you have a cell phone?" Pam asked.

"Lady, this is a taxi, not a hotel room."

"I need to call ahead and make sure someone is home," she explained.

He whispered another oath, then handed a cell phone into the backseat.

Glen was waiting on the street when the taxi pulled up. He had a blanket that he wrapped around Pam; then he walked her to the elevator, which the doorman was holding. Peter tagged along with nothing more than a cursory greeting.

Inside the apartment, Glen rushed Pam into the master bathroom, leaving Peter dripping on the carpet by the front door. Glen returned carrying a terry-cloth robe and told Peter that he could use the laundry and toss his clothes in the washing machine. He followed him and, as his guest peeled off his trousers, asked, "What in hell happened to you?" His tone was disapproving.

Peter tried to introduce himself, but Glen cut him short. "I know who you are. I was up at your apartment where Pam was hiding out. I tried to talk her into coming home with me. I guess I should have dragged her."

"She doesn't drag easily," Peter answered. Then, as he stripped and tossed his clothes into the washing machine, he told Glen the short version of what they had been through. He explained how the publisher's daughter had been taken, and the instructions they had been given for her return. He told how he and Carl had begged Pam not to go, that she had insisted, and that he had determined to follow her.

"He threw her over?" Glen asked in disbelief.

Peter put on the robe and pulled the belt tight. He told of going in after her, finding her, then sharing the life ring as they drifted in to the shore. "She didn't want to be rescued. She wanted them to think that she was dead."

"You saved her life," Glen realized. "She's alive because of you."

"She probably would have made it without me," Peter answered.

They left his clothes tumbling in the washer and went into the living room, where Glen poured Peter a double of a very expensive Scotch. "You can stay for as long as you want. There's a bed in the den."

"No, I have to get back in the morning. I have classes. Pam can have the bed. I'll sack out on your sofa, if you don't mind. Living with Pam, you get used to a sofa."

"Sure! Okay!" Glen had thought that he would stay with Pam in the master suite. Peter's arrangement was much more considerate of her privacy.

Pam came out to join them, wearing a robe identical to the one Glen had given Peter. Glen stood to embrace her, then hurried to get her something to drink.

"He was at my apartment?" Peter asked Pam.

She nodded. "Several days ago. He wanted me to drop the book and come back here with him."

Peter made a show of glancing around the room and taking in its furnishings. "You would have been more comfortable here," he said wryly.

"I had more freedom there," she answered instantly.

Glen interrupted their conversation as he returned with a brandy for Pam. "Mr. Salerno told me what happened tonight. You're lucky to be alive." He toasted toward Peter. "To your health. We owe you a great deal."

"Just my standard service," Peter said, deflecting the praise. But he heard the "we" loud and clear. Glen and Pam were an item. He'd be leaving in the morning.

THIRTY-SEVEN

Pam woke up in the master bedroom, still wearing the robe Glen had given her. There was daylight between the slats of the blinds, and voices outside the bedroom door. She dragged herself up and stepped out into the living room. Glen and Peter were standing by the front door, both fully dressed.

"Pete was just about to leave," Glen said.

Pam feigned anger. "Without saying good-bye?"

Peter came to her. "I didn't want to wake you." He brushed a kiss across her cheek. "And I have to go. I have a class."

She pulled him into an embrace. "That was a see-you-later kiss. You saved my life." She kissed him fully on the mouth and then whispered, "That was a thank-you kiss."

"I guess I won't be seeing you later," Peter said, "what with you being dead and all that."

Pam smiled, and admitted "It wouldn't be

safe for either of us. But when the book comes out . . . When all this is over . . ."

"Maybe you'll send me a postcard," he suggested, putting an ending to her thought. "I'll still be waiting to get my thesis read." When he turned, Glen had already opened the door.

The two men shook hands, then embraced, Glen acknowledging the debt he owed Peter. "If I can ever do anything. Show my appreciation in any way . . ."

"Maybe you could publish my thesis," Peter teased. "At least no one would set fire to your office." He gave a final wave to Pam, and then he was gone.

Glen closed the door and turned the huge dead-bolt lock. He went to Pam, pushed her hair away from her face, and teased, "You really do look like you died. Why don't you go back to bed? I'll be here when you get up. I'm taking the day."

She found the damp, dirty clothes she had taken off puddled on the bathroom floor, scooped them up, and carried them out to the laundry. Glen was in a phone conversation and acknowledged her with a wave. Then she was back in his bathroom and began running a scalding tub.

She lowered herself in carefully, enjoying the heat on her skin. Ten hours ago, she had been sinking into the murk of New York Harbor. Now she was luxuriating in the bath of a trendy apartment. There was no doubt which lifestyle she preferred. It was easy to regret that she had ever thought of writing a book.

But in the last few days her world had flipped completely over. Until now, writing her story had put her in mortal danger. Now, finishing the story was her only way to safety. Once the book was out, she would be a known figure, with her enemies called out into the open. It would be much harder for them to make her disappear. There wouldn't be any reason for them to try.

With the book being read, and her allegations being discussed, the Washington crowd would go into damage control. A few sacrificial lambs would be selected. Someone who had surreptitiously gathered money, someone who had passed it under a table, and someone who had pocketed it. Everyone would pretend to be aghast that private interests were actually buying elected officials. Outraged voices would call for a "complete investigation" of the scapegoats. A politician might even lavish praise on Pam for her great public service in exposing the transgressors. Suddenly, she would be untouchable.

Glen tapped on the bathroom door and opened it slowly. "Okay if I come in?"

She slouched down in the water. "I was just getting out," she answered.

He took a towel from the linen closet and brought it to the edge of the tub. "Take your time," he said. "Your things just went into the dryer." He ran his fingers through her wet hair. "I can't tell you how much I've missed you. How worried I've been. It's good to have you here. I'm hoping you plan to stay." He put the towel on the edge of the tub and left the room.

Pam stood and stepped out, dried herself, and put on the terry-cloth robe. She tied a smaller towel around her wet head.

Glen was in the den at his desk, a telephone handset cradled under his chin. Pam went to the kitchen, poured coffee, and put a slice of bread into the toaster. She carried her breakfast into the den. Glen pushed aside his papers and swiveled his chair around to face her. "Now you look alive," he said.

She began with an apology. She was sorry that she had involved him again, but she didn't have any other place to go. "We were standing in the street, soaked to the skin and beginning to shiver. We couldn't go back to Peter's apartment. They had found us there just the way you said they would."

He took her hand. "I'm happy you came here. I would have been devastated if you had thought of anyplace else." Then he leaned back and coaxed the full story from her.

Pam gave him the details of the proposed exchange on the ferry. She told him how she had deposited everything concerning the book into the back of a panel truck and walked away from it. She had noticed the man who passed her on the stairs but never thought to study his face. "It took about two seconds to flip me over the rail," she remembered. "I never knew what hit me."

"So they have everything — the book, all your files, and they think they have you. As far as they know, it's a clean sweep. The crisis is over. They're home free."

"Yes," she answered thoughtfully. "As long as I stay in hiding for the rest of my life, which is not an attractive prospect."

"Not for your life," he said, derisive of her exaggeration. "Just for a time. Until they go on to something else."

"It would have to be for a long time. You're talking about a year. Maybe even longer, before I could risk showing my face. Even then, I would have to make it obvious that I hadn't written anything and wasn't planning on writing anything. How would I do that?"

"Easy," Glen said. "Marry me. You would have my name and a place to live. I could probably find you a job where it would be obvious that you weren't still working on your book."

"Glen, you're president of a publishing company. People are going to want to meet your new wife."

"We can have a private wedding. I won't tell anyone I'm married until it's safe for you to reappear. It will work, Pam. Believe me, I've given this a lot of thought."

"I know you have," she said, her tone showing her gratitude. "I've thought about it too. I appreciate you making it sound so simple. But it's not. We would both be in danger. I think there's a safer way."

He leaned back, his manner showing his interest.

"I think I have to finish the book," she said.

His eyes widened in surprise. "You can't be serious. You know —"

She held up a hand to silence him. "Just listen," she said. "I know it sounds crazy, but hear me out." Glen fell back into his attentive posture.

She took him through her reasoning, and

he nodded in appreciation of each point. She concluded that she would be truly safe only when the book was on the shelves. Then it was his turn.

He drew a deep breath. "All well and good," he said, "but what makes you think that they'll ever let you finish the book?"

"They won't know I'm working on it. They think I drowned last night."

"If . . . you stay drowned. But if you go back to that book, your name will start popping up. There will be meetings, telephone calls, data transmissions, press proofs, sample copies. This is my business, Pam, and I know you can't keep something like this quiet. Think about it! Your own publisher will be leaking the news to book buyers all over the world in order to build up the initial print run. It's like having a baby. People generally notice that you're pregnant before the event."

"I'll take it overseas," she countered. "I'll live right there with the project. Glen, I'm finished with the writing. The pages already exist in type. I'm thinking of a few weeks rather than a few years."

His gaze narrowed. "You said you put everything into the back of a panel truck."

"Not everything. Everything they could possibly know about."

His face lowered into his hands. "Pam, you have no idea what you're up against. The government will know what plane you're on five minutes after you present your passport. And even if you do get out of the country, they're listening in on half the world's phone calls. They can get copies of everyone's e-mails."

"I can't believe that anyone can use all the government's resources to stop a book from being published."

"Who do you think killed your friend Marion? Who tossed you off the ferry? Do you think they were amateurs? Pam, by now the people you're planning to name have convinced the military and the spies that what you're writing is a danger to national security. They don't even need a court order to break in on you. They can get the full cooperation of the spooks and the police of any country in the world just by saying that you're delivering information to terrorists. Damn it, they broke into your home. They set fire to my office. They killed your friend in Washington, and they came one life ring short of killing you. You know what? No one has been arrested. No one has even been brought in for questioning. And no one ever will be."

He took the folded newspaper from the

side of his desk and waved it in her face. "Do you know what you are in this morning's paper? You're an 'unconfirmed report' that someone might have fallen from the Staten Island ferry. Officials are 'skeptical' because the person who reported the incident was apparently 'deranged.' He jumped into the water and killed himself."

She pulled the paper from his hand and stared at the article. "Jesus, how can they do this?"

"They can do whatever they want, and most of the time they can get away with it. And if they get caught, they'll find someone else to blame. That's one thing you're right about. There's always a scapegoat."

The clothes dryer pinged. Pam set the paper down and walked slowly out of the den. She carried her clothes into Glen's bedroom. He was right, she thought. There was no safe way. They had found her twice. They could find her again. The difference was that one plan put Glen in danger.

Pam believed he was willing to assume that danger. She had no doubt that, whether she married him or not, he would lend her the protection of his name and home. In her moment of greatest need, he was the one she had called on, and, as always, he had come to her aid without hesitation.

But the book was so close to being finished. A few weeks, maybe a month. People had invested themselves in it. Glen, to be sure, but also Peter Salerno, and Marion Murray, and Carl Weiss. Didn't she owe it to all of them to finish what she had started?

She did her best to make herself presentable without makeup. Then she told Glen that she had to go out to make a call. When he started to protest, she reminded him that Ronda was being held against her delivery of the book. "I have to know that she made it home safely."

She walked across town, putting several streets between herself and Glen's apartment. Then she took a bus downtown, paying with bills that had been washed and dried. She went to her strong box, where she took out the CDs she had hidden. She slipped them into a mailing envelope. She also pocketed her passport. Next, she went to the ATM machine in the bank lobby and withdrew a thousand dollars. Eventually, her pursuers would find the transaction. But by then she would be thousands of miles away.

She began looking for a telephone. She could call Carl Weiss's office. If Ronda answered, she could simply hang up. If Carl answered, she wouldn't know whether

Ronda was still missing or was at home recovering from her ordeal. If she asked, there was every chance that Carl would blab out her name. Like the rest of the world, he thought she was dead.

She tried Peter's apartment, where the telephone kept ringing. Then she called his office, and he answered instantly. "Hi, it's Marie from the restaurant," she said, hoping he would recognize her voice.

"Marie?" He was puzzled for an instant. Then, "Oh, hi, Marie! What can I do for you?"

"I was just wondering if our friend made it home."

"Yep! Safe and sound. Got a ride into Brooklyn and took the subway."

"Great," she said with obvious relief.

"What about you?"

"We'll have to get together," she said. "If you're out walking this afternoon, give me a call at my new address."

On her way back to the apartment, she stopped at an overnight-shipping desk and sent her CDs to an address in London.

Glen was anxious when he let her into the apartment. "Any problems?"

"No, I just didn't want to call from around here. But she's fine."

"Thank God for that. And that you're back safely."

She told him how she had debated whom to call and had decided on Peter because he wouldn't be shocked by the sound of her voice.

"You know, Pam, you're playing spy games with these guys. You're an amateur, and they're professionals. You can't call phones they're bugging and think you're safe just because you use another name."

She nodded. He was right. There was nowhere she could go, no one she could talk to without putting herself at some risk.

Glen had gone back to his office when Peter called. "It's me," he said as his only identification. There was a great deal of noise around him.

"Where are you? I can hardly hear you."

"In a bar. You wouldn't care for the place." He asked how she was feeling, and if there were any effects from last night's party. They exchanged assurances that they both had survived their ordeal. "Anything I can do for you?" he asked.

"There is, but I hate to ask."

"If you lost an earring last night, I'm not going back for it."

She didn't acknowledge his attempt at humor. "I have to get to London, to the people we were working with."

He knew she meant the publisher who was handling the printing for Carl Weiss. "You're going ahead with it." He didn't sound surprised.

"I have no choice," she answered, "unless I want to be permanently dead."

Peter understood her decision. "It sounds as if your host isn't too keen on your choice."

"He's worried about me."

"So am I. But, personally, I think I'll be a lot safer with you on the other side of the ocean. What do you need?"

"I need a ticket, in my name, on your credit card."

"Okay. Do you mind flying coach?"

This time she laughed. "That would be fine."

"One coach ticket to London," Peter said, confirming the arrangement.

"No! To Paris. I don't want to leave a paper trail."

Now he laughed. "Ah, but you're a devious woman. When are you leaving?"

"How's tonight sound?"

THIRTY-EIGHT

She would need things for her trip. A suitcase that would fit in an overhead rack, some drugstore cosmetics, a couple of changes of underwear, and at least another all-purpose outfit. She did her shopping and arrived back at the apartment just as Glen was returning from his office. He noticed the new suitcase.

"You're not staying?" he asked.

"I can't," she said. She brought her new things into his bedroom, and he followed at her heels.

"Does that mean you don't want to stay?"

"No," she answered, turning and falling into his welcoming arms. He kissed her and held her tight for a moment. Then he opened his arms and let her go.

"What it means," she continued, "is that I can't go into hiding for a year, and that I won't let you put yourself and your career at risk."

"I don't care —" he started.

"I know you don't, because you love me. But I care very much, because I love you." She hadn't rehearsed telling him that she loved him, and she didn't weigh the importance of what she'd said until after the words had left her lips. Was it true? She liked him, enjoyed his company, and was grateful for all he had done. But did she love him?

"At least tell me where you're going," he said.

"London," she answered. She explained how Carl Weiss used typesetters and printers all over the world. "Masters, in London, has the book. They were going to print it for Weiss. I think I can revive the project."

He nodded. "I know Masters. It's a good outfit. I might be able to speak with them on a personal basis."

"If you can help, fine," she said. But then she begged, "Just don't compromise yourself. You've been told to drop the project, and I don't want anyone to think that you're still pushing it."

"I'll be discreet." He smiled and took her back into his arms.

Glen asked when she was going. He was shocked when she told him that she was catching a plane that night.

"Do you need anything? Money? A place to stay? I have friends in London."

Pam refused and reminded him once again that she didn't want his fingerprints on any part of the venture. "If all goes well, I'll be back here within a month and there will be nothing to hide. Then we can talk about the future."

"Be careful," he said but quickly corrected himself. "If you were careful, this would be the last thing you'd be doing. But I'll be thinking about you, and rooting for you."

Peter called an hour later. She was on an Air France flight leaving at 8:00 P.M. But he would have to show his credit card to pick up the tickets. They would have to meet at the airport.

Pam taxied to JFK and found the Air France gates at the international terminal. It was buzzing in preflight confusion, so that she had no idea whether she was being watched. She went to the telephone kiosk in the center of the terminal, where Peter had suggested meeting. He was in one of the booths holding a phone receiver to his face. Pam waited behind him until he hung up. "Have a nice flight," he whispered as he stepped around her.

She delayed him for an instant. "Peter . . ."

"It's Pete, and you're never going to be

able to thank me." Then he was gone into the crowd.

She saw an envelope under the telephone. Her ticket was inside. She walked to the check-in counter, answered the security questions, then presented her ticket and passport. The clerk gave her a cursory glance and handed back the passport. Her documents wouldn't be checked again until she reached Paris.

The plane was a wide-body with nearly every seat taken. For all she knew, she was surrounded by government agents. But it didn't seem likely. By now they had checked through the material she had put into the panel truck and knew it was all genuine. The search and rescue effort would have found nothing, so it would be easy to assume that she was dead. She hadn't gone near Carl's office, or Peter's apartment, and all her telephone conversations had been from public phones. The only ones who knew she was alive, and where she was heading, were the two men who were helping her.

But she couldn't let herself get too giddy. They had found her twice before in supposedly safe houses, and, as Glen had reminded her, they were the professionals. She was the amateur. They might have followed

Peter to the airport. It was even possible that they had bugged Glen's phone.

She was exhausted when the plane set down in Paris the next morning. She had tossed and turned all night in the narrow seat and had been able to manage only an hour of sleep. But she focused her attention at passport control. European Union passports had the largest section, and people passed through quickly. The line for non-Europeans was long and torturously slow.

The clerk looked several times from her photo to her face, then scrolled down a long list on the screen of his computer. For the first time it dawned on her that she might be on a list of persons to be denied entry, or to be held for security reasons, and her fears grew as names continued to scroll. But finally her passport was pushed back to her.

The customs clerk glanced at her declaration and waved her through without opening her carry-on. Then she was outside, walking confidently to the line of waiting taxis. She asked for the Gard du Nord station that served the Channel trains and arrived there in half an hour. Once again she faced an official inquiry. She noticed the Europeans filing through without showing any documents and decided to risk crowding in with them. Within minutes she was aboard a train easing out of the station. Her gamble had paid off. Her passport trail ended in Paris.

When she came out of the station, she spotted the queue of London taxis. This time she had an address on a street in Soho, which turned out to be a walkup over a fashionable store. Jean Abbott opened the door with a welcoming embrace.

Living in London had converted her to tea, and she had a pot steeping within seconds. "We'll have a bite, you can tell me what on earth is going on, and then you have to get some sleep. I know it's not flattering, but you look awful."

The apartment was a close copy of the one Jean had rented to Pam in New York, compact, minimally furnished, and tastefully decorated. They sat at a high table in a very small kitchen, looking over a plate of scones and a jar of jam. Pam tried to condense the horrors since they had first met into just a few incidents. Even the abbreviated version had Jean gasping. Her comments alternated between near disbelief at the actions of the government and bewilderment over why Pam had taken on such a challenge. "You could have just walked away from it," she said, reminding Pam that she was somewhat to blame for her own predicament.

"I should have," Pam agreed. She told Jean about her romantic disappointment at the hands of the director of the institute, without admitting that she had been virtually living with a married man. She had begun the book as an act of revenge. "You rotten bastard, you can't treat me like this." Next it had become a contest, with her determined that a bunch of crooks wasn't going to frighten her into quitting. "Now it's a debt that I owe to people who supported me. It's also my only straight line to safety."

She slept on top of the bedspread while Jean worked at a desk in the living room, which overlooked a backyard. When Pam awoke, the two women went shopping and came home with fish and fresh vegetables. They cooked together, then opened an inexpensive French Chablis.

Pam laid out her plans. Masters Publishing had the first page proofs and intended to print the book. There would have been a month of back-and-forth as the English house had Pam approve edits and authenticate footnotes. Now she hoped to have Masters take over the project. She could work with them and cut the preparation time in half.

"You can stay here," Jean offered. Her tone was genuine and enthusiastic. She began discussing the few changes that would be needed to accommodate her guest. Pam refused the offer. "If Masters agrees, they're going to have to find me a place to work. Based on everything that's happened, I'd be a very dangerous houseguest."

In the morning, Pam refreshed herself in the shower, then dressed for her visit to the English publisher. Masters was in the phone book, and luckily in the West End, no more than a fifteen-minute cab ride from Jean's apartment.

At the reception desk, Pam asked for the name she had seen on some of the correspondence and gave her own name as Ronda Weiss. After a few minutes she was handed over to a tall, efficient-looking young woman in high heels and taken back to a large office with a cluster of casual furniture as well as an oversized desk. The man who stood to greet her was gray haired, mustached, and wore a cardigan sweater over a dress shirt. Central casting couldn't have provided a more credible character to play the role of an English literary figure.

He gestured her to the sofa, closed the office door behind the secretary, and took a chair opposite her. "Well," he began, "this mystery is certainly getting more interesting."

"Mystery?" she asked.

"Yes. I'm going to begin by guessing that you're Pamela Leighton."

Her heart sank. How could they know already?

He introduced himself as Gordon Frasier, the firm's senior partner, then cheerfully admitted, "That wasn't entirely a guess, because I know you're not Ronda Weiss. I've met Miss Weiss both here and in New York." Pam apologized and started to explain, but he cut her off. "Quite all right," he assured her. "I was puzzled by the turn of events. Weiss canceling the book with no explanation. No one answering his phone. And then, just this morning, I received your CDs in the mail."

"They got here," she said with relief.

"Yes. Much as I hate to admit it, I hadn't read a word of your book until this morning. We simply print for Carl Weiss and others like him. The print runs are small, and there's not much in it for us. But it keeps our vendors happy, and occasionally it gives us access to a promising title."

He got up from the chair and sauntered back to his desk. "But when your disks came this morning, I was curious to find out exactly what it was that we were printing." He came back to his chair, carrying a stack of typeset pages. "I learned that we already had some of it typeset, and the rest awaiting editorial corrections. So I decided to read what we have in hand." He put the pages on the coffee table. "That certainly is incendiary material. I can see why you needed a boutique publisher like Carl Weiss."

He leaned back. "Books like this invite libel suits. Is that why Weiss decided to drop it? And if so, what on earth are you doing here pretending to be someone else?"

"Carl Weiss dropped the book because his daughter was kidnapped to stop publication," Pam answered. The publisher's expression turned skeptical. "I think you've read enough to know that representatives and lobbyists in Washington would rather not see this in print. They've called in their enforcers to make sure that it never sees the light of day."

"Really," he said, but his expression remained skeptical. "I can understand why they'd rather not read about themselves in such an unflattering light. But to call out the Marines . . ."

"Let me start at the beginning," she said. "I find most of what's happened hard to believe myself." Gordon smiled, leaned back, and crossed his knees. Pam took a deep breath and went back to her career at the Electric Energy Institute. She described her work in detail, along with her collaborative efforts with other lobbyists. The only thing she left out was her long-running affair. Gordon listened for fifteen minutes without interruption. It was clear that the woman before him was an insider.

Pam jumped to her decision to write an exposé without telling him precisely why the idea had come to her. There was nothing admirable about turning the tables on an ex-lover. She simply stated that she had taken the idea to Glen Hubbard at Thomas Howell, and that Howell had put the book under contract.

"I know Thomas Howell very well," Gordon allowed, "and I've had several meetings with Glen Hubbard." The name of a reputable publisher had caught his interest. If Howell had been willing to publish the book, it might be hasty for him simply to walk away from the opportunity.

But however interested he might have been, the rest of Pam's story gave him good reason to refuse. He followed the veiled threats that had come from John Duke, the assaults on her, and the fire that had destroyed her edited manuscript. "Thomas Howell had to drop it," she admitted. "They were threatened with union problems and then were attacked by an arsonist. The parent company ordered Hubbard to drop the book."

Next, she got to Marion Murray. "She had made copies of hundreds of files and records. Times, places, amounts, and receipts," she said. Gordon registered shock when Pam told him of Marion's murder.

"Surely you're not alleging that the United States government . . ."

"I couldn't believe it myself," she said, anticipating his question. "But then it happened to me."

She told him of the relationship with Carl Weiss, and how everything seemed to be going well until her picture had appeared in the paper. That brought her to Ronda's disappearance, and the detailed instructions from her kidnappers. They wanted the book and they wanted Pam. Obviously, when they threw her over the side, they had meant to kill her. That fact added credence to the possibility that they had killed Marion Murray.

Gordon was plainly confused by the details of her story. "It just doesn't seem possible," he said. "It has the flavor of James Bond. Very exciting but totally implausible. I'm afraid my colleagues would never believe it. I mean, all this just to stop some bad publicity?"

"It may be more than that," Pam countered. She took him through the Arthur Ries affair, and the possibility that Ries had been killed to protect a politician who had taken a record payoff. "Someone may be trying to cover up complicity in a murder."

"Still . . ." Gordon was wavering but still far from being convinced.

"I can support every charge in the book. Names, places, dates!"

"I'm afraid your experience and your book are intertwined," he said. " 'The book that the U.S. government doesn't want you to read' and all that." He rose as if to dismiss her. "Where are you staying? I'll have to give this some thought and get back to you." She knew it was a polite letdown. His doubts about her story made him doubt the authenticity of the book.

She spotted a large stack of newspapers on the credenza behind his desk. "Do you get the New York papers?"

He nodded. "The *Times* and *The Washington Post.*"

"Do you have yesterday's *Times?*"

"Possibly. I didn't get to it this morning. Your book, you know." He shuffled through the papers and pulled one out. "Yes, here it is."

"Look at page eight. The title says something about ferry service being disrupted."

He found the article and read it through. When he looked up, amazement showed on his face.

THIRTY-NINE

Gordon Frasier wasn't convinced, but he was very interested. If Pamela Leighton had actually been thrown from a ferry, then it was likely the other incidents she had described were also true. But he still couldn't understand why American elected officials, who were regularly pilloried in the press and insulted by one another, would go to such lengths to stop an unflattering book. Unless it was the murder she had described. He had the remaining material that Pam had mailed to his company printed out, so he now had a complete manuscript. He sat up all night reading the book.

When Pam came in the next morning, he announced that he was taking her out for breakfast. "Quite a book," he began over plates of watery eggs and bulging sausages. "You realize, of course, that you're charging criminal acts."

"Maybe here they're criminal, but in the

United States they're just business as usual," she countered. "In some countries, an official who accepted a ten-thousand-dollar contribution would be carted off to jail. But American politicians are proud to take your money. They'll even send you a thank-you note."

"Then why would they care about your book?"

"Because I'm able to link the payoff with the vote. I can show that the payoff comes first." She reminded him of an incident he had read about just hours earlier. A senator had begged the majority leader not to bring a bill to a vote. He wanted it delayed so that he could collect more contributions by appearing to be undecided on how he was going to vote. Settling the issue quickly, he said, could cost him as much as $25,000.

Gordon remembered the incident and then reminded her of Senator Lawrence sending back the institute's check and telling them it needed another zero. "I thought that was extremely brazen when I read it," he commented. "But still, to make the book more than a tirade, you would need iron-clad substantiation for each incident."

"I think I have everything you would need." Pam seemed confident rather than brash.

Gordon asked if she could stay a week. "We'll put you up in a hotel. I intend to have my solicitors go over your manuscript page by page and challenge you on every charge. By the end of the week I'll know what holds up and what goes too far. Are you willing?"

"Of course. When can we get started?"

"First thing is to get you settled. We keep a small suite for visiting dignitaries," he said. "I'm sure you'll find it comfortable."

Comfortable proved an understatement. The Hilton was a modern tower overlooking Green Park. Services included a spa, a fitness center, several restaurants encompassing most of the world's cuisine, and a private club for casino gambling.

Pam's few belongings filled one drawer in a dresser and needed only one hanger in the closet. The bed was huge and soft, the bath a tribute to the possibilities of plumbing, and her sitting room nearly as big as Jean Abbott's entire apartment. Judging by the accommodations he was providing, Gordon Frasier took her very seriously indeed.

Her budget wasn't up to the hotel. Unless she used her credit card, the menus posted outside the restaurant were unaffordable. Neither of her outfits was suitable even for the bar. She needed to buy clothes. Her problem was that her pursuers might still be monitoring her charge account. If they were, how long would it take them to trace the posting?

Pam had already taken too many risks. Meeting Peter at the airport had been dangerous because he might have been followed. Checking through passport control in Paris had announced that she was alive. If they were alert, and Glen had convinced her that they were, then they already knew she had fled to Europe.

She had gotten a break in boarding the tunnel train without presenting a passport, so her trail ended in France. But if, as Glen had told her, they had access to Carl Weiss's records and his arrangements for publishing the book, they would know that he was dealing with Masters in London. That could lead them to her.

Even if there might be enough evidence to lead them to Masters's front door, Pam didn't want to make it any easier for them. She would go outside to modest restaurants that she could cover with the cash she had brought with her. The clothes she had would have to do. Her recreation would be limited to long walks in the park.

Gordon called her at the end of the day. "Could you come in tomorrow, around ten?" he wondered. "I'll have some questions for you." She agreed, went out for a sandwich and a bottle of beer and dined in front of the television. By bedtime she felt lonely and abandoned. Glen's offer to take her into his life began looking better than the plan she had chosen.

The next morning, Pam wore her other outfit, a modest skirt and a long cotton sweater, to the publishing house. When she reached the reception desk, she wondered what name she should use and, opting for caution, gave Ronda Weiss's. Once again the tall woman in high heels came out to lead her back to the office's suites. Pam felt like a cleaning lady as she walked behind the stylish and statuesque secretary. Her only consolation was that she knew she wasn't attracting any attention.

Gordon was waiting in a small conference room with two young men in coat and tie who were models of English tailoring. He introduced them as lawyers from a firm he retained, offered tea, then left Pam to their mercy. Their role was to attack every incident she had revealed and every charge she had implied. Her task was to convince them that she had credible documentation. She had her annotated text marked with footnotes and the copies of the records she had taken from the safe-deposit box. It promised to be a very long day.

Her inquisitors were polite and friendly but, at the same time, ruthlessly thorough. When she cited something from Marion's files, they wondered if she might show them the file. Then, when she explained that the originals were with the institute, they asked if the institute might be kind enough to provide copies. When she mentioned the amount of a check, they asked for the check, and when she answered that she had worked from a copy, they wanted the copy. She felt ridiculous explaining that she had placed the copy in the back of a panel truck, and that, no, she had no idea who was in the truck or where they had gone.

Gordon sent in tea and biscuits early in the afternoon, and wine and cheese at the end of the workday. The two lawyers packed up their things and told her cheerily that they would see her in the morning. "Is ten o'clock good for you?" one of them asked considerately.

Gordon asked if she had dinner plans. Nothing special, she said casually. Pam had no intention of telling him that she was short of money. He promised to pick her up at seven o'clock. "Nothing too elaborate," she said. "This is as dressy as I can get."

It was very elaborate. Gordon took her to his club, a dining room hushed with decorum and waiters with white gloves. The men wore jackets and ties, and a few were in white tie. The women, with the exception of one underage vamp who showed cleavage nearly to her navel, were distinguished, feathered and bejeweled.

Gordon didn't seem in the least embarrassed, but Pam needed to tell him why she hadn't dressed for the occasion. He smiled when she explained that she was afraid to use her credit cards. "My God," he allowed, "you really are terrified." Then he remembered her list of assaults. "But, of course, after what you've been through."

They dined gracefully, with easy, nondemanding conversation. When she could stand the suspense no longer, Pam asked, "How did I do with your lawyers?"

"They seemed pleased," he answered. "But solicitors never venture a quick opinion. They bill by the hour, you know."

Twice something dawned on him, and he got up and left the table. When dinner was finished, he ordered a port for Pam and a brandy for himself. Then they adjourned to a lounge where cigars were being puffed with ritual reverence.

"One thing puzzles me," Gordon said.

"Why did you ever decide to write such an unpopular book? It seems to burn the bridges to your career, to your friends, to so much that you might have aspired to."

How should she answer? Like the courageous whistle-blower, determined to save her government from corruption? Or like the woman scorned, determined to burn the man who had wronged her? "Hard to say," she finally decided. "I'm not sure I know why. But if I figure it out, I'll try to explain it to you."

He hailed a taxi and took her to her hotel. "Check at the front desk," he told her. "I had something sent over that might make your time with us a bit more enjoyable." He stayed in the taxi while she got out, then called through the open window, "I may be late arriving in the morning, but the gentlemen you met today will be waiting for you." Then he wished her a good night.

Pam stood smiling as the taxi pulled away. She liked Gordon and his business style. He had understood that she had been through a great deal and given her exactly what she needed — a relaxing evening in the comfort and safety of his club. She wasn't yet one of his authors, but he was already treating her with consideration and respect. She had reached the elevators when she remembered that she was to stop at the front desk. The clerk knew her name and gave her an envelope that had "arrived only half an hour ago."

Pam opened it on the elevator and found a Masters check for five hundred pounds made out to her. It was drawn on a bank that had an office in the lobby, so the entire transaction would be within the bank.

FORTY

"London. She's in London." John Duke couldn't believe what he was hearing.

"So I'm told," Senator Lawrence said, acting as if the information was of no consequence. "Supposedly, she's trying to get an English house to publish her book."

They had met late in the evening in the lobby of the Hotel Washington, Lawrence's favorite place to conduct business that he didn't want paraded through his offices. He always had the same table, in the corner past the bar, where a drape and a potted plant gave him a bit of privacy.

John shook his head slowly. "She assured me that this whole issue was over. She was dropping the book. I was going to try to connect her with a good job."

The senator rolled his ice cubes around the inside of the glass, tasted his sour mash, and smiled in approval. Then his attention went back to John. "She seems to have changed her mind. My source is well placed and very reliable."

"I'm sure you're right," John said quickly. The senator usually was right and didn't appreciate contradiction. "I'm just stunned."

"The problem is," Lawrence continued, "she's put herself beyond our reach. There are steps we can take within the country that would be a blatant violation of another nation's sovereignty. I was hoping you might have a suggestion."

John took a moment to sip his own drink. Then he admitted, "As an industry, we don't have very close ties with the UK. As far as the department goes, I'm sure there are contacts and international associations. But there's no one I know personally." Then he had a thought: "How about the publisher? He probably has no reason to offend the United States. He must sell books here, and have American authors."

"I have that covered as best we can. But it's not very reassuring. We can't develop a trade policy that addresses just one company." The senator paused for another sip. "I was hoping you might intervene personally, since you're the one who has the most to lose."

"Yes, yes," John agreed, stuttering in his

sudden anxiety. Was Lawrence warning him that if there was a scandal he'd be the one who would take the fall? Or was he just reminding John that, since the author had gathered her story at his trade association, he was bound to be at the center of the story? "I could call her, or even find some reason to fly to London and see her. But would it do any good? She's already lied to me."

"We would hope that, you can be more persuasive than you were last time," Lawrence said. "Or maybe you could enlist the aid of one of your associates at the institute. There must be a few multinational companies that have clout in Europe, or labor unions with connections. The point is, John, the book is close to publication, and you're the obvious choice to see that it never gets printed. Many of us are counting on you."

The senator looked at his watch. Then he told John that he was expecting another visitor to stop by for a drink. "I hope you'll excuse me."

John finished off his drink, stood, and offered his hand. "I'll keep you informed," he promised.

"No need! I'll know just how persuasive you are."

John was reeling as his driver navigated the traffic into Georgetown. What was Lawrence telling him to do? Was he supposed to find a labor union enforcer in England who would break Pam's legs? Or promise a favor to a corporation in turn for its using its clout in Europe to threaten the publisher? He's counting on me to be *more persuasive,* John thought, remembering the senator's mocking tone. Was he supposed to throw her out of a window? Or was Lawrence suggesting that he rekindle his affair with the woman? That would be his personal scandal, saving the senator and his friends from a far broader scandal. Maybe that was it. They were telling him to take the bullet and save the others.

When he arrived home, Catherine was out, apparently enjoying chamber music at one of his colleagues' homes. She had moved gracefully into the social scene with other Washington wives. They saw more of one another than their husbands did. The maid had left him a sandwich, which he brought into the kitchen along with an oversized martini.

John had no trouble admitting to himself that he had made a terrible mistake. He had paid too high a price for this job. In his greed to become a cabinet officer, he had made himself Catherine's prisoner, and had abandoned Pam after giving her everything she needed to destroy him. At the first hint that he was a candidate for the post, he should have confronted Catherine and told the president's aides that he was about to change wives. They might still have nominated him, but even if they passed him by, he would have been better off. He would still have been one of the capital's top deal makers, would have had a wife who cared about him, and wouldn't have been jumping into Senator Lawrence's lap like a toy poodle.

What could he say to Pam that would persuade her to drop the book? That he had found he loved her and needed her? Why should she believe that when he had said it all before and then reneged on his commitment? That he was initiating divorce proceedings immediately? Catherine, he knew, could drag a divorce out for a year, and punish Pam and him every day it took. His best chance might be simply to beg her. He could appeal to what they had once meant to each other and tell her that her book would ruin him forever in Washington. But after the way he had treated her, why should she care?

He could threaten her. Not personally, of

course, but with what others would do to stop her. "The fact that I'm here," he could tell her in London, "is proof that your cover has been blown." He could remind her of how many movers and shakers would pay any price to stop her, and that her life was in danger. But so far, danger hadn't daunted her. So maybe he would have to give her an up-close demonstration of what could happen. But he didn't expect that anything would frighten her off, particularly when she was so close to publication. That brought him back to the terrible thought that he might have to push her out a window.

FORTY-ONE

Pam cashed Gordon's check as soon as the bank opened and made a brief shopping foray to add a business suit and a plain black dress to her wardrobe. She wore the suit to her meeting with the lawyers, who seemed to appreciate her more conventional attire. Gordon's secretary brought in tea, and they got down to work.

It was a repeat of the previous day. The lawyers had read through the next hundred pages, underlining each assertion. They wanted the data or records that would substantiate what Pam had written. Reference numbers were added throughout, and, for each number, the documentation was provided.

They broke for lunch, a tray of sliced meats and cheeses that was brought in with china plates, silverware, and cloth napkins. The conversation turned personal, with the men wondering about Pam's background.

They had assumed that she was an investigative reporter and that she had enjoyed an exciting and controversial career. Both seemed disappointed that she had been an active player in the corruption she was revealing.

"I suppose there's some of that over here," one of them admitted, "but on a much smaller scale. The length of campaigns is limited by law, so there's less time to spend money."

"There's lobbying, of course," the other said. "But if an MP were caught taking expensive gifts, or demanding money, there would be hell to pay."

Then they were back to work quickly, with the lawyers bringing up the disappearance of Arthur Ries. Was she charging that Ries had been murdered?

"No. I don't know that for a fact. All I can prove is what I've written; that he was about to testify in the matter of a congressional bribe, that he disappeared, and that the prosecutor who persisted with the case was killed in a plane crash." Pam continued, "Given the circumstances and my own experience, it's not too hard for me to believe." The attorneys suggested wording that would make it plain she was not charging that a crime had been committed, and

Pam agreed. "Maybe your report will inspire someone else to take up the investigation," one of them suggested.

The grilling went on, interrupted by tea in the afternoon and wine while they were wrapping up. The lawyers stayed behind for an evening meeting with Gordon Frasier when Pam returned to her hotel.

She felt good about her performance during the grilling. With very few exceptions, she had been able to answer the attorneys' most penetrating questions. She had little doubt that the book would pass whatever criteria for authenticity Gordon might demand. She was confident that it would go to press before the month was out. But then what? She had been so immersed in the project all summer and fall that she had never considered what might happen after the book was published.

Her worst fear was that nothing would happen. The book might be greeted by a collective yawn from people grown totally cynical about their government who found nothing upsetting in her revelations. "We already know they're crooks" might be the reaction. "Tell us something we don't know."

More likely, the book would get the notice of political pundits, who would use it for an attack on the lobbyists and their cronies. That must have been what the Washington insiders expected. Why else would they be going to such lengths to stop publication? The charges would force denials, and the denials would lead to controversy. The controversy, in turn, would drive interest in the book and build sales. But, in the United States, political controversies had very short lives. Pundits and their media needed new, shocking revelations every day. Her book might blaze like a firestorm, but it would burn out very quickly.

Pam was resigned that her moment in the limelight would be very brief. She knew she would be castigated as a liar and a traitor to her friends. Her affair with John Duke might well be dredged up to explain why she had attacked so viciously. Others would rally around her and praise her for blowing the whistle on the constant corruption of government. In her best-case scenario, she had to be prepared for the battering she would take at the center of the storm she had created. But when it was all over, would anything change? Would the book be worth the anguish it had caused? Would it be worth Marion Murray's life?

And then what? Would any business want to hire her, given her disloyalty to her prior employer? Could she expect open arms from civic organizations once she was painted as the other woman, whose motive was revenge? She had a future with Glen Hubbard, who thought of her as an outraged citizen rather than as a woman scorned. But she couldn't enter a lifelong relationship without bringing value to it. She had to have a purpose of her own.

Her telephone rang, and Gordon spoke from the hotel lobby. Could she join him for a cocktail and perhaps dinner? There were a few things he had to discuss with her.

Pam was delighted to accept, even though Gordon's tone hadn't indicated that they would be celebrating a contract for her book. He sounded like someone about to deliver bad news.

She wore the black dress and heels with a few simple pieces of costume jewelry. Her hair was the best she could do under the circumstances, and her makeup was hurried. When she saw herself reflected in the elevator mirror, she was very presentable but several points short of glamorous.

Gordon ordered a whiskey neat with water on the side. Pam chose a flinty Chablis. There were a few minutes of small talk. She thanked him for the generous check, and he admired what she had done with it. "Lovely dress. Very becoming." When they were halfway into their drinks and settled comfortably, he began with the conventional opener that he had both good news and bad news. Which would she like first? She chose the good news to break the gloom of the dire thoughts she had left in her room.

"Your work is holding up beautifully. My solicitors tell me that, with very few exceptions, the documentation is ample and convincing. Some of the source material is open to interpretation; politicians hardly ever say anything without leaving themselves a path of escape. But the important thing is that the book stands up nicely to challenge." He allowed that they still had over a hundred pages to review, and that the process would take another day or two, but there was no reason to believe the rest of her material wouldn't hold up as well.

"Then you'll publish it," she said.

"That brings me to the bad news," he answered. Her expression clouded over. "Oh, not terrible news. Just distressing, I would say. You've been located, and Masters has been identified. It seems the people who drove you out of America are reaching over here to stop you."

She nodded. "It had to happen eventually.

A dear friend reminded me that they were professionals while I was just an amateur. I shouldn't count on outsmarting them." Then she asked how he had found out that they were compromised.

"Pressure from an unlikely source," Gordon told her. "One of our partners is on the board of an international communications conglomerate. Another board member raised the issue. He had heard we were considering your book and advised our partner that it wouldn't be good for our reputation. Apparently he had been told that it was a scurrilous attack on leading figures in the U.S."

Pam responded with a self-conscious smile that seemed a graceful acknowledgment of defeat.

"Of course, we hear dire warnings about many of the things we publish. Just a few months ago we had a recording company up in arms about a biography of one of their big earners, a particularly nasty little punk. They threatened to lead the nation's music audience in a boycott of our books. But in this case the man was delivering a threat on behalf of a government."

"So you can't risk publishing it," Pam said, going straight to where Gordon seemed to be heading.

"Oh, no, nothing that drastic. To me, it's just further confirmation of what you've been saying. Washington will go to any length to stop publication." He smiled and shook his head. "I certainly hope Masters isn't targeted for a cruise missile."

"Thomas Howell had a fire," she admitted.

"Nevertheless, I'm solidly behind the book," Gordon assured her. "But I did make copies for my senior partners. They'll read it over the weekend, and we'll get together on Monday." As an afterthought, he asked, "You can stay the weekend, can't you?"

She could. But while they went on talking, Pam was trying to handicap the decision he would make. Blaming it on the concerns of his partners was a painless way for him to back away from the commitment he had been implying. Was he saying "I love it, but my hands are tied. Sorry, and all that"? Or should she believe his jaunty tone? Was this just an annoying delay, nothing more than a courtesy to his partners?

When he suggested dinner, she used her long day with his lawyers as an excuse. "I'm exhausted, and I have another day of it tomorrow," she said. He walked her as far as the elevators and promised to look in on her during the next day's meeting. His demeanor was upbeat, which she found encouraging.

When she returned to her room, her telephone was blinking that she had a message. She was stunned when she heard John Duke's recorded voice. He was in town, staying at her hotel. It was important that he see her right away.

FORTY-TWO

He picked up on the first ring. "Pam?" he said, knowing that she would be the only one to call."

"Yes, John. How are you, and what brings you to London?"

"I have to see you right away. Can you meet me in the lounge in fifteen minutes?" He made his question sound more like an order.

"Tonight?" she asked. "No, I really don't think so. I had a long day today, and I'm due for another grinding day tomorrow. Maybe we can get together tomorrow night. Or over the weekend."

"Pam, you're in terrible danger," John said. "Your assassins are on their way here. Get down to the lounge as quickly as you can." He hung up, without giving her a chance to reply.

She stared at the phone before she set it back in the cradle. Gordon had told her she had apparently been discovered. Now John had come all the way from the States to save her. Things were happening in a rush. She picked up her handbag and left her room. She found herself glancing behind her as she made her way to the elevator. At the third floor, the elevator stopped, and the door opened. Pam stiffened as two men stepped on and moved to the back, one standing on either side of her. They could take her arms as soon as they reached the lobby and walk her out the front door. She was ready to scream when the doors opened.

Neither man moved. She glanced at one of them from the corner of her eye, only to hear "After you" in a pleasant English accent. She stepped off slowly and stopped. They rushed by her on their way to the taxi entrance.

The hotel lounge was at the far end of the lobby, a long walk between groupings of furniture. Clusters of people were gathered, and she looked from left to right to see if anyone was paying unusual attention to her. They all seemed completely unaware of her passing. She stepped into the lounge, which had a long, dark bar running the length of the room, opposite small tables and half-circle, padded booths. The decor was trying hard to be impressive. John stood in one of the booths and motioned for her to join him. He stood at the table until she slid in, then sat next to her.

"Hello, Pam. I'm glad you came down."

"Why wouldn't I? That was probably the most frightening phone call I've ever had. My assassins are on the way. I haven't stopped shaking."

John waved to a waiter. Pam ordered a port, and he named a brandy. As soon as the waiter stepped away, he began. "They've found you, Pam. They know you're going ahead with the book. They're not going to let it happen."

"Who found me?" she asked. "Who in hell are 'they'? I'd like to know who's going to kill me."

"Who found you? I don't know. The FBI? The CIA? Homeland Security? What does it matter? They knew your flight number before you even got on the plane. Who are they? I'm sure about two senators, an important congressman, and two top-dollar lobbyists. I think there's also a labor union leader. Who's going to kill you? People with absolutely no connection to anyone in government. They're probably hired by Defense Department contractors."

"How do you know all this?" Pam demanded.

"I was at a meeting last night with Senator Lawrence. Just the two of us in the Hotel Washington. He told me where you were and the name of the publisher you were working with. Hell, he even knew which hotel you were staying at."

Pam interrupted him. "Why did he tell you?"

"Because I had assured him that you were dropping the book. That's what you told me after our last meeting. Remember?"

She nodded.

"He wanted me to know that you had lied to me and that he and his friends no longer had confidence in my ability to handle the matter. He said they were going to shut you down immediately."

"Shut me down?"

"You and your book. They're putting the screws on your publisher and ending the possibility that you might ever go to another publisher."

Pam processed this information. Then she asked, "When did they decide to kill me?"

"Yesterday, I suppose. Or maybe the day before. I found out about it last night. That's why I caught an early morning plane. Pam, for God's sake, none of this is my doing. I've been assuring them that you would come to your senses. But now I'm out of the loop and you're out of time. They're not going to let you dredge up Arthur Ries's disappearance."

There was something wrong with his story, Pam thought. John didn't seem to know about the attack on the ferry. They had tried to kill her days before they had told him that they would have to take the final step. So he wasn't at the center of the conspiracy. Others were working much harder than he was.

"What should I do?" she asked.

"For starters, let's get you out of your room. You don't want to be here when the killers arrive. Then we'll get out of London."

"What about my publisher?"

"Forget your publisher. He's going to have his own problems. He'll be happy when he realizes that you're not coming back."

"Where would I go?"

"Back to the States with me. You can tell the congressmen and the lobbyists personally that they have nothing to worry about. Then, just maybe, you and I can make a fresh start."

She pulled back as if she had been slapped. "You and I?"

"I'm going to ask Catherine for a divorce," John said. "I don't give a damn what it does to my career. Pam, pushing you away was the biggest mistake I've ever made. I don't want to live with it for the rest of my life."

Her head was spinning. John was right about his friends putting the screws on his publisher. Gordon had told her as much only an hour ago. That lent credibility to the rest of his warning. "Where can I go?" she repeated.

"We'll trade rooms tonight," John said without hesitation. "I'm checked in under another name. If they come, they won't find you. In the morning we can check out when the desk is crowded."

"They'd find you in my room. That would be dangerous for you."

He laughed, breaking the tension. "Even government agents are bright enough to know that I'm not Pam Leighton."

"You're a public figure in the States. They might recognize you and report back to your friends."

John started to protest but then acknowledged that she was right. "We can both stay in my room." He stood abruptly. "C'mon, I'll get you settled and then get your things." He led her to his room, borrowed her key, and left for her room.

Pam had an uneasy feeling when she stepped into his suite. There were lingering memories of the hotels they had shared on weekends away from the capital. His clothes were in the closet, and his shaving gear was on the bathroom sink top. She was aware of a sense of belonging that she had always felt when they were together. Even after months of being apart, it seemed somehow right that they should be with each other. Still, there was the ease with which he had put her aside. She couldn't believe he would risk his career to restart their relationship. Yet wasn't that what he was doing right now? If his colleagues learned he had switched sides, wouldn't that end his rise in politics? She went into the bathroom, locked the door behind her, and turned on the shower. Under the relaxing massage of hot water, she tried to put together her plans for the next day.

She had to get back to Masters and meet with Gordon Frasier. Did he plan to go ahead with the book? If there was a chance that Masters was going to drop it, then she wasn't going to wait until Monday for a decision. If he thought they would go ahead with publication, then she would stay in London, but at another hotel and under another name. She wouldn't let Gordon know where. As far as she could tell, no one outside Masters knew she was in a company suite at the Hilton. But somehow that information had gotten back to Washington.

What about John Duke? How much of his alleged transformation could she believe? He had tried twice to talk her out of the book. Maybe now he was trying to frighten her away from it. Still, there was no doubt that he had rushed to London as soon as he learned his friends had found her. It made sense that something had frightened him.

She wrapped herself in a towel and leaned out of the bathroom. John was at the desk, talking on the telephone. The casual outfit she had bought that morning was on the bed, along with her underwear. Her jewelry and makeup kit were on the dresser. "We're on British Airways' two o'clock flight to New York," he told her. "There's not much chance of anyone in Washington knowing about us until we land and go through passport control."

"I have to go out in the morning," she said. "I have to meet with people at Masters to tell them that I'm breaking our arrangements."

"You can call from the airport."

"No," she said with determination. "This has to be face-to-face."

John bit his lip, then nodded that he understood. "We'll still check out of here first thing in the morning," he said. "We can meet someplace when you're finished."

"You left some of my things in my suite," she observed, more as a question than as a rebuke.

"I did. In the armoire, and some things out in plain sight on the sink. I also mussed up the bed a bit to make it look as if you were still there. There's no point in telling anyone who comes looking that you've already left."

He went into the sitting room and settled into a soft chair where he couldn't be seen from the bed. She appreciated that he was offering her as much privacy as the layout allowed, but she still wasn't completely comfortable. She went back into the bedroom and dressed in the outfit she had just taken off. Then she pulled the bedspread down and stretched out across the top of the bed.

Pam couldn't be sure how much sleep she had gotten. It seemed that she had been tossing and turning throughout the night, awake most of the time. She was almost relieved when she saw the morning light behind the bedroom curtains. She went into the bath, splashed water on her face, and changed out of her rumpled clothes and into the business suit. Then she did her best to put some color into her face. When she came out, John called from the seclusion of the den, "Are you decent?"

"Yes, of course." It was a strange question from a man she had slept with for two years. "I'm going to my room to get the rest of my things."

"Leave them," he advised.

"It will only take a second."

"Okay, but I'm coming with you." They closed the door quietly behind them and took the elevator to her floor. John put out a hand to keep her in the car while he stepped into the hallway. He looked in all directions, then nodded that it was safe for her to come out.

The bedroom was in darkness but clearly outlined by the pale light seeping through the curtains. They stepped in, John going ahead to check in the sitting room. Pam opened the armoire door, took out the two outfits he had left hanging, and tossed them onto the bed. Then she gasped. "John," she managed in a weak voice.

When he rushed into the bedroom, she pointed down at the bed. The spread had been pulled back, and the pillows arranged under the blanket in a human shape. There were three round bullet holes punched through the blanket. Feathers from one of the pillows were sticking out.

Forty-Three

John checked out of the hotel, and Pam simply left her key at the desk. He took a taxi to another hotel where he could catch a van to the airport.

"Be at the airport by noon," he told her when they separated.

"If I'm leaving London, I'll be there," she answered. "If not, get on the plane without me."

"You can't stay here," he said angrily. "You're a dead woman if you do."

"Just get on the plane," she said. "And, John, thank you for coming to warn me. I'm sure I'll see you again."

She knew it was too early for Masters's offices to be open, so she chose to walk, starting out with a stroll through the park. It was a public place where she felt safe. The color in the trees was faded, and leaves were swirling as they fell. She walked with her arms folded against the wind, passing early morning pedestrians moving along the paths in every direction. She saw nothing suspicious, nor did she feel threatened. But still, she couldn't shake the horror of what she had just seen.

They had been in her room. They had tried to kill her without waking her or letting her speak even a word. Without John coming to her aid, they would have succeeded. Did they think she was dead? Probably not. The hired killer would have walked to the bed, fired his shots, then pulled back the blanket to be certain that the shots were lethal. He would have seen the pillow and known that she had escaped.

Then what? Did he wait in the room for her to return? How long? Perhaps an hour. Sometime in the middle of the night he would have decided that she wasn't coming back. If she ever did return, the bullet holes would drive her deeper into hiding. What was his fallback plan?

They knew the name of her printer, so that would be the logical place to pick up her trail. They would see her go in, and they would wait for her to come out. She would have to call Gordon and arrange to meet him somewhere. But there was another nagging thought. Was it possible that Gordon had joined the enemy camp?

He had told her his company had been warned, and there were probably a thousand business reasons why they wouldn't want to ignore the warning. Pam was ready to hear that she wouldn't get a book contract. But there was more. Someone had revealed that she was at the Hilton, in the company's suite. That raised the question of when Gordon had first been made aware of the warning. If he had told someone where she could be found, that information had to have reached John before he took off from the States. That would suggest that Gordon knew Masters wouldn't do the book at least a day before he had told her of his partners' hesitancy.

Pam couldn't believe he had known he was fingering her for an assassin. Whatever else might have happened, Gordon wouldn't have thrown in with a murder conspiracy. But it was entirely possible that he didn't want to get involved with her book.

She had to phone Gordon and take her chances. There was no one else except John Duke, who was waiting to bring her home so that she could surrender. Whether she was ready to drop the project and beg for forgiveness depended on what she heard from Gordon.

Pam came out of the park, crossed Park

Lane, and went into the lobby of the Dorchester Hotel, where the fussy Victorian decor was in stark contrast to the high, soaring lines of the Hilton lobby. She found a public telephone and checked her watch. Then she gave the hotel operator the number.

A woman answered in a voice that she recognized as that of Gordon's secretary. She asked for Gordon, waited for what seemed an eternity, and then heard his voice.

"I need to see you," she said.

"Of course. You're coming in this morning, aren't you?"

"I can't. Someone tried to kill me last night. He's probably watching your building."

There was a moment of stunned silence. Then "My God," in a tone that registered shock. "Who? What happened?"

"I'll tell you when you get here. I'm in the Dorchester lobby at the concierge desk. How long will it take you?"

"Fifteen minutes. Twenty at the most."

She took an escalator up to the mezzanine, where a balcony looked down on the entrance level. She found a place near a cocktail lounge where she could see the front doors. The lounge was still closed, so the location put her in shadows. She could see without being seen.

Time passed slowly. When she rechecked her watch, it was only two minutes since she had taken up her position. The next check was only five minutes after that. There was constant traffic through the front door. All she wanted to do was make sure that, when Gordon arrived, he arrived alone.

He finally appeared next to a uniformed doorman who pointed him to the concierge desk. Pam eased out of the shadows to get a better look and watched him cross to the desk. Then he stood back and looked around. She knew he was looking for her, and there didn't seem to be anyone searching with him. She went to the escalator, caught his eye, and motioned him into a coffee shop.

"What happened?" he asked in a stage whisper as soon as they were seated.

She glanced around. There was no one sitting near, and no one paying any attention to them. "Someone came into my suite during the night and fired three shots into my bed. Fortunately, I wasn't there. A friend from the States had called to warn me, and I moved to another room."

Gordon sat back, his eyes wide and fixed on hers. Pam thought his shock was genuine. A waitress brought them coffee. Neither ordered anything to eat. When she left, Gordon leaned forward over the table. "Did you call the police? Did you tell them at the hotel?"

"No. I got out of there and called you. There are things I need to know before I decide what to do. Will you help me?"

"Of course. Any way I can."

Her first question was about the book. Was Masters going to publish it? She had to know now, because it was too dangerous for her to stay around for the weekend.

"I'm not sure my associates have even started reading it," he began.

"Gordon, there are three bullet holes in the pillows of your guest suite. If you're not going to do the book, I have to run, and I'd better get started right now."

"Well, yes, I'm almost sure we will. I'll have to make a phone call just to be certain that there are no serious objections. And we'll need to agree on a contract."

"I'm not worried about the contract. What I'm worried about is how the people who tried to kill me found my hotel, and my room. Did you tell anyone where I was staying?"

"No! No one," he said positively. But then, in a less authoritative voice, he continued,

"Well, except my secretary, of course. She made the arrangements. And our business manager. He's the one who drew up your bank draft and sent it to the hotel. Oh, and my driver. We did pick you up and drop you off."

Pam raised her hand to stop him. She didn't need to hear any more particulars. It was apparent that many people at Masters knew she was in the company's hotel suite. Anyone who knew Masters was her publisher could have gotten the information in a dozen ways.

"The last thing I need to know is when you found out that your partner was being pressured to drop the book."

"Yesterday morning. He stopped by just before noon."

Pam smiled. That meant that John Duke and his Washington friends didn't learn from Gordon that his company was being pressured. That information had to have come from another source. "Thank you, Gordon. Now maybe you can make that phone call so we'll know if we're working together."

She ordered a muffin and more coffee while she waited for Gordon to return.

He came back to the table with a self-satisfied grin. "Well, they're not completely happy with it, but they're yielding to my judgment. Masters will do your book. With your help, we can finish vetting all the details over the weekend and start production on Monday. Now the only question is, Where are we going to put you up?"

"Wherever it is, you and I can be the only ones who know about it."

He thought for a moment and then asked, "What about here? The Dorchester?"

"They could follow you here," Pam reminded him.

"I wouldn't have to come here. There's a business services office. You could set up a mailbox and send your material on the Internet. With e-mail and telephone conferencing, we could work without anyone knowing where you are."

"I'd have to stay in my room," Pam mused.

Gordon shook his head. "Nonsense. Your American friends can't watch every hotel in London. You could come and go as you please so long as you didn't come near my office. Maybe you'd need a raincoat with a turned-up collar, and some sort of hat to hide your hair, but you could be totally anonymous."

"How would I register? Hotel desk clerks don't always keep secrets."

"My card," he said but instantly changed his mind. "No, I suppose my name would be the one they would ask for right after yours. It can't be anyone from Masters."

"Certainly not a partner," Pam added.

Gordon's eyes brightened, and he flashed a generous smile. "My secretary," he said. "I'll borrow her card and make a deposit to her account. Your name won't be anywhere. Worst case, someone will think that I'm shagging her!"

They spent a few minutes weighing all that might go wrong. The plan was the best they could come up with. Gordon went back to the office to get his secretary's credit card, which he would send to the concierge's desk in an envelope marked with Pam's name. She would need to show identification to claim the envelope. Then she would use the secretary's name, Emma Rose, when she registered. Even Emma would have no idea of where Pam was staying until her statement came in.

Pam went back to the shadows outside the closed lounge on the mezzanine. On her way, she stopped at a telephone booth and put in a call to British Airways to have them page a passenger at Heathrow. The message she left was, "I'll be staying around for a few more days. Have a safe trip, and thanks for your help."

She stayed in hiding for a few hours, taking a booth in the cocktail lounge as soon as it opened for business. Then she went to the desk and claimed the envelope. Emma Rose's credit card was inside, along with a handwritten note from Gordon.

It was Emma who spilled the beans. She was called by someone claiming to be a friend of yours who was in town just for the evening. She told him where you could be found.

Needless to say, she has no idea where you're staying now.

Pam went to the desk and checked in without incident. From her room high up in the hotel, she could see all of Hyde Park, with its Serpentine Lake. In the first-class lounge at Heathrow, John Duke listened to his message and cursed under his breath. He took his bag and went to the courtesy desk. "Change of plans," he said, sounding pained. "I won't be flying with you this afternoon." He handed over his two tickets. "Can you take care of these for me?"

FORTY-FOUR

Glen had run out of patience. Pam had been gone for a week with no word whatsoever. He didn't know whether she had reached London and made contact with Masters, or whether her book had been accepted or rejected. He couldn't live with the silence. He had to know.

He placed a phone call to Masters and asked for the editor who was working with Pam Leighton. He was told that there was no work in progress authored by a Pam Leighton. Next he pushed up the executive ladder, using his position as president of Thomas Howell to reach the executive offices. Again he wondered whether Masters was planning on doing anything with a book by Pam Leighton. "The reason I ask is that I've heard rumors you were working with her. I think you ought to know that we have her under contract."

The implied threat of a legal problem got

the attention of an officer who immediately had him connected with Gordon Frasier. Gordon denied that he had a contract with Pam Leighton but allowed that she "had a most interesting book." He was, of course, concerned that she might be contracted to another publisher.

" 'Might' isn't the word I would use," Glen said. "I have the contract right here in my hand. Her book, tentatively titled *Fouling the Air,* belongs to Thomas Howell."

Fortunately, Glen said, he was heading to London on another matter. Perhaps Gordon could arrange a meeting with Miss Leighton and the two of them. "I'm sure we can work this out."

Gordon agreed and asked Glen to call him when he arrived in London. Then he sent Pam an e-mail:

I have been contacted by the president of Thomas Howell, Mr. Glen Hubbard, who claims that he has your book under contract. He wants to meet with you and me. How should I respond?

Glen had his travel agent make reservations for a flight that night to London. He also booked a reservation in a small but tidy business hotel on the edge of Soho.

He went to his apartment, packed a change of clothes in a suitcase, and added some of the things that Pam had left at his place — a nightgown, an atomizer of perfume, and bath soap. Then his limo arrived to take him to Kennedy International Airport. At nine P.M. his plane took off, scheduled for a five A.M. landing at Heathrow. As he settled into the overnight flight, he thought of what he might say to Pam to get her to drop the project. He knew his contract was no longer valid, because he had personally signed the release of all Thomas Howell's obligations to Pam. But Pam, because of her rushed departure, certainly wasn't carrying a copy of the release. They would have to talk, face-to-face.

They had discussed the issues already. He was in love with her and wanted her to marry him. They had every reason to hope for a happy life together. Except for her book. It was the book that kept them apart. Even after it was published, it would make her a pariah among the rich and powerful and hardly a perfect partner for the president of a prestigious publishing house. She had to drop the project.

This, Glen felt sure, would be his last chance to stop her. He had to sit her down and make her listen to reason.

Pam had decided to test Gordon Frasier's assurance that it would take an army to cover all the hotels in London and that she was perfectly safe to come and go. She had wandered around the cavernous lobby, left through one door and returned through another until she was sure that no one was moving with her. Then she had walked a short way to Oxford Street and found a clothier with reasonable prices showing in the window. She bought a bottom-of-the-line trench coat and a stylish dark blue beret. When she came out into the street, she could see that she blended in with the pedestrian flow.

She felt safe. As far as she could tell, Gordon was the only person in the city who knew where to find her. Her would-be killers at the Hilton might well be checking hotel registers, but they wouldn't find her name. Probably they would be camped out at Masters's offices, but she wasn't going to be there. And if they were watching the streets around the main West End hotels, they wouldn't recognize her. Still, she remembered Glen's warning. She was the amateur. The professionals had assets that she couldn't even imagine. She might feel free, but she couldn't let herself become complacent. She couldn't afford a mistake.

She returned to the Dorchester and went to its business center. The room was buzzing as traveling executives sat at computers or paced impatiently around giant copiers. The attendant, a middle-aged woman with all the authority of an office manager, directed her to an available computer. Pam went into her e-mail and found a list of questions that demanded answers. The last item was Gordon's note about Glen Hubbard and his claim of a contract with Thomas Howell. She responded:

Glen Hubbard knows that Howell canceled our agreement. It's best if he doesn't learn where I am until after the book is published.

She spent the next two hours answering Masters's editorial comments and requests for documentation. But her thoughts kept drifting back to Glen. He was one of only two people in the States who had known that she had survived her fall from the ferry. She had told him she was going to London, and had told him about Masters, information that had been relayed within hours to her enemies in Washington. Once again she had to consider that the people who were reporting her every move had to be in his office. She could suspect Glen himself, except that he loved her, had supported her from the beginning, and had nearly killed himself trying to save her manuscript.

The only other person who knew where she was and what she was up to was Peter Salerno. When she met him, he had been the obvious candidate to be a government agent, and he had been in the perfect position to reveal her connection with Carl Weiss and arrange the kidnapping of Ronda. But he, too, had put himself at great risk for her. If his mission was to stop the publication of *Fouling the Air,* he never would have jumped off the ferry to save her.

That left John Duke, who knew her much better than either of the other two men. John wanted the book stopped for personal as well as political reasons, and he had access to all the resources of the government. He was the logical one for frightened lobbyists and lawmakers to turn to. But John had rushed across the ocean to warn her of the dangers, and had probably saved her from assassination. She believed he had been sincere when he promised to use his influence to get her exonerated, and maybe even when he confessed his mistake and asked her to come back into his life.

Or maybe none of them was against her. They might be victims just as she was, with their phones tapped, their e-mail copied, and their offices watched. Pam had taken every possible precaution. But the government and military spooks might be laughing hysterically over her stupid cloak-and-dagger efforts.

If that was true, perhaps even Masters was in on the scheme. Couldn't the Americans have enlisted their British counterparts in the name of international security? Was it possible that Gordon knew very well he was never going to publish Pam's book? Perhaps he was just gathering every shred of support she had for her charges and planning to turn it over to the authorities. He had admitted that the location of her hotel room had come from his office.

The more Pam considered the possibilities, the more paranoid she became. But there was nothing she could do. She couldn't run, because they were always only a step behind her. She couldn't hide, because they were always able to find her. She could press ahead at her own peril. Or she could fly back to John Duke and beg forgiveness from his friends.

FORTY-FIVE

Peter sat at the reception desk in Carl Weiss's offices, chatting about his doctoral thesis, which had just been approved. He needed a quote for printing a very limited edition. "One for the library and one for me," he teased. "Oh, and maybe another for my mother."

"What about me?" Ronda said. "I'd like to read it."

"All you'd do is tear off the cover and hang it on the wall with all the other titles that no one reads."

Ronda had come back to work two days after her kidnapping, physically unharmed and mentally no worse off for her ordeal. She was distressed that Pam had lost her book, and assumed that Pam had simply walked off the ferry and chosen to vanish. "I really thought you two were an item," she had told Peter. "I can't believe she just walked away from you."

Peter had shrugged. "Just a friend. A very interesting lady, and she had written a very explosive book. All I was doing was giving her a place to hide."

As Ronda had told it, her kidnapping was a model of efficiency, handled by men who seemed more like business executives than dangerous thugs. They had opened the rear door of a parked car in her face as she walked to her bus stop. A man standing by the car had simply pushed her in, and another man, already in the car, had put a handkerchief over her face. "It was like a dentist," she had explained. "He tells you to count to ten, but you never get past three. Time just stops for a little while."

She had awakened in a hotel room. Anything with the name of the hotel on it had been taken out, but the decor was luxurious. Her kidnappers had a generous expense account. They apologized for detaining her and told her exactly what was involved. Pam Leighton had no right to publish her book, and they were going to take it from her.

They had kept her in the room all morning, parked in front of the television to keep her entertained. A young woman who had joined them sat in a chair on the other side of the bed. One of the men sat patiently at the desk. The other man came and left several times, bringing lunch on one occasion. The telephone had rung a couple of times, and the man at the desk had answered with "Yes, okay, will do" and other responses that told her nothing. It was in the evening when they asked her to make the telephone call that set up the exchange.

The three had driven her across the bridge to Staten Island, then brought her to the ferry slip. They directed her to a bench and told her to wait there until Pam came and got her. "Everything is going well," one of them had told her. "Just don't move and screw things up."

That was the last she saw of any of them. When Pam didn't show up, she had taken a taxi back over the bridge to the closest subway station.

Would she recognize the men? her father had asked. "Of course."

Could she describe them? Not well. They were tall, dark, and reasonably good looking. There were no distinctive features or mannerisms. The same went for the woman. Ronda might be able to pick her out of a lineup, but she couldn't describe her in enough detail to let a sketch artist do his work.

When he had listened to Ronda's story, Peter remembered the man who had lifted

Pam over the rail. He might recognize him even though he had gotten only the quickest glimpse. But he couldn't describe him. The guy was too ordinary. He had also thought that there wouldn't be much point in Ronda describing her captors to the police. They were probably operatives brought in from another city who were on their way home before she had gotten tired of waiting at the ferry terminal.

Now Peter was hoping that Ronda and her father had learned something about Pam's whereabouts. He had not heard a word since they had met at Kennedy Airport. Surely if she had struck a publishing deal with Masters in London, someone would have contacted Carl Weiss for a contract release. Peter raised the issue casually, as if he had no particular interest.

"We transferred the rights to Masters," Ronda told him. "We wouldn't do anything to keep her from publishing in England, and we wouldn't dare take the book after everything that has happened."

But had Masters taken up the book that Weiss had released? Glen Hubbard would know. Peter had recognized the close relationship between Pam and Glen. If Pam was going to talk to anyone on this side of the ocean, Glen was a likely candidate.

When he got back to his office, Peter called Glen's apartment, only to find himself talking to a machine. He hung up, not wanting to leave his signature on the answering machine. Then he phoned Glen's office, acting as a friend trying to reach him. All he could learn was that Mr. Hubbard was away and wouldn't be back until sometime the following week. Did he want to leave a message?

What were his options? If Peter wanted to stay on top of Pam's activities, he would have to go to London. But where in London? The only possible lead was Masters's offices. It was already late in the evening in London, too late for a business call. He set his alarm for four A.M., which would be the beginning of the workday in England. When the alarm sounded, he got up and poured himself a cup of coffee in the hope of sharpening his mind. Then he dialed Masters's number.

A cheerful voice answered. He asked if it might be possible to speak with the editor handling a new book by Pam Leighton. "Oh, I'd have no way of knowing who that might be," the woman answered. She told him how many books were being processed through Masters at any given time. He asked for a senior editor and found himself talking to a very self-important English voice. "Certainly not," the man said. "This isn't a telephone directory service."

Peter waited until the opening of business in New York. When he was routed through to Glen's office, he claimed to be an associate of Mr. Hubbard. Hubbard, he said, had failed to arrive at a scheduled meeting in London. Did she know where he might be reached? "Of course," the secretary said. "He's staying at the Mandarin at Hyde Park."

So, Glen Hubbard *had* gone to London, Peter thought, where all he could do was screw up arrangements that had long been in place. He called the university's travel service and booked a tourist reservation on an afternoon flight.

FORTY-SIX

Glen Hubbard marched into Gordon Frasier's office with a wide smile and a strong handshake. He was jovial and charming, not at all like a man who had come into the enemy's den to press a lawsuit. Gordon, for his part, was pleasant but cautious. If Pam was right in assuring him that her contract with Thomas Howell had been voided, then Hubbard had to be here on a different mission. Perhaps, now that the book was to become a reality, he was hoping to offer Pam a better price, or negotiate for U.S. rights.

Then, too, there was a romantic angle. Glen was the man who, according to Pam, had been steadfast in his support for her, both professionally and emotionally. He had welcomed her into his apartment, given her use of his summer house, and nearly gotten killed trying to save her manuscript. All this went well beyond the business obligations

of a publisher, sounding more like the hero-
ics of a lover. Perhaps Hubbard thought she
was slipping away from him.

The meeting had to start with Glen's alleged reason for flying across the ocean, so
Gordon leaned forward and made a bridge
with his fingertips on the edge of his desk.
Glen accepted a cup of coffee from a secretary, opened his briefcase, and took out the
contract in question. "Pretty much our
standard agreement with new authors," he
told Gordon. "I'm sure your version isn't
very different." He called particular attention to the paragraphs that gave Thomas
Howell exclusive world publishing rights
and gave them a full year to publish the
book after the manuscript was submitted.
"We received the manuscript only a month
ago, and, at that, it wasn't complete. So it
will be a long time before Miss Leighton is
free to take the book to someone else."

Gordon responded with facts that he was
certain Glen already knew. Howell had
executed a release freeing them from the
obligation to publish the book and, at the
same time, giving up all claims to it. In addition, the book had already gone to another
publisher, Carl Weiss in New York. He then
put on the table a document from Carl
Weiss transferring the rights to his company.

Glen claimed that his legal people knew of no release. "Surely if a release existed, Miss Leighton would have given you a copy." Gordon explained the circumstances under which Pam had left the United States and the reasons why she hadn't brought her legal files with her.

Glen was sympathetic to all of Gordon's points, and he offered "an obvious solution." The two of them should meet with Pam Leighton, and, if she insisted that she had a release, she should be given the opportunity to produce it. It was at this point that Gordon told him he couldn't summon Pam to a meeting because she didn't want to reveal her whereabouts. "We're corresponding through Internet mailboxes," Gordon said, implying that even he didn't know where Pam could be found.

"Use the mailbox," Glen suggested. "You can tell her how important this is. We can meet in secret. No one has to know where she's staying."

Gordon said he would leave her an e-mail telling her exactly that. "But," he cautioned, "I don't think she'll agree. She has already seen evidence that people bent on stopping the book are here in London."

Glen's surprise was apparent. "Who?"

"We don't know that. If we did, we'd be

more able to protect her."

"But you are protecting her, aren't you?" Glen demanded. "Surely you have security people or bodyguards."

"I wouldn't know where to send them," Gordon lied. "All we have is an electronic mailbox address." He agreed to send her the e-mail and to contact Glen with her answer. "Where are you staying?" Gordon asked.

"The Mandarin," Glen said. "I'll be in all afternoon."

Pam was hard at work in the Dorchester's business center, answering the final editorial and legal questions that Gordon's lawyers had sent her. She stretched in her chair, fighting the fatigue in her shoulders and back, then put the finishing touches on her work. She was in the process of shutting down when she saw the new message from Gordon:

You were right. Mr. Hubbard is here hoping for a meeting with you. He was stunned to hear that you were attacked in London and concerned for your safety. I told him any meeting would be up to you. Please advise me of your wishes.

Glen had come anyway. She had refused the meeting and was sure that Gordon would have relayed her decision to New York. Still, he had come all this way to see her. Did it make any sense to avoid him? She had separated from him precisely to keep him from becoming involved. Obviously, that was a risk he wanted to take. She was afraid of giving him any information that might pass through his office. But if he was in London, that was not a concern. He could certainly be trusted to take her name and address off any message that he sent back to New York. When she had stood on the rotting dock, wet and frozen, he had been the only one she could trust.

Why had he come? She was only a few days away from completing her work in London. She would be seeing him in New York shortly. There had been no reason for him to suspect that danger had followed her across the ocean, so he wasn't here to protect her. Nor did it seem likely that he was still hoping to persuade her to stop the book. They had been through that several times, and he knew how determined she was. When he'd wished her success as she was leaving for London, he knew she wouldn't be talked out of it.

She had to think clearly and decided a

long walk in the fresh air would help. There was a light rain falling, but with her coat collar turned up, she didn't even need an umbrella. She walked briskly along Oxford Street to Regent, then down to Piccadilly, where crowds were gathering for the matinees.

Glen didn't have the same sources of information as John did. Glen's effort to find her had been clumsy and transparent, nothing like the government agents who, according to John, had known where she was going before she had gotten on the plane. The more she thought about it, the more obvious it became that Glen wasn't part of any conspiracy.

Still, she kept going back to the thought that there were only two people who had known she was alive — Glen and Peter. One of them must have blown her cover. Maybe unintentionally. Glen could have talked in his office. Peter might have been followed to the airport when he gave her the plane ticket. Or maybe one of them was working with John's friends.

She made a few cautionary turns on her way back to the hotel, stopping at several store windows on Oxford Street to check the people around her. Once back at the Dorchester, she sent Gordon an e-mail telling him that he could bring Glen to her suite that night for a late supper. She said it was best if he didn't know the hotel until he arrived. She didn't want him calling his office to tell them where he could be reached.

John Duke had been keeping a close watch on the front door of the Masters offices. Pam, he thought, would show up there sooner or later. He also had good photos of Gordon Frasier, courtesy of the publisher's publicity material and coverage in the business press. If Pam didn't come to Masters, then Gordon might go to Pam. John was prepared to follow either one of them.

Last night John had followed Gordon in a taxi and been led to an apartment in Kensington. That turned out to be Gordon's in-town home. This morning he had watched the arrival at Masters of a man who seemed American and had difficulty with the English money he needed to pay his fare. It took John a few moments to place him, but then he realized it was Pam's New York publisher. When the American came out an hour later, John had gambled that he must have come to see Pam and followed him to the Mandarin Oriental. He had wasted the rest of the morning there and, when the publisher came down alone for lunch in the hotel dining room, decided that Pam wasn't there. Now he was back at the taxi stand across from Masters's doorway, waiting for either Pam or Gordon.

The light rain had been falling steadily, and even with an umbrella he was damp and chilly. He knew that he couldn't keep this up much longer. Stakeouts, he had been told, could take days, even weeks. He had to be back in Washington on Monday.

John dreaded returning to the capital a failure. Senator Lawrence had not been subtle in advising him that, if the book came out, his career would be in jeopardy. He desperately needed one more chance with his former mistress.

FORTY-SEVEN

Peter had landed late at night at Heathrow and taxied to the Mandarin Oriental Hotel. He planned to check in until he saw the rates and realized that he could go through his entire savings account in just a few days. Instead, he gave his bag to the bell captain and settled into a leather chair.

In the morning, he had kept a sharp eye on the lobby and caught Glen Hubbard coming down for breakfast. Then he had followed Glen until he entered the Masters building. He was still waiting when Glen came out and went back to the Mandarin. Once again Peter settled into a soft leather chair.

At noon he retrieved his bag from the bell captain and went into the men's room, where he shaved and changed his shirt. He was watching from the lobby when Glen came down for lunch and dined alone. Peter had been tempted to walk up to Glen, reintroduce himself, and ask where Pam was staying. But there was something illogical about Glen Hubbard being in London and calling on Masters Publishing. Obviously, he knew that Masters had taken over Pam's book. But just as obviously, he didn't know where Pam was. Peter had assumed that Glen would have been the first person she called when she settled in London. He checked into the least expensive room the Mandarin could offer, and even then found himself with a rate that went far beyond his imagination. Then he went back down to the lobby and took up his vigil for Glen, or for Pam. There were no other leads for him to follow.

He didn't recognize Gordon Frasier when he came into the lobby, nor did he notice John Duke, who came through the door only seconds later. Gordon went to the house phone and spoke at some length to one of the guests. John hovered at a distance, watching Gordon's every move.

Glen stepped out of an elevator, spotted Gordon, and walked to meet him. They spoke for an instant, then stepped into the lobby bar. It was then that Peter caught sight of John. He had no idea who he was, but it was obvious that he was following Glen and his friend. Peter let the two men find their place and waited until the man following them had slipped into a booth behind them. Did Glen know he was being followed? And, most important, where was Pam?

Peter sat outside the bar for nearly an hour. He could see Glen and his friend chatting amiably and had to assume that the second person through the door was still watching them. He could guess that Glen's companion was someone from his London office, or someone from Masters. But who was the one following them?

Glen and his associate came out, and seconds later the man following them appeared. Peter joined in at the end of the line and smiled at the thought that everyone seemed to be following everyone else. He remembered Pam telling him that she was being hounded by people who seemed to be government agents. The man with Glen appeared too relaxed to be an American enforcer. His casual attire and shaggy haircut suggested an artist more than a Secret Service robot. But the third man was well turned out, in dark suit and crisp white shirt. His face was painfully shaven, and his haircut was perfectly tapered. He could very well belong to some country's army of special agents.

The taxis were lined up in the hotel driveway, moving to the door only when the doorman blew his whistle and gave them permission. Peter watched while Glen and his friend slid into one taxi. The third man rushed to commandeer the next cab in line. Peter took the following taxi and told the driver to follow the cab ahead. He hoped that he could hang on to the government-agent type, and he hoped that the man was professional enough to keep up with Glen's taxi. It would be ridiculous if no one could keep up the chase, and if the line of cabs didn't lead to Pam.

Enveloped in traffic, they crawled along Kensington. Peter could see the first taxi half a block ahead, and the next one separated from him by only three cars. But this was no high-speed chase. The West End traffic made midtown Manhattan seem like a speedway.

The first car worked its was to the left and then turned onto Park Lane. The second taxi was hemmed in and couldn't follow. Peter pointed out the first car to his driver and told him to follow. For a moment it seemed that Glen was getting away, but then his car turned in to the entrance of the Dorchester Hotel. Peter paid off his driver in the middle of the street. Dodging traffic, he got to the hotel entrance just in time to sec Glen and his companion going through the enormous revolving doors. He hesitated, not wanting to get close enough for Glen to recognize him. When he entered, the two men had just reached the house phones. Glen's associate took a phone, waited, then spoke to someone. He nodded to Glen, and the two walked to a waiting elevator.

Again Peter had to hold back, knowing that he couldn't get into the same car with Glen. Instead, he found the lights that indicated the floor each car was on and followed the progress of Glen's car until it stopped at the tenth floor. He waited tensely for the light to move again. If it continued upward, he wouldn't know whether they had gotten off at the tenth floor or whether someone else had gotten on. When the light started down again, he stepped into the next car that arrived. He pushed the button for ten.

The corridor was quiet and empty, but there were turns in the hallway that made it impossible to see from one end to the other. He could move slowly, listening for a moment at each door, but anyone stepping out of a room would take notice of a man with his ear pressed to a nearby door. Then he noticed a trace of light under one of the doors and, farther away, an identical light under another. He realized the lights identified the rooms that were occupied. He began moving to his left, hesitating for just a second at each of the rooms marked by light. At one he caught the sound of a voice that he didn't recognize. At another there were children's voices. He kept moving, careful at each turn to take a quick glimpse ahead. His greatest danger would be getting caught in a long stretch of hallway when Glen Hubbard stepped out of a room.

John had watched in frustration as the taxi he was following made a sudden turn into Park Lane. His own cab was hemmed in by unyielding traffic and had to go well past the intersection before the driver could make it to the curb. John jumped out, pressed a five-pound bill into the driver's hand, and rushed back. He turned into Park Lane hopeful of catching up with the two men. He knew immediately that he would never find their car in the sea of identical London taxis creeping up the street. But if he was lucky, the men had gotten out and were in the entrance of one of the buildings.

He reached the Dorchester, pulled another five-pound note from his pocket, and went to the doorman. He flashed the money, then asked if two men had just arrived in a taxi. "One is an American," he said and did his best to describe what Glen had been wearing.

"Yes, just a few minutes ago. An American and an English gentleman," the doorman remembered. His well-trained hand eased up toward the five-pound note.

"Where did they go?"

"Into the hotel. I didn't follow them, and they didn't need a porter, but perhaps one of my friends inside would remember." He didn't make a move until John had handed over the tip, then suggested, "You might check at the registration desk and the concierge's desk. I'll call ahead and tell them you're coming." He reached for the outside telephone that kept him in touch with the world inside.

The lobby was cavernous, and it took John a few seconds to get his bearings. He went to the front desk, waited for a clerk to become available, then asked if anyone had just made an inquiry. The clerk acknowledged the call from the doorman but regretted that no one had stopped by to ask for a guest. John went to the concierge, where he got the same courteous answer. "Of course, they might have gone into the bar," the man

492

said, pointing across the lobby.

John walked through the bar as if considering a drink but stealing glances at the occupied tables. They weren't there. He went back into the lobby and walked from one end to the other, glancing at the faces of people he passed and those sitting in the many furniture groupings. He had to conclude that if the doorman had really remembered the two, they had gone straight up to a room.

He settled into a soft chair near the front door that commanded a view of the main bank of elevators. It might be a very long wait, and he couldn't be positive Pam was even in the building. But it was the only chance he had. He had to find her, and do whatever it took to stop her from publishing her book.

FORTY-EIGHT

Pam was thrilled when Glen stepped through the doorway into her suite. She rushed into his arms and held him close. "You shouldn't have come," she said. "I wanted to keep you out of this."

"I had to come," he whispered in her ear. "I couldn't let you do this. It ruins everything."

Gordon, who was still standing in the doorway, discreetly cleared his throat. It was obvious that there was something going on between Pam and her former publisher, and that the two of them would rather be alone. But, the meeting was supposed to be to discuss the contract Glen had left with him. Gordon hoped that it would be at least part of the agenda.

Glen walked Pam to a sofa and settled down beside her. Gordon took an upholstered chair across from them. "Should we discuss the contract now," he asked, "or would you rather wait until after dinner?"

"I don't think the contract is the issue," Pam answered, looking to Glen for confirmation.

Glen spoke directly to Gordon. "I didn't come to debate a contract. I'm here to help Pam understand that her book will be our undoing. Hers, certainly. And yours and mine in all probability."

Pam focused on Glen. "We've had this conversation before. I'm doing what I think I have to do."

Gordon stood. "Perhaps a cocktail," he offered. He stepped over to the bar and began pulling down glasses. Glen and Pam were face-to-face. Pam was starting to explain all the reasons why she felt the book had to go to press. "I'll have them send up our dinner," Gordon said. "It should be only a few minutes. I've already ordered."

Glen accepted a Scotch with a bit of ice, and Pam agreed to a glass of wine. Gordon joined them with a whiskey. "Here's to *Fouling the Air*," he toasted. "May it climb to the top of the bestseller lists." Glen countered with a toast of his own. "Here's to common sense."

They walked to the glass doors that looked out over the park. Glen released the lock and stepped outside, where he could look up and down the length of Park Lane. To his right, Marble Arch was bathed in a bright, white light. Pam followed him out to the edge of the balcony, and Gordon moved up next to her. He began pointing out the landmarks, looking down to Green Park and the distant Houses of Parliament. Wherever they turned, Gordon found a history lesson and began piecing together the story of the great city.

They were interrupted by a knock on the door and opened it to a room service waiter who pushed in a stainless-steel cart. Instantly he went to work, setting a table in the sitting room and pulling up three chairs. Within just a few minutes, they were seated while their waiter explained the evening's selection.

They were to begin with cold cucumber soup, served in cups set in beds of ice. Next he promised a salad, seasoned with balsamic vinegar and oil and shavings of pungent cheese. And then the Dover sole that he had taken the liberty of boning and flaming. The desert was to be a bread pudding that was a specialty of the house.

Glen could certainly have done without an elaborate dinner. He would gladly have pushed the table aside and launched into his argument against publishing the book.

Pam silently agreed that the topic of conversation was more important than the meal. Gordon thought he might excuse himself but decided he couldn't walk out on a meal served by the Dorchester. "Now, about this contract," he began as soon as the waiter had served the soup and withdrawn from the table. Pam explained that Howell had decided not to publish the book and had released all rights back to her. Glen agreed that his company had indeed let the book go, but with the right to bid again if another company agreed to publish.

"Are you planning to reacquire Pam's book?" Gordon asked.

Glen admitted that his company had no such plan. "The problem is that some of the most powerful people in the United States think the book is an outrageous slander," he said. "They have tried to destroy it, attacked Pam, and perhaps already killed one of her important sources. I have no doubt they'll try again."

"These are government officials?" Gordon asked.

"Some of them are. But there are others: lobbyists, union heads, corporate officers."

"Do you know who these people are?"

Glen was about to answer, but the waiter came forward to serve the next course. They sat in silence while the soup dishes were removed and the salad served. Then Glen got back to the subject. "We know who some of them are. But that's the next problem. There's no hard proof. All the records have been destroyed. The woman with the most damaging files has been killed, and Pam was forced to surrender her files. You can be sure that, by now, the Electric Energy Institute has shredded all the originals." He turned to Pam. "In the end, it's just going to be your word on what you remember from the files."

"I've told Gordon all this," Pam said.

"And our solicitors," Gordon added. "They're quite pleased with her testimony and her recollection of places and dates."

Glen sighed with impatience. "Gordon, they'll cut her to pieces if she ever has to testify. They'll make it look as if the whole book is the bitchy revenge of a woman trying to get back at the man who dumped her."

Gordon focused on Pam. "What man?"

"John Duke, director of the institute. He and I were . . . lovers."

"Oh, dear," Gordon allowed.

"I'm sorry," Pam said. "I should have told you."

Gordon probed for the details of Pam's

affair. He seemed disturbed when she said that she and John had been lovers for two years, and flabbergasted when he learned that John had left Pam to rejoin his wife. "This puts you in a very bad light," he said. "You'll undoubtedly be raked over the coals."

Pam nodded. "I expect I will. Back when I started this project, that fear would have been more than enough to get me to quit. But now there are other people involved. One of them is dead."

Glen had seen the flicker of doubt in Gordon's expression. The Masters partner seemed to be wavering in his commitment, perhaps looking for a graceful exit from what he now understood could be an embarrassing and degrading venture. Glen still had other arguments that could turn Gordon away from publication.

"There are certainly going to be libel suits," he said. "My firm figures as many as thirty, with defamed persons seeking millions, plus more in punitive amounts. They won't go after Pam. They'll go after the deep pockets. They could put both of us out of business."

"Why both of us?" Gordon asked. "You just told me that Thomas Howell had decided not to publish."

"We edited the book," Glen said, "and provided assistance to the author. We could be dragged in."

Pam stiffened abruptly. Her eyes flashed at Glen and then narrowed in anger. "Is that what this is all about? You want me to stop because you might get dragged in?"

"Of course not," he snapped back. "It's what it has always been. I don't want you to get hurt, or maybe killed. Even if you aren't attacked directly, I don't want you to get tarred and feathered. Damn! How many ways can I prove to you that I love you?"

Once again Gordon cleared his throat to remind them that he was present. He signaled the waiter, who hurried over to clear the salads, creating an ominous silence.

"Well, I think we've aired the issues," Gordon said. "I have a much clearer picture of the problems, and, at least for the moment, I've lost my appetite." He stood and came around the table to Glen. "I wish you a pleasant trip home," he said, offering his hand. "I appreciate your coming all the way over to enlighten me." He smiled at Pam. "I suppose we'll talk on Monday, just as we'd planned." She nodded, feeling sure that Monday's meeting would be brief, polite, and totally negative.

Pam and Glen stayed at the table until the

door clicked shut. The flustered waiter lingered for instructions. Glen told him that they were finished and asked him to clear everything away. Then he went to the bar, where the glasses and bottles Gordon had taken down were still standing, and fixed himself another Scotch, this time with a generous helping of ice. He turned to find Pam standing close.

"It was you all along," she said as a simple statement of fact.

"What are you talking about?"

"When your bosses told you to drop the project, they also told you to make damn sure it never got published anywhere."

"Don't be ridiculous." He turned from her and marched out onto the balcony. She followed at his heels. "You didn't just contract the book. You edited it. You collaborated every step of the way. The book makes you a target, and Thomas Howell has the deep pockets. That's why you had to talk me out of it."

"Pam, you're saying crazy things. I love you. I want to marry you. For God's sake, I nearly got burned to death trying to save your book."

Her eyes dropped. "You know, you're the second man in the last few days who has told me he loves me, as long as I don't do anything to hurt his career. You'd think I would have caught on by now."

She turned away, but Glen grabbed her wrist and pulled her back. "Don't you see what you're throwing away just to write your damn book? I'm the top man in a subsidiary of a global giant. I haven't even come close to my potential. We could have anything we want. We could have each other. You wouldn't always be looking over your shoulder to see if anyone was following you."

Pam pulled her wrist out of his grasp. "It's too late for that. Two nights ago someone tried to kill me. He fired three bullets into my bed. My only chance is to get the book out so that there's no reason to kill me."

"You can have your life back in a minute. All I have to do is make one phone call and tell them that the book is dead. They don't want . . ." His voice trailed off when he saw the flash of recognition in her eyes. In his rush to persuade her, he had added a fact that he'd never told her. Glen knew who "they" were. He knew who to call.

"Who would you call, Glen?" she asked calmly. "Who is it who can decide in a minute that I'm no longer a threat?" She was standing directly in front of him and waiting for his answer.

FORTY-NINE

Peter had walked the corridor to one side of the main elevators without hearing a familiar voice. Now, back at the central elevator bank, he had a choice. He could start down the other end of the hallway using the same routine. Or he could give up the search, reasoning that the few voices he had heard were probably people close to the door, and that he couldn't hear voices well inside the rooms.

Maybe a better strategy was to return to the lobby and keep a close watch on the elevator doors. The two men would have to come down sooner or later. If they came to one of the lobby restaurants, Pam might be with them.

Peter's decision was made when he caught sight of the Englishman coming around a distant turn in the corridor and headed toward him. He turned away, walked back into the hallway he had just searched, and stopped at a dark door, pretending to be fumbling with a key. He expected that Glen would be just a few steps behind his friend, and he didn't want to confront him. With a quick glance, he saw that the Englishman was alone, but still he waited. Not until the man stepped into an elevator car did he turn back.

The room they had gone to was in that direction, and was at least beyond the first turn in the hallway. Peter started down the corridor at a brisk pace until he made the turn. A long section of corridor stretched before him, and he moved slowly now, lingering briefly at just the doors that showed light.

He could guess at what had happened. Glen, as desperate as he was himself for some word from Pam, had flown over to London. Glen, too, knew of the Masters connection but had the clout to demand an appointment with one of the publisher's senior executives, probably the man who had escorted him the hotel. He had spent the past hour in a meeting with Pam, and then the Masters executive, having delivered the visitor to Pam's hiding place, had decided to leave them together.

There wasn't anything left for him to accomplish, Peter realized. The night he had rescued her from the river, it had been obvious that Pam and Glen were in a relationship. Glen had taken the risk of compromising Pam's hiding place, but apparently Pam had been happy to see him. Peter could hardly hope for an enthusiastic welcome if he walked in on their reunion.

But he couldn't be certain that Pam was in the room with Glen. It had not been an unreasonable assumption that Glen had come to London to find her. Nevertheless, it was only an assumption. Glen Hubbard was a major figure in publishing who very likely had numerous business reasons to show up at Masters. The English publisher might well have introduced him to other parties in a business deal.

It was time for Peter to give up the search. Still, it would be reassuring to know that Pam was safe. If she wasn't in a room on this corridor, he could go back to the Masters building in the morning. He could identify the Masters manager who had brought Glen to the hotel and press him for news about Pam. He walked to the next doorway that showed a light and lingered to eavesdrop.

John Duke spotted Glen's partner as soon as the elevator door opened. He stayed in his chair while the man crossed the lobby and went to the front door. Then he stood and moved into position to follow.

The problem was that Glen was still upstairs. Should he wait for his only certain link with Pam, or should he stick with the lead that was available?

The Englishman went through the revolving doors and was greeted by the doorman. John pushed outside and stood a few steps behind them while they discussed a taxi. Then the doorman waved to the next cab in the queue. John pressed closer and heard the doorman repeat a street address. Then the doorman led Glen's companion down the steps to the car and pulled open the door. John recognized the address as the one where he had followed the Englishman the night before. Should he go there again, or should he stay here and wait for Glen Hubbard? He had just one night left to find Pam and put a stop to the book. He had to make the right choice.

FIFTY

Pam assembled all the pieces. Glen wasn't just on the edges of the Washington plot that had tried to kill her. He was at the center, with access to the key players. That was what she had learned from his careless mention of what he could achieve with one phone call. Yet it was impossible. He loved her, had been her first supporter, and had risked his life for her.

"Pam, you have to believe me. I'm trying to save both of us. We're in this together."

"You knew everything," she said in disbelief.

"Yes! Not in the beginning, but ever since we canceled your book. I knew what you were up against, and I was playing along with them to keep you out of danger."

"You knew they were going to kill Marion?" Her voice was turning icy.

"No. For God's sake, no!"

"But you told someone that Marion was

helping me, didn't you?"

"In a general way, I mentioned that John Duke's former secretary had some information for you. But I never guessed they would harm her. I was shocked when I heard she was dead. That's when I first realized how serious they were and what horrible danger you were in."

Pam was still face-to-face with him, standing in the opening to the balcony. "Who are *they*, Glen?" she demanded. "Who was it that you told?"

He hesitated. He shouldn't tell her, but there was no way to avoid it. "Intermedia. The chairman and his chief executive officer." He could tell by her expression that she didn't understand. "Intermedia doesn't care about you or your book. They're just doing what they have to do for friends in Washington." She still seemed bewildered. "They're in television. They need federal licenses. They're in newspapers. They need exemptions from federal restrictions. They make billions abroad and they need tax breaks. They give millions of dollars to the people who make the rules. It's the way they stay in business."

She was beginning to understand, but she couldn't believe what she was hearing. "Intermedia killed Marion Murray to stay in business?"

"No. Intermedia pulled the plug on your book because their congressional friends told them how embarrassing it would be. They've been watching the industry to make sure that no one publishes it. They expect a big payback."

"*You've been watching me!*" she exclaimed in anger. "That's why you suddenly became such a big man in the company. You told them you could keep me quiet. All of a sudden, you were important to the big boys."

He snapped back, "I told them I could keep you quiet in order to keep you alive. All the while I was assuring them I was warning you. I told you that you couldn't win. I warned you that you had no idea of what you were up against."

"You were screwing me, you bastard. You were fucking me to keep me quiet." She slapped him in the face. "Get out of my room. Go back to your handlers and tell them I'm going to add another chapter. This one is going to be about how killing someone is good for business."

She wheeled and rushed to the door, turned the knob, and started to open it. "Get out of my life," she ordered.

Glen grabbed her from behind, one arm

around her waist and the other around her shoulders. "You're being crazy!" he hissed into her ear. "Come back inside. Listen to me, for God's sake."

She screamed. His hand clamped over her mouth, and he lifted her back into the room. "I've told you the truth. I didn't kill anyone. I didn't throw you off a ferry. All I've ever done is try to save you."

She was struggling in his grasp, tearing at his arms. She freed her mouth for an instant and screamed, "Let go of me." Then he covered it with an even tighter grip.

"I had to stop you. I set myself on fire just to show you that it was too dangerous. The only one I hurt was myself."

Pam stopped struggling. Glen relaxed his grip a bit but still kept her locked in his arms. He slipped his hand away from her mouth. "It was all for you," he told her.

"You're a liar. A murderer. That's what my book will say."

"Pam, I can't let you publish that book. It will destroy everything. Everything!"

"Murderer," she screamed into his face.

He again clamped a suffocating hand across her mouth and locked her arm behind her back. "You can't say that. I won't let you." His voice suddenly took on an insane tone. "I won't let you destroy everything!"

He was pressing harder on the arm he held behind her back, driving her toward the balcony door. She could see the stone railing supported by decorative columns. Beyond it were the twinkling lights of the city. Far below was the darkness of Hyde Park.

FIFTY-ONE

Peter was moving slowly along the hallway when he heard a commotion beyond the next turn. He stopped to listen; two people were shouting. A man and a woman. Then it stopped as suddenly as it had started.

He moved quickly down the hallway and turned at the jog. He was sure it had been a man and a woman, maybe Glen and Pam. Ahead, on the right side, a door was ajar, light seeping out around the edges. Suddenly the momentary quiet was shattered by a woman's scream. He heard the word "Murderer!" and recognized Pam's voice.

Peter rushed to the partially open door and swung it open. He was looking directly across the sitting room at the open doors to the balcony. Glen had Pam in a hammerlock, her legs pressed against the stone railing, her head hanging over the edge. He was forcing her farther out, reaching down to her legs so that he could lift her over.

"Pam!" Peter screamed and rushed across the room. Glen spun around, still holding on to Pam's arm. His jaw was set and his face iron in his rage. Peter reached out to get a grip on Pam, leaving himself vulnerable to Glen's free arm. Glen slammed a fist into his side, deflecting the momentum of Peter's charge. Peter spun against the railing. His lower back struck the stone, and he lost his balance. For a moment, he was falling backward, his arms windmilling as he reached for a handhold. He snapped a grip on Pam's free hand and tipped back onto the balcony. Glen leaned out with another punch, which was short of the mark. Then Pam twisted away and was able to break free from his hold. He turned away from Peter and got a grip on her hair. She swung at him, and he pulled back for just an instant. It was at that instant, as he was leaning backward, that Peter landed a wild punch on the point of Glen's jaw. Glen fell back and toppled over the edge.

For an instant he was balanced on the top of the rail, with his weight and momentum pulling him out into the darkness. Pam made a grasp for his leg and caught the cuff of his trousers. Peter got both hands onto Glen's other foot. But they couldn't stop his fall. The fabric of his trousers slipped through Pam's grasp. The shoe came off. There was no scream as he fell. He was too stunned by the blow that had sent him over. Pam turned away. "Oh God. Oh my God!" she cried. She made it inside the doorway and then fell to her knees. Peter looked over and followed Glen's body as it disappeared into the night. He held the shoe in his hand.

John had stepped out to the sidewalk weighing his options. He had decided he should stay put at the hotel and wait for either Glen or Pam to appear. But he was stopped by a quick scream from somewhere high in the building. He looked up and saw farther down the wing of the hotel that there was a balcony door open with light streaming out. As he looked there was another scream, this one more piercing, definitely from a woman. The doorman came out from his post and looked in the direction John was looking.

Suddenly there were people struggling on the balcony, a man and a woman fighting wildly. "Jesus," the doorman gasped and ran back to the front door. John stood where he was, transfixed by the battle above. As the woman was pushed out over the edge of the rail, John knew exactly what was happening. He had found Pam's room, and now he was looking directly at her.

Then there was another person, a man who joined in the struggle. Pam screamed again, and it seemed that the two men were fighting. Then one of them fell backward over the decorative rail.

John followed the falling body for what seemed like an eternity. He thought he could make out every detail, see every motion of an arm or leg as it twisted in the wind. He felt his own scream of horror as it rose in his chest and caught in his throat. He heard an explosion as the body crashed against the ground. He was standing on the same spot when the doorman rushed past him. People came running from all directions.

John walked cautiously toward the place where the body had landed, afraid of what he might find. Glen had landed on hotel property, inside the fence that separated it from the sidewalk. The area was under construction. A trench had been covered by sheets of plywood.

The body had hit the plywood, shattering it with the force of a cannonball. Splintered wood was caved into the ditch. Glen was sitting, his back against the wall of the ditch, his vacant eyes looking up to the balcony he had fallen from. His face was nearly unmarked. Below his shoulders, the body was crumpled to half its size, mercifully covered by the remnants of his suit. Blood and gore were spattered out in every direction. John stood back, not at all anxious to press to the front of the crowd. He was gradually roused from his stupor by the warble of approaching sirens.

This was not the place for him to be. An American cabinet member who was supposed to be in Washington shouldn't be found at a crime scene in London. He didn't want to be in the background of a photograph, nor did he want to provide a statement for the police. He couldn't let himself be linked to a death that he felt sure would eventually be connected with a book that accused him of corrupting his government. It was time to cut his losses.

He turned and walked past the front door of the hotel. There were taxis in line, but the drivers had left them idling and run to get a look at the remains of the jumper. John was nearly to Marble Arch when he hailed a cab and went back to his hotel. "Keep the meter running," he said. "I'm checking out. I'll need a ride to the airport."

Peter had lifted Pam from her knees and helped her to the sofa. He went to the bar and brought back a whiskey, which she accepted without seeming to notice. It hung from her fingers while she stared blankly into space.

A hotel porter rushed into the room, paused as he passed Pam and Peter, then continued to the open balcony doors. He stepped out cautiously and strained his neck to look over the edge. He was afraid to get too close to where someone had just fallen over.

Then there was a hotel manager in formal dress, who ordered the porter away from the window and sat down beside Pam. "Are you all right, Miss Rose? There's a doctor on his way up." Peter was surprised when he heard "Miss Rose." It took him a second to realize that there were a lot of things he didn't understand about Pam Leighton.

FIFTY-TWO

The police were courteous, even though the circumstances were suspicious. Pam, they noted, had checked into the hotel under an assumed name after having entered the country illegally. They hoped she wouldn't bypass their immigration officials once again and leave the country until their inquiry was completed. Peter had entered the hotel looking for Pam, even though he had no reason to believe that she was staying there, and under an alias he didn't know. He described himself as "a friend of Miss Leighton," who had borrowed his apartment back in the States. They both confirmed that the dead man was a very close friend of Pam's who had suddenly turned on her and tried to kill her. Their stories hinted at a ménage à trois that had turned violent.

Gordon Frasier was interviewed as the last person who had seen Miss Leighton and

Mr. Hubbard together. He explained Hubbard's reason for coming to London and the discussion they'd had over rights to a book Miss Leighton had written. He had surmised there was a "personal relationship" between the publisher and the writer. They'd differed as to whether she should publish her book, but he had absolutely no reason to suspect that their difference would turn violent. He had no idea how Mr. Salerno fit into the relationship and, in fact, had never heard his name mentioned. The police took Peter's passport and warned him, too, against leaving the country.

The London tabloids were anything but courteous. Leading with photos of Glen's crumpled corpse in the excavation ditch, they described him as an American publisher who had died at the hands of his mistress and her new lover. Never missing a chance to embarrass the establishment, they also dragged in Gordon Frasier, identifying him as a member of the bizarre circle of international publishing figures who had obviously had a falling out.

The next day's interviews were held not in the comfort of the Dorchester Hotel but rather in sparsely furnished interrogation rooms. The common thread of the witnesses' testimony was the issue that the police found most difficult to grasp. Why would an American publisher rush across the ocean to stop publication of a book his firm had already decided not to publish? Why would Masters Publishing be interested in a book that was certain to prompt libel suits? Why would the American government be so determined to stop publication? The suspects' stories made no sense.

Yet as the day wore on, they began to gather evidence that corroborated the stories. The doorman and several onlookers were certain that the man who ended up falling into the street had been trying to force the young woman over the railing. Guests in nearby rooms had heard the commotion and were sure that the woman had screamed "murderer" at the man. Most sobering was the evidence found in Miss Leighton's room, still registered under her name, at the Hilton. Three bullets that had been fired into the bedding had been traced to a gun legally owned by an American cabinet official. Airline records showed that the official, Energy Secretary John Duke, had flown from America two days earlier and had returned on a morning flight hours after Mr. Hubbard's death.

By midweek Glen's death was officially labeled accidental. Not that the police could prove anything with great certainty, but simply that they had no more reliable account than the one Pam had given them. It wasn't a murder because Pam and Peter had apparently tried to save Glen. She held the cuff torn from his trousers, and Peter had been holding a matching shoe. Nor was it a suicide, because Glen Hubbard had never intended to throw himself from the balcony. By buying into Pam's story, the police were agreeing that Hubbard had tried to murder her, and was technically guilty of aggravated assault and attempted murder. But with Hubbard having already paid the price for his crime, the charges became moot.

Discreetly, the London police wondered if the United States government might be willing to assist in the investigation by providing one of the missing pieces. Did American authorities have any idea why the Secretary of Energy might have fired three shots into the pillows of one of London's better hotels?

Pam and Peter had been kept apart during the investigation to prevent them from collaborating on their accounts and fashioning an alibi. As soon as all restrictions were lifted, Pam rushed to the hotel where the police had kept Peter, hoping to express her gratitude. Twice during the previous week he had saved her life. She had been sinking into New York Harbor when he had come to her out of the darkness. She had been hanging over the edge of a tenth-story balcony when he had come bursting through the door. On both occasions he had been a guardian angel, watching over her without her knowing it. She had to look him straight in the eye and tell him "thank you for all that you've risked for me."

But when she reached his hotel, he had already checked out. "A United flight, I think," the clerk told her, "but I have no record of the flight number."

Pam checked with the airline and found that there was a plane for New York leaving in an hour. She rushed into the street to hail a taxi. "How fast can we get to Heathrow?" she asked the driver.

"This time of day, an hour, maybe a bit more and sometimes a little less."

It took over twenty minutes to work their way out of the London streets and pick up the highway. They made excellent time until the traffic came to a halt within sight of the airport. Still, Pam had ten minutes when she reached and charged into the main terminal. She was stopped in her tracks by the confusion of gates and counters, and the traffic of confused passengers and racing porters. She found the United check-in counters and rushed ahead of the long waiting line.

"The flight to New York. What gate is it?"

The clerk gave her the gate number but reminded her that she couldn't go up to the boarding area without a pass.

"There's someone I have to see!"

"If you jump one of the security queues, they'll take you out of here in a bomb carrier," the clerk told her. "Besides, that flight is already boarding."

The young woman saw Pam's face drop into despair. "You might page him," she recommended, assuming that Pam's distress must involve a man. "He still might be able to get to a phone."

Pam asked for a page, and a few seconds later, among the endless announcements and warnings, she heard Peter's name called with a request that he pick up the nearest courtesy phone.

She waited until the plane was in the air. Peter didn't respond to the page.

FIFTY-THREE

There was more disappointment awaiting Pam at Masters Publishing. "You can see the position you're putting us in," Gordon said. "What we have is a highly vituperative book written by a woman who had a hand in the death of a man who refused to publish her book. That's a whole new dimension to a woman who is trying to smear the lover who rejected her."

"I didn't have a hand in Glen Hubbard's death. He was the one who was planning murder."

Gordon was nodding. "Yes, of course. But you saw how the newspapers interpreted the events, so you can imagine how your American lobbying industry will portray you. These people, as you so accurately point out, are the master liars. They're never concerned with what happened. All they ever ask is, 'How are we going to spin this to our advantage?' Our tabloids have given them the blueprint."

Pam knew she was losing the argument. "I can verify everything that's in the book. They can say what they want, but I can stand up to them with names, times, and places."

"I know that," Gordon said. "But you're one voice crying in the wilderness. In the real world, John the Baptist loses his head. King Herod wins every time."

She stood slowly, understanding that, after all her efforts, the doors were being closed in her face. "I should thank you," she said to Gordon. "I know I had your vote."

"Not today," he admitted, turning his focus away from her. "I'd like you to think kindly of me, but I had to agree with my partners. Yesterday in New York, Intermedia bought a controlling interest in our U.S. distributor. If they want, they can pretty much put Masters out of business."

Pam settled slowly back into her chair. "God, I'm sorry, Gordon. I had no idea they could —"

"Of course you didn't," he said. "In truth, neither did I. We're an old company with a solid reputation for publishing controversial books by controversial authors. But we're no match for Intermedia, particularly if they have the U.S. government behind them. All of the partners were furious. But we had no choice. We simply couldn't have our name on your book."

She stood again, reached across his desk, and shook his hand. "I'll be cleared out of the hotel in the morning," she promised.

"Where will you go? Back to the States, I presume."

"Eventually, but not right away. There won't be any welcoming committee, and I'm in no hurry to eat crow. I think I'd like to just disappear for a while."

Her defeat was complete. The book was dead. The man she thought loved her had betrayed her. Her financial resources were pretty well exhausted. She knew she could bunk in with Jean Abbott for a few days. But that was hardly enough time to climb out of the pit she had dug for herself. John had told her she couldn't win and had offered to shield her from the people pursuing her. Glen had promised he could free her with one phone call. Either offer seemed much better than the public humiliation she had brought down on her own head.

Masters had moved her away from the crime scene to another suite in the Dorchester Hotel. At first she had thought that it was a vote of confidence in how much her book was going to make for the partners.

Now, she realized, it was simply a courtesy to someone whose hopes they had raised and then abandoned.

She nursed her melancholy with a long soak in a hot tub, a glass of champagne in hand and the bottle resting on the floor. The more she tried to ease the pain, the more dismal her prospects seemed to get. Everything that had happened to her seemed to have earthshaking repercussions. But to the Washington establishment she had been nothing more than an annoying fly on the wall, dispatched quickly with a snap of the flyswatter. When she finally crawled into bed, Pam didn't really care whether she woke up in the morning or not.

The next morning she called room service for her breakfast and packed her few things while she waited for it to be delivered. She had a table brought to the open doors of her balcony and watched the waiter while he arranged a pot of coffee, a fruit crepe, and a plum scone. The crepe and the coffee revived her. The scone stuck in her throat.

She was at the desk checking out when Gordon came through the revolving doors, looked around, and spotted her. He had brought his car to take her wherever she was going. Pam thanked him but explained that her friend's apartment was only a ten-minute taxi ride away. He insisted on being her chauffeur and carried her bag. "You know," he began as soon as they were together in the backseat, "the contract for your book still belongs to Carl Weiss." Pam hadn't thought of it but assumed that Gordon was right. "If Weiss wants his mark on the book, we would be happy to have our printer work with him. We would turn over everything, without charge, of course."

Pam was grateful, but she explained how small Weiss's operation actually was. "If they could shut down Masters, imagine what they could do to an old man and his daughter."

Gordon wished her well as he left her at Jean Abbott's doorstep. "I must seem a terrible coward," he said. Pam answered that she must seem a ridiculous fool.

Jean was less joyous in her welcome than she had been when Pam first arrived. "Are you okay?" were her first words. She had followed the gruesome coverage in the tabloids from the death of her former employer through Pam being cast as the woman in a sordid love triangle. "You've been through hell," she said in consolation.

Pam filled her in on everything that had happened since she had left the apartment and called on Masters. Jean's expression changed to horror when she heard about the phone message that the assassins were on their way to London. "Apparently John Duke was desperate to stop the book. The carrot was the possibility that we could get back together. The stick was the shots fired into my pillow, something he did when he went to my room to get my things."

"That's when you moved to the Dorchester," Jean surmised.

"Yes, under a false name. That seemed to be working until Glen Hubbard came to see me. I had no reason to fear Glen. He had always been supportive. At least I thought he had, until I found out that he was the spy in his own office. Everything I told him found its way to Washington within hours."

Jean shook her head slowly. "What a bastard!"

"I'm not sure," Pam allowed. "Glen claimed he loved me and was trying to keep me from getting hurt."

"He was a liar," Jean said. "The only one Glen Hubbard ever loved was himself."

Now it was Pam's turn to be shocked at the vehemence of Jean's outburst. "I suppose —" she started, but Jean cut her off.

"Glen and I had a steamy affair," she said. "He was charming, attentive, and romantic, and I fell for it completely. I thought how lucky I was to have found true love with a man who seemed enthralled with my every gesture, hypnotized by my every word. I was so happy to be in love that I never gave a thought to the fact that my uncle was Thomas Howell's right-hand man. Glen was using me to suck up to his boss. And I guess it paid off for him. He was promoted into every job that opened up ahead of him. My uncle was treating him like a son."

"What happened?" Pam asked.

Jean sighed, hesitated, and then said, "My uncle died. Got up in the middle of the night with a screaming headache and fell on the bathroom floor. The funeral was awful, but Glen was by my side every moment. Then, in a matter of weeks, he was gone. He just became less and less attentive until I was hardly seeing him. When I confronted him, he said it had been over for him for quite a while. He just didn't want to say anything abrupt while I was still mourning my uncle.

"He was friendly, even solicitous for my welfare. He just didn't love me, and I realized that he never had. I had been used, fool that I was. When I saw an opportunity to get away from New York, I jumped at it."

"I'm so sorry," Pam whispered.

"Thanks, but don't be sorry for Glen. He

was a *serial* bastard."

"Serial bastards seem to be the story of my life," Pam said with a half smile. "Do you suppose I'll ever learn?"

She spent two days with Jean, getting over her ordeal and learning how to laugh again. They talked fancifully about the next step each of them might take. Jean had changed her mind about going back to America and pretty much decided to join an English publisher. Pam speculated on the joys of trapping a rich husband. "At least I'd get paid for being screwed." They decided that her best prospects would be on the French Riviera, where it was easy to gauge a man's wealth by the size of his yacht.

They were walking home from a theater, chatting about the play they had just seen, when they became aware of the limo parked in front of Jean's apartment. "Maybe it's your billionaire coming to call," Jean teased, but her laughter stopped when a distinguished-looking man climbed out and waved in their direction.

"Pam!"

She recognized Gordon immediately.

"I've been back and forth to this address all day," he complained cheerfully. "Are you never at home?"

Pam introduced Jean and immediately

added that she was a fine editor looking to work for a London publisher.

"Oh, how nice. You must come by for a chat," Gordon answered, but then his attention focused on Pam. "Good news, I think, about your book."

She was stunned.

"We've put our printer in touch with Carl Weiss. They've worked out arrangements for Weiss to publish *Fouling the Air.*"

He came up to the apartment for tea and explained the details. Masters was completely out of the loop, as was Thomas Howell. No one would know that the book was about to be published until it appeared. There would be announcement ads in Washington and New York. Pam would have to be on hand to do the television talk shows. The controversy would create interest, and the interest would create sales. "I truly expect that the book will do very nicely," Gordon said in summary.

"Where is the money coming from?" Pam asked warily.

"A private investor," he answered. "As I said, *Fouling the Air* should bring a handsome return."

FIFTY-FOUR

Fouling the Air was announced with full-page ads in *The New York Times* and *The Washington Post*. Within hours the Washington crowd launched a counterattack, branding the book libelous on their usual outlets and organizing a groundswell of indignation from various citizens' groups. By the end of the day, the book was a twenty-second report on the late news.

Pam appeared live on a morning show and came across as bright, articulate, and honest. What was most apparent was her grasp on the facts. "You write that a United States senator actually put a price on his vote," the interviewer said.

"No, he said that the amount donated by the Electric Energy Institute wasn't enough and suggested that another zero be added to the check. That took the amount from ten thousand dollars to a hundred thousand. At the institute, we estimated that the vote saved our member companies close to $2 billion. I can give you the name of the senator, the date of the memo, and the check number involved."

"Please don't," the interviewer said. "We have legal restrictions. . . ."

"Of course," Pam answered. "But all that information is in the book."

"You also describe phony charities and civic groups created to hide payments to public officials," the interviewer prompted.

"Yes. For example, Citizens for Safe Automobiles was founded in April 2001. It had a director and three staffers working out of an office at the oil industry's lobbying organization. Its purpose was to prevent light trucks from being subjected to emissions controls. It received contributions from the petroleum, automobile, and electric power lobbies, and made donations to four congressmen and two senators who were considering the bill." She gave the dates of the payments and the date on which the bill was killed in committee. "Should I give you the names?"

"No, we do have legal limitations."

"They're all in the book."

Washington insiders realized very quickly that they didn't want to debate Pam Leighton in any open forum. Her command of the facts would put them immediately on the defensive, trying to explain why such money-laundering institutions were in the public interest, and why public officials needed so much money from special-interest groups in order to serve their constituents. It was an argument they couldn't win. There were a few voices claiming that lobbyists were simply acting on their First Amendment right to free speech. But if the money was merely an expression of belief, it seemed odd that the donors would go to such lengths to hide it.

Deprived of the public forum, the power brokers began casting about for someone to blame. As in the shell game, the purpose was to distract the mark from the real issue and give the columnists and interviewers something else to talk about.

Senator Lawrence told a press conference that *Fouling the Air,* for all its inaccuracies and distortions, had uncovered abusive activities by a well-connected lobbyist within the electric power industry. "It seems certain that John Duke, the Secretary of Energy, while director of the Electric Energy Institute, improperly disguised donations to elected officials' campaign funds." Elected officials, he explained, had no way of tracing the source of every donation made to their campaigns and no ability to investigate the legitimacy of every citizens' association that made donations. John Duke had taken advantage of this gray area. Lawrence called for his resignation. Reporters raised their hands, but the senator didn't take any questions.

Another defense was to attack the source. Pam Leighton, it was leaked, had seduced the vulnerable director to get grist for her mill. She had destroyed a happy marriage to a noble lady from a great American family, and involved innocent employees of the institute in gathering the rumors and unsubstantiated allegations for her book. Pro-business commentators were appalled that the ranting of a money-mad whore should be dignified by public discussion.

Pam stood up well under the blitz. "Yes, I did have a relationship with John Duke, but not to gather material for a book. I didn't think of a book until after I left the institute." Wasn't she involved in another scandalous affair in London that caused the death of her publisher? "No, there was no affair in London. The man killed came to stop me from publishing the book. He tried to throw me from the hotel balcony and lost his footing in the process. It was just one of many attempts made to stop me from publishing." She had the police records of the burglary at her apartment, and the attack in the warehouse. She had the newspaper report of being tossed from the ferry, and the original ransom note for the return of Ronda Weiss. Instead of smearing her reputation and destroying her credibility, her detractors were turning her into a hero and raising questions about the conduct of the government. Did they really use federal agents to stalk her? Did they hire contract killers? Pam's personal story became as controversial as her book.

There was a key witness who would have added to her credibility. Peter Salerno could have vouched that she was thrown from a New York ferry, and that she was being lifted over a balcony railing when he burst into her London hotel room. He had been an eyewitness to nearly all of her torturous effort to tell the public how Washington really worked. But she never called on him, never mentioned his name or ever referred to his role. Peter was a private person who would build his reputation by the brilliance of his work. He didn't deserve to have his name tarnished by association with the sordid details of her story.

Twice he had tried to reach her. Once it had been a note forwarded through a television interviewer:

I see your book everywhere. You must be filthy rich, so the next dinner is on you. Pete.

On another occasion she had gotten a package forwarded through Ronda Weiss. In it was a thin book with a picture of a roulette ball falling onto the spinning wheel: *The Odds Against the Odds of Probability.* The author was Peter T. Salerno, Ph.D. He signed it,

Nobody cares about the odds. We just take our chances. Pete.

FIFTY-FIVE

"Was it worth it?" Peter asked.

Pam hesitated, then raised her hands in a gesture of hopelessness. "I'm not sure. I guess it depends on worth *what*."

They were sitting at a back table in the same student joint they had used for their first rendezvous. It was just as noisy, with speakers in the corners blaring out hard rock and hip-hop. The hundred conversations at the bar and various tables were blended into a dull roar. It wasn't the ideal setting for serious conversation.

Pam, who was finally old news on the talk-show circuit, had called Peter's office. "I tried to catch you at the airport," she had said as her opening line. "I even had you paged."

"I heard the page," he had answered. "I was just boarding, and I thought that it was probably you. But I knew what you were going to say. I didn't want to miss a flight with a discounted ticket."

"I was going to say 'thank you.' "

"That's what I figured. You're welcome."

Pam had said that she would like to meet with him. "I have the first copy off the press. I've been saving it for you."

He had suggested the student bar as a meeting place.

Now Pam handed him the book, open to her inscription: "For Peter, a true life saver."

"I didn't do anything special," he said with a smile. "It's just the normal service that someone who lives as dangerously as you do has every right to expect."

"It was hellish," she agreed.

"Was it worth it?" he asked again.

Her response was a question instead of an answer. "Was it worth Marion Murray's life? No, not by any calculation. It wasn't worth the life of that poor guy who fell down the elevator shaft. It sure as hell wasn't worth all the danger and humiliation that I've been through, nor was it worth you risking your life. By every important measure, I should have abandoned the book the first time I saw signs that someone wanted it stopped."

"You did have some successes," Peter said.

"Sure. Senator Lawrence was a success. He's been censured, removed from his committees, and may end up facing criminal charges. But I bet he'll never be indicted. He knows too much for his colleagues to risk what he might say in cross-examination.

"The same thing is true for Congressman Porter. I don't think anyone will ever be able to prove who killed Arthur Ries. But now everyone knows why he was killed. That has to be the reason the majority whip has decided not to run for another term."

"You can take credit for the new lobbying rules," Peter reminded her.

"If they stick. But the only people who get to enforce the rules are the senators and congressmen. They have a history of finding ways around their own rules when it comes to lining their pockets."

Peter finished his beer, took her bottle and his own, and started to the bar. But he stopped. "What about John Duke? You sure kicked his ass." Then he was off to get another round, which left Pam with lots of time to consider the fate of her former lover.

John, she had learned as the details of her ordeal were filled in by a variety of sources, had been a victim of his own ambition. His troubles with Catherine had begun early in their marriage, as he was absorbed into her large and politically prominent family. In circles of power, he became nothing more than "What's his name? The fellow who married the youngest Porter girl." Washington was his escape from her shadow and his hope of establishing his own identity.

Catherine had foiled his escape. Her detectives had reported that he was seeing another woman and provided all the evidence she would need for a divorce. But a divorce would give John just what he wanted. Catherine had a better idea. She pulled her political strings to get him nominated to the cabinet, knowing full well that once he accepted the post she would have complete control of him. Just to be sure, she had kept the detectives on retainer, watching both John and the woman she knew he loved. It was her detectives who discovered that Pam was writing a book which would end John's public career and his wife's hold on him.

To stop the book, Catherine had turned to her cousin Benjamin. Wouldn't he want to block publication of a book that exposed all the dirty dealings of elected officials? He would, but for reasons far more important than helping a cousin control her husband. His own career was built on industry backing and financed by lobby money. He was nearly certain that the man who had come closest to exposing him, a union official named Arthur Ries, had been eliminated to preserve the arrangement that bought his support for the coal industry. Benjamin Porter had shared his concerns with Thomas Lawrence and a few other government officials who shared his need for secrecy. Those closest to the Pentagon had sold the idea that Pam's book was a threat to national security. The military had launched its secret operatives — Special Forces, Navy SEALS — to seize the book. It had been one of those who lost his footing and fell down the elevator shaft. Politicians with oversight of communications regulations simply mentioned to Intermedia directors that they would hate to see such a scurrilous book published. A director told Glen Hubbard how much he would appreciate it if Glen could make certain the book never found a home.

After stopping at a gathering of students to exchange pleasantries, Peter came back to the table. "God, it's so easy to go to jail," he said, tipping his head back toward the students. "I've just been propositioned by a girl who can't be a day over sixteen. I think she's in one of my calculus classes."

"About John Duke," Pam said, answering the question he had asked before. "I certainly did bring him down, and I suppose he had it coming. But the fact is that John was as much a victim as I was. I'm not sure he deserved such a humiliating finale. At any rate, if I had my moment of vengeance, it was a petty victory. You don't win points by destroying a weakling."

"You're too kind," Peter told her. "The son of a bitch tried to have you killed."

She shook her head. "That wasn't John's doing."

"Who, then? Glen Hubbard?"

"No! Neither of them had the clout to have me killed. But they both knew that I had run afoul of special interests and knew that I could get myself killed. I think they were both telling the truth when they said they were trying to save me. No, the orders to kill me had to come from high up in government. It had to be someone who could get to the Pentagon, or one of the agencies. My guess is either Senator Lawrence or Congressman Porter. Maybe both of them."

Peter's eyes widened. "Government officials ordered you murdered? They killed your friend Marion? I can't believe it!"

"I thought Marion's death must have been unintentional. I thought that they just wanted her records and that she put up a struggle. But then someone tossed me off a ferry *after* I had given him the records. My

544

guess is that the killers were contractors hired by the Pentagon, or the CIA, or some agency that had been told I was a danger to national security. There are a lot of outfits hired by the government that lurk in the shadows. You can't trace the money they get, and no one has oversight of their activities. But governments fall, planes crash, and whistle-blowers vanish. No one ever asks why or how."

Peter's next question was about the Justice Department inquiry into the activities of the lobbyists who were destroying any semblance of representative government. "Do you think it might be stopped? God knows you've ignited a public outcry."

She laughed. "The inquiry is just a diversion. They'll call witnesses, slap hands, and announce new rules. But nothing will change."

"Why not, if the people want reform?"

"Because the elected officials don't give a damn about what the people want or need. They don't want anything to change. They've created a system that pays top dollar. Why should they change it?"

On his third beer, Peter ventured into dangerous territory, asking her about Glen Hubbard. "Did you love him?"

She shook her head slowly. "I'm really not

sure. I told him I did once, and, in his own way, I think he loved me. Right to the very end, when he claimed he was reporting on me in order to keep me safe, I think he wanted to marry me. The trouble was that Glen wanted it all — the position, the power, the wealth, and me to share it with him. He kept talking about the wonderful life we could have together, and he couldn't understand why I was throwing it away just for the book."

"He almost killed you," Peter reminded her.

"That was when he saw that he was going to lose everything. I was throwing him out, and he knew that when the book came out he would no longer be Intermedia's golden boy. In the end, that was the one thing he couldn't live without."

"Do you still love him?"

"My, you do pry," Pam teased.

Peter raised his hands defensively. "Sorry! I withdraw the question."

He offered to see her home to the apartment she had inherited when Jean Abbott landed a position at Masters.

"No, I'll take a cab. I have money now, enough even to buy that dinner I owe you. Pick out a nice place."

"How about my apartment?" he suggested. "You could stop at the Italian place and bring in some seafood pasta. I'll get the wine."

"It's a date," she answered as she slid into a taxi. The car pulled away.

Pam's schedule filled in quickly. She signed a contract for a once-a-week television appearance in which she would report on the money flow in capital politics. Her spot was introduced as "The Weekly Report of Our Washington Watchdog." She did a column with a small syndicated following. There was also an offer for another book, this one based on her frightening experiences in writing *Fouling the Air.*

Peter took on two more classes, along with the title Associate Professor, and began work on a new book, tentatively titled *Improbability.* He added to his workload by casting about for college and university openings that would put him on a faster track to tenure.

The date they made wasn't kept. Pam called once, suggesting a time that was impossible for Peter. When he called back, all he could do was leave a message. Pam was out of town.

Still, she thought about him often. She had no doubt that he was the most straightforward man she had ever met. But every thought of Peter was tainted with the terrible background of their relationship. It was impossible to picture him without also conjuring up images of dark water closing over her head, or a body flailing in the air as it fell to destruction. He was part of the life that she was trying forget, a player in an era she was struggling to leave behind.

Peter often thought about Pam, and on many occasions picked up the telephone to call her. But his logical mind wouldn't let him make assumptions about her feelings toward him. He had rescued her twice, but that didn't mean she ought to love him. A swimmer dragged out of the surf doesn't have to fall in love with the lifeguard. Besides, she had become something of a celebrity, and Peter was protective of his privacy. There were reasons to let the past stay in the past.

It was spring before Pam was able to shake the thoughts and feelings that had imprisoned her. When she looked back over the year since she had left Washington, Peter Salerno was the only bright spot. It wasn't because of the times he had saved her life. Those moments didn't entitle her to a special relationship with him. Peter was the kind of person who would have jumped from a ship to save a cat that had fallen overboard. What she remembered were the nights when he slept on the sofa so she could have the bed. She remembered him tiptoeing in and out of the bathroom so as not to disturb her. She remembered his way of putting things into perspective, and his ability to find something humorous in even the darkest events. Most of all, Pam remembered that he didn't need to be anything more than he was. He liked mathematics and he did what he liked. He didn't seem to care who might not be impressed.

It was Pam who was finally able to pick up the phone. "Are you still interested in that dinner I owe you?"

"Sure! When?"

"Are you free tonight?"

"Wow, that isn't much notice. Let me check my social calendar." After a long pause, he announced, "You're in luck. My eight o'clock had to cancel."

"Eight it shall be. I'm bringing dinner and you're doing the wine."

"Do you like really fine wine?"

"Of course," Pam answered.

"Then you better bring the wine, too. My book sales haven't been nearly as high as yours."

As the time drew near, Pam began to

regret her hasty decision to call. There would certainly be awkward moments after they had let so many months pass. What in hell are we going to talk about? she asked herself. Imaginary numbers?

She got to the restaurant early, placed an order for lobster ravioli, antipasto, salad, and two bottles of an expensive Pinot Grigio. While the order was being prepared, she sat at the bar and sipped a Chianti. Her anxieties began to vanish. When she rang his bell, it took several seconds for Peter to answer. "Hello," he said, as if he had no idea who was calling.

"It's me, with your dinner."

"Dinner? I didn't order any dinner."

She laughed. "I ordered dinner, and the package is burning my hands. If you don't push that buzzer, I'm going to start eating it on your front step."

The door clicked open, and she climbed the two flights to the third floor. Peter was leaning into the open doorway. "What did you bring me?" he asked when she finally arrived. Pam recited the menu. "Lobster ravioli," he repeated with pleasure. "Your book is *certainly* outselling mine."

The table was set as it had been for their first dinner at his apartment. The only change was that the fall leaves in the center were now spring flowers. Peter took the wine and set it in a coffee-can ice bucket. Pam found dishes for the food and set the antipasto on the table.

"What are these?" he asked, lifting a silvery fish on a fork.

"Sardines," she said.

"I've never seen them outside those little cans."

They ate with gusto, rhapsodizing over the food and sipping the wine as if it was too precious to drink. Peter spent some time describing his new book, which he thought might be even duller that his earlier effort.

"You must have gotten good reviews from your peers," Pam encouraged.

Peter smirked. "We sold one each to about half the university libraries. As far as I know, no one has ever signed out a copy."

"You're teasing me," Pam answered.

"Well, maybe one. I got one good review, so I hope he actually read the book."

"I read it," she said. "At least the first third of it. Then you lost me. I was hoping you might find time to take me through it page by page."

"Tonight?"

"No!" she answered. "I was thinking of the first two weeks in August." He had no idea what she was talking about, so she explained. "One of the fond memories I have of last summer's ordeal was that house in the Hamptons. So, I was thinking of taking a place out there for two weeks. I thought if you visited me, you could explain everything I didn't understand."

Peter gave her a long, questioning look. "It's complicated stuff. It would take a lot longer than two weeks."

"I'd like that," Pam said.

"We could start tonight," he suggested.

"Peter, I want to be sure that I get this right. I've screwed up so badly, and I —"

He put a finger to her lips. "You don't have to give me another long, convoluted explanation of why I'm not going to get laid. All you have to say is that you have a headache."

She took his hand. "I don't have a headache," she said. "You shouldn't give up so easily."

ABOUT THE AUTHOR

Diana Diamond is the pseudonym of a critically acclaimed mystery and thriller writer. She is also the author of *The Stepmother, The First Wife, The Trophy Wife, The Daughter-in-Law, The Babysitter,* and *The Good Sister.*

The employees of Thorndike Press hope you have enjoyed this Large Print book. All our Thorndike and Wheeler Large Print titles are designed for easy reading, and all our books are made to last. Other Thorndike Press Large Print books are available at your library, through selected bookstores, or directly from us.

For information about titles, please call:

(800) 223-1244

or visit our Web site at:

www.gale.com/thorndike
www.gale.com/wheeler

To share your comments, please write:

Publisher
Thorndike Press
295 Kennedy Memorial Drive
Waterville, ME 04901